The Man in the Moone

Ce Globe partira incessamment pour les Echelles du Levant ; et a son retour il annoncera ses autres Voyages, tant pour les 2 Poles que pour les extremités de l'Occident. P. S. Il ne faut se mettre en peine de rien tout est prévu et tout ira bien. Il y aura un tarif exact pour tout les lieux de passage ; mais les prix seront les mêmes pour les Contreés les plus éloignées de notre Hemisphere. Scavoir, Mil Louis pour un des dits voyage, quelquonque. et l'on peut dire que cette somme est tres modique eu égard à la Célérité à la Commodité et aux agréments dont on jouira dans le dit aërostat. Agréments que l'on ne peut trouver ici bas, attendu que dans ce balon chacun y trouvera les choses selon son imagination. Cela est si vrai que dans le meme lieu les uns seront au bal et les autres en Station ; Les uns feront chere exquise et les autres jeuneront ; Les uns feront l'amour, et les autres le detesteront tout enfin sera là à souhait quiquonque voudra s'entretenir avec des gens d'esprit trouvera a qui parler, quiconque sera bête ne manquera pas d'égal. ainsi de maniere ou d'autre le plaisir sera l'ame de la Societé Aerienne, comme il l'est parmi nous et comme il le fut jadis chez l'ancienne

INDICATION DE TOUT CE QUI PEUT INTERRESSER LES VOYAGEURS

AAA. *Le Globe*	G. *Vaisseau enchanté servant de Logement universel pouvant contenir 4000 personnes*	OO. *Echelles de Cordes auquelle le Vaisseau est attaché*	Y. *Musicien de l'equipage sur leur balcon*
B. *L'Observatoire*	H. *Le Gouvernail*	P. *Logement des phisiciens Conducteurs*	Z. *Petit balon de 30 pieds en guise de Chaloupe*
C. *Fanal*	I. *Logement du Garde Gouvernail*	Q. *Grand Magasin de Matiere Combustible*	2 *Grand telescope public* 3. *Grand Orgue pour donner des Serenades* 4 *Canon pour eveiller les habitant des Villes qui auront souscrit pour entendre nos palilles* 5. *Tente des Surveillans, Inspecteur et Ordonnateurs des Manoeuvres &c.* 6. *Casernes des Matelot Aerien, Pompiers Mousses et autres Subalterne.*
D. *La Galerie*	K. *Sale de Spectacle avec ses dependances*	R. *Filles faciles avec l'escalier qui aboutit a leur Cages* S. *Demeure des Chirurgiens*	
E. *Tuyau pour laisser exaler l'air Inflammable*	L. *Lieu des rendés vous*	T. *Ailerons d'ornement* U *Traiteur Restaurat Caffés* X *Cabinet d'aisance.*	
F. *Officiers Aeriens*	M *Grand Tuyau Aerostatique* N N. *Voiles*		

Ce Globe le plus étonnant que l'on ait vu sur papier se trouve a Paris chez Pithou Md d'Estampes No 138 des Galeries neuves du Palais Royal.

This engraving, reproduced from François-Louis Bruel's *Histoire Aeronautique par les Monuments, Points, Sculptés, Dessinés et Gravés des Origines à 1830* (Paris, 1909), bears the following legend, here translated from the French:

INVENTED FOR THE GOOD OF THE PRESENT AND THAT OF POSTERITY

This balloon will depart regularly for the seaports of the Levant, and upon its return other excursions will be announced, to the two Poles as well as the far reaches of the Western world. One need not trouble himself about anything, because everything has been provided for and all will go well. There will be an exact fare for all accommodations, but the price will be the same for the most distant reaches of our hemisphere—i.e., one thousand *louis* for any one of the aforementioned voyages—and, considering the speed, comfort, and pleasure offered by this aircraft, it is a very modest sum. Because in this balloon each will find things according to his own imagination . . . in the same place some will be attending a ball while others will be standing still; some will dine on exquisite fare while others will fast; some will make love while others despise them; finally, whoever wishes to converse with witty men will find them there to his heart's content, and whoever will be a fool will never lack an equal; and thus, in one way or another, pleasure will be the essence of the Celestial Society, as it is among us and used to be with our forefathers.

The list printed below the legend, which contains "Information on Everything That Might Interest Travelers," identifies parts of the ship indicated on the engraving by letters or numbers, such as "main lodging quarters for 4,000 people" (*G*) and "main aerostatic valve" (*M*), or provisions for the enjoyment of passengers and crew, such as "easy women with stairs leading from their cages" (*R*), "restaurant and café" (*U*), and "grand organ for serenades" (*3*).

The Man in the Moone

AN ANTHOLOGY OF ANTIQUE SCIENCE FICTION AND FANTASY

Edited by

FAITH K. PIZOR AND T. ALLAN COMP

Introduction by Isaac Asimov

SIDGWICK & JACKSON
LONDON

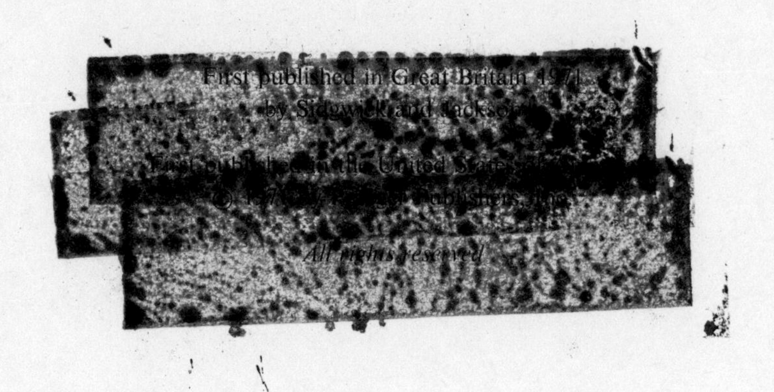
First published in Great Britain 1971
by Sidgwick and Jackson

First published in the United States [illegible]
© [illegible] Publishers, Inc.

ISBN 0 283 97815 5

Printed in the United States of America
for Sidgwick and Jackson Limited
1 Tavistock Chambers, Bloomsbury Way,
London W.C.1

Acknowledgments

Many of the works included in this collection are quite rare and consequently difficult to obtain. We are most grateful to those libraries which have been willing to allow us to borrow or copy these books and to reprint portions of them here. The editions of Godwin, Brunt, Vivenair, Daniel, and "The Great Steam-Duck" are all housed in the Lammot du Pont, Jr., Collection of Aeronautics in the Eleutherian Mills Historical Library of the Hagley Museum, Greenville, Wilmington, Delaware. The original (1640) edition of Wilkins was supplied by the Library Company of Philadelphia, and an 1899 edition of the earlier Lovell translation of Cyrano de Bergerac was supplied by Bryn Mawr University. The University of Delaware Library provided the Griggs edition of Richard Adams Locke's moon story, and the University of Pennsylvania permitted us to reproduce the original edition of Edgar Allan Poe's "Hans Phaall."

In particular, we are indebted to Dr. Richmond Williams, Director of the Eleutherian Mills Historical Library, who gave us access to the Lammot du Pont, Jr., Collection of Aeronautics; to Mrs. B. Bright Low, Research and Reference Librarian at the Eleutherian Mills Historical Library, and her assistants, Mrs. Carol Hallman and Miss Shirley Thompson, all of whom filled that dual role of super-detective and omniscient mother hen that makes a great librarian; and to Mrs. Gladys Topkis, our editor, whose patience, encouragement, and suggestions were always gratefully received. Finally, we wish to express our appreciation to Gordon L. Pizor for his help and support and to Dr. John Hurt for his empathy and advice.

F.K.P.
T.A.C.

Contents

List of Illustrations ix

Reaching for the Moon: An Introduction Isaac Asimov xi

From *The Man in the Moone, or A Discourse of a Voyage Thither by Domingo Gonsales The Speedy Messenger* (1638) Francis Godwin 3

From *The Discovery of a New World, . . . with a Discourse Concerning the Possibility of a Passage Thither* (1640) John Wilkins 41

From *The Comical History of the States and Empires of the World of the Moon* (1656) Cyrano de Bergerac 59

From *A Voyage to Cacklogallinia* (1727) "Captain Samuel Brunt" 103

From *The Life and Astonishing Transactions of John Daniel . . .* (1751) Ralph Morris 126

A Journey lately performed through the Air, in an Aerostatic Globe . . . To the newly discovered Planet, Georgium Sidus (1784) "Vivenair" 146

Hans Phaall—A Tale (1835) Edgar Allan Poe 162

From *Great Astronomical Discoveries Lately Made by Sir John Herschel . . . at the Cape of Good Hope* (1835) Richard Adams Locke 190

The Great Steam-Duck (1841) "A Member of the L.L.B.B." 217

List of Illustrations

Satirical engraving of a balloon fitted out for space travel (Paris, 1830) frontispiece

Frontispiece of the 1768 edition of *The Man in the Moone* 6

Frontispiece of the 1640 edition of *Discovery of a New World in the Moone* 44

Frontispiece of a Dutch edition of *The Works of Cyrano de Bergerac,* Volume II (Amsterdam, 1709) 63

Frontispiece of the original (1727) edition of *A Voyage to Cacklogallinia* 106

An artist's conception of John Daniel's "Flying Eagle" 128

Satirical English engraving of 1784, probably showing the pioneer balloonists Blanchard and Jeffries 148

Italian engraving (Naples, 1836), showing Sir John Herschel's supposed scheme for the "Flying Diligence" 194

Illustration from *The Great Steam-Duck* (Louisville, Ky., 1841) 219

ISAAC ASIMOV

Reaching for the Moon: An Introduction

Nobody knows when men first dreamed of flight. Undoubtedly, the longing to be free of the harsh unevenness of the earth's surface was universal. The birds showed the way as they dipped and soared in easy flight. If they could do it, why not man?

Wings were needed, and perhaps feathers. It was an easy leap of the imagination to conceive of a light framework of wood with skin attached to the arms, coated with wax into which feathers could be fixed. It was by just such a device that Daedalus and Icarus, in the Greek myth, flew out of imprisonment in Crete.

In the Greek imagination, the invention worked. (Icarus's later disaster was, of course, his own fault.) There was an innocence concerning aerodynamics among the ancients—no knowledge even of the square-cube law, which states that, as the size of a flying creature increases, the surface of its wings (which do the lifting) increases only as the square of the linear dimensions, while its mass (which must be lifted) increases as the cube. As a bird increases in size, the shape of its wings must change to allow for a more efficient use of updrafts. Even so, the albatross and the condor approach the upper limit of size for a flying creature.

We know now that, for a man to fly by Icarus's method, his wings would have to be so large that in repose they would wrap round and round the body many times or flap so furiously that the muscles required would pad out his chest for several feet. Yet, in the Greek myth, Daedalus and Icarus flew. Indeed, Icarus rose so triumphantly high that he approached the sun. Its heat then melted the wax, loosened the feathers of his device, and sent him hurtling downward to his death.

Fantasy, you see, takes a rather cavalier approach to reality. It adopts those products of sober observation and careful deduction that it needs for its dreaming but ignores or rejects what will not fit the dream.

Those who conceive fantasies observe the effortless flight of small birds and the fact that these alone among living creatures have wings and feathers, and deduce from this the supposed requirements for human flight. If the fantasts ever remarked the difficulty with which crop-gorged large birds launch themselves, they might have suspected that an upper limit of size for flight exists, a limit far below the human mass. But mythmakers ignored this evidence.

Indeed, to them, even creatures larger than men were by no means too heavy for winged flight. There was Pegasus the beautiful flying horse and huge flying dragons, sometimes pictured with tiny wings, to say nothing of the independent flight attributed to inanimate carpets and broomsticks.

What of the goals of flight? Once a man flies, where does he go? To strange and distant countries thousands of miles away, undoubtedly, but why not to that stranger and seemingly no more distant land we see in the sky—the moon?

To the child, reasoning from appearances, the moon is quite close. He will credit the story that a cow can jump over it, or that it is sometimes caught in the branches of a tall tree.

Primitive adults may have suspected that the moon was not *that* close; it cleared the tops of the hills, but perhaps not by much. It was a shining silver plate at a middling distance, they may have supposed, on which smudge marks could be seen.

The smudges needed explanation. Perhaps they were the dimly perceived figure of a man—a man who, because the moon was so small, filled its entire circle. In the Book of Numbers, there is the tale of a man who, during the stay of the children of Israel in the wilderness, desecrated the Sabbath by gathering sticks on that day. By the decree of God, he was stoned to death. Yet somehow the tale arose (perhaps by the adaptation of a pre-Christian legend to the Biblical story) that he was hurled to the moon as a punishment. There one can make out not only the man but the bundle of sticks he is gathering as well. Some, with particularly vivid imaginations, can see a dog too.

The ancient Greeks added touches of sophistication to man's view of the moon. (Undoubtedly, the Babylonians and Egyptians preceded them in this, but our records of pre-Hellenic astronomy are too skimpy to give us the necessary detail.)

The Greek astronomers made it absolutely clear that the moon shone by the reflected light of the sun, that only half of its surface could be lit by the sun at any one time, and that the changing phases of the moon were the result of its changing position in relation to the sun. When the moon was only a thin crescent, this was because it was almost directly between the sun and ourselves, and most of the sunlight was spread out upon the other side of the moon, the side away from us, which we could not see.

More important still, the Greeks were able to determine the distance of the moon from the earth. The first to come out with a roughly accurate answer, as far as we know, was Aristarchus of Samos, about 270 B.C. A better value, virtually the correct one, was obtained by Hipparchus of Rhodes, in about 150 B.C.

It turned out that the moon is no short distance away at all. No cow, nor any bird either, is likely to approach it, for it is nearly a quarter of a million miles away.

But, to be that far away and still appear as large as it does, the moon must be not merely a silver plate, not merely a shining boulder, but much more. It has to be a world of considerable dimensions. Indeed, from what was known about its distance and its apparent size, it could be calculated at once that the moon was a little over 2,000 miles in diameter.

About 250 B.C., the Greek geographer Eratosthenes of Cyrene had correctly estimated the earth's diameter to be about 8,000 miles. The moon is distinctly smaller than the earth, therefore, and yet still of respectable size.

At once, the possibility of flight to the moon gained greater credibility. Surely, if the moon is a world, it must be full of life; it must contain plants, animals, intelligent beings, nations, governments, cultures, and customs. Tales of moon flight can be (and were) written. One of the earliest that has survived was written in A.D. 150 by the Greek satirist Lucian of Samosata. With the typical selectivity of the fantast, Lucian accepted the size of the moon, which he needed for his story, but ignored its distance from the earth.

If Lucian's tale represented (as some maintain) the beginnings of science fiction, it proved a false dawn. In his time, Greek science was withering, and, by the fourth century, when Christianity took over the Roman Empire, a new kind of "truth" blanketed the West. For nearly a millennium and a half thereafter, no statement could be allowed flatly to contradict anything in Holy Writ. That meant retreat, for the Biblical view of the universe was less advanced than the Greek view had been. It was easy to demonstrate, by selecting appropriate passages from the Bible, that the earth we live on is the only world that could possibly exist and that the moon and the sun are merely "lights" intended to serve as calendars for man.

The notion of the moon as an earthlike world vanished. It became instead, as in Dante's *Divine Comedy,* part of the divine heavens.

It took more than a Polish astronomer to change this. In 1543, Nicholas Copernicus published a revolutionary book explaining how much simpler it would be to suppose that the sun, not the earth, was the center of the universe. He would have it that the huge and heavy earth was flying through space in a circle around the sun.

But the Copernican theory had nothing to say about the nature of the various worlds or their true distances from each other. The moon might be part of a Copernican universe rather than a Greek or a Christian one and yet still not necessarily be a world.

The turning point came in 1609.

An Italian scientist, Galileo Galilei, having heard rumors that in the Netherlands a device consisting of lenses at the ends of a hollow tube had served to make distant objects seem close, experimented for himself and quickly reinvented what we now call the telescope. Galileo then did something the initial Dutch discoverer had never thought of doing: He turned his telescope toward the sky.

Virtually the first object Galileo observed was the moon, and indeed it appeared closer and therefore larger than with the unaided eye, so that he could see it in much greater detail.

What he saw were mountains! The moon was no shining circle of light, perfectly smooth and perfectly spherical. It was, instead, like the earth, rough and uneven and imperfect.

There was some objection from the die-hards, but telescopes of a quality good enough to substantially improve observation of the moon were so easy to make, so easy to look through, and so convincing once they were used that there was no chance at all for the conservatives to hold the line. The moon has been accepted as a world ever since.

So it came about that the seventeenth century was the first Golden Age of moon flight, at least in imagination. The fact that the moon has at least some of the attributes of earth was the inspiration for fancy so glorious that no disheartenment was allowed to take hold, no difficulties allowed to interfere.

To reach the moon, for instance, one had to face the difficulty of rising against the gravitational pull of the earth. Very little was known about the nature of that pull. The great work of Isaac Newton, *Principia Mathematica,* which was to make rational the machinery of the universe, was not published until 1683. Therefore, it seemed perfectly plausible in the decades before to maintain that the gravitational pull rapidly weakened as one rose from the earth and that it ceased altogether above the level of the clouds.

It followed that, if a man hitched a chariot to a team of strong birds, he could be lifted to the clouds and beyond, with less and less trouble, all the way to the moon. This was the device Domingo Gonsales used to reach the moon in the fantasy Bishop Francis Godwin wrote in 1638.

Of course, such a bird flight presupposes the existence of an atmosphere all the way to the moon, but why not? It was not until 1643, five years after the publication of Godwin's fantasy, that the Italian physicist Evangelista Torricelli measured the pressure of the atmosphere. From that measurement it was easy to show that, if the earth's atmosphere were uniformly of the density it is at the earth's surface, it could extend only five miles above that surface.

To be sure, the atmosphere is not uniformly of surface density but grows less dense as one rises to greater heights. This allows it to extend to considerably greater heights than five miles, but certainly not a quarter of a million miles, all the way to the moon. And anyway, within a very short space, by growing less dense, the atmosphere becomes too rarefied for men to breathe.

Yet, on what were these conclusions based? The pressure of the atmosphere results from the gravitational pull of the earth on the air, and that pull can exist only in the immediate vicinity of earth. Beyond the clouds there might be plenty of air that did not make its weight felt. At least the moon-flight writers could assume so.

But, even if there is air between the earth and the moon, is there air *on* the moon? Does the moon have an atmosphere?

Even the earliest telescopic observations of the moon offered disheartening evidence against that possibility. The surface of the moon is always clearly and sharply in evidence as long as the earth's atmosphere is clear. No clouds, no mist, no haze ever obscure the tiniest visible feature of the moon's surface. The boundary between the sunlit portion of the moon's surface and the night-hidden portion is always sharp too, with none of the hazy half-light that one associates with twilight—something that would be necessary if there were an atmosphere. When the moon approaches a star, that star shines bright and undimmed until the very moment the body of our satellite passes before it, when it vanishes all at once. There is no gradual dimming just before the eclipse as there would have to be if an atmosphere, clinging to the moon's edge, covered the star first.

And on a world without an atmosphere, any sea would boil away under the sun's heat. If there was no air and no water—there would be no life.

But a world with no life seemed a wasted world. Mankind was still under the spell of the idea of a purposeful universe. The universe had been created by God, and surely no part of it could be wasted or purposeless.

And somehow man's imagination did not extend to a purpose that did not include living, intelligent beings very like himself.

So the fantasts had to cling firmly to the notion of a moon with an atmosphere and seas, regardless of astronomical evidence to the contrary.

John Wilkins in 1638–40 published a long rationalization of the new ideas of the moon's worldhood, arguing strongly in favor of a lunar atmosphere. In these arguments, Wilkins labored under two disadvantages. In the seventeenth century, the ancients were still given exaggerated and almost uncritical worship. For every point Wilkins considers, every possible ancient author was trotted out with opinions for or against. Secondly, it had to be taken for granted that no proposition could be true if it flatly contradicted Scripture. Endless ingenuity had to be utilized therefore to demonstrate that something that seemed to be at variance with the Bible really did not contradict it.

Within the confines, then, of the Greek philosophers, the Hebrew prophets, and the Christian fathers (and the observations of Galileo and others of his generation, too), Wilkins set about to show that it was both reasonable in a secular sense and orthodox in a religious sense to believe in a plurality of worlds, and in the habitability of the moon in particular.

To prove that the moon had an atmosphere, he noted that the sunlit portion seemed larger than the darkened portion (as one can see during the crescent phase or during a lunar eclipse). He explained this observation by contending that the atmosphere is illuminated by the sun, that the solid body of the moon plus its atmosphere are larger than the solid body alone, that the moon therefore has an atmosphere. (Alas, the argument is faulty. The moon's sunlit portion seems larger than its darkened portion because of a well-known optical illusion that makes any light object seem larger than a dark object of the same shape and dimensions. The phenomenon has nothing to do with a lunar atmosphere one way or the other.)

The French poet, duelist, and wit Cyrano de Bergerac (yes, he really lived, large nose and all) did not confine himself to bird flight but devised several alternative methods for reaching the moon. One that was surely not meant to be taken too seriously (after all, his book is entitled *The Comical History . . .*) was to strap bottles of dew about his waist. Because the sun draws dew upward, it followed that he would be drawn upward with it—and, according to his story, so he was.

He also suggested the use of rockets for the purpose, and this is certainly one of the most fascinating pieces of intuitive foresight in literature. The rocket principle represents the only method of carrying on directed flight through a vacuum, and that was the method that, three centuries after Cyrano's time, was actually used to carry men to the moon.

But the usefulness of rockets in this respect was to become plain only when Newton published his book in 1683. Yet Cyrano published his fantasy in 1656, over a quarter of a century before Newton's revelation of the workings of the universe.

To be sure, Cyrano eventually abandoned rockets, finding them too difficult to control. More to his taste was the device of hurling a strong magnet up in the air while he was standing on a light iron chariot. The chariot rose in response to the pull of the magnet, and, when Cyrano reached the magnet, he threw it up again, and so on. Perfect control.

This sort of pulling-oneself-up-by-one's-own-bootstraps is expressly forbidden by the second law of thermodynamics, but the second law was not to be understood until two centuries after Cyrano had written his book, so he is scarcely to be blamed for that.

When Newton's great book came out at last, the intellectual life of Europe was utterly revolutionized. Newton explained the principles of motion, both on earth and in the heavens, so clearly and irrefutably that the exaggerated reverence for the ancient philosophers was broken forever. However insightful their views of morals and ethics, however valuable their observations and thoughts, where their conclusions differed from those of Newton, they were wrong and Newton was right. Even the authority of the Bible could not stand against the clear reason of Newton's demonstrations. For the first time, then, men of science could move forward with confidence, no longer held back by the constant fear of contradicting the great ancients or the great prophets and fathers.

Furthermore, an understanding of the workings of the universe limited the hypotheses one could pull out of thin air in order to bolster a pet theory. One could not suppose that, because no one had ever climbed beyond the clouds, the earth's gravitational pull weakened and ceased beyond that point. Even without going beyond the clouds, one could be certain then that the pull extended far beyond—weakening at a fixed rate, to be sure, but extending, at substantial values, all the way to the moon's orbit and beyond. What is more, the moon has a gravitational pull of its own. On the moon's surface, that pull could be calculated to be just one-sixth of the earth's pull at its own surface.

Because it is by gravitational pull that the earth holds its atmosphere, and because the extent and intensity of that pull were then known, it could be shown clearly that the atmosphere is quite limited in extent and that almost all the stretch of space between the earth and the moon is vacuum.

Furthermore, the moon's comparatively feeble gravity is very unlikely to hold much of an atmosphere, and that bolstered with logic the astronomical observations that showed the moon to be virtually without an atmosphere.

The arguments in favor of a habitable and reachable moon thus vanished. If the seventeenth century was the Golden Age of moon flight, the eighteenth century should, by rights, have seen an eclipse of that literary genre. Why should anyone be interested in the idea of flight to a barren rock—waterless, airless, lifeless?

It did not happen that way, however, for most of the tales of moon flight before the days of Newton were not science fiction in the modern sense but social satire. There had been no attempt, in describing the political and social customs on the moon, to adapt them to the physical surroundings of that imaginary world. There seems to have been no consideration of the possibility that lunar society, assuming such a thing existed, might be utterly unrelated to that of the earth. No, indeed, lunar society, as described, mirrored the earth's. Its existence was designed to illuminate our society. It served to magnify earthly faults or to exemplify virtues we lacked—in either case, in order to shame us.

When it became clear that the moon could not possibly be inhabited by any creatures we would recognize as similar to ourselves, the satirists shrugged and went on with their work anyway. What difference did it make if the world called the moon bore no relationship to the real moon at all, so long as the satire remained useful?

Jonathan Swift, in 1726, published his book *Gulliver's Travels,* which dealt with islands on the earth's own surface on which six-inch-tall men lived, with vast continents on which huge giants wandered, with lands where dwelt intelligent talking horses, and with others over which a flying rock hovered. These were all impossible, all known to be impossible, all accepted as impossible at every point—but the accuracy and bitterness of the social satire made the book (and has kept it) a classic.

Why should the moon not serve the same purpose as Swift's Lilliput and Brobdingnag? In the eighteenth century, therefore, moon-flight tales survived easily, but with their satire sharpened and the science reduced to a vestige. Thus, "Captain Samuel Brunt," in his *Voyage to Cacklogallina,* is not bothered by the moon's airlessness and uses fantasy freely. He even talks of the earth's "magnetic influences," although the story appeared forty years after Newton's great book. Morris, writing a quarter of a century later, notes the moon's long days and nights but not its lesser gravity. No one seemed to be concerned about how strong or weak the moon's gravitational pull might be.

Indeed, why limit to the moon these fanciful flights? In 1781, the German-English astronomer William Herschel discovered a new planet, which he named Georgium Sidus ("George's Star"), in honor of George III of Great Britain, from whom he expected (and later received) generous support. Eventually that grossly flattering name was dropped, and the new planet was called Uranus.

In 1784, however, the planet's existence was exploited for the sake of social satire by an Englishman using the French nom-de-plume Vivenair. After all, Georgium Sidus would do as well for the purpose as the moon.

To be sure, from the very first observations of the new planet, it was clear that it was far beyond Saturn's orbit, never closer to the earth than 1.6 billion miles, and therefore 6,400 times more distant than the moon. But why need a satirist care about that? If one's mythical astronauts are heading for the moon, they can come across Georgium Sidus just as easily.

So well, indeed, did the satirists do their work, and so much better known to the general public were their entertaining tales than the dry-as-dust conclusions of astronomers, that to most lay people the moon remained a habitable world, and one very likely to be inhabited. Indeed, this unwillingness to accept demonstrated fact lasted well into the nineteenth century and led to one of the most entertaining hoaxes in the history of human folly.

In 1834, John Herschel (a son of the discoverer of Uranus and himself an astronomer of note) traveled to the Cape of Good Hope in order to observe the southern stars with better instruments than had until then been available. He expected to gain much data of interest to astronomers, but nothing startling and certainly nothing that might be expected to fascinate the general public.

While he was in South Africa, however, an American journalist published a series of articles in the New York *Sun* purporting to describe a telescope of unprecedented power, designed and built by Herschel, with which he had observed the moon in great detail, having even been able to make out individual structures and living beings upon it.

The public fell for the tale in masses and hordes. Very few spotted it as a fraud (one of those who did was the fledgling writer Edgar Allan Poe), and it seemed to bother no one that the reports were riddled with astronomical fallacies. The New York *Sun* sold in tremendous quantities to a feverishly excited public for the duration of the hoax.

Yet a new age was dawning, and true science fiction was on the verge of being born. Edgar Allan Poe, for example, wrote several stories in which he was much more interested in using authentic science as a background for fiction than in manufacturing social satire. These, however, were overshadowed by his much more successful horror stories. The nineteenth-century writer could not ignore scientific advances. Poe used a balloon to carry his astronaut to the moon in "Hans Phaall," whereas, in *The Great Steam-Duck,* what is essentially a steam-driven airplane is used.

It fell to the French writer Jules Verne to popularize true science fiction. In 1865, for instance, his *From the Earth to the Moon* was published. The focus of the story was the trip itself. Verne did not care that the moon was uninhabited; he did not even bother to have his heroes land on the moon. It was space flight, the effects on the astronauts, what they could see and feel, that interested him.

And this changed everything. While social satire still exists in science fiction (consider Aldous Huxley's *Brave New World*), it is no longer in the mainstream of that field.

In this volume, then, we have a generous selection of writings on space flight published after Galileo and before Jules Verne—a two-century period in which something that resembled science fiction was used largely as a vehicle for social satire. Its fascination to those who today are interested in astronomy, in space flight, in science fiction should be analogous to the fascination that primitive cultures hold for those interested in psychology and sociology.

The Man in the Moone

FRANCIS GODWIN

From *The Man in the Moone, or A Discourse of a Voyage Thither by Domingo Gonsales The Speedy Messenger* (1638)

[As Isaac Asimov has pointed out, men have dreamed of flying for thousands of years, and, according to mythology, a few men have actually attempted it, usually by trying to emulate the flight of birds. But it was not until Galileo refined the telescope in 1609 and turned his instrument upon the moon that men began once again to consider flying as a real possibility. The first work to capitalize on the revival of popular interest in moon flight was Francis Godwin's *The Man in the Moone, or A Discourse of a Voyage Thither by Domingo Gonsales The Speedy Messenger,* a tale of fantasy and satire sprinkled with science, first published in London in 1638.

Godwin was not a scientist by profession but a man of the cloth. Born in 1562, he was educated at Christ Church College of Oxford University. In 1601 he published his well-received *Catalogue of the Bishops of England.* Perhaps in recognition of his achievement, Queen Elizabeth appointed him Bishop of Llardoff and later Bishop of Hereford.

The Man in the Moone was not published until five years after Godwin's death in 1633, and it was issued anonymously. That Godwin chose to withhold publication during his lifetime and sought to conceal his authorship even afterward is not surprising in view of his position in the Anglican church and his reputation as a historian. He may well have been reluctant to put his name to so frivolous and possibly even blasphemous a tale. This view is implied in the Epistle to the work, which was purportedly written by "E.M." (Edward Mahon), a colleague of Godwin's. ("E.M." may be a pseudonym used by Godwin himself.) The Epistle points out that Columbus met scorn at first and asks the reader to refrain from ridicule until he has given the "speedy messenger" a hearing.

At the time Godwin's story was being written, the study of nature and the universe was passing into the hands of experimental scientists, and attacks on abstract, Aristotelian theories were becoming frequent and vigorous. For centuries men had accepted Ptolemy's view of the cosmos, which placed the earth in the center of the universe, with the sun and stars revolving about it. Theologians as well as Aristotelian philosophers had readily accepted this theory, attempting to make it agree with the Biblical account of the Creation. In 1543, the Copernican theory appeared, challenging Ptolemy by claiming that the earth rotated upon its axis and that the sun was in the center of the universe. Scientists and theologians alike regarded the work as mere speculation; it was not until 1614, when Galileo claimed that his observations supported Copernican theory, that controversy arose. Godwin was certainly familiar with Copernicus's work and even had his fictional narrator support portions of Copernican theory (although Godwin the churchman could not go so far as to have Gonsales believe that the earth revolved around the sun).

In Godwin's story, Gonsales is a shipwrecked mariner who, while waiting for a ship to take him back to his native Spain, spends his time in training birds, which he calls gansas, to carry him into the air. Unlike Daedalus, Icarus, and other early mythical travelers, Gonsales does not attempt to fly by flapping his arms or building winglike extensions onto his body but uses actual birds to pull him aloft. Godwin's suggestion that man might be carried into space by means other than the power of his own body inspired at least one scientist. John Wilkins, author of *The Discovery of a New World,* supposedly added his "A Discourse Concerning the Possibility of a Passage Thither," which introduces a mechanical chariot, to the 1640 edition of his work after having read Godwin's book.

Some of the ideas expressed by Gonsales were no doubt based on the scientific knowledge and theories of the day, but many were the product of Godwin's fertile imagination. He writes of a flying device not unlike the helicopter and airplane, an instrument to send and receive messages that brings to mind the telegraph, and another instrument similar to the telephone. His description of his feeling of weightlessness while traveling at great speed and of the atmosphere he passes through, the brightness of the stars, and the view of the earth from outer space is not unlike the reports of pioneer space travelers of the twentieth century.

Gonsales's world on the moon is Utopia, a satirical reverse image of the imperfect society of early seventeenth-century England. On the moon there is no war or hunger; man is monogamous, faithful at all times to his wife; cures exist for every illness and injury; and all men live in perfect harmony. Moon society is stratified by height, not by money. The monarch, Irdonozur, is the tallest of all moondwellers. It is not only height that gives tall lunars the right to rule but intelligence and age as well. The taller a lunar is, the more intelligent he is and the longer he lives. Learning is held in very high esteem, and those who lie and cheat are severely punished.

Contrary to Godwin's expectations, the tale of Domingo Gonsales's moon voyage became very popular. It was reprinted, according to varying estimates, from twenty to twenty-five times during the seventeenth and eighteenth centuries and was also translated into French, Dutch, and German. Both Edgar Allan Poe and Jules Verne read the work in its French translation and believed, as did many others, that the original was written by a Frenchman. Still others credited it to a Spaniard because of the narrator's name.

In 1656, Domingo Gonsales reappeared, this time as a character in Cyrano de Bergerac's *The Comical History of the States and Empires of the World of the Moon,* reprinted in this volume. Many of the phenomena suggested by Godwin, such as an edible leaf and a language based on tunes, are found on Cyrano's moon as well. Gonsales and his gansas were mentioned in poems by Samuel Butler and William Merton, among others, and played roles in Thomas D'Urfey's comic opera *Wonders in the Sun* (1706) and in Aphra Behn's play *The Emperor of the Moon* (1687).

The text reprinted here is from the extremely rare first edition (1638), of which only four copies are believed to exist. The copy used is in the Lammot du Pont, Jr., Collection of Aeronautics in the Eleutherian Mills Historical Library, Greenville, Wilmington, Delaware.]

The Epistle to the Reader

Tis fit thou allow him a liberty of conceite; where thou takest to thy self a liberty of judgment. In substance thou hast here a new discovery of a new *world,* which perchance may finde little better entertainment in thy opinion, than that of *Columbus* at first, in the esteeme of all men. Yet his than but poore espiall of *America,* betray'd unto knowledge soe much as hath since encreast into a vaste plantation. And the then unknowne, to be now of as large extent as all other the knowne world.

That there should be *Antipodes* was once thought as great a *Paradox* as now that the *Moon* should bee habitable. But the knowledge of this may seeme more properly reserv'd for this our discovering age: In which our *Galilaeusses,* can by advantage of their spectacles gaze the Sunne into spots,

Frontispiece of the 1768 edition of *The Man in the Moone,* retitled *The Strange Voyage and Adventures of Domingo Gonsales to the World in the Moon.* The engraving shows Gonsales en route to his lunar destination. The figures around him are the devils that attacked him while he was in the "middle region."

& descry mountaines in the *Moon*. But this, and more in the ensuing discourse I leave to thy candid censure, & the faithfull relations of the little eye-witnesse, our great discoverer.

E.M.

The Man in the Moone

It is well enough and sufficiently knowne to all the countries of *Andaluzia,* that I *Domingo Gonsales,* was borne of Noble parentage, and that in the renowned City of *Sivill,* to wit in the yeare 1552, my Fathers name being *Therrancio Gonsales,* (that was neere kinsman by the mothers side unto *Don Pedro Sanchez* that worthy Count of *Almenara,*) and as for my Mother, she was the daughter of the Reverend and famous Lawyer, *Otho Perez de Sallaveda,* Governour of *Barcellona,* and *Corrigidor of Biscaia:* being the youngest of 17 Children they had, I was put to schoole, and intended by them unto the Church. But our Lord purposing to use my service in matters of farre other nature and quality, inspired me with spending sometime in the warres.[1] It was at the time that *Don Ferrando,* the Noble and thrice renowned *Duke D'Alva,*[2] was sent into the Low Countries, viz. the yeare of Grace 1568. I then following the current of my foresaid desire, leaving the Universitie of *Salamanca,* (whither my Parents had sent mee) without giving knowledge unto any of my dearest friends, got mee through *France,* unto *Antwerp,* where in the moneth of *June* 1569, I arrived in something poore estate. For having sold my Bookes and Bedding, with such other stuffe as I had, which happily yeelded me some 30 duckats and borrowed of my Fathers friends some 20 more, I brought mee a little nagge with which I travelled more thriftily than young Gentlemen are wont ordinarily to doe; Untill at last arriving within a league of *Antwerp,* certaine of the cursed *Geuses*[3] set upon mee, and bereaved me of Horse, monie, and all: Whereupon I was faine (through want and necessitie,) to

[1] The wars referred to were, no doubt, the civil wars in France and the Low Countries in which Spain fought to preserve Catholicism against the Huguenots and the Calvinists, respectively.

[2] The Duke of Alva, often referred to as the "Iron Duke," was Philip II of Spain's most trusted commander. When the Calvinists in the Low Countries threatened to overthrow Philip's Catholic rule, he dispatched the Duke and ten thousand soldiers to stop the insurrection.

[3] The Guises, princes of Lorraine, represented fanatical Catholicism in France. In their desire to rid the country of the Huguenots, they brought about a civil war in which Philip II of Spain came to the aid of the Catholics and Queen Elizabeth of England supported the Huguenots. The men who attacked Gonsales might have mistaken him, because of his rather shabby attire, for an insignificant traveler rather than an ally.

enter into the service of Marshal *Cofsey* a French Nobleman, whom I served truly in honourable place, although mine enemies gave it out to my disgrace that I was his horse-keepers boy. But for that matter I shall referre my selfe unto the report of the Count *Mansfield*,[3] *Mounsieur Tavier*[4] and other men of knowne worth and estimation; who have often testified unto many of good credit yet living, the very truth in that behalfe, which indeed is this, that *Mounsieur Cossey*, who about that time had been sent Embassador unto the Duke *D'Alva*, Governour of the Low Countries, he I say, understanding the Nobility of my birth, and my late misfortune; thinking it would bee no small honour to him, to have a Spanyard of that qualitie about him, furnished mee with horse, armour, and whatsoever I wanted, using my service in nothing so much (after once I had learned the French tongue) as writing his Letters, because my hand indeed was then very faire. In the time of warre, if upon necessitie I now and then dressed mine owne Horse, it ought not to be cast in my teeth, seeing I hold it the part of a Gentleman for setting forward the service of his Prince, to submit himselfe unto the vilest office. The first expedition I was in, was against the Prince of *Orange*,[6] at what time the Marshall my friend aforesaid, met him making a roade into France, and putting him to flight, chafed him even unto the walls of *Cambray*. It was my good hap at that time to defeat a horseman of the enemy, by killing his Horse with my pistoll, which falling upon his leg, so as he could not stirre, hee yeelded himselfe to my mercie; but I knowing mine owne weaknesse of bodie, and seeing him a lustie tall fellow, thought it my surest way to dispatch him, which having done, I rifled him of a chaine, monie, and other things to the value of 200 ducats: no sooner was that money in my purse, but I began to resume the remembrance of my nobilitie, and giving unto *Monsieur Cossey* the *Besa Los Manos* [obeisance], I got my selfe immediately unto the Dukes court, where were divers of my kindred, that (now they saw my purse full of good Crownes) were ready enough to take knowledge of mee; by their meanes I was received into pay, and in processe of time obtained a good degree of favour with the Duke, who sometimes would jeast a little more broadly at my personage than I could well brook. For although I must acknowledge my stature to be so little, as no man there is living I thinke lesse, yet in as much as it was the work of God and not mine, hee ought

[4] Peter Ernst, Fürst von Mansfeld, who was governor of Luxembourg, led his troops to the aid of the Catholics in France.

[5] Gaspard de Saulx Tavannes, governor of Provence and marshal of France, was very repressive in his dealings with the Huguenots.

[6] William of Orange, a member of the Council of State in the Low Countries, led the insurgents against the established (Catholic) rule.

not to have made that a meanes to dishonour Gentleman with all. And tho things which have happened unto mee, may bee an example, that great and wonderfull things may be performed by most unlikely bodies, the mind be good, and the blessing of our Lord doe second and follow the endeavours of the same. Well, howsoever the Dukes merriments went against my stomacke, I framed my selfe the best I could to dissemble my discontent, and by such my patience accomodating my selfe also unto some other his humors, so won his favour, as at his departure home into *Spaine,* (whither I attended him) the Year 1573 by his favour and some other accidents, (I will say nothing of my owne industry, wherein I was not wanting to my selfe) I was able to carry home in my purse the value of 3000 Crownes. At my returne home my Parents, that were marvellously displeased with my departure, received mee with great joy; and the rather, for that they saw I brought with mee meanes to maintaine my self without their charge, having a portion sufficient of mine owne, so that they needed not to desalk [take away] any thing from my brethren or sisters for my setting up. But fearing I would spend it as lightly as I got it they did never leave opportuning mee, till I must needs marry the daughter of a *Portugais* a Merchant of *Lisbon,* a man of great wealth and dealings, called *John Figueres.* Therein I satisfied their desire, and putting not onely my marriage money, but also a good part of mine owne Stock into the hands of my father in Law, or such as hee wished mee unto, I lived in good sort, even like a Gentleman, with great content for divers yeares. At last it fell out, that some disagreement happened between me and one *Pedro Delgades* a Gentleman of my kinne, the causes whereof are needlesse to be related, but so farre this dissention grew betweene us, as when no mediation of friends could appease the same, into the field wee went together alone with our Rapiers, where my chance was to kill him, being a man of great strength, and tall stature. But what I wanted of him in strength, I supplied with courage, and my nimblenesse more then countervailed his stature. This fact being committed in *Carmona,* I fled with all the speed I could to *Lisbone,* thinking to lurke with some friend of my Father in-lawes, till the matter might bee compounded, and a course taken for a sentence of Acquittall by consent of the prosecutors. This matter fell out in the Yeare 1596, even at that time that a certaine great Count of ours came home from the West-Indies, in triumphant manner, boasting and spending out his declarations in print, of a great victory hee had obtained against the *English,* neere the *Isle of Pines.* Whereas the truth is, he got of the *English* nothing at all in that Voyage, but blowes and a great losse.

Would to God that lying and Vanitie had beene all the faults he had; his covetousnesse was like to bee my utter undoing, although since it hath proved a meanes of eternizing my name for ever with all Posteritie, (I verily hope) and to the unspeakeable good of all mortall men, that in succeeding ages the world shall have if at the leastwise it may please God that I doe returne safe home againe into my Countrie, to give perfect instructions how those admirable devices, and past all credit of possibilitie, which I have light upon, may be imparted unto publique use. You shal then see men to flie from place to place in the ayre; you shall be able, (without moving or travailing of any creature,) to send messages in an instant many Miles off, and receive answer againe immediately; you shall bee able to declare your minde presently unto your friend, being in some private and remote place of a populous Citie, with a number of such like things: but that which far surpasseth all the rest, you shall have notice of a new World, of many most rare and incredible secrets of Nature, that all the Philosophers of former ages could never so much as dreame off. But I must be advised, how I be over-liberall, in publishing these wonderfull mysteries, till the Sages of our State have considered how farre the use of these things may stand with the Policy and good government of our Countrey, as also with the Fathers of the Church, how the publication of them, may not prove prejudiciall to the affaires of the Catholique faith and Religion, which I am taught (by those wonders I have seen above any mortall man that hath lived in many ages past) with all my best endeavours to advance, without all respect of temporall good, and soe I hope I shall.

But to goe forward with my narration, so it was that the bragging Captaine above named, made shew of great discontentment, for the death of the said *Delgades,* who was indeed some kinne unto him. Howbeit hee would have been intreated, so that I would have given him no lesse than 1000. Ducats (for his share) to have put up his Pipes [been quiet], and surceased all suite in his Kinsmans behalfe; I had by this time (besides a wife) two sonnes whom I liked not to beggar by satisfying the desire of this covetous braggart and the rest, and therefore constrained of necessity to take another course, I put my selfe in a good Caricke[7] that went for the East *Indies,* taking with me the worth of 2000. Ducats to traffique withall, being yet able to leave so much more for the estate of my wife and children, whatsoever might become of me, and the goods I carried with me. In the *Indies* I prospered exceeding well, bestowing my stocke in *Jewells,* namely, for the most part in *Diamonds, Emeraulds,* and great *Pearle;* of which I had such peniworths, as my stocke being safely returned into

[7] A very large, heavy, well-armed merchant ship that could carry several hundred passengers.

Spaine, (so I heard it was) must needs yeeld ten for one. But my selfe upon my way homeward soone after we had doubled the East of *Buena Speranza* [the Cape of Good Hope], fell grievously sicke for many daies, making account by the same sicknesse to end my life, as undoubtedly I had done, had we not (even then as we did) recovered that same blessed *Isle of S. Hellens,* the only paradice, I thinke, that the earth yeeldeth, of the healthfulnesse of the Aire there, the fruitfulnesse of the soile, and the abundance of all manner of things necessary for sustaining the life of man, what should I speake, seeing there is scant a boy in all *Spaine,* that hath not heard of the fame? I cannot but wonder, that our King in his wisdome hath not thought fit to plant a Colony, and to fortifie in it, being a place so necessary for refreshing of all travaillers out of the *Indies,* so as it is hardly possible to make a Voyage thence, without touching there.

It is situate in the Altitude of 16. degrees to the South, and is about 3. leagues[8] in compasse, having no firme land or continent within 300. leagues, nay not so much as an *Island* within 100. leagues of the same, so that it may seeme a miracle of Nature, that out of so huge and tempestuous an Ocean, such a little peece of ground should arise and discover it selfe. Upon the South side there is a very good harborough, and neere unto the same divers edifices built by the *Portingals* [Portuguese] to entertaine passengers, amongst the which there is a pretty Chappell handsomly beautified with a Tower, having a faire Bell in the same. Neere unto this housing there is a pretty Brooke of excellent fresh water, divers faire walkes made by hand, and set along upon both sides, with fruit-Trees, especially Oranges, Limmons, Pomgranats, Almonds, and the like which beare Fruit all the yeare long, as doe also the fig-Trees, Vines, Peare-Trees, (whereof there are divers sorts,) Palmitos, Cocos, Olives, Plumms; . . . as for Apples I dare say there are none at all; of garden Hearbs there is good store, as of Parsely, Cole-worts [kale], Rosemary, Mellons, Gourds, Lettice, and the like; Corne likewise growing of it selfe, incredible plenty, as *Wheate, Pease, Barley* . . . but chiefly it aboundeth with *Cattell,* and *Fowle,* as *Goates, Swine, Sheepe,* and *Horses, Partridges,* wilde *Hens, Phesants, Pigeons,* and wild *Fowle,* beyond all credit; especially there are to be seene about the Moneths of *February,* and *March,* huge flocks of a certaine kinde of wild *Swans* (of which I shall have cause heerafter to speake more) that like unto our *Cuckoes,* and *Nightingales,* at a certaine season of the yeare, doe vanish away, and are no more to be seene.

On this blessed *Island* did they set mee ashore with a Negro to attend

[8] A league is presently equivalent to three miles, though it has varied in different periods of history and from country to country.

me, where, praised bee God, I recovered my health, and continued there for the space of one whole yeare, solacing my selfe (for lacke of humane society) with *Birds,* and brute beasts, as for Diego (so was the *Blackmoore* called,) he was constrained to live at the West end of the *Island* in a Cave. Because being alwayes together, victuals would not have fallen out so plenty: if the Hunting or Fowling of the one had suceded well, the other would finde means to invite him, but if it were scant with both, we were faine both to bestirre our selves; marry that fell out very seldome, for that no creature there doe any whit more feare a man, then they doe a *Goate* or a *Cow;* by reason thereof I found meanes easily to make tame divers sorts both of *Birds* and *Beasts,* which I did in short time, onely by muzzeling them, so as till they came either unto me, or else *Diego,* they could not feede. At first I tooke great pleasure in a kinde of *Partridges,* of which I made great use, as also of a tame *Fox* I had. For whensoever I had any occasion to conferre with *Diego,* I would take me one of them, being hungry, and tying a note about his necke, beat him from me, whereupon strait they would away to the Cave of *Diego,* and if they found him not there, still would beat up and downe all the West end of the *Island,* till they had hunted him out; yet this kinde of conveyance not being without some inconvenience needlesse heere to be recited; after a certaine space I perswaded Diego (who though he were a fellow of good parts, was ever content to be ruled by me,) to remove his habitation unto a promontory or cape upon the North West part of the *Island,* being though a league off, yet within sight of my house and Chappell and then, so long as the weather was faire, we could at all times by signalls, declare our minds each to other in an instant, either by night, or by day; which was a thing I tooke great pleasure in.

If in the night season I would signifie any thing to him, I used to set up a light in the Tower or place where our bell hung: It is a pretty large roome, having a faire window well glased, and the walls within being plaistered, were exceeding white; by reason thereof, though the light were but small it gave a great shew, as also it would have done much further off if need had beene. This light after I had let stand some halfe houre, I used to cover: and then if I saw any signall of light againe from my companion at the cape, I knew that he waited for my notice, which perceiving, by hiding and shewing my light, according to a certaine rule and agreement between us, I certified him at pleasure what I list: The like course I tooke in the day to advertise him of my pleasure, sometimes by smoake; sometimes by dust, sometimes by a more refined and more effectual way.

But this Art containeth more mysteries then are to be set downe in few words: Hereafter I will perhaps afford a discourse for it of purpose, assuring my selfe that it may prove exceedingly profitable unto mankind, being rightly used and well imployed: for that which a messenger cannot performe in many dayes, this may dispatch in a peece of an houre. Well, I notwithstanding after a while grew weary of it, as being too painfull for me, and betook me againe to my winged messengers.

Upon the Sea shore, especially about the mouth of our River, I found great store of a certain kinde of wild *Swan* (before mentioned) feeding almost altogether upon the prey, and (that which is somewhat strange,) partly of Fish, partly of Birds, having (which is also no lesse strange) one foote with Clawes, talons, and pounces, like an *Eagle,* and the other whole like a Swan or water fowle. These birds using to breed there in infinite numbers, I tooke some 30. or 40. young ones of them, and bred them up by hand partly for my recreation, partly also as having in my head some rudiments of that device, which afterward I put in practise. These being strong and able to continue a great flight, I taught them first to come at call affarre off, not using any noise but onely the shew of a white Cloth. . . . It were a wonder to tell what trickes I had taught them, by that time they were a quarter old; amongst other things I used them by little and little to fly with burthens, wherein I found them able above all credit, and brought them to that passe, as that a white sheet being displayed unto them by Diego upon the side of a hill, they would carry from me unto him, Bread, flesh, or any other thing I list to send, and upon the like call returne unto mee againe.

Having prevailed thus farre, I began to cast in my head how I might doe to joyne a number of them together in bearing of some great burthen: which if I could bring to passe, I might enable a man to fly and be carried in the ayre, to some certaine place safe and without hurt. In this cogitation having much laboured my wits, and made some triall, I found by experience, that if many were put to the bearing of one great burthen, by reason it was not possible all of them should rise together just in one instant, the first that raised himselfe upon his wings finding himselfe stayed by a weight heavier than hee could move or stirre, would by and by give over, as also would the second, third, and all the rest. I devised (therefore) at last a meanes how each of them might rise carrying but his owne proportion of weight only, and it was thus.

I fastned about every one of my Gansas[9] a little pulley of Corke, and putting a string through it of meetly [suitable] length, I fastened the one

[9] Godwin's name for the wild swans described above.

end thereof unto a blocke almost of eight Pound weight, unto the other end of the string I tied a [weight of] some two Pound, which being done, and causing the signall to be erected, they presently rose all (being 4 in number,) and carried away my blocke unto the place appointed. This falling out according to my hope and desire, I made proofe afterwards, but using the help of 2. or 3. birds more, in a Lamb, whose happinesse I much envied, that he should be the first living creature to take possession of such a device.

As last after divers tryalls I was surprized with a great longing, to cause my selfe to be carried in the like sort. *Diego* my Moore was likewise possessed with the same desire, and but that otherwise I loved him well, and had need of his helpe, I should have taken that his ambitious affection in very evill part: for I hold it farre more honour to have been the first flying man, then to bee another *Neptune* that first adventured to sayle upon the Sea. Howbeit not seeming to take notice of the marke hee aymed at, I onely told him (which also I take to be true) that all my Gansa's were not of sufficient strength to carry him, being a man, though of no great stature, yet twice my weight at least. So upon a time having provided all things necessary, I placed my selfe with all my trinckets, upon the top of a rocke at the Rivers mouth, and putting my selfe at full Sea upon an Engine (the description whereof ensueth) I caused *Diego* to advance his Signall: whereupon my Birds presently arose, 25 in number, and carried mee over lustily to the other rocke on the other side, being about a Quarter of a league.

The reason why I chose that time and place, was that I thought somewhat might perchance fall out in this enterprise contrary to my expectation, in which case I assured my selfe the worst that could bee, was but to fall into the water, where being able to swim well, I hoped to receive little or no hurt in my fal. But when I was once over in safety, O how did my heart even swell with joy and admiration of mine owne invention! How often did I wish my selfe in the midst of *Spaine,* that speedily I might fill the world with the fame of my glory and renowne? Every hower wished I with great longing for the *Indian* Fleet to take mee home with them, but they stayed (by what mischance I know not) 3 Moneths beyond the accustomed time.

At last they came being in number 3 Carickes sore weather-beaten, their people being for the most part sick and exceedingly weak, so as they were constrained to refresh themselves in our Island one whole moneth.

The Captaine of our Admirall was called *Alphonso de Xima,* a Valiant man, wise, and desirous of renowne, and worthy [of] better fortune then afterward befell him. Unto him I opened the device of my *Gansa's,* well knowing how impossible it were otherwise to perswade him to take in so many Birds into the Ship, that would bee more troublesome (for the nicenesse of provision to be made for them,) then so many men; Yet I adjured him by all manner of Oaths, and perswasions, to afford mee both true dealing, and secrecy. Of the last I doubted not much, as assuring my selfe, he would not dare to impart the device to any other, before our King were acquainted with it. Of the first I feared much more, namely, lest Ambition, and the desire of drawing unto himselfe the honour of such an invention, should cause him to make mee away; yet I was forced to run the hazard, except I would adventure the losse of my Birds, the like whereof for my purpose were not to be had in all Christendome. . . . Well, that doubt in proofe fell out to be causeless: the man I thinke was honest of himselfe: but had he dealt treacherously with me, I had laid a plot for the discovery of him, as he might easily judge I would, which peradventure somewhat moved him, yet God knowes how he might have used me, before my arrivall in *Spaine,* if in the meane course wee had not been intercepted, as you shall heare. Upon Thursday the 21. of *June,* to wit in the yeare, 1599. wee set saile towards *Spaine,* I having allowed me a very convenient Cabin for my *Birds,* and stowage also for mine Engine, which the Captaine would have had me leave behinde me, and it is a mervaile I had not, but my good fortune therein saved my life, and gave me that which I esteeme more then an hundred lives, if I had them: for thus it fell out, after 2. moneths saile, we encountered with a fleet of the *English,* some 10. leagues from the *Island of Tenerik* [Tenerife] one of the *Canaries,* which is famous through the World, for a Hill upon the same called *el Pico* [Pico de Teide, a volcanic peak 12,000 feet high] that is to be discerned and kenned upon the Sea no lesse then 100. leagues off. We had aboord us 5. times the number of people that they had; we were well provided of munition, and our men in good health. Yet seeing them disposed to fight, and knowing what infinite riches wee carried with us, we thought it a wiser way to fly, if we might, then by encountring a company of dangerous fellowes to hazard not onely our owne lives, (which a man of valour in such a case esteemeth not) but the estates of many poore Merchants, who I am affraid were utterly undone by miscarriage of that businesse. Our fleete then consisted of 5 sayle, to wit, 3. Carickes, a Barke, and a Caravell,[10] that comming from the Isle of Saint *Thomas,* had (in an evill houre for him) overtaken us some few dayes before.

The *English* had 3. Ships very well appointed, and no sooner spied, but they began to play for us, and changing their course, as wee might well

[10] A small, fast vessel.

perceive, endeavoured straight way to bring us under their lee,[11] which they might well doe (as the wind stood) especially being light nimble vessells, and yare of Sayle [maneuverable], as for the most part all the *English* shipping is, whereas ours was heavy, deepe laden, foule with the Sea: our Captaine therefore resolved peradventure wisely enough (but I am sure neither valiantly, nor fortunately) to flie, commanding us to disperse our selves: the Caravell by reason of too much hast fell foule upon one of the Carickes, and bruised her so, as one of the *English* that had undertaken her, easily fetcht her up and entred her: as for the caravell shee sanke immediately in the sight of us all. The Barke (for ought I could perceive) no man making after her, escaped unpursued; and another of our carickes after some chase, was given over by the *English,* that making account to finde a booty good enough of us, and having us betweene them and their third companion, made upon us with might and maine. Wherefore our Captaine that was aboord us, gave direction to runne aland upon the *Isle,* the Port whereof we could not recover, saying that hee hoped to save some of the goods, and some of our lives, and the rest he had rather should bee lost, then commit all to the mercy of the enemie. When I heard of that resolution, seeing the Sea to worke high, and knowing all the coast to bee full of blind Rockes, and Shoales, so as our Vessell might not possibly come neere land, before it must needs be rent in a thousand peeces, I went unto the Captaine, shewing him the desperateness of the course hee intended, wishing him rather to trie the mercy of the enemie, then so to cast away himselfe, and so many brave men: but hee would not heare me by any meanes; whereupon discerning it to be high time to shift for my selfe, first, I sought out my Box or little Casket of stones, and having put it into my sleeve, I then betooke me of my *Gansa's,* put them upon my Engine, and my selfe upon it, trusting (as indeed it happily fell out) that when the Shippe would split, my Birds, although they wanted their Signall, of themselves, and for safegard of their owne lives (which nature hath taught every living creature to preserve to their power) would make towards the Land; which fell out well (I thanke God,) according to mine expectation. The people of our Ship mervailed about what I went, none of them being acquainted with the use of my *Birds,* but the Captaine, for *Diego* was in the *Rosaria,* the Ship that fled away unpursued, (as before I told you:) some halfe a league we were from the Land, when our Carick strake upon a Rocke, and split immediately: whereupon I let loose unto my Birds the raines, having first placed my selfe upon the highest of the Decke: and with the shock they all arose, carrying mee fortunately unto

[11] That is, to a position such that the wind would blow from the English to them.

the Land, . . . but a pittifull sight it was unto me, to behold my friends and acquaintance in that miserable distresse of whom (notwithstanding) many escaped better then they had any reason to hope for. For the *English* launching out their cockboates [tenders], like men of more noble, and generous disposition then wee are pleased to esteeme them, taking compassion upon them, to helpe such as had any meanes to save themselves from the furie of the waves and that even with their owne danger: amongst many, they tooke up our Captaine, who . . . having put himselfe into his Cock with 12. others, was induced to yeeld himselfe unto one Captaine Rymundo, who carried him together with our Pilote along in their voyage with them, being bound for the East *Indies;* but their hard hap [luck] was by a breach of the Sea neere the cape of *Buona Esperanca* [Good Hope], to be swallowed of the mercilesse Waves, whose fury a little before they had so hardly escaped. The rest of them (as I likewise heard) and they were in all some 26. persons that they took into their ship, they set them a land soone after at *Cape Verde.*

As for my selfe, being now a shore in a Country inhabited for the most part by *Spaniards,* I reckoned my selfe in safety. Howbeit I quickly found the reckoning, I so made, mine Host had not beene acquainted with all; for it was my chance to pitch upon that part of the Isle, where the hill before mentioned, beginneth to rise. And it is inhabited by a Savage kinde of people, that live upon the sides of that hill, the top whereof is alwayes covered with Snow, and held for the monstrous height and steepnesse not to be accessible either for man or beast, Howbeit these Savages fearing the *Spaniards,* (betweene whom and them there is a kinde of continuall warre) hold themselves as neere the top of that hill as they can, where they have divers places of good strength, never comming downe into the fruitfull Valleys, but to prey upon what they can finde there. It was the chance of a company of them to espie mee within some howers space after my Landing: They thinking they had light upon a booty, made towards mee with all the speed they could, but not so privily as that I could not perceive their purpose before they came neere to me by halfe a Quarter of a League; seeing them come downe the side of a Hill with great speed directly towards mee, divers of them carrying Long Staves, besides other weapons, which because of their distance from mee I might not discerne. I thought it high time to bestirre mee, and shift for my selfe, and by all meanes, to keepe my selfe out of the fingers of such slaves, who had they caught mee, for the hatred they beare to us *Spaniards,* had surely hewed me all to peeces.

The Country in that place was bare, without the coverture of any wood:

But the mountaine before spoken of, beginning even there to lift up itselfe, I espied in the side of the same a white cliffe, which I trusted my *Gansa's* would take for a signall, and being put off, would make all that way, whereby I might quickly bee carried so farre, as those barbarous Cullions [knaves] should not be able to overtake mee, before I had recovered the dwelling of some *Spaniard,* or at least-wise might have time to hide my selfe from them, till that in the night, by helpe of the starres, I might guide my selfe toward *Las Loeguna,* the City of that Island, which was about one league off, as I thinke. Wherefore with all the celeritie that might be I put my selfe upon mine Engine, and let loose the raines unto my *Gansa's.* It was my good fortune that they tooke all one way, although not just that way I aymed at. But what then. O Reader, . . . prepare thy selfe unto the hearing of the strangest Chance that ever happened to any mortall man, and that I know thou wilt not have the Grace to beleeve, till thou seest it seconded with Iteration of Experiments in the like, as many a one, I trust, thou mayest in short time; My *Gansa's,* like so many horses that had gotten the bitt betweene their teeth, made . . . not towards the cliffe I aymed at, although I used my wonted meanes to direct the Leader of the flocke that way, but with might and maine tooke up towards the top of *El Pico,* and did never stay till they came there, a place where they say never man came before, being in all estimation at least 15 leagues in height perpendicularly upward, above the ordinary levell of the Land and Sea.

What manner of place I found there, I should gladly relate unto you, but that I make hast to matters of farre greater Importance. There when I was set downe, I saw my poore *Gansa's,* fall to panting and blowing, gaping for breath, as if they would all presently have died: wherefore I thought it not good to trouble them a while, forbearing to draw them in, (which they never wont to indure without strugling) and little expecting that which followed.

It was now the season that these Birds were wont to take their flight away, as our Cuckoes and swallowes doe in *Spaine* towards the Autumne. They (as after I perceived) mindfull of their usual voyage, even as I began to settle my selfe for the taking of them in, as it were with one consent, rose up, and having no other place higher to make toward, to my unspeakeable feare and amazement strooke bolt upright, and never did linne [lean] towring upward, and still upward for the space, as I might guesse, of one whole hower; toward the end of which time, mee thought I might perceive them to labour lesse and lesse; till at length, O incredible thing, they forbare moving any thing at al! and yet remained unmoveable, as stedfastly, as if they had beene upon so many perches; the Lines slacked;

neither I, nor the Engine moved at all, but abode still as having no manner of weight.

I found then by this Experience that which no Philosopher ever dreamed of, to wit, that those things which wee call heavie, do not sinke toward the Center of the Earth, as their naturall place, but as drawen by a secret property of the Globe of the Earth, or rather some thing with in the same, in like sort as the Loadstone draweth Iron, being within the compasse of the beames attractive.

For though it bee true that there they could abide unmoved without the proppe or sustentation of any corporall thing other then the ayre, as easily and quietly as a fish in the middle of the water, yet forcing themselves never so little, it is not possible to imagine with what swiftnesse and celeritie they were carried, and whether it were upward, downward, or sidelong, all was one. Truly I must confesse, the horror and amazement of that place was such, as if I had not been armed with a true *Spanish* courage and resolution, I must needs have died there with very feare.

But the next thing that did most trouble me, was the swiftnesse of Motion, such as did even almost stop my breath; If I should liken it to an Arrow out of a Bow, or to a stone cast downe from the top of some high tower, it would come farre short, and short.

An other thing there was exceeding, and more then exceeding, troublesome unto mee, and that was the Illusions of Devills and wicked spirits, who, the first day of my arrivall, came about mee in great numbers, carrying the shapes and likenesse of men and women, wondring at mee like so many Birds about an Owle, and speaking divers kindes of Languages which I understood not, till at last I did light upon them that spake very good *Spanish,* some *Dutch,* and othersome *Italian,* for all these Languages I understood.

And here I saw onely a touch of the Sunnes absence for a little while once, ever after having him in my sight. Now to yeeld you satisfaction in the other, you shall understand that my *Gansa's,* although entangled in my lynes, might easily find means to sease upon divers kinds of flyes and Birds, as especially Swallowes, and Cuckoes, whereof there were multitudes, as Motes in the sunne; although to say the truth I never saw them to feed any thing at all. As for my selfe, in truth I was much beholding unto those same, whether men or Divels I know not, that a mongst divers speeches, which I will forbeare a while to relate, told me, that if I would follow their directions, I should not onely bee brought safely to my home, but also be assured to have the command of all pleasures of that place, at all times.

To the which motions not daring to make a flat deniall, I prayed a time to thinke of it, and with all intreated them (though I felt no hunger at all, which may seeme strange) to helpe mee with some victualls, least in the meane while I should starve. They did so, readily enough, and brought me very good Flesh, and Fish, of divers sorts well dressed, but that it was exceeding fresh, and without any manner of relish or salt.

Wine also I tasted there of divers sorts, as good as any in *Spayne,* and Beere, no better in all *Antwerp.* They wished me then, while I had meanes to make my provision, telling me, that till the next Thursday they could not helpe me to any more, if happily then; at what time also they would find meanes to carry me backe and set mee safe in *Spayne* where I would wish to be, so that I would become one of their fraternity, and enter into such covenants and profession as they had made to their Master and Captaine, whom they would not name. I answered them gently for the time, telling them, I saw little reason to be very glad of such an offer, praying them to be mindfull of me as occasion served.

So for that time I was ridd of them, having first furnished my Pocketts with as much Victuall as I could thrust in, among the which I fail not to afford for a little Botijo[12] of good Canary wine.

Now shall I declare unto you the quality of the place, in which I then was. The Clouds I perceived to be all under me, betweene mee and the earth. The starres, by reason it was alwaies day, I saw at all times alike, not shining bright, as upon the earth, we are wont to see them in the night time; but of a whitish Colour, like that of the moone in the day time with us: And such of them as were to be seene (which were not many) . . . shewed farre greater then with us, yea (as I should ghesse) no lesse then ten times so great. As for the Moone being then within two daies of the change, she appeared of a huge and fearefull quantitie.

This also is not to be forgotten, that no starres appeared but on that part of the Hemispheare that was next the Moone, and the neerer to her the bigger in Quantity they shewed. Againe I must tell you, that whether I lay quiet and rested, or else were carryed in the Ayre, I perceived my selfe still to be alwaies directly betweene the Moone and the earth. Whereby it appeareth, not only that my *Gansa's* took none other way then directly toward the Moone, but also, that when we rested (as at first we did for many howers,) either we were insensibly carryed, (for I perceived no such motion) round about the Globe of the Earth, or else that (according to the late opinion of *Copernicus,*) the Earth is carried about, and turneth round perpetually, from *West* to the *East,* leaving unto the Planets onely that motion which Astronomers call naturall. . . .

[12] An earthen pitcher.

The ayre in that place I found quiet without any motion of wind and exceeding temperate, neither hot nor cold, as where neither the Sunne-beames had any subject to reflect upon, neither was yet either the earth or water so neere as to affect the ayre with their natural quality of coldnesse. As for the imagination of the Philosopher attributing heat together with moystnesse unto the ayre, I never esteemed it otherwise then a fancy. Lastly now it is to be remembered that after my departure from the earth, I never felt any appetite or hunger or thirst. Whether the purety of the Ayre our proper element not being infected with any Vapor of the Earth and water might yeald nature sufficient nutriment; or what else might be the cause of it, I cannot tell but so I found it, although I perceived my selfe in perfect health of body, having the use of all my Limmes and senses; and strength both of body and minde, rather beyond and above, then any thing short of the pitch, or wonted vigor. Now let us goe on: and on we shall go more then apace.

Not many howers after the departure of that divelish company from me, my *Gansa's* began to bestir themselues, still directing their course toward the Globe or body of the Moone: And they made their way with that incredible swiftnesse, as I thinke they gained not so little as Fifty Leagues in every hower. In that passage I noted three things very remarkeable: one that the further we went, the lesser the Globe of the Earth appeared unto us; whereas still on the contrary side the Moone shewed her selfe more and more monstrously huge.

Againe, the Earth (which ever I held in mine eye) did as it were mask it selfe with a kind of brightnesse like another Moone, and even as in the Moone we discerned certaine spots or Clouds, as it were, so did I then in the Earth. But whereas the forme of those spots in the Moone continue constantly one and the same; these little and little did change every hower. The reason thereof I conceive to be this, that whereas the Earth according to her naturall motion, (for that such a motion she hath, I am now constrained to joyne in opinion with *Copernicus,*) turneth round upon her owne Axe every 24 howers from the *West* unto the *East:* I should at the first see in the middle of the body of this new starre a spot like unto a Peare that had a morsell bitten out upon the one side of him; after certaine howers, I should see that spot slide away to the East side. This no doubt was the maine [coast] of *Affrike.*

Then should I perceive a great shining brightnesse to occupy that roome, during the like time (which was undoubtedly none other then the great *Atlantick* Ocean). After that succeeded a spot almost of an Ovall form, even just such as we see America to have in our Mapps. Then another vast cleernesse representing the *West* [Pacific] *Ocean;* and lastly a medly of spots, like the Countries of the *East Indies.* So that it seemed unto me no other then a huge Mathematicall Globe, leasurely turned before me, wherein successively, all the Countries of our earthly world within the compasse of 24 howers were represented to my sight. And this was all the meanes I had now to number the dayes, and take reckoning of time.

Philosophers and *Mathematicians* I would should now confesse the wilfulnesse of their owne blindnesse. They have made the world beleeve hitherto, that the Earth hath no motion. And to make that good they are fain to attribute unto all and every of the celestial bodies, two motions quite contrary each to other; whereof one is from the *East* to the *West,* to be performed in 24 howers; the other from the *West* to the *East* in severall proportions.

O incredible thing, that those same huge bodies of the fixed stars in the highest orbe, whereof divers are by themselves confessed to be more then one hundreth times as bigge as the whole earth,[13] should as so many nayles in a Cart Wheele, be whirled about in that short space, whereas it is many thousands of Yeares (no lesse, I trowe, they say, then 30 thousand) before that orb do finish his Course from *West* to *East,* which they call the naturall motion. Now whereas to every of these they yeeld their naturall course from *West* to *East;* therin they doe well. The *Moone* performeth it in 27 daies; the *Sunne, Venus,* and *Mercury* in a Yeare or thereabouts, *Mars* in three Yeares, *Jupiter* in twelve Yeares, and *Saturne* in 30. But to attribute unto these celestial bodies contrary motions at once, was a very absurd conceit, and much more, to imagine that same Orbe wherein the fixed stars are, (whose naturall course taketh so many thousand of yeares) should every 24 howers be turned about. I will not go so farre as *Copernicus,* that maketh the Sunne the Center of the Earth, and unmoveable, neither will I define any thing one way or other. Only this I say, allow the Earth his motion (which these eyes of mine can testifie to be his due) and these absurdities are quite taken away, every one having his single and proper Motion onely.

But where am I? At the first I promised an History, and I fall into disputes before I am aware. There is yet one accident more befell me worthy of especiall remembrance: that during the time of my stay I saw as it were a kind of cloud of a reddish colour growing toward me, which continually growing nearer and nearer, at last I perceived to be nothing else but a huge swarme of Locusts.

[13] The smallest stars are believed to be the size of planets. One of the larger stars, Antares, has a diameter reportedly 390 times as large as the sun, whose diameter is roughly 100 times larger than the earth's.

He that readeth the discourses of learned men . . . how that they are seene in the Ayre many dayes before they fall upon a countrey, adding unto that which they deliver, this experience of mine, will easily conclude, that they cannot come from any other place then the Globe of the Moone. But give me leave now at last to passe on my journey quietly, without interruption for Eleven or Twelve daies, during all which time, I was carried directly toward the Globe or body of the Moone with such a violent whirling as cannot bee expressed.

For I cannot imagine that a bullet out of the mouth of a Cannon could make way through the vaporous and muddie aire neere the earth with that celerity, which is most strange, considering that my *Gansa's* moved their wings but even now and then, and sometimes not at all in a Quarter of an hower together; only they held them stretched out, so passing on, as we see that *Eagles,* and *Kites* sometimes will doe for a little space, . . . and during the time of those pauses I beleeve they tooke their napps and times of sleeping; for other (as I might easily note) they had none.

Now for my selfe, I was so fast knit unto my Engin, as I durst commit my selfe to slumbring enough to serve my turne, which I tooke with as great ease (although I am loath to speake it, because it may seeme incredible) as if I had beene in the best Bed of downe in all *Antwerp.*

After Eleven daies passage in this violent flight, I perceived that we began to approach neare unto another Earth, if I may so call it, being the Globe or very body of that starre which we call the Moone.

The first difference that I found betweene it and our earth, was, that it shewed it selfe in his naturall colours: ever after I was free from the attraction of the Earth; whereas with us, a thing removed from our eye but a league or two, begins to put on that lurid and deadly colour of blew.

Then, I perceived also, that it was covered for the most part with a huge and mighty Sea, those parts only being drie Land, which shew unto us here somewhat darker then the rest of her body (that I mean which the Country people cal *el hombre della Luna,* the Man of the Moone).

As for that part which shineth so clearly in our eyes; it is even another Ocean, yet besprinckled heere and there with *Islands,* which for the littlenesse, so farre off we cannot discern.

So that same splendor appearing unto us, and giving light unto our night, appeareth to be nothing else but the reflexion of the Sun beames returned unto us out of the water, as out of a glasse: How ill this agreeth with that which our *Philosophers* teach in the schooles I am not ignorant.

But alas how many of their Errors hath time and experience refuted in this our age, with the recall whereof I will not stand to trouble the reader.

Amongst many other of their vaine surmises, the time and order of my narration putteth me in mind of one which now my experience found most untrue.

Who is there that hath not hitherto beleeved the uppermost Region of the Ayre to be extreame hot, as being next forsooth unto the natural place of the Element of Fire.

O Vanities, fansies, Dreames!

After the time I was once quite free from the attractive Beames of that tyrannous Loadstone the earth, I found the Ayre of one and the selfe same temper, without Winds, without Raine, without Mists, without Clouds, neither hot nor cold, but continually after one and the same tenor, most pleasant, milde, and comfortable, till my arrivall in that new World of the Moone.

As for that Region of Fire our *Philosophers* talke of, I heard no newes of it; mine eyes have sufficiently informed me there can be no such thing.

The Earth by turning about had now shewed me all her pasts twelve times when I finished my course: For when by my reckoning it seemed to be (as indeed it was) Tuesday the Eleventh day of *September,* (at what time the Moone being two daies old was in the Twentieth degree of *Libra,*) my *Gansa's* staied their course as it was with one consent, and tooke their rest, for certaine howers; after which they tooke their flight, and within lesse then one hower, set me upon the top of a very high hill in that other world, where immediately were presented unto mine eyes many most strange and unwonted sights.

For first I observed, that although the Globe of the Earth shewed much bigger there then the Moone doth unto us, . . . yet all maner of things there were of largenesse and quantity, 10. 20. I thinke I may say 30. times more then ours.

Their trees at least three times so high as ours, and more then five times the breadth and thicknesse.

So their herbes, Beasts, and Birds; although to compare them with ours I know not well how, because I found not any thing there, any *Species* either of *Beast* or *Bird* that resembled ours any thing at all, except *Swallowes, Nightingales, Cuckooes, Woodcockes, Batts,* and some kindes of wild *Fowle,* as also of such *Birds* as my *Gansa's,* all which, (as now I well perceived,) spend the time of their absence from us, even there in that world; neither do they vary any thing at all either in quantity or quality from those of ours heere, as being none other then the very same, and that not onely *Specie, but numero.*

But of these novelties, more hereafter in their due places.

No sooner was I set downe upon the ground, But I was surprised with a most ravenous hunger, and earnest desire of eating. Wherefore stepping unto the next tree, I fastened thereunto my engine, with my *Gansa's,* and in great haste fell to searching of my pockets for the Victuals I had reserved as aforesaid but to my great amazement and discomfort, I found in stead of *Parridge,* and *Capon* which I thought to have put there, a mingle mangle of drye leaves, of *Goats hayre, sheepe,* or *Goats-dung, Mosse,* and such like trash.

As for my *Canary Wine,* it was turned to a stinking and filthie kind of liquor like the Urine of some *Beast.*

O the illusions of wicked spirits, whose helpe if I had been faine only to rely upon, you see how I had been served.

Now while I stood musing and wondering at this strange *Metamorphosis,* I heard my *Gansa's* upon the sudden to make a great fluttering behind me. And looking back, I espied them to fall greedily upon a certaine shrub within the compasse of their lines, whose leaves they fed upon most earnestly; where heretofore, I had never seene them to eat any manner of greene meate whatsoever. Whereupon stepping to the shrubb, I put a leafe of it between my teeth: I cannot expresse the pleasure I found in the tast thereof; such it was I am sure, as if I had not with great discretion moderated my appetite, I had surely surfetted upon the same.

In the meane time it fell out to be a baite that well contented both my *Birds* and me at that time, when we had need, of some good refreshing.

Scarcely had I ended this banquett, when upon the sudden I saw my selfe environed with a kind of people most strange, both for their feature, demeanure, and apparell.

Their feature was most divers but for the most part, twice the height of ours: their colour and countenance most pleasing, and their habit such, as I know not how to expresse.

For neither did I see any kind of *Cloth, Silke,* or other stuffe to resemble the matter of that whereof their Clothes were made; neither (which is most strange, of all other) can I devise how to describe the colour of them being in a manner all clothed alike.

It was neither blacke, nor white, yellow, or redd, greene nor blew, nor any colour composed of these.

But if you aske me what it was then; I must tell you, it was a colour never seen in our earthly world, and therefore neither to be described unto us by any, nor to be conceived of one that never saw it.

For as it were a hard matter to describe unto a man borne blind the difference between blew and Greene, lo can I not bethinke my selfe any meane how to decipher unto you this *Lunar* colour, having no affinitie with any other that ever I beheld with mine eyes.

Onely this I can say of it, that it was the most glorious and delightfull, that can possibly be imagined; neither in truth was there any one thing, that more delighted me, during my abode in that new world, then the beholding of that most pleasing and resplendent colour.

It remaineth now that I speake of the Demeanure of this people, who presenting themselves unto me upon the sudden and that in such extraordinary fashion as I have declared being strucken with a great amasement, I crossed my selfe, and cried out, *Jesus Maria.*

No sooner was the words *Jesus* out of my mouth, but young and old, fell downe upon their knees, (at which I not a little rejoyced) holding up both their hands on high, and repeating all certaine words which I understood not.

Then presently they all arising, one that was farre the tallest of them came unto me, and embraced me, with great kindnesse, and giving order (as I partly perceived) unto some of the rest to stay by my *Birds,* he tooke me by the hand, and leading me downe toward the foote of the hill, brought me to his dwelling, being more then halfe a league from the place where I first alighted.

It was such a building for beauty and hugenesse, as all our world cannot shew any neere comparable to it.

Yet such I saw afterwards elsewhere, as this might seeme but a Cottage in respect of them.

There was not a doore about the house, that was not 30. foote high, and twelve in breadth.

The roomes were between 40. and 50. foote in height, and so all other proportions answerable.

Neither could they well be much lesse, the Master inhabiting them, being full 28 high.

As for his corporature, I suppose verily that if we had him here in this world to be weighed in the ballance, the poyse of his body would shew it selfe more ponderous then Five and Twenty, peradventure thirty of ours.

After I had rested my selfe with him the Value [equivalent] of one of our dayes, he ledd me some Five leagues off, unto the *Palace* of the *Prince* of the country.

. . . .

This *Prince* whose stature was much higher then the former, is called (as neere as I can by Letters declare it, for their sounds are not perfectly to be expressed by our Characters) *Pylonas,* which signifieth in their Language, *First,* if perhaps it be not rather a denotation of his dignity and authority, as being the prime Man in all those parts.

In all those parts, I say. For there is one supreme *Monarch* amongst them, of stature yet much more huge then hee, commanding over all that whole *Orbe* of the world, having under him 29 other Princes of exceeding great power, and every of them 24 others, whereof this *Pylonas* was one.

The first ancestor of this great *Monarch* came out of the earth (as they deliver) and by marriage with the inheretrice of that huge Monarchy, obtaining the government, left it unto his posteritie, who ever since have held the same, even for the space of 40 thousand daies or *Moones,* which amounteth unto 3077. Yeeres.

And his name being *Irdonozur,* his heires, unto this day, doe all assume unto themselves that name, hee, they say having continued there well neere 400 *Moones,* and having begotten divers children, returned (by what meanes they declare not) unto the Earth againe: I doubt not but they may have their Fables, as well as we.

And because our Histories afford no mention of any earthly man to have ever beene in that world before my selfe, and much lesse to have returned thence againe, I cannot but condemne that tradition for false and fabulous; yet this I must tell you, that learning seemeth to be in great estimation among them: And that they make semblance of detesting all Lying and falsehood, which is wont there to be severely punished.

Againe, which may yeeld some countenance unto their historicall narrations, many of them live wonderfull long; even beyond all credit, to wit even unto the age as they professed unto mee of 30000 Moones, which amounteth unto 1000 Yeares and Upwards, (so that the ages of 3. or 4. men might well reach unto the time of the first *Irdonozur,*) and this is noted generally, that the taller people are of Stature, the more excellent they are for all indowments of mind, and the longer time they doe live.

For whereas (that which before I partly intimated unto you) their stature is most divers, great numbers of them little exceeding ours; such seldome live above the age of a 1000 *moones,* which is answerable to 80. of our Yeares, and they account them most base creatures, even but a degree before bruite beasts, imploying them accordingly in all the basest and most servile offices, terming them by a word that signifieth bastard men, counterfetts, or Changelings; so those whom they account Genuine, naturall, and true *Lunars,* both in quantitie of bodie, and length of life, they have for the most part 30 times as much as wee, which proportion agreeth well with the quantities of the day in both worlds, theirs containing almost 30 of ours.

Now when shall I declare unto you the manner of our travell unto the Palace of *Pylonas,* you will say you scarce ever heard any thing more strange and incredible.

Unto every one of us there was delivered at our first setting forth, two Fans of *Feathers,* not much unlike to those that our Ladies doe carrie in *Spaine,* to make a coole Ayre unto themselves in the heat of *Summer.* The use of which Fans before I declare unto you, I must let you understand that the *Globe* of the *Moone* is not altogether destitute of an attractive Power: but it is so farre weaker than that of the earth, as if a man doe but spring upward, with all his force, (as Dancers doe when they shew their activity by capering) he shall be able to mount 50. or 60 foote high, and then he is quite beyond all attraction of the *Moones* earth, falling downe no more, so as by the helpe of these Fans, as with wings, they conveigh themselves in the Ayre in a short space (although not with that swiftnesse that Birds doe) even whither they lift.

In two howers space (as I could guesse) by the helpe of these fans, wee were carried through the Ayre those five Leagues, being about 60 persons. Being arrived at the Pallace of *Pylonas,* after our conductor had gotten audience, (which was not presently) and had declared what manner of present he had brought; I was immediately called in unto him by his attendance: the statelinesse of his Palace, and the reverence done unto him, I soone discerned his greatnesse, and therefore framed my selfe to win his favour the best I might. You may remember I told you of a certaine little *Box* or *Caskett* of *Jewels,* the remainder of those which being brought out of *East Indies,* I sent from *Isle* of St. *Hellen* into *Spaine.*

These before I was carried in unto him I tooke out [of] my pockett in a corner, and making choice of some of every sort, made them ready to be presented as I should think fit.

I found him sitting in a most magnificent chaire of Estate, having his Wife or *Queene* upon one hand, and his eldest sonne on the other, which both were attended, the one by a troope of Ladies, and the other of young men, and all along the side of the roome stood a great number of goodly personages, whereof scarce any one was lower of stature then Pylonas, whose age they say is now 21000 *moones.* At my first entrance falling downe upon my knees, I thought good to use unto him these words in the Latine tongue, *Propitius sit tibi Princeps Illustrissime Dominus noster Jesus Christus c.* As the people I first met withall, so they hearing the holy name of our *Saviour,* they all, I say, *King, Queene,* and all the rest fell downe upon their knees, pronouncing a word or two I understood not. They being risen againe I proceeded [to reckon] up a number of Saints, to see if there were any one of them that they honoured as their patron, at last reckoning among others *St. Martinus,* they all bowed their bodies, and held up hands in signe of great reverence: the reason whereof I learned to bee, that *Martin* in their language signifieth God: Then taking out my *Jewells,* prepared for that purpose, I presented unto the King or Prince (call him how you please) 7 stones of so many severall sorts, a *Diamond,* a *Rubie,* an *Emerauld,* a *Saphire,* a *Topaze,* a *Turquez,* and an *Opall,* which he accepted with great joy and admiration, as having not often seene any such before.

Then I offered unto the Queene and Prince some other, and was about to have bestowed a number of more, upon other there present, but *Pylonas* forbade them to accept, thinking (as afterwards I learned) that they were all I had, and being willing they should be reserved for *Irdonozur* his Soveraigne.

This done he imbraced me with great kindnesse, and began to inquire of me divers things by signes, which I likewise answered by signes as well as I could.

But not being able to give him content, he delivered me to a guard of a 100 of his Giants (so I may wel call them) commanding straightly,

First that I should want nothing that might be fit for me. Secondly that they should not suffer any of the dwarfe *Lunars* (if I may so tearme them) to come neere mee:

Thirdly that I should with all diligence to be instructed in their Language.

And lastly, that by no meanes they should impart unto me, the knowledge of certaine things, particularly by him specified, marry what those particulars were, I might never by any meanes get knowledge.

It may bee now you will desire to understand what were the things *Pylonas* inquired of mee.

Why what but these? whence I came, how I arrived there, and by what meanes? what was my name? what my Errand, and such like?

To all which I answered the very truth as neere as I could.

Being dismissed, I was affoorded all manner of necessaries that my heart could wish, so as it seemed unto me I was in a very *Paradise,* the pleasures whereof notwithstanding could not so overcome mee, as that the remembrance of my wife and Children, did not trouble mee much.

And therefore being willing to foster any small sparke of hope of my returne, with great diligence I tooke order for the attendance of my *Birds,* (I meane my *Gansa's*) whom my selfe in person tended every day with great carefulnesse; All which notwithstanding had fallen out to little purpose, had not other mens care performed that which no indeavour of mine owne could.

For the time now approached, when of necessity all the people of our stature, (and so my selfe among the rest) must needes sleepe for some 13. or 14. whole dayes together.

So it commeth to passe there by a secret power, and unresistable decree of nature, that when the day beginneth to appeare, and the Moone to bee enlightened by the *Sunne* beames, (which is at the first Quarter of the Moon) all such people as exceed not very much our stature inhabiting those parts, they fall into a dead sleepe, and are not possibly to be wakened till the *Sun* be sett, and withdrawne out of their sight, even as *Owles,* and *Batts,* with us cannot indure the light, so wee there at the first approach of the day, begin to be amazed with it, and fall immediately into a slumber, which groweth by little and little, into a dead sleepe, till this light depart from thence againe, which is not in 14. or 15 daies, to wit, untill the last quarter.

Mee thinkes now I heare some man to demand what manner of light there is in that world during the absence of the *Sunne,* to resolve you for that point, you shall understand that there is a light of two sorts.

One of the *Sun* (which I might not endure to behold,) and another of the Earth: that of the Earth was now at the highest; for that when the Moone is at the Change, then is the Earth (unto them in the Moon) like a full Moone with us, and as the Moone increaseth with us; so the light of the Earth decreaseth with them: I then found the light there (though the Sunne were absent) equall unto that with us, in the day time, when the *Sun* is covered with clouds, but toward the quarter it little and little diminisheth, yet leaving still a competent light, which is somewhat strange.

But much stranger is that which was reported unto me there, how that in the other Hemispheare of the *Moone* (I meane contrary to that I happened upon,) where during halfe the Moone, they see not the sunne, and the Earth never appeareth unto them, they have notwithstanding a kinde of light (not unlike by their description to our Moon light) which it seemeth the propinquitie of the starres and other Planets (so much neerer unto them then us) affoordeth.

Now you shall understand that of the true Lunars there bee three degrees.

Some beyond the pitch of our stature a good deale, as perhaps 10 or 12 foote high, that can indure the day of the Moone, when the earth shineth but little, but not endure the beames of both; at such time they must be content to bee laid asleepe.

Others there are of 20 foote high, or somewhat more, that in ordinary places indure all light both of earth & Sun. Marrie there is a certaine *Island,* the mysteries wherof none may know whose stature is at least 27 foot high . . . if any other come a Land there in the Moones day time, they fall asleepe immediately: This Island they call Gods *Island,* or *Insula Martini* in their language: they say it hath a particular governour, who is (as they report) of age 65000 Moones, which amounteth to 5000 of our Yeares, his name is said to be *Hiruch,* and he comandeth after a sort over *Irdonozur* himselfe, especially in that *Island* out of which he never commeth.

There is another repairing much thither, they say is halfe his age and upwards, to wit, about 33 thousand Moones, or 26 hundreth of our Yeares, and hee commandeth in all things (throughout the whole Globe of the Moone) concerning matters of Religion, and the service of God, as absolutely as our holy Father the *Pope* doth in any part of *Italy.* I would faine have seene this man, but I might not be suffered to come neere him: his name is *Imozes.*

Now give mee leave to settle my selfe to a long nights sleepe: My attendants take charge of my *Birds,* prepare my lodging, and signifie to mee by signes, how it must bee with mee. It was about the middle of *September,* when I perceived the Ayre to grow more cleare then ordinary, and with the increasing of the light, I began to feele my selfe first dull, then heavy and willing to sleepe, although I had not lately been hindred from taking mine ease that way.

I delivered my selfe at last into the custody of this sister of Death, whose prisoner I was for almost a fortnight after; Awaking then, it is not to bee beleeved how fresh, how nimble, how vigorous, I found all the faculties both of my bodie and minde.

In good time, therefore, I setled my selfe immediately to the learning of the language which (a marvellous thing to consider) is one of the same throughout all the regions of the Moone, yet so much the lesse to be wondred at, because I cannot thinke all the Earth of Moone to Amount to the fortieth part of our inhabited Earth: partly because the Globe of the Moone is much lesse then that of the Earth, and partly because their Sea or Ocean covereth in estimation Three parts of Foure, (if not more) whereas the *Superficies* [surfaces] of our land may bee judged Equivalent and comparable in Measure to that of our Seas.

The Difficulty of that language is not to bee conceived, and the reasons thereof are especially two:

First, because it hath no affinitie with any other that ever I heard.

Secondly, because it consisteth not so much of words and Letters, as of tunes and uncouth sounds, that no letters can expresse.

For you have few wordes but they signifie divers and severall things, and they are distinguished onely by their tunes that are as it were sung in the utterance of them, yea many wordes there are consisting of tunes onely, so as if they list they will utter their mindes by tunes without wordes: for Example, they have an ordinary salutation amongst them, signifying

(*Verbatim*) Glorie be to God alone, which they expresse (as I take it, for I am no perfect Musician) by [a] tune without any words at all.

Yea the very names of Men they will expresse in the same sort.

. . . .

By occasion hereof, I discerne meanes of framing a Language . . . as copious as any other in the world, consisting of tunes onely, whereof my friends may know more at leasure if it please them.

This is a great Mystery and worthier the searching after then at first sight you would imagine.

Now notwithstanding the difficulty of this language, within two moneths space I had attained unto such knowledge of the same, as I understand most questions to be demanded of mee, and what with signes what with words, make reasonable shift to utter my mind, which thing being certified unto *Pylonas,* hee sent for mee oftentimes, and would bee pleased to give mee knowledge of many things that my *Guardians* durst not declare unto me.

Yet this I will say of them, that they never abused mee with any untruth that I could perceive, but if I asked a question that they liked not to resolve mee in, they would shake their heads and with a Spanish shrugge passe over to other talke.

After 7 moneths space it happened that the great *Irdonozur* makeing his progresse to a place some 200 leagues distant from the Palace of *Pylonas,* sent for mee. . . . Hee would not admit me into his presence, but talked with me through a Window, where I might heare him, and hee both heare and see mee at pleasure. I offered him the remainder of my Jewells, which he accepted very thankfully; telling mee that hee would requite them with gifts of an other manner of value.

It was not above a Quarter of a Moone that I stayed there, before I was sent backe unto *Pylonas* againe; and so much the sooner, because if we had stayed but a day or two longer, the Sunne would have overtaken us, before wee could have recovered our home.

The gifts he bestowed on me were such as a Man would forsake mountaines of Gold for, and they were all stones, to wit 9 in number, and those of 3 sorts, whereof one they call *Poleastis,* another *Machrus,* and third *Ebelus,* of each sort three. The first are of the bignesse of an *Hazell-nutt,* very like unto jett, which among many other incredible vertues hath this property that being once heat in the Fire, they ever after retaine their heat (though without any appearance) untill they be quenched with some kinde of liquor, whereby they receive no detriment at all, though they bee heat and quenched 10 thousand times.

And their heat is so vehement, as they will make red hot any mettall that shall come within a foot of them, and being put in a Chimney, will make a roome as warme, as if a great Fire were kindled in the same.

The *Machrus* (yet farre more precious then the other) is of the colour of *Topaze,* so shining and resplendent as (though not past the bignesse of a beane, yet) being placed in the midst of a large Church in the night time, it maketh it all as light, as if a 100 Lamps were hanged up round about it.

Can you wish for properties in a stone of greater use then these? Yes my *Ebelus* will affoord you that which I dare say will make you preferre him before these, yea and all the *Diamonds, Saphyres, Rubies,* and *Emeralds* that our world can yeeld, were they laid in a heap before you;

To say nothing of the colour, (the Lunar whereof I made mention before, which notwithstanding is so incredibly beautifull, as a man should travell 1000 Leagues to behold it) the shape is somewhat flat of the breadth of a *Pistolett,*[14] and twice the thicknesse. The one side of this which is somewhat more Orient [lustrous] of Colour then the other, being clapt to the bare skin of a man, in any part of his bodie, it taketh away from it all weight or ponderousnesse; whereas turning the other side it addeth force unto the attractive beames of the Earth, either in this world or that, and maketh the bodie to weigh halfe so much againe as it did before; do you marvell now why I should so overprize this stone? before you see mee on earth againe, you shall understand more of the value of this kinde and unvaluable Jem.

I inquired then amongst them, whether they had not any kind of Jewell or other meanes to make a man invisible, which mee thought had beene a thing of great and extraordinary use.

And I could tell that divers of our learned men had written many things to that purpose.

They answered that if it were a thing faisible, yet they assured themselves that God would not suffer it to be revealed to us creatures subject to so many imperfections, being a thing so apt to be abused to ill purposes; and that was all I could get of them.

Now after it was known that *Irdonozur,* the great Monarch, had done me this honour, it is strange how much all men respected mee more than before: my Guardians which hitherto were very nice [reticent] in relating any thing to mee, concerning the government of that world, now became

[14] Probably refers to a gold coin used in Spain.

somewhat more open, so as I could learn (partly of them and partly of *Pylonas,*) what I shall deliver unto you concerning that matter, whereof I will onely give you a taste at this time. . . .

In a thousand yeares it is not found that there is either Whoremonger amongst them, whereof these reasons are to bee yeelded, There is no want of any thing necessary for the use of man.

Food groweth every where without labour, and that of all sorts to be desired.

For rayment, howsing, or any thing else that you may imagine possible for a man to want, or desire, it is provided by the command of Superiors, though not without labour, yet so little, as they doe nothing but as it were playing, and with pleasure.

Againe their Females are all of an absolute beauty: and I know not how it commeth to passe by a secret disposition of nature there, that a man having once knowne a Woman, never desireth any other. As for murther it was never heard of amongst them; neither is it a thing almost possible to bee committed: for there is no wound to bee given which may not bee cured, they assured mee, (and I for my part doe beleeve it,) that although a mans head be cut off, yet if any time within the space of Three Moones it bee put together, and joyned to the Carkasse againe, with the appointment of the Juyce of a certain hearbe, there growing, it will be joyned together againe, so as the partie wounded shall become perfectly whole in a few houres.

But the chiefe cause, is that through an excellent disposition of that nature of people there, all, young and old doe hate all manner of vice, and doe live in such love, peace, and amitie, as it seemeth to bee another Paradise. True it is, that some are better disposed then other: but that they discerne immediately at the time of their birth.

And because it is an inviolable decree amongst them, never to put any one to death, perceiving by the stature, and some other notes they have, who are likely to bee of a wicked or imperfect disposition, they send them away (I know not by what meanes) into the Earth, and change them for other children, before they shall have either abilitie or opportunitie to doe amisse among them: But first (they say) they are faine to keepe them there for a certain space, till that the ayre of the Earth may alter their colour to be like unto ours.

And their ordinary vent for them is a certain high hill in the North of *America,* whose people I can easily beleeve to be wholly descended of them, partly in regard of their colour, partly also in regard of the continuall use of Tobacco which the *Lunars* use exceeding much, as living in a place abounding wonderfully with moysture, as also for the pleasure they take in it, and partly in some other respects too long now to be rehearsed. Sometimes they mistake their aime, and fall upon Christendome, *Asia* or *Africke,* marry that is but seldome. . . .

. . . .

May I once have the happinesse to returne home in safety, I will yeeld such demonstrations of all I deliver, as shall quickly make void all doubt of the truth hereof.

If you will aske mee further of the manner of government amongst the Lunars, and how Justice is executed?

Alas what need is there of Exemplary punishment, where there are no offences committed: they need there no Lawyers, for there is never any contention, the seeds thereof, if any begin to sprout, being presently by the wisedome of the next superior puld up by the roots.

And as little need is there of Physitians; they never misdiet themselves, their Ayre is alwaies temperate and pure, neither is there any occasion at all of sicknes, as to me it seemed at least, for I could not heare that ever any of them were sicke.

But the time that nature hath assigned unto them being spent, without any paine at all they die, or rather (I should say) cease to live, as a candle to give light, when that which nourisheth it is consumed.

I was once at the departure of one of them, which I wondred much to behold; for notwithstanding the happy life hee led, and multitude of friends and children hee should forsake, as soone as certainely hee understood and perceived his end to approach, hee prepared a great feast, and calling about him all those hee especially esteemed of, hee bids them be merry and rejoyce with him, for that the time was come he should now leave the counterfeit pleasures of that world, and bee made partaker of all true joyes and perfect happinesse.

I wondred not so much at his constancy, as the behaviour of those his friends: with us in the like case, all seeme to mourne, when often some of them doe but laugh in their sleeves, or as one sayes under a visard [mask].

They all on the other side, young and old, both seemingly, and in my conscience, sincerely did rejoyce thereat, so as if any dissembled, it was but their owne griefe conceived for their owne particular losse.

Their bodies being dead putrifie not, and therefore are not buried, but kept in certaine roomes ordained for that purpose; so as most of them can shew their Ancestors bodies uncorrupt for many generations.

There is never any raine, wind, or change of the Ayre, never either Summer or Winter, but as it were a perpetuall Spring, yeelding all pleasure, all content, and that free from any annoyance at all.

O my Wife and Children, what wrong have you done mee to bereave mee of the happinesse of that place; but it maketh no matter, for by this voyage am I sufficiently assured, that ere long the race of my mortall life being run, I shall attaine a greater happinesse elsewhere, and that everlasting.

It was the Ninth day of *September* that I began to ascend from El Pico; twelve dayes I was upon my Voyage, and arrived in that Region of the Moone, that they call *Simiri, September* the 21 following.

The 12 day of May being Friday, wee came unto the Court of the great *Irdonozur,* and returned backe the Seventeenth unto the Palace of *Pylonas,* there I continued till the moneth of March, in the yeare 1601, at what time I earnestly besought *Pylonas* (as I had often done before) to give mee leave to depart, (though with never so great hazard of my life) backe into the earth againe.

Hee much disswaded mee, laying before mee the danger of the voyage, the misery of that place from whence I came, and the abundant happinesse of that I now was in; But the remembrance of my Wife and Children overweighed all these reasons, and to tell you the truth, I was so farre forth moved with a desire of that deserved glory, that I might purchase at my return, as me thought I deserved not the name of a *Spanyard,* if I would not hazard 20 lives, rather then loose but a little possibility of the fame. Wherefore I answered him, that my desire of seeing my Children was such, as I knew I could not live any longer, if I were once out of hope of the same. When then he desired one yeares stay longer, I told him it was manifest I must depart now or never: My *Birds* began to droope, for want of their wonted migration, 3 of them were now dead, and if a few more failed, I was for ever destitute of all possibilitie of returning.

With much adoe at last hee condescended unto my request, having first acquainted the great *Irdonozur* with my desire, then perceiving by the often baying of my Birds, a great longing in them to take their flight; I trimmed up mine Engine, and took my leave of *Pylonas,* who (for all the courtesie hee had done mee) required of mee but one thing, which was faithfully to promise him, that if ever I had meanes thereunto, I should salute from him *Elizabeth,* whom he tearmed the great *Queene of England,* calling her the most glorious of all women living, and indeed hee would often question with mee of her, and therein delighted so much, as it seemed hee was never satisfied in talking of her; hee also delivered unto mee a token or present for her of no small Value: Though I account her an enemy of *Spayne,* I may not faile of performing this promise as soone as I shall bee able so to doe: upon the 29 day of *March* being Thursday, 3 dayes after my awakening from the last Moones light, I fastened my self to mine Engine, not forgetting to take with mee, besides the Jewels *Irdonozur* had given mee (with whose use and vertues *Pylonas* had acquainted mee at large) a small quantitie of Victual, whereof afterward I had great use as shall bee declared.

As infinite multitude of people, (and amongst the rest *Pylonas* himselfe) being present, after I had given him the last *Bezalos manos,* I let loose the raines unto my *Birds,* who with great greedinesse taking wing quickly carried mee out of their sight, it fel out with me as in my first passage, I never felt either hunger or thirst, till I arrived in *China* upon a high mountaine, some 5 Leagues from the high and mighty City of *Pachin.*

This Voyage was performed in lesse then 9 dayes; I heard no newes by the way of these ayrie men, which I had seen in my ascending.

No thing stayed my journey any whit at all: Whether it was the earnest desire of my *Birds,* to return to the Earth, where they had missed one season, or that the attraction of the Earth so much stronger then that of the Moone, furthered their labour; so it came to passe, although now I had 3 *Birds* wanting of those I carried forth with mee.

For the first 8 dayes my *Birds* flew before, and I with the Engine was as it were drawn by them.

The Nineth day when I began to approach unto the Clouds, I perceived my selfe and mine Engine to sincke towards the Earth, and goe before them.

I was then horribly afraid, lest my *Birds* not being able to beare our weight, they being so few, should be constrained to precipitate both mee and themselves headlong to the Earth: wherefore I thought it no lesse then needfull to make use of the *Ebelus* (one of the stones bestowed upon me by *Irdonozur,*) which I clapped to my bare flesh within my hose: and it appeared manifestly thereupon mee that my *Birds* made their way with much greater ease then before, as being lightned of a great burthen; neither doe I thinke it possible for them to have let mee downe safely unto the Earth without that helpe.

China is a Country so populous, as I thinke there is hardly a peece of ground to bee found, (in the most barren parts of the same) though but thrice a mans length, which is not most carefully manured. I being yet in the Ayre, some of the country people had espied mee, and came running unto mee by troopes, they seised upon mee, and would needs, by and by, carrie mee unto an Officer. I seeing no other remedy, yeelded my selfe unto them. But when I assayed to goe, I found my selfe so light, that I had much adoe, one foote being upon the ground, to set downe the other, that was by reason of my *Ebelus,* so applyed, as it tooke quite away all weight and ponderousnesse from my body: Wherefore bethinking my selfe what was to be done, I fained a desire for performing the necessitie of nature, which by signes being made knowen unto them (for they understood not a word of any Language I could speake) they permitted mee to goe aside among a few bushes, assuring themselves that for mee to escape from them it was impossible; Being there I remembred the directions *Pylonas* had given mee, concerning the use of my stones, and first I tooke them all together, with a few Jewells yet remaining of those I had brought out of *India,* and knit them up in my handkerchiefe, all, except one the least and worst *Ebelus.*

Him I found meanes to apply in such sort unto my body, as but the halfe of his side touched my skin, whereby it came to passe that my body then had but halfe the weight, that being done I drew towards these my Guardians, till seeing them come somewhat neere together they could not crosse my way, I shewed them a faire paire of heeles.

This I did to the end I might recover an opportunitie of finding my Stones, and Jewells, which I knew they would rob mee off, if I prevented them not.

Being thus lightned I bid them such a chase, as had they been all upon the backes of so many *Zebra's,* they could never have overtaken me: I directed my course unto a certaine thicke wood, into which I entred some a quarter of League, and then finding a pretty spring, (which I tooke for my marke,) hard by it, I thrust my jewells into a little hole. . . .

Then I tooke out of my pocket my Victualls (to which in all my Voyage I had not till then any desire) and refreshed my selfe therewith, till such time as the people pursuing mee, had overtaken mee, into whose hands I quietly delivered my selfe.

They led mee unto a meane [low-ranking] Officer, who (understanding that once I had escaped from them that first apprehended mee,) caused a certaine seat to be made of boords, into which they closed mee in such sort, as onely my head was at liberty, and then carried mee upon the shoulders of 4 slaves, (like some notorious malefactor) before a man of great authority, (whom in their language as after I learned, they called a *Mandarine*), abiding 2 dayes journey off, to wit one League distant from the great and famous City of *Pachin.* . . .

Their language I could no way understand; onely this I could discerne, that I was for something or other accused with a great deale of vehemence.

The substance of this accusation it seemes was, that I was a *Magician,* as witnessed my strange carriage in the ayre; that being a stranger, as appeared by my both language and habit, I contrary to the Lawes of *China,* entred into the Kingdome without warrant, and that probably with no good intent. The *Mandarine* heard them out, with a great deale of composed gravitie; and being a man of quicke apprehension, and withall studious of novelties, hee answered them, that hee would take such order with mee, as the case required, and that my bold attempt should not want its deserved punishment. But having dismissed them he gave order to his Servants, that I should be kept in some remote parts of his vast Palace, and bee strictly watched, but courteously used: This doe I conjecture, by what at the present I found, and what after followed. For my accomodation was every way better, then I could expect; I lodged well, fared well, was attended well, and could not fault any thing, but my restraint. In this manner did I continue many moneths, afflicted with nothing so much as with the thought of my *Gansa's;* which I knew must be irrecoverably lost, as indeed they were. But in this time, by my owne industry, and the forwardnesse of those that accompanied me, I was growne indifferent ready in the ordinary language of that Province, (for almost every Province in *China,* hath its proper Language) whereat I discerned they tooke no small content I was at length to take the ayre, and brought into the spacious garden of that Palace, a place of excellent pleasure, and delight, as being planted with herbes and Flowers of admirable both sweetnes and beauty, and almost infinite variety of fruits both *European* and others, and al those composed with that rare curiositie, that I was ravished with the contemplation of such delightfull objects. But I had not here long recreated my selfe, yet the *Mandarine* entered the Garden, on that side where I was walking, and being advertised thereof by his servants, and wished to kneel down unto him (as I after found it to be the usuall publique reverence to those great Officers) I did so, and humbly craved his favour towards a poore stranger, that arrived in those parts, not by his own destination, but by the secret disposall of the heavens: He in a different language (which al the *Mandarines,* as I have since learned, do use) and that like that of the Lunars did consist much of tunes, but was by one of his servants interpreted to mee. Hee, I say, wished mee to bee of good comfort, for that he intended no harme unto mee, and so passed on. The next day was I commanded to come before him, and so conducted into a sumptuous dining roome exquisitely painted and adorned. The *Mandarine* having commanded all to avoid the roome, vouchsafed conference with mee in the vulgar language; inquiring first the estate of my Country, the power of my

Prince, the religion and manners of the people; wherein being satisfied by mee, hee at last descended to the particulars of my education and studies, and what brought mee into this remote country: Then did I at large declare unto him the adventure of my life, only omitting here and there; what particulars I thought good, forbearing especially any mention of the stones given me by *Irdonozur*. The strangenes of my story did much amaze him. And finding in all my discourse nothing any way tending to Magique; (wherein he had hoped by my means to have gaind some knowledge) he began to admire the excellence of my wit, applauding me for the happiest man, that this world had ever produced: and wishing me to repose my selfe after my long narration, he for that time dismissed me. After this, the *Mandarine* tooke such delight in me, that no day passed, wherein he sent not for me. At length he advised me to apparell my selfe in habit of the Country (which I willingly did) and gave mee not onely the liberty of his house, but took mee also abroad with him, when he went to *Paquin* [Pachin], whereby I had the opportunitie by degrees to learn the disposition of the people, and the policie of the Country. . . . Neither did I by this my attendance on him gaine only the knowledge of these things, but the possibility also of being restored to my native soyle, and to those deare pledges which I value above the world, my Wife and children. For by often frequenting *Paquin,* I at length heard of some Fathers of the Society that were become famous for the extraordinary favour by the King vouchsafed them, to whom they had presented some *European* trifles, as Clockes, Watches, [sun] Dials, and the like, which with him passed for exquisite rarities. To them by the *Mandarines* leave I repaired, was welcomed by them, they much wondring to see a Lay *Spaniard* there, whither they had with so much difficulty obtained leave to arrive. There did I relate to father *Pantoja,* and those others of the society these fore-related adventures, by whose directions I put them in writing, and sent this story of my fortunes to *Macao,* from thence to be conveighed for *Spaine,* as a forerunner of my returne. And the *Mandarine* being very indulgent unto me, I came often unto the Fathers, with whom I consulted about many secrets with them also did I lay a foundation for my returne, the blessed houre whereof I doe with patience expect; that by inriching my Country with the knowledge of hidden mysteries, I may once reape the glory of my fortunate misfortunes.

Finis.

JOHN WILKINS

From *The Discovery of a New World, . . . with a Discourse Concerning the Possibility of a Passage Thither* (1640)

[Unlike the other works reprinted in this volume, John Wilkins's is neither satire nor fantasy but a serious attempt to apply logic and the available scientific information to certain persistent questions about the moon. *The Discovery of a New World,* first published in 1638, examines thirteen "propositions." In each instance, Wilkins presents the prevailing arguments, then refutes them, and finally presents the scientific evidence in support of his position. The thirteen propositions (none of them reprinted here) are as follows:

1. That the Moone may be a World.
2. That a plurality of Worlds doth not contradict any principle of Reason or Faith.
3. That the Heavens do not consist of any such pure matter which can priviledge them from the like charge of corruption as these inferiour bodies are liable to.
4. That the Moone is a Solid compacted opacous Body.
5. That the Moone hath not any Light of her own.
6. That there is a World in the Moone hath been the direct opinion of many ancients with some modern mathematicians and may probably be deduced from the tenents of others.
7. That those Spots and brighter parts which by our sight may be distinguished in the Moone do shew the differences betwixt the Sea and Land in that other World.
8. That the Spots represent the Sea; and the brighter parts the Land.
9. That there are high Mountains, deep vallies, and spacious plains in the body of the Moone.

10. That there is an Atmosphere, or an orbe of grosse vaporous aire, immediately encompassing the body of the Moone.
11. That as their world is our Moone, so our world is their Moone.
12. That tis probable there may be such Meteors belonging to that world in the Moone, as there are with us.
13. That tis probable there may be inhabitants in this but of what kinde they are, is uncertaine.

Shortly after *Discovery* was published, Wilkins chanced to read Godwin's *Man in the Moone* and was impelled to write a sequel to his own book setting forth a fourteenth proposition:

14. That tis possible for some of our posteritie, to find out a conveyance to this other world; and if there be inhabitants there, to have commerce with them.

This proposition was published as "A Discourse Concerning the Possibility of a Passage Thither" and included in the third edition of *Discovery,* issued in 1640.

In the fourteenth proposition, more speculative than his prior proposals, Wilkins suggests that a flying chariot would be more practical than attempting to fly under one's own power by means of artificial wings attached to the body or than using birds (an obvious reference to Godwin's tale). Erroneously believing the distance between the earth and the moon to be 178,712 miles, he claimed that a chariot traveling a thousand miles a day could make the trip in 180 days, or half a year. Wilkins's chariot would be large enough to accommodate several men, a supply of food, and commodities to trade with the lunar inhabitants. His suggestion that the chariot be powered by mechanical means was later used by Ralph Morris in *The Life and Astonishing Transactions of John Daniel . . . ,* reprinted in this volume.

Wilkins was well qualified by education and inclination to undertake a sober inquiry into the possibility of lunar travel. Born in 1614, he was educated at Oxford, where he distinguished himself as a scholar and mathematician. While at Oxford he participated in weekly meetings with leading philosophers, which led in 1662 to the founding of the Royal Society, with Wilkins as its first secretary. By the time he died, at the age of fifty-eight, he had been master of Wadham College, Oxford, and of Trinity College, Cambridge, and, finally, Bishop of Chester. And he had published not only *Discovery* and its sequel but, in 1648, *Mathematical Magick,* a book dealing in still greater detail with various aspects of flight. In 1684, twelve years after Wilkins's death, a collection of his *Mathematical and Philosophical Works* appeared, including *Discovery* and *Discourse.* The book was reissued in 1708 and again in 1802.

Wilkins's scientific interests and accomplishments were so well known that the anonymous publication of *The Discovery of a New*

World apparently fooled few of his contemporaries. Throughout his life, he manifested a lively curiosity about scientific matters and a willingness to adopt a scientific approach. He claimed that much of the data on which his book is based was produced by the use of Galileo's telescope. And, although Wilkins was a high-ranking churchman, he constantly tells his readers that the mysteries of the universe can be solved only by continued experimentation and invention, insisting that modern, learned men need not and should not take the Scriptures literally. The mere fact that something is not mentioned in Holy Writ, he argues, does not mean that it cannot exist.

Wilkins, like Godwin, underestimated the reception of his work. *Discovery* and *Discourse* were widely read, in English and in French translation (published in 1655). Along with the story of Domingo Gonsales, to which it gave a certain credibility, *The Discovery of a New World* inspired many fictional moon voyages in the later seventeenth and the eighteenth centuries. For example, the hero of Robert Paltock's *Life and Adventures of Peter Wilkins, a Cornish Man,* published in 1751, is believed to have been named after Bishop John Wilkins. Paltock's hero is no astronaut, however, but finds his adventures in a strange land *within* the earth.

Fewer than ten copies of the 1640 edition of *The Discovery of a New World* with "A Discourse Concerning the Possibility of a Passage Thither" are believed to be in the United States. The copy used in preparing this book is to be found in the collection of the Library Company, Philadelphia, Pennsylvania.]

Proposition 14

That tis possible for some of our posteritie, to find out a conveyance to this other world; and if there be inhabitants there, to have commerce with them.

All that hath been said, concerning the people of the new world, is but conjecturall, and full of uncertainties; nor can we ever looke for any evi-

Frontispiece of the 1640 edition of John Wilkins's *Discovery of a New World in the Moone.*

dent or more probable discoveries in this kind, unlesse there bee some hopes of inventing means for our conveyance thither. The possibilitie of which, shall be the subject of our enquiry in this Last Proposition.

And, if we doe but consider by what steps and leasure, all arts doe usually rise to their growth, we shall have no cause to doubt why this also may not hereafter be found out amongst other secrets. It hath constantly yet been the method of providence, not presently to shew us all, but to leade us on by degrees, from the knowledge of one thing to another.

'Twas a great while, ere the Planets were distinguished from the fixed stars and some time after that, ere the morning and evening starre were found to be the same. And in greater space (I doubt not) but this also, and other as excellent mysteries will be discovered. Time, who hath alwayes been the father of new truths, and hath revealed unto us many things, which our Ancestors were ignorant of, will also manifest to our posteritie, that which wee now desire, but cannot know. . . . Time will come, when the indeavors of after ages, shall bring such things to light as now lie hid in obscuritie. . . . As wee now wonder at the blindnesse of our Ancestors, who were not able to discerne such things, as seeme plaine and obvious unto us; so will our posterity, admire our ignorance in as perspicuous matters.

In the first ages of the world the Ilanders thought themselves either to bee the only dwellers upon earth, or else if there were any other, they could not possibly conceive how they might have any commerce with them, being severed by the deepe and broade Sea. But after times found out the invention of ships, in which notwithstanding, none but some bold, daring men durst venture. . . .

. . . .

And yet now, how easie a thing is this even to a timorous and cowardly nature? And questionlesse, the invention of some other means for our conveiance to the Moone, cannot seeme more incredible to us, than this did at first to them, and therefore we have no just reason to bee discouraged in our hopes of the like successe.

Yea, but (you will say) there can be no sayling thither, unlesse that were true which the Poets doe but faine, that she made her bed in the Sea. Wee have not now any *Drake,* or *Columbus,* to undertake this voyage, or any *Daedalus* to invent a conveiance through the ayre.

I answer, Though wee have not, yet why may not succeeding times, rayse up some spirits as eminent for new attempts and strange inventions, as any that were before them? Tis the opinion of *Keplar,*[1] that as soone as the art of flying is found out, some of their nation will make one of the first Colonies, that shall transplant into that other world. I suppose, his appropriating this preheminence to his owne Countreymen, may arise from an overpartiall affection to them. But yet thus far I agree with him, That when ever that Art is invented, or any other, wherby a man may be conveyed some twenty miles high, or thereabouts, then, tis not altogether improbable that some or other may be successefull in this attempt.

For the better clearing of which I shall first lay downe, and then answer those doubts that may make it seeme utterly impossible.

These are chiefly three.

The first, taken from the naturall heavinesse of a mans body, whereby it is made unfit for the motion of ascent, together with the vast distance of that place from us.

2. From the extreme coldnes of the aethereall ayre.

3. The extreme thinnesse of it. Both which must needs make it impassible, though it were but as many single miles thither, as it is thousands.

For the first. Though it were supposed that a man could flie, yet wee may wel think hee would be very slow in it, since hee hath so heavy a body, and such a one too, as nature did not principally intend, for that kind of motion. Tis usually observed, that amongst the varietie of birds, those which doe most converse upon the earth, and are swiftest in their running, as a Pheasant, Partridge, &c. together with all domesticall fowle, are lesse able for flight, than others which are for the most part upon the wing, as a Swallow, swift, &c. And therefore wee may well think, that man being not naturally endowed with any such condition as may inable him for this motion; and being necessarily tied to a more especiall residence on the earth, must needs be slower than any fowle, and lesse able to hold out. This it is also in swimming; which Art though it bee growne to a good eminence, yet he that is best skilled in it, is not able either for continuance, or swiftnesse, to equall a fish; Because he is not naturally appointed to it. So that though a man could fly, yet hee would be so slow in it, and so quickly weary, that hee could not think to reach so great a journey as it is to the Moone.

But suppose withall that hee could fly as fast, and long, as the swiftest bird: yet it cannot possibly bee conceived, how he should ever be able to passe through so vast a distance, as there is betwixt the Moone and our earth. For this Planet, according to the common grounds, is usually granted

[1] Johannes Kepler (1571–1630), the German theoretical astronomer who showed correctly how the planets move in ellipses.

to bee at the least, 52 semidiameters of the earth from us. Reckoning for each semidiameter 3456 English miles, of which the whole space will be about 179712.[2]

So that though a man could constantly keep on in his journey thither by a straite line, though he could fly a thousand miles in a day; yet he would not arrive thither under 180 dayes, or halfe a yeare.

And how were it possible for any to tarry so long without dyet or sleep?

1. For Diet. I suppose there could be no trusting to the . . . musick of the spheares [to] supply the strength of food.

Nor can wee well conceive how a man should be able to carry so much luggage with him, as might serve for his *Viaticum* in so tedious a journey.

2. But if he could: yet he must have some time to rest and sleep in. And I believe hee shall scarse find any lodgings by the way. No Inns to entertaine passengers, nor any castles in the ayre (unlesse they bee inchanted ones) to receive poore pilgrims or errant Knights. And so consequently, he cannot have any possible hopes of reaching thither.

Notwithstanding all which doubts, I shall laye downe this position.

That supposing a man could fly, or by any other meanes, raise himselfe twenty miles upwards, or thereabouts, it were possible for him to come unto the Moone.

As for those arguments of the first kind, that seeme to overthrow the truth of this, they proceed upon a wrong ground. Whilst they suppose, that a condensed body, in any place of the ayre, would alwayes retaine in it a strong inclination of tending downewards, towards the center of this earth. Whereas 'tis more probable, that if it were but somewhat above this orbe of vaporous ayre, it might there rest immoveable, & would not have in it any propension to this motion of descent.

For the better illustration of this, you must know, that the heavinesse of a body, or (as *Aristotle* defines it) the pronesse of it to tend downe unto some center, is not any absolute quality intrinsicall unto it, as if where ever the body did retaine its essence, it must also retaine this qualitie: or as if nature had implanted in every condensed body *Appetitionem centri, & fugam extremitatis* (such a love to the center and hatred to the extremities). Because one of these being less than a quantitie, and the other no more, cannot have any power of attraction of depulsion in them. . . .

But now the true nature of gravitie is this. Tis such a respective mutuall desire of union, whereby condensed bodies, when they come within the sphere of their owne vigor, doe naturally apply themselves, one to another

[2] The actual distance between the earth and the moon is currently computed as approximately 240,000 miles.

by attraction or coition. But being both without the reach of eithers vertue [power], they then cease to move, and though they have generall aptitude, yet they have not any present inclination or pronesse to one another. And so consequently, cannot bee styled heavy.

The meaning of this will bee more clearly illustrated by a similitude. As any light body (suppose the Sunne) dos send forth his beames in an orbicular forme; So likewise any magneticall body, for instance a round loadstone dos cast abroad his magneticall vigor in a spheare. . . .

. . . .

To apply then what hath been said. This great globe of earth and water, hath been proved by many observations, to participate of Magneticall properties. And as the Loadstone dos cast forth its owne vigor round about its body, in a magneticall compasse: So likewise dos our earth. The difference is, that it is another kind of affection which causes the union betwixt the Iron and Loadstone, from that which makes bodies move unto the earth. The former is some kind of neerenesse and similitude in their natures, for which, Philosophie as yet has not found a particular name. The latter dos arise from that peculiar qualitie, whereby the earth is properly distinguished from the other elements, which is its Condensitie. Of which the more any thing dos participate, by so much the stronger will bee the desire of union to it. So gold and other metalls which are most close in their composition, are likewise most swift in their motion of discent.

And though this may seeme to bee contradicted by the instance of metalls, which are of the same weight, when they are melted, and when they are hard: As also of water, which dos not differ in respect of gravitie, when it is frozen and when it is fluid: yet we must know that metalls are not rarified by melting, but mollified [softened]. And so too for frozen waters, they are not properly condensed, but congealed into a harder substance, the parts being not contracted closer together, but still possessing the same extension. But yet (I say) tis very probable, that there is such a spheare about the earth, which dos terminate its power of attracting other things unto it. So that suppose a body to bee placed within the limits of this sphere, and then it must needs tend downewards, towards the center of it. But on the contrary, if it be beyond this compasse, then there can bee no such mutuall attraction; & so consequently, it must rest immoveable from any such motion.

For the farther confirmation of this, I shall propose two pertinent observations.

The first taken in the presence of many Physitians, and related by an eminent man in that profession, *Hieron. Fracastorius.*[3] There being divers needles provided of severall kindes, like those in a Mariners Chart, they found, that there was an attractive power, not only in the magnet; But that iron also and steele, and silver did each of them draw its owne mettle. Whence hee concludes, *Omne trahit quod sibi simile est.* [Like attracts like.] And as these peculiar likenesses, have such a mutuall efficacy; so tis probable, that this more generall qualification of condensitie, may bee the cause, why things so affected desire union to the earth. And though 'tis likely that this would appeare betwixt two lesser condensed bodies, (as suppose two peeces of earth) if they were both placed at libertie in the aethereall ayre, yet being neere the earth, the stronger species of this great globe dos as it were drowned the lesse.

'Tis a common experiment, that such a lump of ore or stone, as being on the ground, cannot be moved by lesse than six men, being in the bottom of a deep mine, may be stirred by two. The reason is, because then tis compassed with attractive beams, there being many above it, as well as below it. Whence we may probably inferre (saith the learned *Verulam*)[4] "that the nature of gravitie, dos worke but weakly also far from the earth; Because the appetite of union in dense bodies, must bee more dull in respect of distance." As we may also conclude from the motion of birds, which rise from the ground but heavily, though with much labor; Whereas being on high, they can keep themselves up, and soare about by the meere extension of their wings. Now the reason of this difference, is not (as some falsly conceive) the depth of ayre under them. For a bird is not heavier when there is but a foote of ayre under him, than when there is a furlong. As appeares by a ship in the water, (an instance of the same nature) which dos not sinke deeper, and so consequently is not heavier, when it has but five fatham depth, than when it has fifty. But the true reason is, the weaknesse of the desire of union in dense bodies at a distance.

So that from hence, there might be just occasion to taxe *Aristotle* and his followers, for teaching that heavines is an absolute qualitie of itselfe, and really distinct from condensitie: whereas it is onely a modification of it, or rather, another name given to a condensed body in reference to its motion.

For if it were absolute, then it should alwayes be inherent in its subject, and not have its essence depend upon the bodies being here or there. But it is not so. For,

[3] Girolamo Fracastoro (1483–1553) was a physician best known for describing the disease known as syphilis.

[4] Francis Bacon, Baron Verulam (1561–1626), the English philosopher, attacked Aristotelian concepts and stressed discovery by observation.

1. Nothing is heavy in its proper place, according to his owne principle. . . . And then

2. Nothing is heavy, which is so farre distant from that proper orbe to which it dos belong, that it is not within the reach of its vertue. . . .

But unto this it may be objected. Though a body being so placed, be not heavy *in actu secundo;* yet it is *in actu primo:* because it retaines it in an inward proness to move downewards, being once severed from its proper place. And this were reason enough why the quality of heavinesse should have an absolute being.

I answer, this distinction is only appliable to such naturall powers as can suspend their acts; and will not hold in Elementary qualities, whose very essence dos necessarily require an exercise of the second act, as you may easily discerne by an induction of all the rest. I cannot say, that body has in it the quality of heate, coldnesse, drinesse, moisture, hardnesse, softnesse, &c. Which for the present, has not the second act of these qualities. And if you meane by the essence of them, a power unto them: why, there is not any naturall body but has a power to them all.

From that which hath been said concerning the nature of gravity, it will follow; That if a man were above the sphere of this magneticall vertue, which proceeds from the earth, hee might there stand as firmely as in the open aire, as he can now upon the ground: And not only so, but he may also move with a farre greater swiftnesse, than any living creatures here below, because then hee is without all gravity, being not attracted any way, and so consequently will not be liable to such impediments, as may in the least manner resist that kinde of motion which hee shall apply himselfe unto.

If you yet enquire, how wee may conceive it possible, that a condensed body should not be heavy in such a place?

I answer, by the same reason as a body is not heavy in its proper place. Of this I will set down two instances.

When a man is in the bottome of a deepe river, though hee have over him a multitude of heavy waters, yet he is not burdened with the weight of them. And though another body, that should be but of an equall gravity, with these waters, when they are taken out, would be heavy enough to presse him to death; yet notwithstanding whilst they are in the channell, they doe not in the least manner, crush him with their load. The reason is, because they are both in their right places; and tis proper for the man being the more condensed body, to be lower than the waters. Or rather thus, Because the body of the man, dos more nearely agree with the earth, in this affection, which is the ground of its attraction, and therefore doth that more strongly attract it, than the waters that are over it. Now, as in such a case, a body may lose the operation of its gravity, which is, to move, or to presse downewards: So may it likewise, when it is so far out of its place, that this attractive power cannot reach unto it.

Tis a pretty notion to this purpose, mentioned by Albertus de Saxonia,[5] . . . That the aire is in some part of it navigable. And that upon this Staticke principle; any brasse or iron vessell (suppose a kettle) whose substance is much heavier than that of the water, yet being filled with the lighter aire, it will swimme upon it, and not sinke. So suppose a cup, or wooden vessel, upon the outward borders of this elementary aire, the cavity of it being filled with fire, or rather aethereall aire, it must necessarily upon the same ground remaine swimming there, and of it selfe can no more fall, than an empty ship can sinke.

Tis commonly granted, that if there were a hole quite through the center of the earth, though any heavy body (as suppose a milstone) were let fall into it, yet when it came unto the place of the center, it would there rest immoveable in the aire. Now, as in this case, its owne condensity, cannot hinder, but that it may rest in the open aire, when there is no other place, to which it should be attracted: So neither could it be any impediment unto it, if it were placed without the sphere of the earths magneticall vigor, where there should be no attraction at all.

From hence then (I say) you may conceive, that if a man were beyond this sphere, hee might there stand as firmely in the open aire, as now upon the earth. And if he might stand there, why might hee not also goe there? And if so; then there is a possibility likewise of having other conveniences for travelling.

And here tis considerable, that since our bodies will then bee devoide of gravity, and other impediments of motion; wee shall not at all spend our selves in any labour, and so consequently not much need the reparation of diet: But may perhaps live altogether without it, as those creatures have done, who by reason of their sleeping for many dayes together, have not spent any spirits, and so not wanted any foode: which is commonly related of Serpents, Crocodiles, Beares, Cuckoes, Swallowes, and such like. To this purpose, . . . divers strange relations [are reckoned up] as that of *Epimenides,*[6] who is storied to have slept 75 yeeares. And another a rusticke in *Germany,* who being accidentally covered with a hay-ricke, slept there for all autumne, and the winter following, without any nourishment.

Or, if this will not serve: yet why may not a Papist fast so long . . . ? Or if there be such a strange efficacy in the bread of the Eucharist, as their

[5] Albert of Saxony (1316–90) was a follower of Aristotelian thought whose theory that the velocity of a falling object would increase in direct proportion to the distance fallen was widely accepted until it was disproved by Galileo.

[6] A poet and prophet of Knossos in Crete in the sixth century B.C.

miraculous relations doe attribute to it: why then, that may serve well enough, for their *viaticum*.

Or, if wee must needs feed upon something else, why may not smells nourish us? Plutarch, and Pliny and divers other ancients, tell us of a nation in *India* that lived only upon pleasing odors. And tis the common opinion of Physitians, that these doe strangely both strengthen and repaire the spirits. Hence was it that *Democritus*[7] was able for divers dayes together, to feede himselfe with the meere smel of hot bread.

Or if it bee necessary that our stomacks must receive the food: why then tis not impossible that the purity of the aethereall aire, being not mixed with any improper vapors, may be so agreeable to our bodies, as to yeeld us sufficient nourishment. . . .

. . . .

Twas an old *Platonicke* principle, that there is in some part of the world such a place where men might be plentifully nourished, by the aire they breathe: Which cannot more properly be assigned to any one particular, than to the aethereall aire above this.

I know tis the common opinion that no *Element* can prove *Aliment* [sustaining], because tis not proportionate to the bodies of living creatures which are compounded. But

1. This aethereall aire is not an element; and though it be purer, yet tis perhaps of a greater agreeablenesse to mans nature and constitution.

2. If we consult experience and the credible relations of others, wee shall finde it probable enough that many things receive nourishment from meer elements.

First, for the earth, Aristotle and Pliny, those two great naturalists, tell us of some creatures, that are fed only with this. And it was the curse of the serpent, *Gen.* 3. 14. *Upon thy belly shalt thou goe, and dust shalt thou eate all the dayes of thy life.*

So likewise for the water. *Albertus Magnus*[8] speaks of a man who lived seven weeks together by the meere drinking of water. *Rondoletius*[9] (to whose diligence these later times are much beholding for sundry observations concerning the nature of Aquatils) affirmes that his wife did keep a fish in a glasse of water, without any other food for three yeares: In which

[7] Democritus (*ca.* 460–370 B.C.), a Greek philosopher, believed that matter consists of indivisible particles, which he called "atoms."

[8] Albert von Böllstadt (*ca.* 1193–1280) was an important German philosopher and biologist. He was a teacher of Thomas Aquinas.

[9] Guillaume Rondelet (1507–66), a physician and professor of anatomy, studied aquatic creatures and showed that fish kept in a container without air would suffocate.

space it was constantly augmented, till at first it could not come out of the place at which it was put in, and at length was too big for the glasse it selfe, though that were of a large capacity. *Cardan*[10] tells us of some wormes, that are bred & nourished by the snow, from which being once separated, they dye.

Thus also is it with the aire, which wee may well conceive dos chiefly concurre to the nourishing of all vegetables. For if their food were all sucked out from the earth, there must needs be then, some sensible decay in the ground by them; especially since they do every yeare renew their leaves, and fruits: which being so many, and so often, could not be produced without abundance of nourishment. To this purpose is the experiment of trees cut down which will of themselves put forth sproutes. As also that of Onyons, & the *Semper-vive,*[11] which will strangely shoot forth, and grow as they hang in the open aire. Thus likewise is it with some sensible creatures; the *Camelion* (saith *Pliny* . . .) is meerely nourished by this: And so are the birds of Paradise,[12] treated of by many; which reside constantly in the aire, Nature having not bestowed upon them any legs, and therefore they are never seene upon the ground but being dead. If you aske, how they multiply? Tis answered, they lay their egges on the backes of one another, upon which they sit till their young ones be fledg'd. *Rondoletius* . . . tels us of a Priest (of whom one of the Popes had the custody) that lived forty yeares upon meer aire. As also of a maide in *France,* and another in *Germany,* that for diverse yeares together did feed on nothing but this: Nay, hee affirmes that hee himself had seene one, who lived till ten years of age without any other nourishment. . . . Now, if this elementary aire which is mixed with such improper vapors, may accidentally nourish some persons; perhaps then, that pure aethereall aire may of it selfe be more naturall to our tempers.

But if none of these conjectures may satisfie; yet there may happily be some possible meanes for the conveiance of other foode, as shall be shewed afterwards.

Againe, seeing we do not then spend our selves in any labour, we shall not, it may bee, neede the resfreshment of sleepe. But if we doe, we cannot desire a softer bed than the aire, where wee may repose our selves firmely and safely as in our chambers.

[10] Giralamo Cardan (1501–76) was an Italian mathematician, physician, and astrologer who claimed that all creation was evolutionary and all animals were originally worms.

[11] Sempervivums or houseleeks are hardy succulent plants. The name, bestowed by Pliny, is derived from *semper* (forever) and *vivo* (to live) and alludes to the tenacity of the plants.

[12] Tis likely that these birds doe chiefly reside in the aethereall aire, wher they are nourished and upheld. [Marginal notation in original.]

But here you may aske, whether there be any meanes for us to know, how far this sphere of the earths vertue dos extend it selfe?

I answer, tis probable that it dos not reach much farther than that orbe of thick vaporous aire, that incompasseth the earth; because tis likely the Sunne may exhale some earthly vapors, near unto the utmost bounds of the sphere alloted to them.

Now there are divers wayes used by Astronomers, to take the altitude of this vaporous aire. As,

1. By observing the height of that aire which causeth the *Crepusculam,* or twilight; For the finding of which, the Antients used this meanes: As soone as ever they could discerne the aire in the east to be altered with the least light, they would by the situation of the starres find out how many degrees the Sun was below the *Horizon,* which was usually about 18. From whence they would easily conclude, how high that aire must be above us, which the Sun could shine upon, when hee was 18 degrees below us. And from this observation, it was concluded to bee about 52 miles high.

But in this Conclusion, the Antients were much decevied, because they proceeded upon a wrong ground, whilst they supposed that the shining of the Suns direct rayes upon the aire, was the only reason of the *Crepusculum;* Whereas tis certain that there are many other things which may also concurre to the causing of it. As,

1. Some bright clouds below the *Horizon,* which being illuminated by the Sunne, may be the means of conveying some light to our aire, before the direct rayes can touch it.

2. The often refraction of the rayes, which suffer a frequent repercussion from the cavitie of this sphere, may likewise yeeld us some light.

3. And so may the orbe of enlightned aire compassing the Sunne, part of which must rise before his body.

2. The second way whereby we may more surely find the altitude of this grosser aire, is by taking the highth of the highest cloud: which may be done, 1. Either as they use to measure the altitude of things that cannot be approached unto, *viz.* by two stations, when two persons shall at the same time, in severall places, observe the declination of any cloud from the vertical point. Or, 2. which is the more easie way, when a man shall choose such a station, where he may at some distance, discerne the place on which the cloud dos cast its shadow, and withall dos observe, how much both the cloud and the Sun decline from the vertical point. From which he may easily conclude the true altitude of it. . . .

. . . .

But if, without making the observation, you would know of what altitude the highest of these are found by observation; Cardan answers, not above two miles; Keplar, not above 1600 paces, or thereabouts.

3. Another way to finde the height of this vaporous aire, is, by knowing the difference of altitude, which it causeth, in refracting the beames of any star neere the *horizon*. And from this observation also, it is usually concluded to bee about two or three miles high.

But now you must not conceive, as if the orbe of magneticall vigor, were bounded in an exact superficies, or as if it did equally hold out just to such a determinate line, and no farther. But as it hath bin said of the first region, which is there terminated where the heat of reflexion dos begin to languish; So likewise is it probable, that this magneticall vigor dos remit of its degrees proportionally to its distance from the earth, which is the cause of it: And therefore though the thicker clouds may be elevated no higher, yet this orbe may be continued in weaker degrees a little beyond them. We will suppose it (which in all likelyhood is the most) to bee about twenty miles high. So that you see the former Thesis remaines probable; that if a man could but fly, or by any other meanes get twenty miles upwards, it were possible for him to reach unto the Moone.

But it may bee again objected: Though all this were true; though there were such an orbe of aire which did terminate the earth's vigor: And though the heavinesse of our bodies could not hinder our passage, through the vast spaces of the aetheriall aire; yet those two other impediments may seeme to deny the possibility of any such voyage.

1. The extreme *coldnesse* of that aire. If some of our higher mountaines for this reason bee not habitable; much more then will those places bee so, which are farther from any cause of heate.

2. The extreme thinnesse of it, which may make it unfit for expiration. For if in some mountaines (as *Aristotle* tells us of Olympus . . .) the aire bee so thin that men cannot draw their breath, unlesse it were through some moistned spunges; much more then must that aire be thin, which is more remotely situated from the causes of impurity and mixture. And then beside, the refraction that is made by the vaporous aire incompassing our earth, may sufficiently prove that there is a great difference betwixt the aethereall aire and this, in respect of rarity.

To the first of these I answer, that though the second region, be naturally endowed with so much coldnesse as may make it fit for the production of meteors; yet it will not hence follow, that all that aire above it, which is not appointed for the like purpose, should partake of the same condition: But, it may seeme more probable that this aethereal aire, is freed from having any quality in the extremes. And this may be confirmed, from those common arguments, which are usually brought to prove the warmnesse of the third region. . . .

This the assertion of *Pererius,*[13] that the second region, is not cold meerly for this reason, because it is distant from the ordinary causes of heat, but because it was actually made so at the first, for the condensing of the clouds, and the production of other meteors that were there to be generated; which (as I conceive) might bee sufficiently confirmed from that order of the creation observed by *Moses,* who tells us that the waters above the firmament (by which, in the greatest probability, we are to understand the clouds in the second region) were made the second day, whereas the Sunne it selfe (whose reflection is the cause of heate) was not created till the fourth day.

To the other objection I answer, that though the aire in the second region (where by reason of its coldnesse there are many thicke vapors) doe cause a great refraction; yet tis probable that the air which is next the earth, is sometimes, & in some places, of a farre greater thinnesse, nay as thin as the aethereall aire it selfe; since sometimes there is such a speciall heat of the Sun, as may rarifie it in an eminent degree; And in some dry places, there are no grosse impure exhalations to mixe with it.

But here it may be objected. If the aire in the second region were more condensed and heavy than this wherein wee breath, then that must necessarily tend downewards and possesse the lower place.

To this some answer, that the hanging of the clouds in the open aire, is no lesse than a miracle. They are the words of *Pliny. Quid mirabilius aquis in caeolo stantibus?* what more wonderfull thing is there than that the waters should stand in the heavens? . . . Because the waters do hang there after such a stupendous inconceivable manner; Which seems likewise to bee favoured by Scripture, where tis mentioned as a great argument of Gods omnipotency, that hee holds up the clouds from falling. *He binds up the waters in his thicke clouds, and the cloud is not rent under them.*

But that which unto me seemes full satisfaction against this doubt, is this consideration; that the naturall vigor whereby the earth dos attract dense bodies unto it, is lesse efficacious at a distance: and therefore a body of lesse density, which is neare unto it, as suppose this thin aire wherein we breath, may naturally bee lower in its situation, than another of a great condensity that is farther of[f]; as suppose the clouds in the second region. And though the one bee absolutely and in it selfe more fit for this motion of

[13] Benedict Pererius (*ca.* 1535-1610) was a philosopher and theologian.

descent; yet by reason of its distance, the earths magneticall vertue cannot so powerfully worke upon it.

As for that relation of *Aristotle*,[14] If it were true; yet it dos not prove this aire to be altogether impassible, since moistned spunges might helpe us against its thinnesse: But tis more likely that hee tooke it upon trust, as hee did some other relations concerning the height of the mountaines, wherein tis evident that he was grossely mistaken. As where he tells us of *Caucasus,* that it casts its shadow 560 miles. And this relation being of the same nature, wee cannot safely trust unto him for the truth of it.

If it be here enquired, what meanes there may bee conjectured, for our ascending beyond the sphere of the earths magneticall vigor.

I answer. 1. Tis not perhaps impossible that a man may be able to flye, by the application of wings to his owne body; As Angels are pictured, as *Mercury* and *Daedalus* are fained, and as hath bin attempted by divers, particularly by a Turke in Constantinople, as *Busbequius*[15] relates.

2. If there bee such a great *Ruck*[16] in *Madagascar,* as *Marcus Polus* [Marco Polo] the Venetian mentions, the feathers in whose wings are twelve foot long, which can soope [scoop] up a horse and his rider, or an elephant, as our kites doe a mouse; why then tis but teaching one of these to carry a man, and he may ride up thither, as *Ganymed* dos upon an eagle.

3. Or if neither of these wayes will serve: Yet I do seriously, and upon good grounds, affirme it possible to make a flying Chariot. In which a man may sit, and give such a motion unto it, as shall convey him through the aire. And this perhaps might bee made large enough to carry divers men at the same time, together with foode for their *viaticum,* and commodities for traffique. It is not the bignesse of any thing in this kind, that can hinder its motion, if the motive faculty be answerable thereunto. We see a great ship swimmes as well as a small corke, and an Eagle flies in the aire as well as a little gnat.

This engine may be contrived from the same principles by which *Archytas*[17] made a wooden dove, and *Regiomontanus*[18] a wooden eagle.

14 This refers to Aristotle's contention (see p. 55) that the air on some mountaintops was too thin to breathe.

15 Ogier Ghislain de Busberg (1522–92) was a Flemish author and collector of Greek manuscripts and coins.

16 A legendary great bird.

17 Archytas (*ca.* 428—*ca.* 347 B.C.) was a Greek philosopher and scientist who claimed to have invented a flying machine.

18 Johann Müller (1436–76) was a German mathematician and astronomer who, with his pupil Bernhard Walther, equipped Europe's first observatory. He also observed Halley's comet in 1472, and his writings on this became the basis of modern cometary astronomy.

I conceive it were no difficult matter (if a man had leisure) to shew more particularly, the meanes of composing it.

The perfecting of such an invention, would be of such excellent use, that it were enough, not only to make a man famous, but the age also wherein hee lives. For besides the strange discoveries that it might occasion in this other world, it would be also of inconceiveable advantage for travelling, above any other conveiance that is now in use.

So that notwithstanding all these seeming impossibilities, tis likely enough, that there may be a meanes invented of journying to the Moone; And how happy shall they be, that are first successefull in this attempt?

From *The Comical History of the States and Empires of the World of the Moon* (1656)

[It will perhaps come as a surprise to many readers that the leading character of Edmond Rostand's five-act comedy *Cyrano de Bergerac,* first performed in Paris in 1897, was based on the life and works of a real man, born almost three centuries earlier. Like the fictional Cyrano, the man was a noted wit. Rostand took many of his hero's speeches from the real Cyrano's writings, which are said to have inspired works by Edgar Allan Poe and Jonathan Swift as well.

Cyrano de Bergerac was born in Paris on March 6, 1619, to a family rich in noble titles and little else. At the College de Beauvais in Paris, where he studied philosophy, he led a wild student's life, taunting tradesmen and engaging in madcap escapades with his friends. Later he joined a company of the famous Gaston Guards and proceeded to establish his reputation as a master of the duel—be it with sword or with wit. Many of his exploits and his remarks became legendary.

While serving with the Guards, Cyrano was wounded twice. The second wound, a sword slash in the neck, forced his retirement from the Gaston Guards in 1640. Returning to Paris, he became a student of Pierre Gassendi—a philosopher, a scientist, and, most important to Cyrano's later writings, a devoted follower of Galileo.

Although little is known of Cyrano's life between his retirement from the Guards and his death at age thirty-six in 1655, several of his posthumously published writings were done at this time. The best known of these—*The Comical History of the States and Empires of the World of the Moon* (1656), excerpted here, and *The Comical History of the States and Empires of the World of the Sun*

(1662)—not only present satirical glimpses of seventeenth-century Parisian life, with sly references to Cyrano's own friends and enemies, but are vehicles for Cyrano's iconoclastic views on religion and for his freewheeling—and sometimes prophetic—speculations about scientific matters.

On the moon, Cyrano finds the Garden of Eden, from which he is soon expelled for his irreverence. In fact, Cyrano is known to have traveled a great deal in the last years of his life, perhaps spurred by the threat of persecution by the Jesuits for his espousal of anti-Aristotelian philosophy and his enthusiastic support of the theories of Copernicus and Galileo.

One of the several methods Cyrano suggests to get to the moon involves the use of rockets that erupt in stages. When the fireworks are spent, the firing mechanism drops away, much as the launching rockets of today's space capsules do. One of his characters breaks the force of his landing by using a kind of parachute, formed by the billowing skirts of his gown. Cyrano proposes a method of illumination resembling the electric light, consisting of incombustible tapers enclosed in glass. His moon characters "read" books without pages, devices that when wound up emit sound or music, as today's phonograph does.

On the subject of mores Cyrano is no less modern. Lunar society, from his point of view, is often much more rational than the France he left behind. On the moon the young are honored and the old obey them (remember, Cyrano was only thirty-six at the time of his death); impartial arbitrators settle all differences between nations, and wars are carefully planned so that the strengths, losses, and gains of both sides are equal; and verse is used as currency instead of money. Characters in Cyrano's fantasy debate the pros and cons of abortion, and Cyrano's "trial" to determine whether he is man or beast is in essence a plea for toleration. Large noses (Cyrano's was in fact monumental, as in the Rostand play) are regarded as signs of wit, courtesy, intelligence, and generosity. (The enlightened moon people measured the noses of all male babies at birth. Those with short noses were castrated so that they could not pass on the miserable trait.)

Cyrano introduces Domingo Gonsales as a character in his book, making it clear that he had carefully read Francis Godwin's work. It also seems likely that he was familiar with John Wilkins's treatise.

The first English translation of Cyrano's lunar tale appears to have been published by T. St. Serf in 1659. Very few copies of this translation exist and, apparently, none in the United States. The next translation, which appeared in 1687 and was the work of A. Lovell, is considered to be the most faithful to the French original in that it preserves the "high fantastical" Bergerac style. The selection printed here is from an 1899 edition of this Lovell translation, annotated by Curtis Hidden Page. Notes have been edited by the present writers from the edition of the Lovell–Page version in the Bryn Mawr College Library, Bryn Mawr, Pennsylvania. Page said of Cyrano, "Exaggeration, sometimes carried to the burlesque, is the essential trait which makes him what he is; and we cannot wish it away." We would be the last to so wish, for the style of these works, like their content, expresses the unfettered imagination of an extraordinary man.]

CHAPTER I
Of how the Voyage was Conceived

I had been with some Friends at Clamard, a House near Paris, and magnificently Entertain'd there by Monsieur de Guigy, the Lord of it; when upon our return home, about Nine of the Clock at Night, the Air serene, and the Moon in the Full, the Contemplation of that bright Luminary furnished us with such variety of Thoughts as made the way seem shorter than, indeed, it was. Our Eyes being fixed upon that stately Planet, every one spoke what he thought of it: One would needs have it be a Garret Window of Heaven; another presently affirmed, That it was the Pan whereupon *Diana* smoothed *Apollo's* Bands; whilst another was of Opinion, That it might very well be the Sun himself, who putting his Locks up under his Cap at Night, peeped through a hole to observe what was doing in the World during his absence.

"And for my part, Gentlemen," said I, "that I may put in for a share, and guess with the rest; not to amuse my self with those curious Notions wherewith you tickle and spur on slow-paced Time; I believe, that the Moon is a World like ours, to which this of ours serves likewise for a Moon."

This was received with the general Laughter of the Company. "And perhaps," said I, "just so they laugh now in the Moon, at some who maintain, That this Globe, where we are, is a World." But I'd as good have said nothing, as have alledged to them, That a great many Learned Men had been of the same Opinion; for that only made them laugh the faster.

However, this thought, which because of its boldness suted [suited] my Humor, being confirmed by Contradiction, sunk so deep into my mind, that during the rest of the way I was big with Definitions of the Moon which I could not be delivered of: Insomuch that by striving to verifie this Comical Fancy by Reasons of appearing weight, I had almost perswaded my self already of the truth on't; when a Miracle, Accident, Providence, Fortune, or what, perhaps, some may call Vision, others Fiction, Whimsey, or (if you will) Folly, furnished me with an occasion that engaged me into this Discourse. Being come home, I went up into my Closet, where I found a Book open upon the Table, which I had not put there. It was a piece of *Cardanus;*[1] and though I had no design to read in it, yet I fell at first sight, as by force, exactly upon a Passage of that Philosopher where he tells us, That Studying one evening by Candle-light, he perceived Two tall old Men enter in through the door that was shut, who after many questions that he put to them, made him answer, That they were Inhabitants of the Moon, and thereupon immediately disappeared.

I was so surprised, not only to see a Book get thither of it self; but also because of the nicking of the Time so patly, and of the Page at which it lay upon, that I looked upon that Concatenation of Accidents as a Revelation, discovering to Mortals that the Moon is a World. "How!" said I to my self, having just now talked of a thing, can a Book, which perhaps is the only Book in the World that treats of that matter so particularly, fly down from the Shelf upon my Table; become capable of Reason, in opening so exactly at the place of so strange an adventure; force my Eyes in a manner to look upon it, and then to suggest to my fancy the Reflexions, and to my Will the Designs which I hatch?

"Without doubt," continued I, "the Two old Men, who appeared to that famous Philosopher, are the very same who have taken down my Book and opened it at that Page, to save themselves the labour of making to me the Harangue which they made to *Cardan*. But," added I, "I cannot be resolved of this Doubt, unless I mount up thither."

"And why not?" said I instantly to my self. "*Prometheus* heretofore went up to Heaven, and stole fire from thence. Have not I as much Boldness as he? And why should not I, then, expect as favourable a Success?"

[1] Jerome Cardan, 1501–76, was a natural philosopher, doctor, astrologer, mathematician, and prolific author famous for his learning and his intense interest in all domains of possible knowledge, including astrology.

Frontispiece of *The Works of Cyrano de Bergerac,* Volume II (Amsterdam, 1709), showing one of the methods Cyrano suggests for getting to the moon: "I have attached all around me a number of vials full of dew upon which the sun darts forth its rays so strongly that the heat which is attracted forms tremendous clouds, raising me so high that I find myself above the mid-region."

CHAPTER II

Of how the Author set out, and where he first arrived

After these sudden starts of Imagination, which may be termed, perhaps, the Ravings of a violent Feaver, I began to conceive some hopes of succeeding in so fair a Voyage: Insomuch that to take my measures aright, I shut my self up in a solitary Country-house; where having flattered my fancy with some means, proportionated to my design, at length I set out for Heaven in this manner.

I planted my self in the middle of a great many Glasses full of Dew, tied fast about me;[2] upon which the Sun so violently darted his Rays, that the Heat, which attracted them, as it does the thickest Clouds, carried me up so high, that at length I found my self above the middle Region of the Air. But seeing that Attraction hurried me up with so much rapidity that instead of drawing near the Moon, as I intended, she seem'd to me to be more distant than at my first setting out; I broke several of my Vials, until I found my weight exceeded the force of the Attraction, and I began to descend again towards the Earth. I was not mistaken in my opinion, for some time after I fell to the ground again; and to reckon from the hour that I set out at, it must then have been about midnight. Nevertheless I found the Sun to be in the Meridian, and that it was Noon. I leave it to you to judge, in what Amazement I was; the truth is, I was so strangely surprised, that not knowing what to think of that Miracle, I had the insolence to imagine that in favour of my Boldness God had once more nailed the Sun to the Firmament, to light so generous [noble] an Enterprise. That which encreased my Astonishment was, That I knew not the Country where I was; it seemed to me, that having mounted straight up, I should have fallen down again in the same place I parted from.

However, in the Equipage I was in, I directed my course towards a kind of Cottage, where I perceived some smoke; and I was not above a Pistol-shot from it, when I saw my self environed by a great number of People, stark naked: They seemed to be exceedingly surprised at the sight of me; for I was the first, (as I think) that they had ever seen clad in Bottles. Nay,

[2] *Cf.* Edmond Rostand's *Cyrano de Bergerac,* act 3, scene II: "One way was to stand naked in the sunshine, in a harness thickly studded with glass phials, each filled with morning dew. The sun, in drawing up the dew, you see, could not have helped drawing me up too!" (Gertrude Hall's translation)

and to baffle all the Interpretations that they could put upon that Equipage, they perceived that I hardly touched the ground as I walked; for, indeed, they understood not that upon the least agitation I gave my Body the Heat of the beams of the Noon-Sun raised me up with my Dew; and that if I had had Vials enough about me, it would possibly have carried me up into the Air in their view. I had a mind to have spoken to them; but as if Fear had changed them into Birds, immediately I lost sight of them in an adjoyning Forest. However, I catched hold of one, whose Legs had, without doubt, betrayed his Heart. I asked him, but with a great deal of pain, (for I was quite choked) how far they reckoned from thence to *Paris?* How long Men had gone naked in *France?* and why they fled from me in so great Consternation? The Man I spoke to was an old tawny Fellow, who presently fell at my Feet, and with lifted-up Hands joyned behind his Head, opened his Mouth and shut his Eyes: He mumbled a long while between his Teeth, but I could not distinguish an articulate Word; so that I took his language for the maffling [mumbling] noise of a Dumb-man.

Some time after, I saw a Company of Soldiers marching, with Drums beating; and I perceived Two detached from the rest, to come and take speech of me. When they were come within hearing, I asked them, Where I was? "You are in *France,*" answered they: "But what Devil hath put you into that Dress? And how comes it that we know you not? Is the Fleet then arrived? Are you going to carry the News of it to the Governor? And why have you divided your Brandy into so many Bottles?" To all this I made answer, That the Devil had not put me into that Dress: That they knew me not because they could not know all Men: That I knew nothing of the *Seine's* carrying Ships to *Paris:* That I had no news for the *Marshal de l'Hôspital,*[3] and that I was not loaded with Brandy. "Ho, ho," said they to me, taking me by the Arm, "you are a merry Fellow indeed; come, the Governor will make a shift to know you, no doubt on't."

They led me to their Company, where I learnt that I was in reality in *France,* but that it was in *New-France.*[4] So that some time after, I was presented before the Governor, who asked me my Country, my Name and Quality; and after that I had satisfied him in all Points, and told him the pleasant Success of my Voyage, whether he believed it, or only pretended to do so, he had the goodness to order me to a Chamber in his Apartment. I was very happy, in meeting with a Man capable of lofty Opinions, and

[3] François de l'Hospital, *Maréchal de France,* was Governor of Paris in 1649, the year when *The Comical History . . . of the Moon* was probably written.

[4] Canada.

who was not at all surprised when I told him that the Earth must needs have turned during my Elevation; seeing that having begun to mount about Two Leagues from *Paris,* I was fallen, as it were, by a perpendicular Line in *Canada.*

CHAPTER III

Of his Conversation with the Vice-Roy of New France; and of the system of this Universe

When I was going to Bed at night, he came into my Chamber, and spoke to me to this purpose: . . . "You know not . . . what a pleasant Quarrel I have just now had with our Fathers; upon your account. They'll have you absolutely to be a Magician; and the greatest favour you can expect from them, is to be reckoned only an Imposter: The truth is, that Motion which you attribute to the Earth[5] is a pretty nice Paradox; and for my part I'll frankly tell you, That that which hinders me from being of your Opinion is, That though you parted yesterday from *Paris,* yet you might have arrived today in this Country without the Earth's turning: For the Sun having drawn you up by the means of your Bottles, ought he not to have brought you hither; since according to *Ptolemy,* and the Modern Philosophers,[6] he marches obliquely, as you make the Earth to move? And besides, what great Probability have you to imagine, that the Sun is immoveable, when we see it go? And what appearance is there, that the Earth turns with so great Rapidity, when we feel it firm under our Feet?"

"Sir," replied I to him, "These are, in a manner, the Reasons that oblige us to think so: In the first place, it is consonant to common Sense to think that the Sun is placed in the Center of the Universe; seeing all Bodies in nature standing in need of that radical Heat, it is fit he should reside in the heart of the Kingdom, that he may be in a condition readily to supply the Necessities of every Part; and that the Cause of Generations should be placed in the middle of all Bodies, that it may act there with greater Equality and Ease: After the same manner as Wise Nature hath placed the Seeds in the Center of Apples, the Kernels in the middle of their Fruits.

[5] In connection with this discussion, it should be remembered that nearly two centuries were required for the Copernican system, promulgated in 1543, to become generally accepted and that, in 1633, only sixteen years before *The Comical History . . . of the Moon* was written, Galileo had been compelled by the Inquisition to deny the motion of the earth.

[6] According to the Ptolemaic system, still generally accepted by "Modern Philosophers" at the time of Cyrano's writing, the fixed stars, the sun, the moon, and each of the five then known planets revolved about the earth in different orbits called "epicycles" and "excentrics."

. . . For an Apple is in it self a little Universe; the Seed, hotter than the other parts thereof, is its Sun, which diffuses about it self that natural Heat which preserves its Globe. . . . Having laid down this, then, for a ground, I say, That the Earth standing in need of the Light, Heat, and Influence of this great Fire, it turns round it, that it may receive in all parts alike that Virtue which keeps it in Being. For it would be as ridiculous to think, that that vast luminous Body turned about a point that it has not the least need of; as to imagine, that when we see a roasted Lark, that the Kitchin-fire must have turned round it. Else, were it the part of the Sun to do that drudgery, it would seem that the Physician stood in need of the Patient; that the Strong should yield to the Weak; the Superior serve the Inferior; and that the Ship did not sail about the Land, but the Land about the Ship.

"Now if you cannot easily conceive how so ponderous a Body can move; Pray, tell me, are the Stars and Heavens, which, in your Opinion, are so solid, any way lighter? Besides, it is not so difficult for us, who are assured of the Roundness of the Earth, to infer its motion from its Figure: But why do ye suppose the Heaven to be round, seeing you cannot know it? . . . To make good your Hypothesis, you are forced to have recourse to Spirits or *Intelligences* that move and govern your Spheres. But for my part, without disturbing the repose of the supreme Being, . . . I say, that the Beams and Influences of the Sun, darting Circularly upon the Earth, make it to turn as with a turn of the Hand we make a Globe to move; or, which is much the same, that the Steams which continually evaporate from that side of it which the Sun shines upon, being reverberated by the Cold of the middle Region, rebound upon it, and striking obliquely do of necessity make it whirle about in that manner. . . .

At these words the Vice-Roy interrupted me: "I . . . have read some Books of Gassendus[7] on that subject: And hear what one of our Fathers, who maintained your Opinion one day, answered me. 'Really,' said he, 'I fancy that the Earth does move, not for the Reasons alledged by *Copernicus;* but because Hell-fire being shut up in the Center of the Earth, the damned, who make a great bustle to avoid its Flames, scramble up to the Vault, as far as they can from them, and so make the Earth to turn, as a Turnspit[8] makes the Wheel go round when he runs about in it.' "

We applauded that Thought, as being a pure effect of the Zeal of that

[7] Gassendi was Cyrano's own teacher of philosophy. He was a bitter opponent of the supposedly Aristotelian philosophy of the time and was the leader of those who followed Epicurus. He was also the most important contemporary supporter of empiricism against the essentially idealistic method of Descartes. He was important, as well, as a popularizer of the Copernican system.

[8] A dog trained to turn a spit by running about in a rotary cage attached to it.

good Father: And then the Vice-Roy told me, That he much wondered, how the Systeme of *Ptolemy,* being so improbable, should have been so universally received. "Sir," said I to him, "most part of Men, who judge of all things by the Senses, have suffered themselves to be perswaded by their Eyes; and as he who Sails along a Shoar thinks the Ship immoveable, and the Land in motion; even so Men turning with the Earth round the Sun have thought that it was the Sun that moved about them. To this may be added the unsupportable Pride of Mankind, who perswade themselves that Nature hath only been made for them; as if it were likely that the Sun, a vast Body Four hundred and thirty four times bigger than the Earth,[9] had only been kindled to ripen their Medlars and plumpen their Cabbage.

"For my part, I am so far from complying with their Insolence, that I believe the Planets are Worlds about the Sun, and that the fixed Stars are also Suns which have Planets about them, that's to say, Worlds, which because of their smallness, and that their borrowed light cannot reach us, are not discernable by Men in this World: For in good earnest, how can it be imagined that such spacious Globes are no more but vast Deserts; and that ours, because we live in it, hath been framed for the habitation of a dozen of proud Dandyprats [idle fops]? How, must it be said, because the Sun measures our Days and Years, that it hath only been made to keep us from running our Heads against the Walls? No, no, if that visible Deity shine upon Man, it's by accident." . . .

. . . .

CHAPTER IV

Or how at last he set out again for the Moon, tho without his own Will

Next Day, and the Days following, we had some Discourses to the same purpose: But some time after, since the hurry of Affairs suspended our Philosophy, I fell afresh upon the design of mounting up to the Moon.

So soon as she was up, I walked about musing in the Woods, how I might manage and succeed in my Enterprise; and at length . . . I went all alone to the top of a little Hill at the back of our Habitation, where I put in Practice what you shall hear. I had made a Machine which I fancied might carry me up as high as I pleased, so that nothing seeming to be

[9] The sun is only 109 times larger than the earth.

wanting to it, I placed my self within, and from the Top of a Rock threw my self in the Air: But because I had not taken my measures aright, I fell with a sosh [splash] in the Valley below.

Bruised as I was, however, I returned to my Chamber without losing courage, and with Beef-Marrow I anointed my Body, for I was all over mortified from Head to Foot: Then having taken a dram of Cordial Waters to strengthen my Heart, I went back to look for my Machine; but I could not find it, for some Soldiers, that had been sent into the Forest to cut wood for a Bonefire [bonfire], meeting with it by chance, had carried it with them to the Fort: Where after a great deal of guessing what it might be, when they had discovered the invention of the Spring, some said, that a good many Fire-Works should be fastened to it, because their Force carrying them up on high, and the Machine playing its large Wings, no Body but would take it for Fiery Dragon. In the mean time I was long in search of it, but found it at length in the Market-place of *Kebeck* [Quebec], just as they were setting Fire to it. I was so transported with Grief, to find the Work of my Hands in so great Peril, that I ran to the Soldier that was giving Fire to it, caught hold of his Arm, pluckt the Match out of his Hand, and in great rage threw my self into my Machine, that I might undo the Fire-Works that they had stuck about it; but I came too late, for hardly were both my Feet within, when whip, away went I up in a Cloud.

The Horror and Consternation I was in did not so confound the faculties of my Soul, but I have since remembered all that happened to me at that instant. For so soon as the Flame had devoured one tier of Squibs [firecrackers], which were ranked by six and six, by means of a Train that reached every half-dozen, another tier went off, and then another; so that the Salt-Peter taking Fire, put off the danger by encreasing it. However, all the combustible matter being spent, there was a period put to the Firework; and whilst I thought of nothing less than to knock my Head against the top of some Mountain, I felt, without the least stirring, my elevation continuing; and adieu Machine, for I saw it fall down again towards the Earth.

That extraordinary Adventure puffed up my Heart with so uncommon a Gladness; that, ravished to see my self delivered from certain danger, I had the impudence to philosophize upon it. Whilst then with Eyes and Thought I cast about to find what might be the cause of it, I perceived my flesh blown up, and still greasy with the Marrow, that I had daubed my self over with the Bruises of my fall: I knew that the Moon being then in the Wain, and that it being usual for her in that Quarter to suck up the Marrow of Animals, she drank up that wherewith I was anointed, with so much the more force that her Globe was nearer to me, and that no interposition of Clouds weakened her Attraction.

When I had, according to the computation I made since, advanced a good deal more than three quarters of the space that divided the Earth from the Moon; all of a sudden I fell with my Heels up and Head down, though I had made no Trip; and indeed, I had not been sensible of it, had not I felt my Head loaded under the weight of my Body: The truth is, I knew very well that I was not falling again towards our World; for though I found my self to be betwixt two Moons, and easily observed, that the nearer I drew to the one, the farther I removed from the other; yet I was certain, that ours was the bigger Globe of the two: Because after one or two days' Journey, the remote Refractions of the Sun, confounding the diversity of Bodies and Climates, it appeared to me only as a large Plate of Gold: That made me imagine, that I byassed [was descending] towards the Moon; and I was confirmed in that Opinion, when I began to call to mind, that I did not fall till I was past three quarters of the way. For, said I to my self, that Mass being less than ours, the Sphere of its Activity must be of less Extent also; and by consequence, it was later before I felt the force of its Center.

CHAPTER V

Of his Arrival there, and of the Beauty of that Country in which he fell

In fine, after I had been a very long while in falling, as I judged, for the violence of my Precipitation hindered me from observing it more exactly: The last thing I can remember is, that I found my self under a Tree, entangled with three or four pretty large Branches which I had broken off by my fall; and my face besmeared with an Apple, that had dashed against it.

By good luck that place was, as you shall know by and by * * * * *[10]

[10] "That place" was unquestionably the Garden of Eden, which Cyrano heretically locates on the moon, and the "Tree" through which he has fallen, an "Apple" of which has besmeared his face, is the Tree of Life. This is the first of a series of gaps that occur in all the French editions as well as the English and to which Cyrano refers in Gertrude Hall's translation of the play as follows: "But I intend setting all this down in a book, and the golden stars I have brought back caught in my shaggy mantle, when the book is printed, will be seen serving as asterisks." It seems altogether improbable, however, that Cyrano himself left the work incomplete. There can be little doubt that the passages were deliberately cut out on account of their "heretical" character. It even seems likely from passages at the beginning of *The Comical History . . . of the Sun* that, when the work was circulated in manuscript, Cyrano had been the object of persecution because of them.

So that you may very well conclude, that had it not been for that Chance, if I had had a thousand lives, they had been all lost. I have many times since reflected upon the vulgar Opinion, That if one precipitate himself from a very high place, his breath is out before he reach the ground; and from my adventure I conclude it to be false, or else that the efficacious Juyce of that Fruit, which squirted into my mouth, must needs have recalled my soul, that was not far from my Carcass, which was still hot and in a disposition of exerting the Functions of Life. The truth is, so soon as I was upon the ground my pain was gone, before I could think what it was; and the Hunger, which I felt during my Voyage, was fully satisfied with the sense that I had lost it.

When I was got up, I had hardly taken notice of the largest of Four great Rivers, which by their conflux make a Lake; when the Spirit, or invisible Soul, of Plants that breath [breathe] upon that Country, refreshed my Brain with a delightful smell: And I found that the Stones there were neither hard nor rough; but that they carefully softened themselves when one trode upon them.

I presently lighted upon a Walk with five Avenues, in figure like to a Star; the Trees whereof seemed to reach up to the Skie, a green plot of lofty Boughs; Casting up my Eyes from the root to the top, and then making the same Survey downwards, I was in doubt whether the Earth carried them, or they the Earth, hanging by their Roots: Their high and stately Forehead seemed also to bend, as it were by force, under the weight of the Celestial Globes; and one would say, that their Sighs and outstretched Arms, wherewith they embraced the Firmament, demanded of the Stars the bounty of their purer Influences before they had lost any thing of their Innocence in the contagious Bed of the Elements. The Flowers there on all hands, without the aid of any other Gardiner but Nature, send out so sweet (though wild) a Perfume, that it rouzes and delights the Smell: There the incarnate of a Rose upon the Bush, and the lively Azure of a Violet under the Rushes, captivating the Choice, make each of themselves to be judged the Fairest: There the whole Year is Spring; there no poysonous Plant sprouts forth, but is as soon destroyed; there the Brooks by an agreeable murmuring, relate their Travels to the Pebbles; there Thousands of Quiristers [choristers] make the Woods resound with their melodious Notes; and the quavering Clubs of these divine Musicians are so universal, that every Leaf of the Forest seems to have borrowed the Tongue and shape of a Nightingale; nay, and the Nymph *Eccho* is so delightful [delighted] with their Airs, that to hear her repeat, one would say, She were sollicitous to learn them. On the sides of that Wood are Two Meadows, whose continued Verdure seems an Emerauld reaching out of sight.

The various Colours, which the Spring bestows upon the numerous little Flowers that grow there, so delightfully confounds and mingles their Shadows, that it is hard to be known, whether these Flowers shaken with a gentle Breeze pursue themselves, or fly rather from the Caresses of the Wanton *Zephyrus:* one would likewise take that Meadow for an Ocean, because, as the Sea, it presents no Shoar to the view; insomuch, that mine Eye fearing it might lose it self, having roamed so long, and discovered no Coast, sent my Thoughts presently thither; and my Thoughts, imagining it to be the end of the World, were willing to be perswaded, that such charming places had perhaps forced the Heavens to descend and join the Earth there. In the midst of that vast and pleasant Carpet, a rustick Fountain bubbles up in Silver Purles, crowning its enamelled Banks with Sets of Violets, and multitudes of other little Flowers, that seem to strive which shall first behold it self in that Chrystal Myrroir [mirror]: It is as yet in the Cradle, being but newly Born, and its Young and smooth Face shews not the least Wrinkle. The large Compasses it fetches, in circling within it self, demonstrate its unwillingness to leave its native Soyl: And as if it had been ashamed to be caressed in presence of its Mother, with a Murmuring it thrust back my hand that would have touched it: The Beasts that came to drink there, more rational than those of our World, seemed surprised to see it day upon the Horizon, whilst the Sun was with the *Antipodes;* and durst not bend downwards upon the Brink, for fear of falling into the Firmament.

I must confess to you, That at the sight of so many Fine things, I found my self tickled with these agreeable Twitches, which they say the *Embryo* feels upon the infusion of its Soul: My old Hair fell off, and gave place for thicker and softer Locks: I perceived my Youth revived, my face grow ruddy, my natural Heat mingle gently again with my radical Moisture:[11] And in a word, I grew younger again by at least Fourteen Years.

CHAPTER VI

Of a Youth whom he met there, and of their Conversation: what that country was, and the Inhabitants of it

I had advanced half a League, through a Forest of Jessamines and Myrtles, when I perceived something that stirred, lying in the Shade: It was a Youth, whose Majestick Beauty forced me almost to Adoration. He

[11] "Natural heat" is body heat, thought to be caused by an internal fire; "radical moisture" refers to the body fluids that circulate in order to cool the internal fire.

started up to hinder me; crying, "It is not to me but to God that you owe these Humilities." "You see one," answered I, "stunned with so many Wonders that I know not what to admire most; for coming from a World, which without doubt you take for a Moon here, I thought I had arrived in another, which our Worldlings call a Moon also; and behold I am in Paradise at the Feet of a God, who will not be Adored." "Except [for] the quality [title] of a God," replied he, "whose Creature I only am, the rest you say is true: This Land is the Moon, which you see from your Globe, and this place where you are is* * * "[12]

"Now at that time Man's Imagination was so strong, as not being as yet corrupted, neither by Debauches, the Crudity of Aliments [food], nor the alterations of Diseases, that being excited by a violent desire of coming to this Sanctuary, and his Body becoming light through the heat of this Inspiration; he was carried thither in the same manner, as some Philosophers, who having fixed their Imagination upon the contemplation of a certain Object have sprung up in the Air by Ravishments, which you call Extasies. The Woman, who through the infirmity of her Sex was weaker and less hot, could not, without doubt, have the imagination strong enough to make the Intension of her Will prevail over the Ponderousness of her Matter; but . . . the Sympathy which still united that half of its whole[13] drew her towards him as he mounted up, as the Amber attracts the Straw, [as] the Load-stone turns towards the North from whence it hath been taken, and drew to him that part of himself, as the Sea draws the Rivers which proceed from it. When they arrived in your Earth, they dwelt betwixt *Mesopotamia* and *Arabia*. . . . So that to inhabit your World, that Man left this destitute; but the All-wise would not have so blessed an Habitation, to remain without Inhabitants; He suffered a few ages after that[14] * * * [until Enoch] cloyed with the company of Men, whose Innocence was corrupted, had a desire to forsake them. This person, however, thought no retreat secure enough from the Ambition of Men, who already Murdered one another about the distribution of your World; except that blessed Land, which his Grand-Father [Adam] had so often mentioned unto him, and to which no Body had as yet found out the way: But his Imagination supplied that. . . . He filled Two large Vessels which he sealed Hermetically, and fastened them under his Arm-pits: So soon as the

[12] A long passage has been lost here, in which the Youth (the Prophet Elijah) probably describes the place where they are as the original Garden of Eden and tells of the Creation, the Fall, and the banishment of Adam and Eve. At the beginning of the next paragraph, he is telling of Adam's transference from the moon to the earth.

[13] The woman to the man, from whose side she was taken.

[14] We may imagine this a short hiatus, to be filled in as follows: "He suffered a few ages after that, *that Enoch,* cloyed with the company of men. . . ." etc.

Smoak began to rise upwards, and could not pierce through the Mettal, it forced up the Vessels on high, and with them also that Great Man. When he was got as high as the Moon, and had cast his Eyes upon that lovely Garden, a fit of almost supernatural Joy convinced him, that that was the place where his Grand-father had heretofore lived. He quickly untied the Vessels, which he had girt like Wings about his Shoulders, and did it so luckily, that he was scarcely Four Fathom in the Air above the Moon, when he set his Fins a going; yet he was high enough still to have been hurt by the fall, had it not been for the large skirts of his Gown, which being swelled by the Wind, gently upheld him till he set Foot on ground.[15] . . .

"I must now tell you, the manner how I came hither. . . . I lived on the agreeable Banks of one of the most renowned Rivers of your World [the Jordan] where amongst my Books, I led a Life pleasant enough not to be lamented, though it slipt away fast enough. In the mean while, the more I encreased in Knowledge, the more I knew my Ignorance. Our Learned Men never put me in mind of the famous *Mada* [Adam], but the thought of his perfect Philosophy made me to Sigh. I was despairing of being able to attain to it, when one day, after a long and profound Studying, I took a piece of Load-stone about two Foot square, which I put into a Furnace; and then after it was well purged, precipitated and dissolved, I drew the calcined Attractive [extract] of it, and reduced it into the size of about an ordinary Bowl [bowling ball].

"After the Preparations, I got a very light Machine of Iron made, into which I went, and when I was well seated in my place, I threw this Magnetick Bowl as high as I could up into the Air. Now the Iron Machine, which I had purposely made more massive in the middle than at the ends, was presently elevated, and in a just Poise; because the middle received the greatest force of Attraction. So then, as I arrived at the place whither my Load-stone had attracted me, I presently threw up my Bowl in the Air over me."[16]

"But," said I, interrupting him, "How came you to heave up your Bowl so streight over your Chariot, that it never happened to be on one side of it?"

"That seems to me to be no wonder at all," said he; "for the Load-stone

[15] Cyrano here anticipates the idea of the parachute.

[16] *Cf.* the "sixth means" in the play: "Or else, I could have placed myself upon an iron plate, have taken a magnet of suitable size, and thrown it in the air! That way is a very good one! The magnet flies upward, the iron instantly after; the magnet no sooner overtaken than you fling it up again. . . . The rest is clear! You can go upward indefinitely." (Gertrude Hall's translation)

being once thrown up in the Air, drew the Iron streight towards it; and so it was impossible, that ever I should mount side-ways. Nay more, I can tell you, that when I held the Bowl in my hand, I was still mounting upwards; because the Chariot flew always to the Load-stone, which I held over it. But the effort of the Iron to be united to my Bowl, was so violent that it made my Body bend double; so that I durst but once essay that new Experiment. The truth is, it was a very surprizing Spectacle to behold; for the Steel of that flying House, which I had very carefully polished, reflected on all sides the light of the Sun with so great life and lustre, that I thought my self to be all on fire. In fine, after often Bowling and following of my Cast, I came, as you did, to an Elevation from which I descended towards this World; and because at that instant I held my Bowl very fast between my hands, my Machine, whereof the Seat pressed me hard, that it might approach its Attractive, did not forsake me; all that now I feared was, that I should break my Neck: But to save me from that, ever now and then I tossed up my Bowl; that by its attractive Virtue it might prevent the violent Descent of my Machine, and render my fall more easie, as indeed it happened; for when I saw my self within Two or three hundred fathom of the Earth, I threw out my Bowl on all hands, level with the Chariot, sometimes on this side, and sometimes on that, until I came to a certain Distance; and immediately then, I tossed it up above me; so that my Machine following it, I left it, and let my self fall on the other side, as gently as I could, upon the Sand; insomuch that my fall was no greater than if it had been but my own height." . . . [*Elijah continues to describe his adventures in the garden, promising Cyrano that a bite of the apple will bring full enlightenment. Cyrano is eventually expelled from the garden because of his irreverence, but he takes an apple with him. He then finds himself "all alone, in a Country I knew not. It was to no purpose for me to stare and look about me; for no Creature appeared to comfort me."*]

CHAPTER VII

Being cast out from that Country, of the new Adventures which Befell him

At length I resolved to march forwards, till Fortune should aford me the company of some Beasts, or at least the means of Dying. She favourably granted my desire, for within half a quarter of a League, I met two huge Animals, one of which stopt before me, and the other fled swiftly to its

Den; for so I thought at least; because that some time after, I perceived it come back again in company of above Seven or Eight hundred of the same kind, who beset me. When I could discern them at a near distance, I perceived that they were proportioned and shaped like us. This advanture brought into my mind the old Wives Tales of my Nurse concerning *Syrenes, Faunes* and *Satyrs:* Ever now and then they raised such furious Shouts, occasioned undoubtedly by their Admiration [astonishment] at the sight of me, that I thought I was e'en turned a Monster. At length one of these Beast-like men, catching hold of me by the Neck, just as Wolves do when they carry away Sheep, tossed me upon his back and brought me into their Town; where I was more amazed than before, when I knew they were Men, that I could meet with none of them but who marched upon all four.

When these People saw that I was so little; (for most of them are Twelve Cubits long,) and that I walked only upon Two Legs, they could not believe me to be a Man: For they were of [the] opinion, that Nature having given to men as well as Beasts Two Legs and Two Arms, they should both make use of them alike. And, indeed, reflecting upon that since, that scituation of Body did not seem to me altogether extravagant; when I called to mind, that whilst Children are still under the nurture of Nature, they go upon all four, and that they rise not on their two Legs but by the care of their Nurses; who set them in little running Chairs, and fasten straps to them, to hinder them from falling on all four, as the only posture that the shape of our Body naturally inclines to rest in.

They said then, (as I had it interpreted to me since) That I was infallibly the Female of the Queen's little Animal. And therefore as such, or somewhat else, I was carried streight to the Town-House, where I observed by the muttering and gestures both of the People and Magistrates, that they were consulting what sort of a thing I could be. When they had conferred together a long while, a certain Burgher, who had the keeping of the strange Beasts, besought the Mayor and Aldermen to commit me to his Custody, till the Queen should send for me to couple me to my Male. This was granted without any difficulty, and that Juggler carried me to his House; where he taught me to Tumble, Vault, make Mouths, and shew a Hundred odd Tricks, for which in the Afternoons he received Money at the door from those that came in to see me.

But Heaven pitying my Sorrows, and vext to see the Temple of its Maker profaned, so ordered it, that one day [when] I was tied to a Rope, wherewith the Mountebank made me Leap and Skip to divert the People,

I heard a Man's voice, who asked me what I was, in Greek. I was much surprised to hear one speak in that Country as they do in our World. He put some Questions to me, which I answered, and then gave him a full account of my whole design, and the success of my Travels: He took the pains to comfort me, and, as I take it, said to me: "Well, Son, at length you suffer for the frailties of your World: There is a Mobile [populace] here, as well as there, that can sway with nothing but what they are accustomed to: But know, that you are but justly served; for had any one of this Earth had the boldness to mount up to yours, and call himself a Man, your Sages would have destroyed him as a Monster."

He then told me, That he would acquaint the Court with my disaster; adding, that so soon as he had heard the news that went of me, he came to see me, and was satisfied that I was a man of the World of which I said I was; because he had Travelled there formerly, and sojourned in *Greece*. . . . "It is not long since I came from thence a second time; within these Hundred Years I had a Commission to Travel thither: I roamed a great deal in *Europe,* and conversed with some, whom possibly you may have known. [*He then names a number of philosophers, poets, and scholars known to have been admired by Cyrano.*] I have known a great many more whom your Age call *Divine,* but all that I could find in them was a great deal of Babble and a great deal of Pride. . . . "

"After all, I am not a Native neither of this country nor yours, I was born in the Sun; but because sometimes our World is overstock'd with people, by reason of the long Lives of the Inhabitants, and that there is hardly any Wars or Diseases amongst them: Our Magistrates, from time to time, send Colonies into the neighbouring Worlds. . . .

"Though the Inhabitants of the Sun be not so numerous as those of this World; yet the Sun is many times over stocked, because the People being of a hot constitution are stirring and ambitious, and digest much.

"You ought not to be surprised at what I tell you; for though our Globe be very vast, and yours little, though we die not before the end of Four thousand Years, and you at the end of Fifty; yet know, that as there are not so many Stones as clods of Earth, nor so many Animals as Plants, nor so many Men as Beasts; just so there ought not to be so many Spirits as Men, by reason of the difficulties that occur in the Generation of a perfect Creature." . . .

He was gone on so far in his Discourse, when my Juggler perceived, that the Company began to be weary of my Gibberish, that they understood not, and which they took to be an inarticulated Grunting: He therefore fell to pulling my Rope afresh to make me leap and skip, till the Spectators having had their Belly-fulls of Laughing, affirmed that I had almost as much Wit as the Beasts of their Country, and so broke up.

CHAPTER VIII

Of the Languages *of the People in the Moon; of the Manner of Feeding there, and of* Paying *the Scot; and of how the Author was taken to Court*

Thus, all the comfort I had during the misery of my hard Usage, were the visits of this officious [kindly] Spirit; for you may judge what conversation I could have with these that came to see me, since besides that they only took me for an Animal, in the highest class of the *Category* of Bruits, I neither understood their Language, nor they mine. For you must know, that there are but two Idioms in use in that Country, one for the Grandees, and another for the people in general.

That of the great ones is no more but various inarticulate Tones, much like to our Musick when the Words are not added to the Air:[17] and in reality it is an Invention both very useful and pleasant; for when they are weary of talking, or disdain to prostitute their Throats to that Office, they take either a Lute or some other Instrument, whereby they communicate their Thoughts as well as by their Tongue: So that sometimes Fifteen or Twenty in a Company will handle a point of Divinity, or discuss the difficulties of a Law-suit, in the most harmonious Consort that ever tickled the Ear.

The second, which is used by the Vulgar, is performed by a shivering of the Members, but not, perhaps, as you may imagine; for some parts of the Body signifie an entire Discourse; for example, the agitation of a Finger, a Hand, an Ear, a Lip, an Arm, an Eye, a Cheek, every one severally will make up an Oration, or a Period with all the parts of it: Others serve only instead of Words, as the knitting of the Brows, the several quiverings of the Muscles, the turning of the Hands, the stamping of the Feet, the contorsion of the Arm; so that when they speak, as their Custom is, stark naked, their Members being used to gesticulate their Conceptions, move so quick that one would not think it to be a Man that spoke, but a Body that trembled.

Every day almost the Spirit came to see me and his rare Conversation

[17] *Cf. The Man in the Moone,* by Francis Godwin, above, pp. 31–32—EDS.

made me patiently bear with the rigour of my Captivity. At length one morning I saw a Man enter my Cabbin, whom I knew not, who having a long while licked me gently, took me in his Teeth by the Shoulder, and with one of his Paws, wherewith he held me up for fear I might hurt my self, threw me upon his Back; where I found my self so softly seated, and so much at my ease, that, [though] being afflicted to be used like a Beast, I had not the least desire of making my escape; and besides, these Men that go upon all four are much swifter than we, seeing the heaviest of them make nothing of running down a Stagg.

In the mean time I was extreamly troubled that I had no news of my courteous Spirit; and the first night we came to our Inn, as I was walking in the Court, expecting [waiting] till Supper should be ready, a pretty handsome young Man came smiling in my Face and cast his Two Fore-Legs about my Neck. After I had a little considered him: "How!" said he in *French,* "do you [not] know your Friend then?" I leave you to judge in what case I was at that time; really, my surprise was so great, that I began to imagine, that all the Globe of the Moon, all that had befallen me, and all that I had seen, had only been Enchantment: And that Beast-man, who was the same that had carried me all day, continued to speak to me in this manner; "You promised me, that the good Offices I did you should never be forgotten, and yet it seems you have never seen me before;" but perceiving me still in amaze: "In fine," said he, "I am that same [one] who diverted you during your Imprisonment, and who, that I may still oblige you, took to my self a Body, on which I carried you to day:" "But," said I interrupting him, "how can that be, seeing that all Day you were of a very long Stature, and now you are very short; that all day long you had a weak and broken Voice, and now you have a clear and vigorous one; that, in short, all day long you were a Grey-headed old Man, and are now a brisk young Blade: Is it then that whereas in my Country, the Progress is from Life to Death; Animals here go Retrograde from Death to Life, and by growing old become young again?"

"So soon as I had spoken to the Prince," said he, "and received orders to bring you to Court, I went and found you out where you were, and have brought you hither; but the Body I acted in was so tired out with the Journey, that all its Organs refused me their ordinary Functions, so that I enquired the way to the Hospital; where being come in I found the Body of a young Man, just then expired by a very odd Accident, but yet very common in this Country. I drew near him, pretending to find motion in him still, and protesting to those who were present, that he was not dead, and that what they thought to be the cause of his Death, was no more but a bare Lethargy; so that without being perceived, I put my Mouth to his, by which I entred as with a breath: Then down dropt my old Carcass, and as if I had been that young Man, I rose and came to look for you, leaving the Spectators crying a Miracle."

With this they came to call us to Supper, and I followed my Guide into a Parlour richly furnished; but where I found nothing fit to be eaten. No Victuals appearing, when I was ready to die of Hunger, made me ask him where the Cloth was laid: But I could not hear what he answered, for at that instant Three or Four young Boys, Children of the House, drew near, and with much Civility stript me to the Shirt. This new Ceremony so astonished me, that I durst not so much as ask my Pretty *Valets de Chamber* the cause of it; and I cannot tell how my Guide, who asked me what I would begin with, could draw from me these two Words, *A Potage;* but hardly had I pronounced them, when I smelt the odour of the most agreeable Soop that ever steamed in the rich Gluttons Nose: I was about to rise from my place, that I might trace that delicious Scent to its source, but my Carrier hindered me: "Whither are you going," said he, "we shall fetch [take] a walk by and by; but now it is time to Eat, make an end of your *Potage,* and then we'll have something else:" "And where the Devil is the *Potage?"* answered I half angry: "Have you laid a wager you'll jeer me all this Day?" "I thought," replied he, "that at the Town we came from, you had seen your Master or some Bo[dy] else at meal, and that's the reason I told you not, how People feed in this Country. Seeing then you are still ignorant, you must know, that here they live on Steams. The art of Cookery is to shut up in great Vessels, made on purpose, the Exhalations that proceed from the Meat whilst it is a dressing; and when they have provided enough of several sorts and several tastes, according to the Appetite of those they treat; they open one Vessel where the Steam is kept, and after that another; and so on till the Company be satisfied.

"Unless you have already lived after this manner, you would never think, that the Nose with Teeth and Gullet can perform the office of the Mouth in feeding a Man; but I'll make you experience it your self." He had no sooner said so, but I found so many agreeable and nourishing Vapours enter the Parlour, one after another, that in less than half a quarter of an Hour I was fully satisfied. When we were got up; "This is not a matter," said he, "much to be admired at, seeing you cannot have lived so long, and not have observed, that all sorts of Cooks, who eat less than People of another Calling, are nevertheless much Fatter. Whence proceeds that Plumpness, d'ye think, unless it be from the Steams that continually environ them, which penetrate into their Bodies and fatten them? Hence it is, that the People of this World enjoy a more steady and vigorous Health, by reason that their Food hardly engenders any Excrements, which are in a manner the original [source] of all Diseases. You were, perhaps, surprised, that before supper you were stript, since it is a Custom not practised in your Country; but it is the fashion of this, and for this end used, that the Animal may be the more transpirable to the Fumes." "Sir," answered I, "there is a great deal of probability in what you say, and I have found somewhat of it my self by experience; but I must frankly tell you, That not being able to Unbrute my self so soon, I should be glad to feel something that my Teeth might fix upon:" He promised I should, but not before next Day; "because," said he, "to Eat so soon after your meal would breed Crudities."

After we had discoursed a little longer, we went up to a Chamber to take our rest; a Man met us on the top of the Stairs, who having attentively Eyed us, led me into a Closet where the floor was strowed with Orange-Flowers Three Foot thick, and my Spirit into another filled with Gilly-Flowers and Jessamines: Perceiving me amazed at that Magnificence, he told me they were the Beds of the Country. In fine, we laid our selves down to rest in our several Cells, and so soon as I had stretched my self out upon my Flowers, by the light of Thirty large Glow-worms shut up in a Crystal, (being the only Candles used) I perceived the Three or Four Boys who had stript me before Supper, One tickling my Feet, another my Thighs, the Third my Flanks, and the Fourth my Arms, and all so delicately and daintily, that in less than in a Minute I was fast asleep.

Next Morning by Sun-rising my Spirit came into my Room and said to me, "Now I'll be as good as my Word, you shall breakfast this Morning more solidly than you Supped last Night." With that I got up, and he led me by the Hand to a place at the back of the Garden, where one of the Children of the House stayed for us, with a Piece [gun] in his Hand much like to one of our Fire-Locks. He asked my Guide if I would have a dozen of Larks, because *Baboons* (one of which he took me to be,) loved to feed on them? I had hardly answered, Yes, when the Fowler discharged a Shot, and Twenty or Thirty Larks fell at our Feet ready Roasted. . . . "Fall too, fall too," said my Spirit, "don't spare; for they have a knack of mingling a certain Composition with their Powder and Shot, which Kills, Plucks, Roasts, and Seasons the Fowl all at once." I took up some of them, and eat them upon his word; and to say the Truth, In all my Life time I never eat any thing so delicious.

Having thus Breakfasted we prepared to be gone, and with a Thousand odd Faces, which they use when they would shew their Love, our Landlord received a Paper from my Spirit. I asked him, if it was a Note for the Reckoning. He replied, No, that all was paid, and that it was a Copy of Verses. "How! Verses," said I, "are your Inn-Keepers here curious of [interested in] Rhime, then?" "It's," said he, "the Money of the Country, and the charge we have been at here, hath been computed to amount to Three *Couplets,* or Six Verses, which I have given him. I did not fear we should out-run the Constable; for though we should Pamper our selves for a whole Week, we could not spend a *Sonnet,* and I have Four about me, besides Two *Epigrams,* Two *Odes,* and an *Eclogue."*

"Would to God," said I, "it were so in our World; for I know a good many honest Poets there who are ready to Starve, and who might live plentifully if that Money would pass in Payment." I farther asked him, If these Verses would always serve, if one Transcribed them. He made answer, No, and so went on: "When an Author has Composed any, he carries them to the Mint, where the sworn Poets of the Kingdom sit in Court. There these versifying Officers essay the pieces; and if they be judged Sterling, they are rated not according to their Coyn; that's to say, That a *Sonnet* is not always as good as a *Sonnet;* but according to the intrinsick value of the piece; so that if any one Starve, he must be a Blockhead; For Men of Wit make always good Chear." With Extasie I was admiring the judicious Policy of that Country, when he proceeded in this manner:

"There are others who keep Publick-house after a far different manner: When one is about to be gone, they demand, proportionately to the Charges, an Acquittance for the other World; and when that is given them, they write down in a great Register, which they call *Doomsday's Book,* much after this manner: *Item,* The value of so many Verses, delivered such a Day, to such a Person, which he is to pay upon the receipt of this Acquittance, out of his readiest Cash: And when they find themselves in danger of Death, they cause these Registers to be Chopt in pieces, and swallow them down; because they believe, that if they were not thus digested, they would be good for nothing."

This Conversation was no hinderance to our Journey; for my Four-legged Porter jogged on under me, and I rid stradling on his Back. I shall not be particular in relating to you all the Adventures that happened to us on our way, till we arrived at length at the Town where the King holds his Residence.

CHAPTER IX

Of the little Spaniard *whom he met there, and of his quaint Wit; of* Vacuum, *Specific Weights, and sundry other Philosophical Matters*

I was no sooner come, but they carryed me to the Palace, where the Grandees received me with more Moderation, than the People had done as I passed the Streets: But both great and small concluded, That without doubt I was the Female of the Queen's little Animal. My Guide was my Interpreter; and yet he himself understood not the Riddle, and knew not what to make of that little Animal of the Queen's; but we were soon satisfied as to that; for the King having some time considered me, ordered it to be brought, and about half an hour after I saw a company of Apes, wearing Ruffs and Breeches, come in, and amongst them a little Man[18] almost of my own Built, for he went on Two Legs; so soon as he perceived me, he Accosted me with "Your excellency's servant." I answered his Greeting much in the same Terms. But alas! no sooner had they seen us talking together, but they believed their Conjecture to be true; and so, indeed, it seemed; for he of all the By-standers, that past the most favourable Judgment upon us, protested that our Conversation was a Chattering we kept for Joy at our meeting again.

That little Man told me, that he was an *European,* a Native of old *Castille:* That he had found a means by the help of Birds to mount up to the World of the Moon, where then we were: That falling into the Queen's Hands, she had taken him for a Monkey, because Fate would have it so, That in that Country they cloath Apes in a *Spanish* Dress; and that upon his arrival, being found in that habit, she had made no doubt but he was of the same kind.

"It could not otherwise be," replied I, "but having tried all Fashions of Apparel upon them, none were found so Ridiculous, and by consequence more becoming a kind of Animals which are only entertained for Pleasure and Diversion." "That shews you little understand the Dignity of our Nation," answered he, "for whom the Universe breeds Men only to be our Slaves, and Nature produces nothing but objects of Mirth and Laughter." He then intreated me to tell him, how I durst be so bold as to Scale the

[18] Domingo Gonsales, hero of Francis Godwin's *The Man in the Moone,* says of himself, "I must acknowledge my Stature is so little, as I think no Man living is less."

Moon with the Machine I told him of. I answered. That it was because he had carried away the Birds, which I intended to have made use of. He smiled at this Raillery; and about a quarter of an hour after, the King commanded the Keeper of the Monkeys to carry us back. The King's Pleasure was punctually obeyed; at which I was very glad, for the satisfaction I had, of having a Mate to converse with during the solitude of my Brutification.

One Day my Male (for I was taken for the Female) told me, That the true reason which had obliged him to travel all over the Earth, and at length to abandon it for the Moon, was that he could not find so much as one Country where even Imagination was at liberty. "Look ye," said he, "how the Wittiest thing you can say, unless you wear a Cornered Cap, if it thwart the Principles of the Doctors of the Robe, you are an Ideot, a Fool, and something worse perhaps. I was about to have been put into the Inquisition at Home, for maintaining to the Pendants Teeth, That there was a *Vacuum,* and that I knew no one matter in the World more Ponderous than another." I asked him, what probable Arguments he had, to confirm so new an Opinion? . . . [*There follows a long discourse by Gonsales concerning the possible existence of a vacuum, and a discussion of fire as the "First Matter," or primary element in nature.*]

These were the things, I think, with which we past the time; for that little *Spaniard* had a quaint Wit. Our conversation, however, was only in the Night time; because from Six a clock in the morning until night, Crowds of the People, that came to stare at us in our Lodging, would have disturbed us: For some threw us Stones, others Nuts, and others Grass; there was no talk, but of the King's Beasts; we had our Victuals daily at set hours. I cannot tell, whether it was that I minded their Gestures and Tones more than my Male did: But I learnt sooner than he to understand their Language, and to smatter [speak] a little of it, which made us to be lookt upon in another guess manner than formerly; and the news thereupon flew presently all over the Kingdom, that two Wild Men had been found, who were less than other Men, by reason of the bad Food we had had in the Desarts; and who through a defect of their Parents' Seed, had not the fore Legs strong enough to support their Bodies.

CHAPTER X

Where the Author comes in doubt, whether he be a Man, *an* Ape, *or an* Estridge [ostrich]; *and of the Opinion of the Lunar Philosophers concerning* Aristotle

This belief would have taken rooting by being spread, had it not been for the Learned Men of the Country, who opposed it, saying, That it was horrid Impiety to believe not only Beasts, but Monsters, to be of their kind. It would be far more probable, (added the calmer Sort) that our Domestick Beasts should participate of the privilege of Humanity and by consequence of Immortality, as being bred in our Country, than a Monstrous Beast, that talks of being born I know not where, in the Moon; and then observe the difference betwixt us and them. We walk upon Four Feet, because God would not trust so precious a thing upon weaker Supporters, and he was afraid lest marching otherwise some Mischance might befall Man; and therefore he took the pains to rest him upon four Pillars, that he might not fall, but disdaining to have a hand in the Fabrick of these two Brutes, he left them to the Caprice of Nature, who not concerning her self with the loss of so small a matter, supported them only by Two Feet.

"Birds themselves," said they, "have not had so hard measure as they; for they have got Feathers at least, to supply the weakness of their Legs, and to cast themselves in the Air when we pursue them; whereas Nature, depriving these Monsters of Two Legs, hath disabled them from escaping our Justice.

"Besides, consider a little how they have the Head raised toward Heaven; it is because God would punish them with scarcity of all things, that he hath so placed them; for that supplicant Posture shews that they complain to Heaven of him that Created them, and that they beg Permission to make their best of our Leavings. But we, on the contrary, have the Head bending downwards, to behold the Blessings whereof we are the Masters, and as if there were nothing in Heaven that our happy condition needed Envy."

I heard such Discourses, or the like, daily at my Lodge; and at length they so curbed the minds of the people as to that point, that it was decreed, That at best I should only pass for a Parrot without Feathers; for they confirmed those who were already perswaded, in that I had but two Legs no more than a Bird, which was the cause that I was put into a Cage by express orders from the Privy Council.

There the Queen's Bird-keeper taking the pains daily to teach me to Whistle, as they do Stares [starlings] or Singing-Birds here, I was really happy in that I wanted [lacked] not Food; In the mean while, with the Sonnets [nonsense] the Spectators stunned me [with], I learnt to speak as they did; so that when I was got to be so much Master of the Idiom as to express most of my thoughts, I told them the finest of my Conceits. The Quaintness of my Sayings was already the entertainment of all Societies, and my Wit was so much esteemed that the Council was obliged to Publish an Edict, forbidding all People to believe that I was endowed with Reason; with express Commands to all Persons, of what Quality or Condition soever, not to imagine but that whatever I did, though never so wittily, proceeded only from Instinct.

Nevertheless, the decision of what I was, divided the Town into Two Factions. The party that stood for me encreased daily; and at length in spight of the *Anathema,* whereby they endeavoured to scare the multitude: They who held for me, demanded a Convention of the States, for determining that Controversie. It was long before they could agree in the Choice of those who should have a Vote; but the Arbitrators pacified the heat, by making the number of both parties equal, who ordered that I should be brought unto the Assembly, as I was: But I was treated there with all imaginable Severity. My Examiners, amongst other things, put questions of Philosophy to me; I ingenuously told them all that my Tutor had heretofore taught me, but they easily refuted me by more convincing Arguments: So that having nothing to answer for my self, my last refuge was to Principles of Aristotle, which stood me in as little stead, as his Sophisms did, for in two Words, they let me see the falsity of them.

"That same Aristotle," said they, "whose Learnings you brag so much of, did without doubt accommodate Principles to his Philosophy, instead of accommodating his Philosophy to Principles; and besides he ought to have proved them at least to be more rational than those of the other Sects you mentioned to us: Wherefore the good Man will not take it ill, we hope, if we bid him God b'w'."

In fine, when they perceived that I did nothing but bawl, that they were not more knowing than *Aristotle,* and that I was forbid to dispute against those who denied his Principles: They all unanimously concluded, That I was not a Man, but perhaps a kind of *Estridge,* seeing I carried my Head upright like them, that I walked on two Legs, and that, in short, but for a little Down, I was every way like one of them; so that the Bird-keeper was ordered to have me back to my Cage. I spent my time pretty pleasantly there, for because I had correctly learned their Language, the whole Court took pleasure to make me prattle. The Queen's Maids, among the rest, slipt always some Boon into my Basket, and the gentilest [nicest] of them all, having conceived some kindness for me, was so transported with Joy, when in private I entertained her with the manners and divertisements of the People of our World, and especially our Bells, and other Instruments of Musick, that she protested to me, with Tears in her Eyes, That if ever I found my self in a condition to fly back again to our World, she would follow me with all her Heart.

CHAPTER XI

Of the Manner of making War in the Moon; and of how the Moon is not the Moon, nor the Earth the Earth

One Morning early, having started out of my Sleep, I found her Taboring [dreaming] upon the grates of my Cage: "Take good heart," said she to me, "yesterday in Council a War was resolved upon, against the King.[19] I hope that during the hurry of Preparations, whilst our Monarch and his Subjects are absent, I may find an occasion to make your escape." "How, a War," said I interrupting her, "have the Princes of this World, then, any quarrels amongst themselves, as those of ours have? Good now, let me know their way of Fighting."

"When the Arbitrators," replied she, "who are freely chosen by the two Parties, have appointed the time for raising Forces for their March, the number of Combatants, the day and place of Battle, and all with so great equality, that there is not one Man more in one Army, than in the other: All the maimed Soldiers on the one side, are lifted in one Company; and when they come to engage, the *Mareshalls de Camp* take care to expose them to the maimed of the other side: The Giants are matched with Colosses, the Fencers with those that can handle their Weapons, the Valient with the Stout, the Weak with the Infirm, the Sick with the Indisposed, the Sturdy with the Strong; and if any undertake to strike at another than the Enemy he is matched with, unless he can make it out that it was by mistake, he is Condemned for a Coward. When the Battle is over, they take an account of the Wounded, the Dead and the Prisoners, for Run-

[19] Cyrano writes all proper names by means of musical notation, in imitation of the language of the moon as he has described it.

aways they have none; and if the loss be equal on both sides, they draw Cuts [lots], who shall be Proclaimed Victorious.

"But though a Kingdom hath defeated the Enemy in open War, yet there is hardly any thing got by it; for there are other smaller Armies of Learned and Witty Men, on whose Disputations the Triumph or Servitude of States wholly depends.

"One Learned Man grapples with another, one Wit with another, and one Judicious Man with another Judicious Man: Now the Triumph which a State gains in this manner is reckoned as good as three Victories by open force. After the Proclamation of Victory, the Assembly is broken up, and the Victorious People either chuse the Enemies' King to be theirs, or confirm their own."

I could not forbear to Laugh at this scrupulous way of giving Battle; and for an Example of much stronger Politicks; I alledged the Customs of our *Europe,* where the Monarch would be sure not to let slip any favourable occasion of gaining the day; but mind what she said as to that.

"Tell me, pray, if your Princes use not a pretext of Right, when they levy Arms?" "No doubt," answered I, "and of the Justice of their Cause too." "Why then," replied she, "do they not chuse Impartial and Unsuspected Arbitrators to compose their Differences? And if it be found, that the one has as much Right as the other, let things continue as they were; or let them play a game at *Picket,* for the Town or Province that's in dispute?"

"But why all these Circumstances," replied I, "in your way of Fighting? Is it not enough, that both Armies are equal in the number of Men?" "Your Judgment is Weak," answered she. "Would you think in Conscience, that if you had the better of your Enemy, Hand to Hand, in an open Field, you had fairly overcome him, if you had had on a Coat of Mail, and he none; if he had had but a Dagger, and you had a Tuck [rapier]; and in a Word, if he had had but one Arm, and you both yours? Nevertheless, what Equality soever you may recommend to your Gladiators, they never fight on even terms; for the one will be a tall Man, and the other Short; the one skilful at his weapon, and the other a Man that never handled a Sword; the one will be strong, and the other Weak: And though these Disproportions were not, but that the one were as skillful and strong as the other; yet still they might not be rightly matched; for one, perhaps, may have more Courage than the other, who being rash and hot headed, inconcerned in danger, as not foreseeing it; of a bilious Temper, a more contracted Heart, with all the qualities that constitute Courage, (as if that, as well as a Sword, were not a Weapon which his Adversary hath not:) He makes nothing of falling desperately upon, terrifying, and killing this poor Man, who foresees the danger; who has his Heat choked in Phlegme, and a Heart too wide to close in the Spirits in such a posture as is necessary for thawing that Ice which is called Cowardise. And now you praise that Man, for having killed his Enemy at odds, and praising him for his Boldness you praise him for a Sin against nature; seeing such Boldness tends to its destruction. And this puts me in mind to tell ye, that some Years ago application was made to the Council of War for a more circumspect and conscientious Rule to be made, as to the way of Fighting. The Philosopher who gave the advice, if I mistake it not, spake in this manner.

" 'You imagine, Gentlemen, that you have very equally balanced the advantages of two Enemies, when you have chosen both Tall Men, both skillful, and both couragious: But that's not enough, seeing after all the Conquerour must have the better on't either through his Skill, Strength, or good Fortune. If it be by Skill, without doubt he hath taken his Adversary on the blind side, which he did not expect; or struck him sooner than was likely, or faining to make his Pass on one side, he hath attacked him on the other: Nevertheless all this is Cunning, Cheating, and Treachery, and none of these make a brave Man: If he hath triumphed by Force, would you judge his Enemy over-come, because he hath been over-powered? No; doubtless, no more than you'll say that a Man hath lost the Victory, when, over-whelm'd by a Mountain, it was not in his power to gain it: Even so, the other was not overcome, because he was not in a suitable Disposition, at that nick of time, to resist the violences of his Adversary. If Chance hath given him the better of his Enemy, Fortune ought then to be Crowned, since he hath contributed nothing to it; and, in fine, the vanquished is no more to be blamed, than he who at Dice having thrown Seventeen, is beat by another that throws three Sixes.'

"They confessed he was in the right; but that it was impossible, according to humane Appearances, to remedy it; and that it was better to submit to a small inconvenience, than to open a door to a hundred of greater Importance."

. . . .

In the mean time, some must needs have revived the Disputes about the Definition of my Being; for whilst I was thinking of nothing else but of dying in my Cage, I was once more brought out to have another Audience. I was then questioned, in presence of a great many Courtiers, upon some points of Natural Philosophy; and, as I take it, my Answers gave some kind of Satisfaction; for the President declared to me at large his thoughts concerning the structure of the World. . . .

. . . .

When he had made an end, all the Hall rung again with a kind of Musical Applause; and after all the Opinions had been canvased, during the space of a large quarter of an hour, the King gave Sentence:

That for the future, I should be reputed to be a Man, accordingly set at liberty, and that the Punishment of being Drowned, should be converted into a publick Disgrace (the most honourable way of satisfying the Law in that Country) whereby I should be obliged to retract openly what I had maintained in saying, That the Moon was a World, because of the Scandal that the novelty of that opinion might give to weak Brethren.

This Sentence being pronounced, I was taken away out of the Palace, richly Cloathed; but in derision, carried in a magnificent Chariot, as on a Tribunal, which four Princes in Harness drew; and in all the publick places of the Town, I was forced to make this Declaration:

"Good People, I declare to you, That this Moon here is not a Moon, but a World; and that that World below is not a World, but a Moon: This the Council thinks fit you should believe."

CHAPTER XII
Of a Philosophical Entertainment

After I had Proclaimed this, in the five great places of the Town, my Advocate came and reached me his Hand to help me down. I was in great amaze, when after I had Eyed him I found him to be my Spirit; we were an hour in embracing one another: "Come lodge with me," said he, "for if you return to Court, after a Publick Disgrace, you will not be well lookt upon: Nay more, I must tell you, that you would have been still amongst the Apes yonder, as well as the *Spaniard* your Companion, if I had not in all Companies published the vigour and force of your Wit, and gained from your Enemies the protection of the great Men in your favours." I ceased not to thank him all the way, till we came to his Lodgings; there he entertained me till Suppertime with all the Engines he had set a work to prevail with my Enemies . . . to desist from so unjust a Prosecution. But as they came to acquaint us that Supper was upon the Table, he told me that to bear me company that evening he had invited Two Professors of the University of the Town to Sup with him: "I'll make them," said he, "fall upon the Philosophy which they teach in this World, and by that means you shall see my Landlord's Son: He's as Witty a Youth as ever I met with; he would prove another *Socrates,* if he could use his Parts [talents] aright, and not bury in Vice the Graces wherewith God continually visits him, by affecting a Libertinism, as he does, out of a Chimerical Ostentation and Affectation of the name of a Wit. I have taken Lodgings here, that I may lay hold on all Opportunities of Instructing him:" He said no more, that he might give me the Liberty to speak, if I had a mind to it; and then made a sign, that they should strip me of my disgraceful Ornaments, in which I still glistered.

The Two Professors, whom we expected, entered just as I was undrest, and we were to sit down to Table, where the Cloth was laid, and where we found the Youth he had mentioned to me, fallen to already. They made him a low Reverence, and treated him with as much respect as a Slave does his Lord. I asked my Spirit the reason of that, who made me answer, that it was because of his Age; seeing in that World, the Aged rendered all kind of Respect and Difference [deference] to the Young; and which is far more, that the Parents obeyed their Children, so soon as by the Judgments of the Senate of Philosophers they had attained to the Years of Discretion.

"You are amazed," continued he, "at a Custom so contrary to that of your Country; but it is not all repugnant to Reason: For say, in your Conscience, when a brisk young Man is at his Prime in Imagining, Judging, and Acting, is not he fitter to govern a Family than a Decrepit piece of Three-score Years, dull and doting, whose Imagination is frozen under the Snow of Sixty Winters, who follows no other Guide but what you call the Experience of happy Successes; which yet are no more but the bare effects of Chance, against all the Rules and Oeconomy of humane Prudence? And as for Judgment, he hath but little of that neither, though the people of your World make it the Portion of Old Age: But to undeceive them, they must know, That that which is called Prudence in an Old Man is no more but a panick Apprehension, and a mad Fear of acting any thing where there is danger: So that when he does not run a Risk, wherein a Young Man hath lost himself; it is not that he foresaw the Catastrophe, but because he had not Fire enough to kindle those noble Flashes, which make us dare: Whereas the Boldness of that Young Man was as a pledge of the good Success of his design; because the same Ardour that speeds and facilitates the execution, thrust him upon the undertaking.

"As for Execution, I should wrong your Judgment if I endeavoured to convince it by proofs: You know that Youth alone is proper for Action; and were you not fully perswaded of this, tell me, pray, when you respect a Man of Courage, is it not because he can revenge you on your Enemies or

Oppressors? And does any thing, but meer Habit, make you consider [respect] him, when a Battalion of Seventy *Januarys* hath frozen his Blood and chilled all the noble Heats that youth is warmed with? When you yield to the Stronger, is it not that he should be obliged to you for a Victory which you cannot Dispute him? Why then should you submit to him, when Laziness hath softened his Muscles, weakened his Arteries, evaporated his Spirits, and suckt the Marrow out of his Bones? If you adore a Woman, is it not because of her Beauty? Why should you then continue your Cringes, when Old Age hath made her a Ghost, which only represents a hideous Picture of Death? In short, when you loved a Witty Man, it was because by the Quickness of his Apprehension he unravelled an intricate Affair, seasoned the choicest Companies with his quaint Sayings, and sounded the depth of Sciences with a single Thought; and do you still honour him, when his worn Organs disappoint his weak Noddle, when he is become dull and uneasy in Company? . . .

"Conclude then from thence, Son, that it is fitter Young Men should govern Families, than Old; and the rather, that according to your own Principles, *Hercules, Achilles, Alexander,* and *Caesar,* of whom most part died under Fourty Years of Age, could have merited no Honours, as being too Young in your account, though their Youth was the only cause of their Famous Actions; which a more advanced Age would have rendered ineffectual, as wanting that Heat and Promptitude that rendered them so highly successful. But you'll tell me, that all the Laws of your World do carefully enjoin the Respect that is due to Old Men: That's true; but it is as true also, that all who made Laws have been Old Men, who feared that Young Men might justly have dispossessed them of the Authority they had usurped.

"You owe nothing to your mortal Architector, but your Body only; your Soul comes from Heaven, and Chance might have made your Father your Son, as now you are his. . . . So that, perhaps, you are no more indebted to your Father for the life he hath given you, than you would be to a Pirate who had put you in Chains, cause he feeds you: Nay, grant he had begot you a Prince, or King; a Present loses its merit, when it is made without the Option of who receives it. . . . Did your Father consult your Will and Pleasure, when he Embraced your Mother? Did he ask you, if you thought fit to see that Age, or to wait for another; if you would be satisfied to be the Son of a Sot, or if you had the Ambition to spring from a Brave Man? Alas, you whom alone the business concerned, were the only Person not consulted in the case. May be then, had you been shut up any where else, than in the Womb of Nature's Ideas, and had your Birth been in your own Opinion, you would have said to the *Parca* [Fate], my dear Lady, take another Spindle in your Hand: I have lain very long in the Bed of Nothing, and I had rather continue an Hundred years still without a Being, than to Be to day, that I may repent of it to morrow: However, Be you must, it was to no purpose for you to whimper and squall to be taken back again to the long and darksome House they drew you out of, they made as if they believed you cryed for the Teat.

"These are the Reasons, at least some of them, my Son, why Parents bear so much respect to their Children: I know very well that I have inclined to the Children's side more than in justice I ought; and that in favour of them, I have spoken a little against my Conscience. But since I was willing to repress the Pride of some Parents, who insult [complain] over the weakness of their little Ones; I have been forced to do as they do who to make a crooked Tree streight bend it to the contrary side, that betwixt two Conversions it may become even: Thus I have made Fathers restore to their Children what they have taken from them, by taking from them a great deal that belonged to them; that so another time they may be content with their own. I know very well also that by this Apology I have offended all Old Men: But let them remember, that they were Children before they were Fathers, and Young before they were Old; and that I must needs have spoken a great deal to their advantage, seeing they were not found in a Parsley-bed. . . ."

[*In the remainder of this chapter, the Youth supports the professor's arguments concerning the generation gap. There follows a debate about whether cabbages and other plants have souls, with Cyrano arguing the affirmative, thus taking the "vegetarian" point of view to its logical extreme. The chapter ends with a discussion of "physiognomists," who are similar to physicians, except that they minister only to the healthy, prescribing their food, the flowers for their beds, and so forth, on the basis of their complexion, agility, hair color, and the like.*]

CHAPTER XIII

Of the little Animals that make up our Life, and likewise cause our Diseases; and of the Disposition of the Towns in the Moon

During all this Discourse, I made Signs to my Landlord, that he would try if he could oblige the Philosophers to fall upon some head of the Science which they professed. He was too much my Friend, not to start an

Occasion upon the Spot: But not to trouble the Reader with the Discourse and Entreaties that were previous to the Treaty, wherein Jest and Earnest were so wittily interwoven, that it can hardly be imitated; I'll only tell you that the Doctor, who came last, after many things, spake as follows:

"It remains to be proved, that there are infinite Worlds, in an infinite World: Fancy to your self then the Universe as a great Animal; and that the Stars, which are Worlds, are in this great Animal, as other great Animals that serve reciprocally for Worlds to other Peoples; such as we, our Horses, &c. That we in our turns, are likewise Worlds to certain other Animals, incomparably less than our selves, such as Nits, Lice, Hand-worms [itch mites], &c. And that these are an Earth to others, more imperceptible ones; in the same manner as every one of us appears to be a great World to these little People. Perhaps our Flesh, Blood, and Spirits, are nothing else but a Contexture of little Animals that correspond, lend us Motion from theirs, and blindly suffer themselves to be guided by our Will, which is their Coachman; or otherwise conduct us, and all Conspiring together, produce that Action which we call Life.

"For tell me, pray, is it a hard thing to be believed, that a Louse takes your Body for a World; and that when any one of them travels from one of your Ears to the other, his Companions say, that he hath travelled the Earth from end to end, or that he hath run from one Pole to the other? Yes, without doubt, these little People take your Hair for the Forests of their Country; the Pores full of Liquor, for Fountains; Buboes and Pimples, for Lakes and Ponds; Boils, for Seas; and Defluxions, for Deluges: And when you Comb your self, forwards, and backwards, they take that Agitation for the Flowing and Ebbing of the Ocean. Doth not Itching make good what I say? What is the little Worm that causes it but one of these little Animals, which hath broken off from civil Society, that it may set up for a Tyrant in its Country? If you ask me, why are they bigger than other imperceptible Creatures? I ask you, why are Elephants bigger than we? And the *Irish*-men, than *Spaniards?*

. . . .

"To prove more plainly that universal *Vermicularity,* you need but consider, when you are wounded, how the Blood runs to the Sore: Your Doctors say that it is guided by provident Nature, who would succour the parts debilitated; which might make us conclude, that, besides the Soul and Mind, there were a third intellectual Substance, that had distinct Organs and Functions: And therefore, it seems to me far more Rational to say,

That these little Animals finding themselves attacked send to demand Assistance from their Neighbours, and thus, Recruits flocking in from all Parts and the Country being too little to contain so many, they either die of Hunger or are stifled in the Press. That Mortality happens when the Boil is ripe; for as an Argument that these Animals at that time are stifled, the Flesh becomes insensible: Now, if Blood-letting, which is many times ordered to divert the Fluxion, do any good, it is because, much being lost by the Orifice which these little Animals laboured to stop, they refuse their Allies Assistance, having no more Forces than is enough to defend themselves at home." . . .

CHAPTER XIV

[*Most of this chapter is a lengthy discourse on scientific and philosophical principles. In the last section, reprinted below, Cyrano anticipates the light bulb. A philosopher is speaking.*]

"Now upon the same Principle will I explain to you the Creation, Harmony, and Influence of the Celestial Globes, with the immutable Variety of Meteors."

He was about to proceed; but the Old Landlord coming in, made our Philosopher think of withdrawing: He brought in Christals full of Glow-worms, to light the Parlour; but seeing those little fiery Insects lose much of their Light, when they are not fresh gathered, these which were ten days old had hardly any at all. My Spirit stayed not till the Company should complain of it, but went up to his Chamber, and came immediately back again with two Bowls of Fire so Sparkling that all wondred he burnt not his Fingers. "These incombustible Tapers," said he . . . are Rays of the Sun, which I have purged from their Heat; otherwise, the corrosive qualities of their Fire would have dazzled and offended your Eyes; I have fixed their Light, and inclosed it within these transparent Bowls. That ought not to afford you any great Cause of Admiration; for it is not harder for me, who am a Native of the Sun, to condense his Beams, which are the Dust of that World, than it is for you to gather the Atomes of the pulveriz'd Earth of this World."

Thereupon our Landlord sent a Servant to wait upon [accompany] the Philosophers home, it being then Night, with a dozen Globes of Glow-worms hanging at his four Legs. As for my Preceptor and my self, we went to rest, by order of the Phisiognomist. He laid me that Night in a Chamber of Violets and Lillies, [and] ordered me to be tickled after the usual manner.

CHAPTER XV

Of the Books *in the Moon; and their Fashion; of Death, Burial, and Burning; of the Manner of telling the Time; and of* Noses

Next Morning about Nine a Clock, my Spirit came in, and told me that he was come from Court, where . . . one of the Queen's Maids of Honour had sent for him, and that she had enquired after me, protesting that she still persisted in her Design to be as good as her Word; that is, that with all her Heart she would follow me, if I would take her along with me to the other World; "which exceedingly pleased me," said he, "when I understood that the chief Motive which inclined her to the Voyage, was to become Christian: And therefore, I have promised to forward her Design, what lies in me; and for that end to invent a Machine that may hold three or four, wherein you may mount to day, both together, if you think fit. I'll go seriously set about the performance of my Undertaking; and in the mean time, to entertain you, during my Absence, I leave you here a Book, which heretofore I brought with me from my Native Countrey; the Title of it is, *The States and Empires of the Sun, with an Addition of the History of the Spark*.[20] I also give you this, which I esteem much more; it is the great Work of the Philosophers, composed by one of the greatest Wits of the Sun. He proves in it that all things are true, and shews the way of uniting Physically the Truths of every Contradiction; as, for Example, That White is Black, and Black White; that one may be, and not be at the same time; that there may be a Mountain without a Valley; that nothing is something, and that all things that are, are not; but observe, that he proves all these unheard-of Paradoxes without any Captious or Sophistical Arguments.

. . . .

[20] Cyrano's own work, published as *The Comical History of the States and Empires of the World of the Sun*. It is full of interesting matters, including a trip through the country of the Birds, which offers many points of comparison with Gulliver's voyage to the country of the Houyhnhnms.

Having said so, he left me; and no sooner was his back turned, but I fell to consider attentively my Books and their Boxes, that's to say, their Covers, which seemed to me to be wonderfully Rich; the one was cut of a single Diamond, incomparably more resplendent than ours; the second looked like a prodigious great Pearl, cloven in two. My Spirit had translated those Books into the Language of that World; but because I have none of their Print, I'll now explain to you the Fashion of these two Volumes.

As I opened the Box, I found within somewhat of Metal, almost like to our Clocks, full of I know not what little Springs and imperceptible Engines: It was a Book, indeed; but a Strange and Wonderful Book, that had neither Leaves nor Letters: In fine, it was a Book made wholly for the Ears, and not the Eyes. So that when any Body has a mind to read in it, he winds up that Machine with a great many Strings; then he turns the Hand to the Chapter which he desires to hear, and straight, as from the Mouth of a Man, or a Musical Instrument, proceed all the distinct and different Sounds, which the *Lunar* Grandees make use of for expressing their Thoughts, instead of Language.

When I since reflected on this Miraculous Invention, I no longer wondred that the Young-Men of that Country were more knowing at Sixteen or Eighteen years Old, than the Gray-Beards of our Climate; for knowing how to Read as soon as Speak, they are never without Lectures, in their Chambers, their Walks, the Town, or Travelling; they may have in their Pockets, or at their Girdles, Thirty of these Books, where they need but wind up a Spring to hear a whole Chapter, and so more, if they have a mind to hear the Book quite through; so that you never want the Company of great Men, living and Dead, who entertain you with Living Voices. This Present employed me about an hour; and then hanging them to my Ears, like a pair of Pendants, I went a Walking; but I was hardly at End of the Street when I met a Multitude of People very Melancholy.

Four of them carried upon their Shoulders a kind of a Herse, covered with Black: I asked a Spectator, what that Procession, like to a Funeral in my Country meant. He made me answer, that [a man] had, being convicted of Envy and Ingratitude, died the day before; and that Twenty Years ago, the Parliament had Condemned him to die in his Bed, and then to be interred after his Death. I fell a Laughing at that Answer. And he asking me, why? "You amaze me," said I, "that that which is counted a Blessing in our World, as a long Life, a peaceable Death, and an Honourable Burial, should pass here for an exemplary Punishment." "What, do you take a Burial for a precious thing then?" replyed the Man. "And, in good earnest, can you conceive any thing more Horrid than a Corps crawling with Worms, at the discretion of Toads which feed on his Cheeks; the Plague it self Clothed with the Body of a Man? Good God! The very thought of having, even when I am Dead, my Face wrapt up in a Shroud, and a Pike-depth of Earth upon my Mouth, makes me I can hardly fetch breath. The Wretch whom you see carried here, besides the disgrace of being thrown into a Pit, hath been Condemned to be attended by an Hundred and Fifty of his Friends; who are strictly charged, as a Punishment for their having loved an envious and ungrateful Person, to appear with a sad Countenance at his Funeral; and had it not been that the Judges took some compassion on him, imputing his Crimes partly to his want of Wit, they would have been commanded to Weep there also.

"All are Burnt here, except Malefactors: And, indeed, it is a most rational and decent Custom: For we believe, that the Fire having separated the pure from the impure, the Heat by Sympathy reassembles the natural Heat which made the Soul, and gives it force to mount up till it arrive at some Star, the Country of Certain people more immaterial and intellectual than us; because their Temper ought to suit with, and participate of the Globe which they inhabit.

"However, this is not our neatest way of Burying neither; for when any one of our Philosophers comes to an Age, wherein he finds his Wit begin to decay, and the Ice of his years to numm the Motions of his Soul, he invites all his Friends to a sumptuous Banquet; then having declared to them the Reasons that move him to bid farewel to Nature, and the little hopes he has of adding any thing more to his worthy Actions, they shew him Favour; that's to say, they suffer him to Dye; or otherwise are severe to him and command him to Live. When then, by plurality of Voices, they have put his Life into his own Hands, he acquaints his dearest Friends with the day and place. These purge, and for Four and Twenty hours abstain from Eating; then being come to the House of the Sage, and having Sacrificed to the Sun, they enter the Chamber where the generous Philosopher waits for them on a Bed of State; every one embraces him, and when it comes to his turn whom he loves best, having kissed him affectionately, leaning upon his Bosom, and joyning Mouth to Mouth, with his right hand he sheaths a Dagger in his Heart."

I interrupted this Discourse, saying to him that told me all, That this Manner of Acting much resembled the ways of some People of our World; and so pursued my Walk, which was so long that when I came back Dinner had been ready Two Hours. They asked me, why I came so late. It is not my Fault, said I to the Cook, who complained: I asked what it was a Clock several times in the Street, but they made me no answer but by opening their Mouths, shutting their Teeth, and turning their Faces awry.

"How," cried all the Company, "did not you know by that, that they shewed you what it was a Clock?" "Faith," said I, "they might have held their great Noses in the Sun long enough, before I had understood what they meant." "It's a Commodity," said they, "that saves them the Trouble of a Watch; for with their Teeth they make so true a Dial, that when they would tell any Body the Hour of the day, they do no more but open their Lips, and the shadow of that Nose, falling upon their Teeth, like the Gnomon of a Sun-Dial, makes the precise time.

"Now that you may know the reason, why all People in this Country have great Noses; as soon as a Woman is brought to Bed the Midwife carries the Child to the *Master of the Seminary;* and exactly at the years end, the Skillful being assembled, if his Nose prove shorter than the standing Measure, which an Alderman keeps, he is judged to be a *Flat Nose,* and delivered over to be gelt [gelded]. You'l ask me, no doubt, the Reason of that Barbarous Custom, and how it comes to pass that we, amongst whom Virginity is a Crime, should enjoyn Continence by force; but know that we do so, because after Thirty Ages' experience we have observed, that a great Nose is the mark of a Witty, Courteous, Affable, Generous and Liberal Man; and that a little Nose is a Sign of the contrary: Wherefore of *Flat Noses* we make Eunuchs, because the Republick had rather have no Children at all than Children like them."

He was still a speaking, when I saw a man come in stark Naked; I presently sat down and put on my Hat to shew him Honour, for these are the greatest Marks of Respect, that can be shew'd to any in that Country. "The Kingdom," said he, "desires you would give the Magistrates notice, before you return to your own World; because a Mathematician hath just now undertaken before the Council, that provided when you are returned home, you would make a certain Machine, that he'l teach you how to do; he'l attract your Globe, and joyn it to this." . . .

. . . .

CHAPTER XVI

[*This chapter deals with miracles and the possibility of "curing by the Imagination."*]

CHAPTER XVII
Of the Author's Return to the Earth

At length my Love for my Country took me off of the desire and thoughts I had of staying there; I minded [desired] nothing now but to be gone; but I saw so much impossibility in the matter, that it made me quite peevish and melancholick. My Spirit observed it, and having asked me, What was the reason that my Humor was so much altered? I frankly told him the Cause of my Melancholy; but he made me such fair Promises concerning my Return, that I relied wholly upon him. I acquainted the Council with my design; who sent for me, and made me take an Oath, that I should relate in our World, all that I had seen in that. My Pass-ports then were expeded, and my Spirit having made necessary Provisions for so long a Voyage, asked me. What part of my Country I desired to light in? I told him, that since most of the Rich Youths of *Paris,* once in their life time, made a Journey to *Rome;* imagining after that that there remained no more worth the doing or seeing; I prayed him to be so good as to let me imitate them.

"But withal," said I, "in what Machine shall we perform the Voyage, and what Orders do you think the Mathematician, who talked t'other day of joyning this Globe to ours, will give me?" "As to the Mathematician," said he, "let that be no hinderance to you; for he is a Man who promises much, and performs little or nothing. And as to the Machine that's to carry you back, it shall be the same which brought you to Court." "How," said I, "will the Air become as solid as the Earth, to bear your steps? I cannot believe that:" "And it is strange," replied he, "that you should believe, and not believe. Pray why should the Witches of your World, who march in the Air, and conduct whole Armies of Hail, Snow, Rain, and other Meteors, from one Province into another, have more Power than we? Pray have a little better opinion of me, than to think I would impose upon you." "The truth is," said I, "I have received so many good Offices from you, . . . that I dare trust my self in your hands, as now I do, resigning my self heartily up to you."

I had no sooner said the word, but he rose like a Whirl-wind, and holding me between his Arms, without the least uneasiness he made me pass that vast space which Astronomers reckon betwixt the Moon and us, in a day and a halfs time; which convinced me that they tell a Lye who say that a Millstone would be Three Hundred Three-score, and I know not how many years more, in falling from Heaven, since I was so short a while in dropping down from the Globe of the Moon upon this. At length, about the beginning of the Second day, I perceived I was drawing near our World; since I could already distinguish *Europe* from *Africa,* and both from *Asia;* when I smelt Brimstone which I saw steaming out of a very high Mountain [Vesuvius], that incommoded me so much that I fainted away upon it.

I cannot tell what befel me afterwards; but coming to my self again, I found I was amongst Briers on the side of a Hill, amidst some Shepherds, who spoke *Italian.* I knew not what was become of my Spirit, and I asked the Shepherds if they had not seen him. At that word they made the sign of the Cross, and looked upon me as if I had been a Devil my self: But when I told them that I was a Christian, and that I begg'd the Charity of them, that they would lead me to some place where I might take a little rest; they conducted me into a Village, about a Mile off; where no sooner was I come but all the Dogs of the place, from the least Cur to the biggest Mastiff, flew upon me, and had torn me to pieces, if I had not found a House wherein I saved my self: But that hindered them not to continue their Barking and Bawling, so that the Master of the House began to look upon me with an Evil Eye; and really I think, as people are very apprehensive when Accidents which they look upon to be ominous happen, that man could have delivered me up as a Prey to these accursed Beasts, had not I bethought my self that that which madded them so much at me, was the World from whence I came; because being accustomed to bark at the Moon, they smelt I was come from thence, by the scent of my Cloaths, which stuck to me as a Sea-smell hangs about those who have been long on Ship-board, for some time after they come ashore. To Air myself then, I lay three or four hours in the Sun, upon a Terrass-walk; and being afterwards come down, the Dogs, who smelt no more that influence which had made me their Enemy, left barking, and peaceably went to their several homes.

Next day I parted for *Rome,* where I saw the ruins of the Triumphs of some great men, as well as of Ages: I admired those lovely Relicks; and the Repairs of some of them made by the Modern. At length, having stayed there a fortnight in the Company of *Monsieur de Cyrano* my Cousin, who advanced me Money for my Return, I went to *Civita vecchia,* and embarked in a Galley that carried me to *Marseilles.*

During all this Voyage, my mind run upon nothing but the Wonders of the last I made. At that time I began the Memoires of it; and after my return, put them into as good order, as Sickness, which confines me to Bed, would permit. But foreseeing, that it will put an end to all my Studies, and Travels; that I may be as good as my word to the Council of that World; I have begg'd of *Monsieur le Bret,* my dearest and most constant Friend, that he would publish them with the History of the *Republick of the Sun,* that of the *Spark,* and some other Pieces of my Composing, if those who have Stolen them from us restore them to him, as I earnestly adjure them to do.

"CAPTAIN SAMUEL BRUNT"

From *A Voyage to Cacklogallinia* (1727)

[In 1727, slightly less than a hundred years after Godwin published the story of Domingo Gonsales and his adventures, an unknown author, using the pseudonym "Captain Samuel Brunt," told a similar tale of shipwreck and a journey to the moon, but this time heavily laced with social satire. Parallels between the initial experiences of Gonsales and Brunt are too close to justify printing the entire Brunt account. Suffice it to say that, after Captain Brunt goes through much the same series of ocean voyages, encounters with pirates, and shipwreck, he is washed ashore on a strange and unknown island. He discovers the island to be inhabited by human-sized birds, or "Cacklogallinians," fully capable of speech and rational thought. Brunt's description of the society, customs, and government of the island bears a remarkable resemblance to descriptions of England in the early eighteenth century.

Brunt knew a great deal more science than Godwin-Gonsales did (Isaac Newton died just before the Brunt book was published), and scientific inquiry was therefore a secondary goal for him. His primary motive for traveling to the moon was economic: to obtain the gold that Cacklogallinian "Empirics" (philosophers) had concluded was hidden in the mountains of the moon.

In the years just before the book's publication, England was in the midst of a commercial upswing. New financial schemes and "projects" appeared almost daily, some of them very shady indeed. Nevertheless, joint stock companies selling shares in these adventures proliferated and prospered. In 1710, the most infamous of them all, the South Sea Company, received a charter from Parliament. Men and women with money rushed to buy shares in the company, and, when the "Great South Sea Bubble" burst in 1720, it ruined many of these people. Judging from Captain Brunt's descriptions of the wild speculation surrounding his own moon venture (even the "Squabbaws," or bird-women, sold their valuables to join the speculation) and the manipulation of the moon-project stock by the Cacklogallinian courtiers, who controlled both the sale of the stock and the release of news concerning Brunt's progress, the anonymous author may well have been one of those caught when the South Sea Company failed and the English stock market crashed.

The selection reprinted here begins after Brunt and the Cacklogallinians have gone through much discussion and philosophical speculation about the possibility of the moon journey and its economic rewards. Finally, after the proper news releases are made, shares in the new project are released and the Cacklogallinian "'Change" (stock market) becomes the scene of frenzied activity, in which the Minister of Finance is a careful and successful manipulator. Brunt, who had protested the moon trip as impossible, is deeply impressed by the clever statesmanship of this minister:

> I found I had been very short-sighted in condemning the Minister for giving Ear to a Project so contrary to Reason: But when I saw the noblest Families, and such whose Ruine was necessary to his own support, sell their Estates to buy shares, I look'd upon him as the wisest Minister in the Known World.

Thus impressed, Brunt gives up his objections and accepts a position as one of the two "Projectors," or leaders of the adventure. (The other "Projector" is Volatilio, the Cacklogallinian who had first conceived of the expedition.)

Much like the earlier voyage of Domingo Gonsales, Brunt's ascent is made from a mountain top. The thin air of the summit requires that all passengers use "humected" (moistened) sponges to ease their breathing, Brunt acclimating to the change more slowly than his Cacklogallinian companions. After several trial flights, the journey is begun with Volatilio leading and Brunt riding in a "Palanquin," or flying car, borne by four Cacklogallinians. Once in space, the adventurers discover and enjoy their weightlessness and a "Universal Spirit" that makes food, drink, and sleep unnecessary. (Brunt refers his reader to Galileo's *Systema Mundi* for further astronomical observations, because he believes that Galileo had visited the moon, "whatever his reasons for not owning it.")

On the moon Brunt and the Cacklogallinians find a world in which the dreams of every earth-bound man are acted out by the man's spirit, which comes to the moon whenever he sleeps. Less frightening inhabitants, the "Selenites" (a term later used by H. G. Wells), treat Brunt's company to a grand feast and tell them all they wish to know about the moon. The Captain quickly learns that his hopes of finding gold will come to naught. Selenites are the souls of the virtuous, freed from their earthly bodies by death. They live in a world without passion or greed and think only of philosophy and religion. In such a world, gold is of no interest whatever. (The deeply serious and devout remarks of Abrahijo, the oldest Selenite, lead us to suspect that the pseudonymous author may well be a cleric, as Godwin and Wilkins were.) The story ends with Brunt and Volatilio returning to land on the Blue Mountain of Jamaica. There they bid each other farewell, Brunt returning to England to write of his adventures, and Volatilio attempting to make his way back to a Cacklogallinia devastated by the financial crash of the great moon project.

The book was apparently very popular. First printed in England in 1727, it was reprinted in 1736, 1751, and 1770. German translations were issued in 1735 and 1799 and a Russian translation in 1788. Our selection is taken from the 1828 edition, printed by J. Watson in England and currently housed in the Eleutherian Mills Historical Library.]

The Author begins his Journey to the MOON

All things necessary being provided, and the *Palanquins* of Provisions being sent before to join us at the Mountain *Tenera,* I had an Audience of Leave of his Imperial Majesty and his *Squabbaws;* after which, I went to receive my last Instructions from his Excellency. He gave me a Paper, with Orders not to open it, till I was arrived at the Mountain, which was about a Thousand Miles from the City. He having wish'd me a good Journey, said he had given Orders to six lusty *Cacklogallinians* to obey those I should give them; that he depended on my Fidelity and Prudence, and therefore, as I would find, had reposed a great Trust in me. I made him a suitable Answer, and retired to my Apartment in the Palace, where I found the Projector, who told me we were to set out the next Morning before Day. I asked him, in Case we succeeded in our Journey, and found the Riches we coveted, how we should bring away any Quantity?

"If," *said he,* "that happens, we shall, in a second Journey, be provided with Vehicles, if there is Occasion; but I propose to extract such a Quantity of the Soul of Gold, which I can infuse into Lead at our Return, that we may be rich enough to pave the Streets with that valuable Metal; for a

Frontispiece of the original edition of "Captain Samuel Brunt," *A Voyage to Cacklogallinia* (London, 1727), showing the traveler on his journey to the moon, escorted by a group of Cacklogallinians. This is the first published aerial illustration of the eighteenth century and quite possibly the last of the good romantic illustrations of flight in an animal-drawn vehicle.

Grain will, infused into Lead, make an Ounce of pure Gold. Now, if a Penny-weight of the Soul will make Twenty four Ounces, or Two Pound of Gold, consider what immense Treasure we may bring back with us, since the *Palanquineers* can fly with Five Hundred Weight in a *Palanquin*."

The next Morning we set forward at about Three o'Clock, and reach'd the Mountain in about Forty six Hours. We first refresh'd our selves, and when I was alone, I open'd my Instructions, which ran thus:

As Experience proves you are not to be led by chimerical Notions, and that your Capacity and Fidelity render you fit to undertake the most difficult and secret Affairs, his Imperial Majesty thought none so fit as yourself to be entrusted in the Management of the present Scheme; which that you may do to his Majesty's Satisfaction, and your own Interest and Credit, you are to observe the following Instructions.

"You are to order *Volatilio,* the first Proposer of the Journey now undertaken, to go to the Top of the Hill a Day before you, and from thence to acquaint you with the Nature of the Air; and if you find it practicable, you are to follow him. If you gain the Summit, and that the Air is too thin for Respiration, you are to descend again, dispatch an Express to his Majesty, and clap *Volatilio* in Irons, then dispatch away one of the six Messengers whom I ordered to attend you: They, *Volatilio,* and the whole Caravan, are to obey you, till you have pass'd the Atmosphere, when you and they are to follow the Directions of *Volatilio,* in what regards the Way only; but, in Case that you can respire on the Top of the Mountain, order *Volatilio* to precede you a Day's Ascent, return the next, and immediately dispatch a second Messenger with the Account he gives, and continue on the Mountain for farther Instructions, before you proceed, should it prove practicable. I need not tell you the Publick must be amused with Hopes of Success, tho' you have Reason to despair of it; nor need I even hint to you what Method you ought to take. I wish you Health, and that your Conduct may answer my Expectations."

I acted pursuant to these Instructions, and sent *Volatilio* forward, who reach'd the Top of the Hill; but finding the Air too thin to continue there, without the Help of humected [moistened] Spunges, he therefore sent those back he carried with him to the mid Space of the Mountain, and an Express to me, by which he informed me what he had done; that he resolved to continue there a natural Day, and then join me where he had sent his Followers, to which Place he desired I would ascend, and defer the dispatching any Express to his Majesty, till he saw me again.

I ascended to the Mid-space, and found a vast Alteration in the Air, which even here was very sensibly rarified.

My Projector came to me at his appointed Time, and told me he did not question the Success of our Enterprise, since he imagined the Air above the second Region rather denser than that near the Earth, and hoped the Cold was not more intense than on the Mountain's Top; and that if this prov'd so, we cou'd breathe and support the Cold with little Difficulty. I answer'd, that it was natural to conclude the Air next the Earth more dense than that above it, as the weightiest always descends the first. "That Reason," *said he,* "is not conclusive, for the Air immediately encompassing the Earth, is more sensible of its attractive Power, than that at a greater Distance, as you may be satisfied, in placing two Pieces of Iron, one near, and the other at a Distance from the Loadstone; the nearest Piece will be strongly attracted, while that at a greater Distance is but weakly affected. Now supposing the Air only of an equal Density thro'out when we have left the Earth, (which, by the Reflection of Heat from the Mountains, rarifies the circumambient Air, and renders it more subtle than that above it) we may respire without Pain; for in less than Six Hours I, by Degrees, withdrew my Spunge."

I dispatch'd an Express with the Account I had received, and set forward, resolving to wait for further Instructions on the top of the Mountain. I was at a good Distance from the Summit, when I was obliged, by the Thinness of the Air, to have Recourse to my wet Spunge, and was Four and Twenty Hours before I could intirely remove it. The *Cacklogallinians* found less Difficulty than I in their Respiration, but more in supporting the rigid Cold, especially at Night, when the Damps fell. We staid here Eight Days, that the Subtlety of the Air might become habitual to us.

On the seventh Day, the Messenger return'd with Credentials for *Volatilio* and my self, to the Potentate in whose Dominions we might happen, and Orders to proceed on our Journey. This Messenger told me, that on the Contents of my Letter being publish'd, the Town was illuminated throughout, and such a Number of Coaches and *Palanquins* bespoke, that he believed, at our Return, we should find none out of them but the Ostriches. Our Credentials ran thus.

"Hippomene-Connuferento, Emperor and absolute Monarch of the greatest Empire in the Terrestrial Globe, Disposer of Kingdoms, Judge of Kings, Dispenser of Justice, Light of the World, Joy of the Sun, Darling of Mortals, Scourge of Tyrants, and Refuge of the Distress'd, to the Puissant Monarch of that Kingdom in the Moon, to which our Ambassadors shall arrive: Or, To the Mighty and Sole Lord of that beautiful Planet, sends Greetings.

"Dearly Beloved Brother, and most Mighty Prince, as it has been long doubted by our Ancestors, as well as by those of our Time, whether the Moon were, or were not inhabited, We, who have ever encouraged those who seek the universal Good of Mortals, supposing it possible, if that Planet were possess'd by such, that an Intercourse between the two Worlds might be of mutual Advantage to both, have send our two Ambassadors, *Volatilio* and *Probusomo* [Captain Brunt's Cacklogallinian name], to attempt a Passage to your World, and to assure you, if they succeed, of the great Desire we have of entertaining with you a reciprocal Friendship, of giving all possible Demonstrations of our Affection, and to invite you to send to our World your Ambassadors, with whom we may consult our common Interest. So recommending ours to your Protection, we heartily bid you farewell.

Given at our Court, *&c.*

According to the Orders we receiv'd, *Volatilio* took his Flight in an oblique Ascent, without a *Palanquin,* but wrapt up as warm as possible, accompanied by two Servants. He parted with great Alacrity, and we soon lost Sight of him. Some Half a Score, in Complaisance, took a Flight of three Hours to see him part of his Way towards his Discovery.

He went off at break of Day, to avoid those Vapours which the Heat of the Sun exhales, and which by Night would have rendered his Passage, he thought, impossible; for he hoped, in a small Space to gain beyond the Heighth they rise to. At the Return of those who convoy'd him, I sent away an Express, to acquaint the Emperor with their Report, which was, That they found no sensible Alteration as to the Rarefaction of the Air, and that the Cold was rather less intense. This News at Court made every one run mad after Shares, which the Proprietors sold at what Rate they pleas'd.

The next Day in the Even[ing], we saw *Volatilio* on his Return: His first Salutation was, *Courage my Friend, I have pass'd the Atmosphere, and, by Experience, have found my Conjecture true; for being out of the magnetick Power of the Earth, we rested in the Air, as on the solid Earth, and in an Air extreamly temperate, and less subtle than what we breathe.*

I sent again this Account to Court, but the Courtiers having no more Shares to sell, gave out, that *Volatilio* did not return as he promis'd, and it was expected, that I despair'd of the Undertaking, and believ'd him lost.

This was such a Damp to the Town, that Shares fell of Half Value, and none of the Courtiers would buy, sell they cou'd not, having (I mean those let into the Secret) already dispos'd of all by their Agents, tho' they pretended the contrary.

The Express return'd, with private Orders for me to confirm this Report, which I was oblig'd to do, and stay eight Days longer, as the publick Instructions to us both commanded.

This was a great Mortification to *Volatilio,* and, I own, the Report he made had rais'd my Curiosity so much, that I was uneasy at this Delay; but we were to obey, and not to enquire into the Reasons of it.

The Messenger returning, told me, that my last Letter had fallen the Shares to five *per Cent.* under *Par,* nothing but Lamentations eccho'd thro' the Streets, and it was impossible to give an Idea of the Change it had occasion'd. The Letter the Minister sent me order'd me to write him Word, that *Volatilio* was returned, had found no Obstacles, and that I was preparing to depart. That the Court had bought up a vast Number of Shares, and that he took Care of my Interest in particular; that I need stay for no farther Instructions, but make the best of my Way.

I gave Notice to the Caravan, that we would set forward the next Morning, which we accordingly did, and as near as I could compute, we flew that Day, 180 Miles. What surpriz'd me was, that in less than an Hour and half's Ascent, *Volatilio,* who would not go in his *Palanquin,* folded his Wings, and came to me on Foot, and told me I might get out and stretch my Limbs. My *Palanquineers* stood still, and confirm'd what he said; and more, that they had not for a Quarter of an Hour past been sensible of my Weight, which had lessen'd by Degrees, so as not to be felt at all.

I left my *Palanquin,* and found what *Volatilio* had conjectur'd, and his Report verified; for I could with as much Ease lift a *Palanquin* of Provisions, which did not on Earth weigh less than 500 Weight, as I could on our Globe raise a Feather. The Cold was much abated, and I found my Spirits rais'd.

I would have here sent back half the *Palanquin*-Bearers, but *Volatilio* was of Opinion we should keep them a Day longer; for, perhaps, said he, we may send them all (except those which carry you) away; for if the Universal Spirit included in the Air should suffice for our Nourishment, we have no Business with Provisions.

I approv'd his Reason, and we proceeded on, sure of falling first into the Attraction of the Moon, it being the nearest Planet to us.

I shall not detain the Reader with my Observations in this aerial Journey; *Gallileus* [Galileo], who by his Writings gives me room to believe he had, before me, visited this Planet, whatever were his Reasons for not owning it, having left nothing, which is not mentioned in his *Systema Mundi.*

I observ'd only, which I take Notice of for those who have not read him, that when the Moon has but a small Part of his Body enlighten'd, that the Earth, the other Moon, has a proportionable Part of its Hemisphere visibly darken'd; I mean a Part in proportion to that of the Moon which is enlighten'd; and that both these Moons, of which ours is much the larger, mutually participate [in] the same Light of the Sun, and the same Obscurity of the Eclipses, and mutually assist each other: For when the Moon is in Conjunction with the Sun, and its *pars superior* receives all the Light, then its inferior Hemisphere is enlighten'd by the Earth's reflecting the Rays of the Sun, otherwise it would be intirely dark; and when those two Planets are in Opposition, then that Part of the Earth which is deprived of the Rays of the Sun, is enlighten'd by a full Moon.

The next Day *Volatilio* was for sending back the Provisions, but I judg'd it proper not to go forward, but to stay the Space of a natural Day, in the same Situation, because in that time, or in no other in the Journey, we should require Sustenance, and also because their Return would be easier, than if we carried them still forward.

This was agreed to, and none of us finding any Appetite, Weakness, or Sinking of our Spirits, dismiss'd all but those who carried my *Palanquin,* and proceeded forward with an incredible Swiftness.

We were about a Month before we came into the Attraction of the Moon, in all which time none of us had the least Inclination to Sleep or Eat, or found our selves any way fatigued, nor, till we reach'd that Planet, did we close our Eyes; the Attraction was so great, that it was all the Bearers and *Volatilio* could do to prevent our being dash'd to Pieces on a Mountain; we descended with that inconceivable Swiftness, that I apprehended it impossible, in our Return, to avoid that Misfortune in the World we left; since the Attraction, if its Virtue was augmented in proportion to its Magnitude, must be much stronger.

This Thought made me very uneasy for those who return'd. I spoke of it to *Volatilio,* who bid me apprehend nothing; for, said he, the Magnetick Virtue [power] of the Load-stone is so far from being in Proportion to its Size, that the very large ones have less attractive Power than those which are middling.

When I had recover'd from the Fright, which the Rapidity of our Descent had put me into, I view'd the circumjacent Country with equal Wonder and Delight; Nature seem'd here to have lavish'd all her Favours; on whatsoever Side I turn'd my Eye, the most ravishing Prospect was offer'd to my Sight. The Mountain yielded a gradual Descent to most beautiful Meadows, enamell'd with Cowslips, Roses, Lilies, Jessamines, Carnations, and other fragrant Flowers, unknown to the Inhabitants of our Globe, which were as grateful to the Smell, as entertaining to the Eye. The chrystal Rivulets which smoothly glided thro' these inchanting Meads, seem'd so many Mirrors reflecting the various Beauties of those odoriferous Flowers which adorn'd their Banks. The Mountain, which was of considerable Height, afforded us a great Variety of our Prospect; and the Woods, Pastures, Meads, and small Arms of the Sea, were intermingled with that surprising Beauty and Order, that they seem'd rather dispos'd by Art, than the Product of Nature; the Earth it self yielded a grateful and enlivening Scent, and is so pure, that it does not sully the Hands. The Cedars, which cloath'd the middle Part of the Summit, were streight, tall, and so large, that seven Men would hardly fathom the Bowl of one; round these twin'd the grateful Honey-suckle, and encircling Vine, whose purple Grapes appearing frequent from among the Leaves of the wide extended branches, gave an inconceivable Pleasure to the Beholder. The Lily of the Valley, Violet, Tuberose, Pink, Julip and Jonquil, cloath'd their spacious Roots, and the verdant Soil afforded every salutiferous Herb and Plant, whose Vertues diffus'd thro' the ambiant Air (without the invenom'd and the griping Fist of the *Cacklogallinian* Empiricks) Preservatives to the blessed Inhabitants of the Lunar World.

The Heavens here were ever serene; no Thunder-bearing Cloud obscur'd the Sky; the whispering Zephyrs wanton'd in the Leaves, and gently bore along the enchanting Musick of the feather'd Choir: The Sea here knew no Storms, nor threatning Wave, with Mountain swell, menaced the Ships, which safely plough'd the peaceful Bosom of the Deep. *Aeolus* [god of the winds] and all his boisterous Sons were banish'd from these happy Seats, and only kindly Breezes fann'd the fragrant Air. In short, all was ravishing, and Nature seem'd here to have given her last Perfection to her Works, and to rejoice in her finish'd Labours.

I found my Spirits so invigorated by the refreshing Odours, of this Paradice, so elated with the Serenity of the Heavens, and the Beauties which every where entertained and rejoiced my Sight, that in Extasy I broke out into this grateful Soliloquy. *O Source of Wisdom, Eternal Light of the Universe! what Adorations can express the grateful Acknowledgments of thy diffusive Bounty! Who can contemplate the Beauty of thy Works, the Product of thy single Fiat, and not acknowledge thy Omnipotence, Omniscience, and extensive Goodness! What Tongue can refrain from singing thy Praise! What Heart so hard, but must be melted into Love! Oh Eternal Creator, pity my Weakness, and since I cannot speak a*

Gratitude adequate to thy Mercies, accept the Fullness of my Heart, too redundant for Expression.

As I spoke this, in the *Cacklogallinian* Tongue, *Volatilio* came up to me, and said, "Alas! *Probusomo,* how can a finite Being return Praises adequate to infinite Mercies! Let us return such as we are capable of; let the Probity of our Lives speak our Gratitude; by our Charity for each other endeavour to imitate the Divine Goodness, and speak our Love to him, by that we shew to Mortals, the Work of his Divine Will, however they may differ from us, and from one another, in their Species. I am glad I am not deceived in my Opinion of you. I believed from the Observation I made of your Life in a corrupt and dissolute Court, that you fear'd the first Being of Beings, and for that Reason chose you Companion of this hitherto unattempted Journey; for I expected a Blessing would attend my Undertaking, while such a one was embark'd with me: For to the Shame of our Nation, we own a Deity in Words, but deny him in our Actions: We acknowledge this Divine Being must be pure and just, and that our Lives (as he must abominate all Impurity and Injustice) ought to be conformable to his Attributes, wou'd we hope his Favour and Protection, notwithstanding we act diametrically opposite, as the most ready Method to procure our Happiness."

Finding our selves press'd by Hunger, we descended the Mountain, at the Foot of which we found a Plantation of Olive Trees, and abundance of Pear, standing Apricock, Nectarn, Peach, Orange, and Lemon Trees, interspers'd. We satisfied our craving Appetites with the Fruit we gather'd, and then getting into my *Palanquin, Volatilio* leading the Way, we went in Search of the Inhabitants. Our Flight was little better than a Soar, that we might with more Advantage view the Country.

After a couple of Hours, he saw a House, but of so great a Height, and so very large, I who was short-sighted in Comparison of the *Cacklogallinians,* took it for a great Hill; I told him my Opinion, but he assured me I was mistaken. We therefore urg'd forward, and I alighted not far from this Palace, for I could term it no other, from the Largeness and Beauty of its Structure. We had been discover'd, as I had reason to believe, some Time, and a Number of People about Thirty, at our alighting, immediately encompass'd me. The gigantick Make of these Inhabitants struck me with a panick Fear, which I also discover'd in the Eyes of the *Cacklogallinians.*

They were of different Statures, from Thirty to an Hundred and Fifty Foot high, as near as I cou'd guess; some of them were near as thick as long, some proportionable, and others shap'd like a Pine, being no thicker than my self, tho' tall of an Hundred Foot.

I resolv'd however to conceal, if possible, the Terror I was in, and coming out of my *Palanquin,* I went to salute the Company, when I observ'd they retired from me in proportion as I advanced, and like a Vapour, or an *Ignis fatuus,* the Air being mov'd by my Motion, drove those which were directly opposite still before me.

I stood still, they did the same; if I was astonish'd at their Make, and at what other things I had observ'd, I was more so, when I saw one of the tallest, dwindle in the Twinkling of an Eye, to a Pigmy, fly into the Air without Wings, and carry off a Giant in each Hand by the Hair of the Head.

They were all differently dress'd at their first Appearance; some like Generals in Armour, some were in Ecclesiastical, and some in Gowns not unlike our Barristers at Law. Some were dress'd as fine as Imagination could make 'em, but with the quickness of Thought, these Dresses were all changed, who was cover'd with Rags one Moment, the next was in Purple, with a Crown on his Head; the Beau in Rags; the Priest assum'd the Air and Dress of a Bully, and the General was turn'd into a demure Figure resembling a *Quaker.*

I was struck dumb with Amazement, and while I was considering with my self what this should mean, I observ'd a Man riding up to us, mounted on a Lion; when he came to the others, I found him of the common Size with the inhabitants of our Globe; he had on his Head a Crown of Bays, which in an Instant chang'd to a Fool's Cap, and his Lion to an Ass. He drew from his Breast a Rowl like a Quire of Written Paper, which using as a Sword, he set upon the others, and dispers'd them. Some ran over the Sea, as on dry Ground; others flew into the Air, and some sunk into the Earth. Then alighting from his Ass, he opened the Jaws of the Animal, went down his Throat, and they both vanish'd.

After I had recover'd [from] my Fright, I told *Volatilio,* that I fear'd this Planet was inhabited by evil Spirits. He answered, that what we had seen, was sufficient to induce us to believe so. We look'd for the House, which we saw rise into the Air, and vanish in Flame and Smoke, which strengthen'd our Opinion. However, we resolv'd to go forward, when one of the *Palanquineers* said he saw a House on the left, and People of my Size and Species making towards us.

We determin'd therefore to wait their Arrival, which was in less than a Quarter of an Hour. They accosted me very courteously, as I could gather from their Gestures, tho' they seem'd surprised at the Size of the *Cacklogallinians.* I was not less amaz'd at the Beauty of their Persons, and the Becomingness of their Dress, either of which I can give no just Idea of. Let it suffice, that I seem'd both in my own, and in the Eyes of the *Cacklogallinians,* something of the same Species, but frightfully ugly.

These People are neither a corporeal, nor an aerial Substance, but (I know not how otherwise to express my self) between both. They spoke to me in a Language I did not understand, but the Tone of their Voices, and the Smoothness of their Syllables, were divinely harmonious. I bow'd my Body to the Ground three times, and offer'd my Credentials, which one of them took, but by the shaking of his Head, I found understood nothing of the Contents. *Volatilio* then address'd himself to them, which made them look on one another, as People who hardly believed their Senses. As I had address'd these *Selenites* [moon people] in the *Cacklogallinian* Language, I had a Mind to try, if speaking in those of the *Europeans,* (for I understood, beside my own, the *French* and *Spanish*) I should have any better Success. I therefore spoke in *English,* and, to my great Joy, one of the Company answer'd me. He ask'd me, Whether I came from the World? if so, how I durst undertake so perilous a Journey? I told him, I would satisfy his Curiosity in answering all his Questions, but desired he would give me some Time; for I had been so terrified by Phantoms, since my Arrival, that I was hardly capable of Recollection.

While I was speaking, a Man on Horseback ran full speed upon me with a drawn Sabre, to cleave me down; but the *Selenite* waving his Hand, he soon vanish'd. "You need," *said he,* "apprehend nothing from these Shades; they are the Souls of the Inhabitants of your World, which being loos'd from the Body by Sleep, resort here, and for the short Space allotted them, indulge the Passions which predominate, or undergo the Misfortunes they fear while they are in your Globe. Look ye," *said he,* "yonder is a Wretch going to the Gallows, and his Soul feels the same Agony, as if it was a real Sentence to be executed on him. Our Charity obliges us, when we see those imaginary Ills, to drive the Soul back to its Body, which we do, by waving our Hand in the Air, and the agonizing Dreamer wakes. We do also retain them by a Virtue peculiar to the *Selenites,* and as they sometimes administer a great deal of Diversion, we do it for our Entertainment, which is the Reason of those long Naps of two or three Days, nay, of as many Weeks, which cause the Wonder of your World. The Souls of your impure Dreamers never reach beyond the middle Region. But we delay too long inviting you to our Habitations, where you shall have all possible Care taken of you. But by what Art have you taught Fowls articulate Sounds? and where could you possibly find them of that Size?"

I told him they were rational Beings, but that the Story was now too long to tell him; he presented me to the rest of the Company, and, at my Request, the *Cacklogallinians* were humanly treated, whom otherwise they had look'd upon as overgrown dunghill Fowls. *Volatilio* did not appear much surpriz'd at this, who had once esteem'd me a Prodigy of Nature. As we walk'd to the House, one of the *Selenites* address'd me in the *Spanish* Language, with the known Affiability and Gravity of that Nation.

"Sir," *said he,* "I cannot consider you as other, than the bravest and wisest of all Mortals, who could find the Way to reach our World, and had the Courage to undertake the Journey; for it's certain, none cloath'd in Flesh ever (before you) made so bold an Attempt, or at least succeeded in it: Tho' I have read the Chimera's of *Dominick Gonzales.* While you stay amongst us, you may depend upon our treating you with all the Respect answerable to so great Merit, and in every thing endeavour, as far as the Power we have will permit, that the Design of your Journey may not be frustrated, which I am apt to believe, is no other than to extend your Knowledge."

I return'd him many Thanks for his Humanity, but told him I durst not attribute to my self the Character he gave me; that I was a Lover of Truth, and would not, on any Account, disguise the real Motive which sent me on an Undertaking I look'd upon [as] impossible to go thro' with, and which I very unwillingly embark'd in: But since, contrary to my Expectations, Providence has guided me to this Terrestrial Paradice, I should esteem my self extreamly happy, if I might be permitted to ask such Questions as my Curiosity might prompt me to.

He answer'd, that nothing I desir'd to know should be kept from me. We soon reach'd the House, which was regular, neat, and convenient. We all sat down in an inner Hall, and he who spoke *English,* desired I would give an Account, both of the Motives, the Manner, and Accidents of my Journey, which I did as succinctly as possible, interpreting the Credentials, which I gave them.

He was astonish'd at the Account I gave him of the *Cacklogallinians,* and said, if my Account was not back'd with ocular Demonstration, he should take their Story for the Ravings of a distemper'd Brain.

"I find," *said he,* "you begin to be drowzy; I would therefore have you and your rational Fowls (as you call them) repose your selves, while I in the *Vernacular* Language, repeat to my Companions the Wonders I have heard from you."

We were indeed very sleepy, and I was heartily glad of the Proposal, as were also the *Cacklogallinians,* when I mention'd it to them. They, as well as my self, were provided each of them with a bed, in very handsome and commodious Rooms. These Beds were so very soft, that I seem'd to lye on a Couch of Air. When we awak'd, the *Selenites* came to my Chamber, and told me it was time to take some Nourishment; that they had provided Corn for my Companions, and desir'd I would sit down to Supper with them, it being their usual time. "Why, Sir," *said I,* to our *English* Interpreter, "do you sup by Day-light?" "You mistake," *said he,* "it is now Night; your World to the Inhabitants of this Hemisphere (which is always turn'd to it, this Planet moving in an Epicycle) reflects so strong the Sun's Light, that your Error is excusable." "What then," *said I,* "do those of the other Hemisphere for Light?" "They have it," *said he,* "from the Planets."

I went with them into a Parlour, where, after a Hymn was sung, we sat down to a Table cover'd with Sallets and all sorts of Fruits.

"You must," *said the Selenite,* "content your self with what we can offer you, which is nothing but the spontaneous Products of the Earth: We cannot invite you to other, since the eating any thing that has had Life, is look'd upon with Abhorrence, and never known in this World: But I am satisfied you will easily accommodate your self to our Diet, since the Taste of our Fruits is much more exquisite than yours, since they fully satisfy, and never cloy." Which I found true by Experience, and I was so far from hankering after Flesh, that even the Thoughts of it were shocking and nauseous to me.

We drank the most delicious Wine, which they press'd from the Grape into their Cups, and which was no way intoxicating. After Supper, the *Selenite* address'd himself to me in Words to this Effect.

"I have acquainted my Friends here present, who are come to pass some days with me, both with the Contents of the *Cacklogallinian* Emperor's Letter, and the Reasons which mov'd this Prince to desire an Intercourse between the two Worlds, and we will all of us wait on you to our Prince's Court, tho' strictly speaking, we neither have, nor need a Governour; and we pay the distant Respect due to your Princes to the eldest among us, as he is the nearest to eternal Happiness. But that I may give you some Idea, both of this World, and its Inhabitants, you must learn, that Men in yours are endued with a Soul and an Understanding; the Soul is a material Substance, and clothes the Understanding, as the Body does the Soul; at the Separation of these two, the Body is again resolved into Earth, and the Soul of the Virtuous is placed in this Planet, till the Understanding being freed from it by a Separation we may call Death, tho' not attended with Fear or Agony, it is resolved into our Earth, and its Principle of Life, the Understanding, returns to the Great Creator; for till we have here purg'd off what of Humanity remains attach'd to the Soul, we can never hope to appear before the pure Eyes of the Deity.

"We are here," *said he,* "in a State of Ease and Happiness, tho' no way comparable to that we expect at our Dissolution, which we as earnestly long for, as you Mortals carefully avoid it. We forget nothing that pass'd while we were cloath'd in Flesh, and Inhabitants of your Globe, and have no other uneasiness, than what the Reflection of our Ingratitude to the Eternal Goodness, while in Life, creates in us, which the Eternal lessens in proportion to our Repentance, which is here very sincere. This will cease your Wonder at hearing the Sublunary Languages.

"We have here no Passions to gratify, no Wants to supply, the Roots of Vice, which under no Denomination is known among us; consequently no Laws, nor Governours to execute them, are here necessary.

"Had the *Cacklogallinian* Prince known thus much, he would have been sensible how vain were his Expectations of getting from us the Gold he thirsts after: For were we to meet with the purest Veins of that Metal, by removing only one Turf, not a *Selenite* would think it worth his while.

"This is a Place of Peace and Tranquillity, and this World is exactly adapted to the Temper of its Inhabitants: Nature here is in an Eternal Calm; we enjoy an everlasting Spring; the Soil yields nothing noxious, and we can never want the Necessaries of Life, since every Herb affords a salubrious Repast to the *Selenites.*

"We pass our Days without Labour, without other Anxiety, than what I mention'd, and the longing Desire we have for our Dissolution, makes every coming Day encrease our Happiness.

"We have not here, as in your World, Distinction of Sexes; for know, all Souls are masculine (if I may be allow'd that Term, after what I've said) however distinguish'd in the Body; and tho' of late Years the Number of those which change your World for this (especially of the *European* Quarter) is very small; yet we do not apprehend our World will be left unpeopled."

"You say," *replied I,* "that none but the virtuous Soul reaches these blissful Seats; what then becomes of the Vicious? and how comes it, that the Soul, when loosed by Sleep, I suppose without Distinction, retires hither?"

"The Decrees," *said he,* "of the Almighty are inscrutable, and you ask me Questions are not in my Power to resolve you."

"Have not," *said I,* "the *Cacklogallinians* Souls, think you, since they're endued with Reason?" "If they have," *said he,* "they never are sent hither."

I repeated this Discourse to the *Cacklogallinians,* which made *Volatilio* extreamly melancholly. *Happy Men! said he, to whose Species the divine Goodness has been so indulgent! Miserable* Cacklogallinians! *if destin'd, after bearing the Ills of Life, to Annihilation. Let us,* Probusomo, *never think of returning, but beg we may be allow'd to end our Days with these Favourites of Heaven.*

I interpreted this to the *Selenite,* who shook his Head, and said it was, he believ'd, impossible. That he did not doubt but Providence would reward the Virtuous of his Species; that his Mercy and Justice were without Bound, which ought to keep him from desponding.

The next Day, a great Number of *Selenites* came to see me, and entertain'd me with abundance of Candour. I seeing no Difference in Dress, nor any Deference paid to any, as distinguish'd by a superior Rank, I took Liberty to ask my *English Selenite,* if all the Inhabitants were upon a Level, and if they had no Servants?

"We have," *said he,* "no Distinctions among us; who in your World begg'd Alms, with us, has the same Respect as he who govern'd a Province: Tho', to say Truth, we have but few of your sublunary Quality among us. We have no Occasion for Servants; we are all Artificers, and none where Help is necessary, but offers his with Alacrity. For Example, would I build a House, every one here, and as many more as were wanting, would take a Pleasure to assist me."

He told me, that the next Day they intended to present me to *Abrahijo,* the oldest *Selenite.* Accordingly, we set out at Sun-rising, and entered a Bark about a League from the House, and having pass'd about four Leagues on a River which ran thro' a Valley beautiful beyond Description, we went ashore within a Hundred Yards of *Abrahijo's* Place of Abode.

When we came in, the venerable old Man, whose compos'd and chearful Countenance spoke the Heaven of his Mind, rose from his Chair, and came to meet us; he was of a great Age, but free from the Infirmities which attend it in our World.

The *English Selenite* presented me to him with few Words, and he received me with Tenderness.

After he was inform'd of my Story, he spoke to me by our Interpreter, to this Effect.

"My Son, I hope you will reap a solid Advantage from the perilous Journey you have made, tho' your Expectation of finding Riches among us is frustrated. All that I have to give you, is my Advice to return to your World, place your Happiness in nothing transitory; nor imagine that any Riches, but those which are Eternal, which neither *Thief can carry away, nor Rust corrupt,* are worthy of your Pursuit. Keep continually in your Eye the Joys prepared for those who employ the Talents they are entrusted with, as they ought: Reflect upon the little Content your World can afford you: Consider how short is Life, and that you have but little Time to spare for Trifles, when the grand Business, the securing your eternal Rest, ought to employ your Mind. You are there in a State of Probation, and you must there chuse whether you will be happy or miserable; you will not be put to a second Trial; you sign at once your own Sentence, and it will stand irrevocable, either for or against you. Weigh well the Difference between a momentary and imperfect, and an eternal and solid Happiness, to which the Divine Goodness invites you; nay, by that Calmness, that Peace of Mind, which attends a virtuous Life, bribes you to make Choice of, if you desire to be among us, be your own Friend, and you will be sure to have those Desires gratify'd. But you must now return, since it was never known, that gross Flesh and Blood ever before breath'd this Air, and that your Stay may be fatal to you, and disturb the Tranquillity of the *Selenites.* This I prophesy, and my Compassion obliges me to warn You of it."

I made him a profound Reverence, thank'd him for his charitable Admonition, and told him I hoped nothing should win me from the Performance of a Duty which carry'd with it such ineffable Rewards. That if no greater were promis'd, than those indulg'd to the *Selenites,* I would refuse no Misery attending the most abject Life, to be enroll'd in the Number of the Inhabitants of that happy Region.

"I wish," *replied he,* "the false Glare of the World does not hinder the Execution of these just Resolutions: But that I may give you what Assistance is in our Power, in hopes of having you among us, we will shew the World unmask'd; that is, we will detain some time the Souls of Sleepers, that you may see what Man is, how false, how vain, in all he acts or wishes. Know, that the Soul loos'd by Sleep, has the Power to call about it all the Images which it would employ, can raise imaginary "Structures, form Seas, Lands, Fowls, Beasts, or whatever the rational Faculty is intent upon. You shall now take some Refreshment, and after that we will both divert and instruct you."

The Table was spread by himself and the other *Selenites,* the *Cackagallinians* and my self invited, and I observ'd it differ'd nothing, either in Quality or Quantity, from that of my *English* Host.

After a solemn Adoration of the ineffable Creator, each took his Place; having finish'd our Meal, at which a strict Silence was observed, *Abrahijo* took me by the Hand, and led me into a neighbouring Field, the Beauty of which far excell'd that of the most labour'd and artificial Garden among us.

"Here," *said he,* "observe yon Shade: I shall not detain it, that you may see the Care and Uneasiness attending Riches."

The Shade represented an old wither'd starv'd Carcass, brooding over Chests of Money. Immediately appear'd three ill-look'd [ugly] Fellows; Want, Despair, and Murder, were lively-pictur'd in their Faces; they were taking out the Iron Bars of the old Man's Window, when all vanish'd of a sudden. I ask'd the Meaning of it; he told me, the Terror the Dream of

Thieves put him into, had awaken'd him; and the Minute he slept again, I should see again his Shade. Hardly had *Abrahijo* done speaking, when I again saw the old Man, with a young well-dress'd Spark standing by him, who paid him great Respect. I heard him say very distinctly, "Sir, do you think I am made of Money, or can you imagine the Treasure of a Nation will supply your Extravagance? The Value I have for you on Account of your Father, who was my good Friend, has made me tire all my Acquaintance, by borrowing of them to furnish your Pockets: However, I'll try, if I cannot borrow One Thousand more for you, tho' I wish your Estate will bear it, and that I don't out of my Love to you, rashly bring myself into Trouble. You know I am engaged for all; and if the Mortgage you have given should not be valid, I am an undone Man. I can't, I protest, raise this Money under Fifteen *per Cent,* and its cheap, very cheap, considering how scarce a Commodity it is grown. It's a Pity so generous a young Gentleman should be straiten'd. I don't question a Pair of Gloves for the Trouble I have. I know you too well to insist on't: I am old and crazy, Coach-hire is very dear, I can't walk, God help me, and my Circumstances won't afford a Coach. A Couple of Guineas is a Trifle with you: I'll get you the Thousand Pound, if I can, at Fifteen *per Cent.* but if my Friend should insist on Twenty (for Money is very hard to be got with the best Security) must I refuse it? Yes; I can't suffer you to pay such an exorbitant Premium; it is too much, too much in Conscience; I can't advise you to it."

The young Gentleman answer'd, he was sensible of his Friendship, and left all to him. "Well, well," *said the Miser,* "come again two Hours hence, I'll see what's to be done."

He went away, t'other barr'd the Door after him, and falls to rummaging his Bags, and telling [counting] out the Sum to be lent to the young Gentleman: When, on a sudden, his Doors flew open, and a Couple of Rogues bound him in his Bed, and went off laden with Baggs. Soon after, a meagre Servant comes in, and unbinds him; he tears his Hair, raves, stamps, and has all the Gestures of a Madman; he sends the Servant out, takes a Halter, throws it over a Beam, and going to hang himself, vanishes.

Soon after, he appear'd again with Officers, who hurry the young Gentleman to Gaol [Jail]. He follows him, gets his Estate made over to him, and then sets his Prisoner at Liberty: The Scene of the Gaol vanishes, and he's in a noble Mansion-Seat with the young Gentleman in Rags, who gives him Possession, and receives a Trifle from him for that Consideration. He turns away all the Servants, and in a Palace he is alone roasting an Egg over a Handful of Fire for his Dinner. His Son comes in, as he is by himself, goes to murder him, and he vanishes again. He returns to our Sight, digging in his Garden, and hiding Money, for Soldiers appear in the neighbouring Village: He has scarce buried it, when they rifle his House; this makes us lose him again for a little Space. His Coachman comes to him, tells him his Son is kill'd; he answers, "No matter, he was a great Expence, I shall save at least Forty Pounds a Year by his Death, it's a good Legacy, *Tom.*"

He tells him a Lord offer'd him Five Hundred Pounds to carry off his young Lady, but that he refused it, and thought himself obliged to acquaint him with his Lordship's Design. "You are a Fool," *replies the old Man;* "take the Money, I'll consent, we'll snack [share] it—Quit of another. My Lord shan't have a Groat [fourpence] with her. What a Charge are Children! This Lord is the best Friend I have, to take her off my Hands. To be sure bring the Money, carry her to my Lord, and bring the Money; go take Time by the Fore-lock, he may recant, then so much Money's lost. Go, run to my Lord, tell him you'll do it."

Here he thrust the Fellow out, and appear'd with a smiling Countenance. A Man comes in, and tells him the Exchequer is shut up, Stocks are fallen, a War declar'd, and a new Tax laid on Land; he beats his Breast, groans aloud, and vanishes.

"By this Wretch," *said Abrahijo,* "you see the Care and Anxiety [that] wait on the Miserable. The Love of Gold in him has extinguish'd Nature; nay, it predominates over Self-love; for he hastens his End, by not allowing his Body either Rest, or sufficient Nourishment, only that he may encrease the Number of his Coffers."

Another Shade appear'd with a great Crowd of People, huzzaing, a *Venditor,* a *Venditor;* he goes before them, steps into every Shop, enquires after the Health of each Family, kisses the Wives, and out of his thrusts Gold into their Mouths. Here he bows to a Tinker, there embraces a Cobler, shakes a Scavinger by the Hand, stands bare-headed, and compliments an Ale-Wife, invites a Score of Shoemakers, Taylors, Pedlars, Weavers and Hostlers, to do him the Honour of their Company to Dinner.

The Scene changes; he's at Court, the Ministers repay him his servile Cringes by theirs; one comes up to him, and says, he hopes, when the Bill comes into the House, he will favour him with his Vote for its passing: He answers, he shall discharge the Trust reposed in him, like a Man of Honour, in forwarding what is for the Good of his Country, and opposing the contrary, tho' the Consequence were his own Ruin: That he begg'd his Lordship's Pardon, if he dissented from him in Opinion, and did not think what he required warrantable in a Man of Honour.

"You are not well inform'd," *replied the Nobleman,* "but we'll talk of that another Day, when I hope I shall convince you, that you did not well understand me; my present Business is to wish you Joy, *Courvite's* Regiment is vacant, and tho' you have never serv'd, your personal Bravery and good Conduct in the Senate have spoke so much in your behalf, that you will to morrow have the Commission sent you." "My Lord," *replied the Patriot,* "this is an unexpected Favour, and I am satisfied I owe it to your Lordship's Goodness. I hope an Opportunity to speak my Gratitude, will present it self; in the mean while count upon me, in whatever I can serve your Interest." At these Words, with a visible Joy in his Looks, he vanished.

Three dirty Mechanicks appeared in a Shoemaker's Shop, who was a Dreamer. He was declaiming to his Companions over a Pot of Beer, after the following Manner. "Look ye, Neighbours, there's an old Proverb says, *It is not the Hood which makes the Monk;* the being born a Gentleman does not make a Man of Sense; and the being bred a Tradesman, does not deprive us of it; for how many great Men have leap'd from the Shop-board, [workbench], sprung up from the Stall, and have, by patching and heel-piecing [fitting] Religion and the State, made their Names famous to After-Ages? I can name many, but I shall mention only *John of Leyden.*[1] Now, I see no Reason, why Meanness of Birth should be an Obstacle to Merit, and I am resolved, as I find a great many Things which ought to be redress'd both in Church and State, if you my Friends will stand by me, to aim at the setting both upright: For you must own, they are basely trod awry. Trade is dead, Money is scarce, the Parsons are proud, rich and lazy; War is necessary for the Circulation of Money; and an honest Man may starve in these Times of Peace and Beggary.

"There are a great many Mysteries in Religion, which, as we don't know what to make of them, are altogether unnecessary, and ought to be laid aside, as well as a great many Ceremonies, which ought to be lopp'd off for being chargeable."

The rest gave their assenting Nod, and seem'd to wonder at, and applaud his Eloquency. In a Moment, I saw him preaching to a Mobb against the Luxury of the Age, and telling them it shew'd a Meanness of Spirit to want Necessaries, while the Gentry, by force of long Usurpations of their Rights, rioted in all manner of Excess. That Providence brought none into the World that he might starve; but that all on Earth had a Right to what was necessary to their Support, which they ought to seize, since the Rich

[1] John of Leyden was a one-time tailor and vigorous Anabaptist who established a strict theocracy with himself as King in the city of Münster in 1534. Catholics recovered the city in 1535, and John of Leyden was tortured to death.

refus'd to share with them. From a Preacher I saw him a Captain of a Rabble, plundering the Houses of the Nobility, was terrible to all; and tho' he declared for levelling, would be serv'd with the Pomp and Delicacy of a Prince; marries his Daughters to Lords, hoards an immense Treasure, and wakes from his golden Dream.

Another Shade I saw suborning Witnesses, giving them Instructions what to swear, packing Juries, banishing, hanging, and beheading all his Enemies, sending immense Sums to foreign Courts, to support his Power at Home, bribing Senates, and carrying all before him without Controul, when he vanish'd. My *English* Friend told me, that Soul belong'd to the Body of a Money-Scrivener, who almost crack'd his Brain with Politicks, and thought of nothing less than being a prime Minister. I knew him while I was in the World; his whole Discourse always ran on Liberty, Trade, Free Elections, *&c.* and constantly inveigh'd against all corrupt and self-interested Practices. I saw Persons descended from the ancient Nobility fawning on Valets who were arrived to great Preferment for Pimping; I beheld others contriving Schemes, to bring their Wives and Daughters into the Company of Persons in Power, and aiming to gain Preferment for themselves, at the Expense of the Vertue of their Families; nor was there a Vice, a Folly or a Baseness, practised in this World below, tho' ever so secret, which I did not see there represented. . . .

In the mean time I was allow'd a Week to satisfy my Curiosity, and make my Observations on all the strange things which were there to be seen, which I may justly reckon the most agreeable Part of my whole Life; and also a further Time to refresh my self: Which being done, we prepared for our Journey, being provided with all things necessary for that Purpose.

As I found in my self that longing Desire (which is natural to all Men, who have been long absent from Home) of returning to see my own Country; and being besides unwilling to go back to *Cacklogallinia,* the Actions and Designs of the first Minister, to which I was privy, having made such Impressions upon me, that I was prejudic'd against their whole Nation; nor was that Prejudice remov'd, by being acquainted with their Laws, Customs and Manners, some of which appear'd to me unreasonable, and others barbarous.

I say, upon the aforesaid Considerations, I apply'd my self to some of the *Selenites,* whose Courtesy I had already experienced, asking them, whether they could direct me to find out some Part of the Terrestrial World, known and frequented to by *Europeans:* They were so good to give me full and plain Instructions what Course to steer thro' the Air for that Purpose, which I was very well able to follow, having a Pocket Compass about me, which I brought from *England,* it having long been my Custom never to stir any where without one.

It being necessary to bring *Volatilio* into the Design, I went to him and told him, that as we were so unfortunate not to succeed in finding out the Country of Gold, it would be adviseable to return home some other Way, in hopes of better Success in going back; otherwise we might, in all Probability, meet with a disagreeable Welcome from the Emperor and the whole Court. *Volatilio* hearken'd to these Reasons, and besides having the true Spirit of a Projector in him, which is, not to be discouraged at Disappointments, he consented to my Proposal.

Accordingly we set out, and after some Days travelling, we meeting with little or nothing in our Journey differing from our former, we lighted safely upon the *Blue Mountain* in *Jamaica.* Here I was within my own Knowledge; for having formerly made several Voyages to *Jamaica,* I was no Stranger to the Place.

Now therefore I thought it time to acquaint the *Cacklogallinians* with the innocent Fraud I had put upon them; they seem'd frighted and surprized, as not knowing how to get home to their own Country: For *Volatilio* appear'd to be quite out of his Element. However, I directed them which Way to steer, which was directly Southward; and having rested for some time, they took their Leave of me, and *Volatilio,* with his *Palanquineers,* began their Flight, as I had directed them, and I never saw them more.

As for my Part, I made the best of my way to *Kingston,* where [be]coming acquainted with one Captain *Madden,* Commander of the *London Frigate,* he was so kind, upon hearing my Story, to offer to give me my Passage *gratis,* with whom having embark'd at *Port Royal,* I reach'd my native Country, after a Passage of Nine Weeks.

Finis.

RALPH MORRIS

From *The Life and Astonishing Transactions of John Daniel . . .* (1751)

[We noted earlier that the hero of Robert Paltock's *Life and Adventures of Peter Wilkins, a Cornish Man* may have been named after Bishop John Wilkins. *The Life and Astonishing Transactions of John Daniel,* published in the same year, also may have been inspired by the Wilkins tale, but it contains original ideas as well. Most significant is the use for the first time of a device that enables a man to fly by his own muscle power rather than by the labor of fowls, be they gansas or Cacklogallinians. Here, as in other accounts of moon trips, a special leaf serves to satisfy the voyager's hunger and thirst, thus eliminating the need for provisions. Gestures are again successful in establishing initial communication with the moon's inhabitants. The work is pure fantasy, with few of the satirical overtones of the Brunt adventure.

The excerpt reprinted here is only a small part of the long story of John Daniel and his son. In the early parts of the book, Daniel tells how he was shipwrecked on an unknown shore with a messmate who, he discovers, is a woman. In the course of time they "marry" and people the island.

Their son Jacob, a boy of "sedentary disposition and amazing ingenuity," is the builder of the flying machine "Eagle," on which he and his father "mount the Aerial World" and then accidentally fly to the moon. The "Eagle," which "looked like a stage or floor" surrounded by calico wings, was the result of "sober, careful, diligent" work. Once launched into flight, Jacob claimed, one was "safe here as on solid ground."

Following the moon adventures related in this selection, John and Jacob return to earth, only to be fired upon by frightened earthlings. The two finally succeed in landing in Lapland and then journey to

Norway, where Jacob engages in whale fishery to earn passage money home for himself and his father. Jacob loses his life in the attempt. John Daniel, "after a life of fatigue and anxiety, reaches England and ends his days in peace and comfort at his native place, aged Ninety-seven Years."

It is interesting that neither of the Daniels realizes that they are on the moon before their return to earth. Searching for some explanation of the long periods of daylight and darkness, Daniel finally concludes that the moon is the only place such would occur. He is then also able to understand why the "Eagle" "pitched quite over" as they moved between the gravitational attraction of the planet and that of its satellite.

The book went through at least three early editions, the first in 1751, a second in 1770, and a third in 1801. The selection reprinted here is drawn from the third edition, which is part of the Lammot du Pont collection of early aeronautical literature housed in the Eleutherian Mills Historical Library. "Mr. Ralph Morris" may or may not have been a pseudonym. In either case the author remains unknown, although later editions call him "Rev."]

. . . .

Jacob had for some years buried himself in a little hovel he had built for his own use in my yard, and was always accounted of *my* family; and though my other children were disposed of, I had commonly one or more grandchildren at home with me and my wife. I was now in the fortieth year of my reign in this island, which I had named, *The Island of Providence;* and the point where I had fixed my residence, I named *Point Fortune* from my receiving so much benefit from the shipwreck on that spot; when *Jacob* came and desired me to give him some of my wax (for I had a vast quantity of it by me, from the bees that I had destroyed for the sake of their honey). I did so, about three pounds, or more, wondering what

An artist's conception of John Daniel's "Flying Eagle" (by Paul Schaub).

use he had in his head to put it to; and I was satisfied it was to no purpose to ask him; but about a week afterward, seeing him come from the mountains with his long poles in his hands; "so, *Jacob,*" says I, "have you been weighing the air again?"—"Father," says he, "it will do, it will do," and away he ran into his work-room.

Some time after, he desired me to lend him my cart and a cow, to draw somewhat [something] up to the mountain. I told him, with all my heart, and as I had little to do, I would go with him; but I soon found I had touched upon a wrong string, he begging I would excuse his company at that time, for he had an experiment to make, which, if it should not succeed, he should be as much ashamed of as he would have reason to rejoice if it prospered. "Well, *Jacob,*" says I, "of all my children, I see you must be the philosopher," and left him, with leave to take the cart, and what else he saw fit. He did so, and stayed out upon the mountain for three days and nights.

I often took a walk, and looked toward it; and as constantly saw some fresh appearance, by which I knew he was alive, or else, by his long delay, I should have expected some accident had befallen him; but on the third day, as I stood below him, I imagined I saw somewhat like a large sail of a ship, flapping about in the air, and began to suspect, that after all the discourse we had about shipping, he had been putting somewhat like it together, on the mountain. I was laughing to myself, at the impropriety of the place he had chose to build his ship on. "Poor lad," thinks I, "how will you be puzzled, when you want to launch into the sea?" I was pleasing myself with these speculations, when I suspected that it must move; and wondered how it was possible for him to beat along a machine of the bulk that seemed to be (for I visibly saw it pass along, faster and faster, till some trees deprived me of the further view of it). I ran therefore to avoid the obstruction of the trees, to a spot, not above sixty paces off, from whence I could command the whole top of the mountain; when turning about, I perceived the ship, as I termed it of myself, standing almost at the further extremity of it, and in about half an hour more (for I stayed determined to observe the issue of it), I perceived it move back again with great velocity to its former station. This motion quite confounded all my former ideas of a ship; for I thought, though it was possible to make something with sails that would be drove along before the wind by its force; yet how this thing could so apparently move with equal celerity against the wind too, I could not imagine.

It being fixed on the first station, in less than an hour, I saw *Jacob,* the cow, and cart, all descending the hill; and being impatient to know what it was he had been doing, I stepped on as fast as I could to meet him. "Son," says I, "pray what conjuration have you been carrying on upon the mountain, for I have seen to my thinking a ship there? Pray, how have you disposed of it, for I cannot see it there now?"—"O father," says *Jacob,* "I will now show you your own country again. I am sure I can go thither with all the safety imaginable, and much speedier than your ship could go."—"But, *Jacob,*" says I, "though from the description of my ship, you may imagine, that having made one so much lighter, it can go swifter; yet you do not consider that you have built it in the worst place you could have contrived for launching it."—"Launching it," says he, "what do you call launching?" —"That is," says I, "letting it down gently into the sea at high water; how do you propose to bring it down from the mountain to the sea?"—"Why," says *Jacob,* "I have brought it down here in the cart." At that I laughed very heartily. "O! *Jacob,*" says I, "when I was a boy, I have made a ship of a bean-shell, and put up a little mast in it; and if yours was to be set a-float in the sea, I suppose it would meet with the same fate as my bean-shell did in a puddle; to be soon turned keel upward."—"Father," says *Jacob,* "I do not understand one word you say, nor can I think what you conceive of me."—"Why," says I, "I saw plain enough what you have been at these three or four days. You have, from the notion I gave you of a ship, been making some little thing, as like one as you can, and are now simple enough to imagine that you can go to sea in it. As for going, I will not be positive but you may; but I am as certain that you will never return again."

"Indeed, father," says he, "you was never more deceived in your life than at present. I have made no ship, nor any thing like one, nor intend I to go to sea at all, for your catastrophe[1] has driven all such thoughts from my mind. No, sir, you shall see that I will travel on a better footing than in a ship." He then told me, he had brought his machine to absolute perfection, and that he had been making an experiment for flying in it. "Flying in it!" says I. "What! And was the motion I saw upon the mountain, flying?" —"It was indeed, father," says he, "and a delightful motion it is too."— "Had you not wheels to your machine?" said I, "or did it not slide somehow on the ground as it went?"—"No, no," says he, "I am sensible that no sliding on the ground can be called flying. Why, father, I actually flew in the air, without any other support than that sea-mew [a kind of gull] hath (pointing at one); and if you will return with me, you shall fly yourself."

I told him, that we would not return now for he must be fatigued, and

[1] The senior Daniel had been shipwrecked, with a female messmate, on the island where the family now lived.

hungry, I supposed, having been four days absent, and that it was time to go home and refresh himself. "Perhaps then, father," says he, "you do not think a man can live without eating or drinking."—"No, truly," says I, "and he that does, must have but a short and sorry life of it."—"Then, father," says he, "you do not think I have been all this while in the mountain without it?"—"No, indeed, do I not," says I, "you must have been starved." —"But I can assure you, I have," says he, "and could have staid ten times longer there, without the least inclination to any. I have lived six weeks together, without the least nourishment, save what I have extracted by chewing these leaves in my mouth," pulling at the same time a handful from his pocket. "Well," says I, "and do you not call that eating?"—"No," says he, "I never swallow it, but let it only lie in my mouth."—"But you have had water," says I. "Not a drop, I assure you," says he; "and if you will make the trial, you will find it answer, as I say."

These facts, so strongly attested by *Jacob,* a sober, careful, diligent young fellow, could leave me very little room to doubt of their certainty. I really stood in admiration of his inquisitive temper, which seemed to promise such wonders; then assuring him, that I would one day go see him make use of his machine on the mountain, we parted for that time, he having before promised me, at my leisure, to explain the whole contrivance to me.

About this time my wife, who had been long talking of it, had come to a resolution of making a progress to visit all her children and grandchildren, at their several settlements round the island, and take her leave of them all; for she said, that growing now in years, it would probably be the last perambulation she should be able to make; as the journey would be very considerable, of at least sixty miles. I told her, that she and two of her grandchildren we had then with us, should ride in the cart, and that I would walk by them. This we having agreed upon, we left *Jacob* to take care of all at home, and set forward. . . .

. . . having, in about six months, taken the circuit of the whole island, and settled its general economy, we returned to my old habitation.

After some small stay at home, I questioned *Jacob* again upon his machine, when he took me into his work-room, and showed me the several pieces of which it consisted, most of which were made of iron; and though exceeding strong and tough, they were so thin, light, and taper, that I could not have imagined so great a force of iron could have been wrought into so little a weight; there were several pieces of wood-work too, and one somewhat like a pump, but all so nicely wrought, as only to preserve strength, without superfluous weight; but then, the whole being in such a number of separate pieces, it was no easy matter to conceive what sort of a figure it would compose, when each was adapted to the other; nor could I, from the best idea of its single parts, dive into several of its consequences; but this I only could observe in the general, that I never saw pieces of work better executed in my life, than the several parts, separately examined, seemed to be.

It was not long after this, that *Jacob* desired me to go with him to the mountain, to see him fly his *eagle,* as he called it; and I, with great expectations, embraced his proposal; telling my wife what I was going about, and placing her properly to be a spectator of it.

We loaded the cart, and conducted it up the hill; when discharging it of its burden, we turned the cow to graze, and began our operation. He first of all struck four poles into the earth at proper distances, measuring them with four bars, in the ends of the two longest of which, on the flat sides, were four holes, into which the four points of the upright poles were to enter, at about three feet high from the ground, then letting the ends of the shorter pieces, of which there were several, all tenanted at the ends, into mortises or grooves on the inward edges of the two long pieces, he pinned them in very tight, leaving about a foot space unfilled up near one end, where he had contrived a trap-door to lift up and shut down at pleasure; so that when the whole woodwork was framed, it looked like a stage or floor, upon which he could mount, by getting under it, and opening the trap-door.

In the middle of this floor was a hole about four inches [in] diameter, to let in a pipe like a pump, to the upper part of which was an handle on each side, and a pendant iron between them, which ran through the pipe beneath the floor; and the pipe itself was held firm in the floor by four long irons fastened to its body, and screwed down to the floor in a square figure. This was the whole form of the upper surface of the floor.

Near the extremities of this floor every way, at proper distances, on the under edge, were driven in several flat and broad-headed staples, into each of which were thrust and screwed in a thin iron rib, about three inches broad next [to] the floor, and from thence tapering to a point, at the length of about three yards, so wrought and tempered, as to be exceeding tough and elastic, with each a female screw at about three feet distant from the edge of the floor; these were all clothed with callico dipt in wax, each running into a sort of scabbard or sheath, made proper in the cloth to receive it; and being all screwed to their staples and the floor, made an horizontal superficies [surface] of callico, including the floor of about eight yards diameter, but somewhat longer than broad.

On the under side of the floor was a circle of round iron, above five feet

[in] diameter, with several upright legs, about a foot long, equal in number to the above described ribs, and standing in the middle space between them; each of which legs entering upward through a recipient hole in the floor, was screwed tight by a nut on the upper side of the floor. Between these legs, on the interspaces of the round iron ring, just under each rib, hung balances, exactly poised upon the ring, with all their ends nearly meeting in the center, under the pipe-hole, each of which, by an iron chain fixed to it, was linked to the sucker iron of the pipe or pump, and the other end was, with a like chain, linked to an iron loop, screwed into the female screw of the rib, just placed over it; and then all the clothing was hooked upon little pegs all around the outward edge of the floor, so close as to keep the air from passing in any quantity.

Thus the whole apparatus being fixed, my son opened his trap-door, and ascending through it, mounted his floor, fixed the handle, and began to play his wings, to see that all was right, but very gently, for fear of rising off his poles till he was quite prepared. I then observed, that when the pump-handle was pressed downward, as in pumping, that in raising the sucker the pendant iron raised the end of the balances next to it, when the other extremities of the balances hooked to the several ribs necessarily descending, drew their corresponding ribs downward; and that the uplifting of the handle consequently gave the ribs liberty, through their springing, to return to their horizontal position again, so that they were raised and depressed, proportionably to the motion and force of the handle, and exactly answered the use and play of wings in birds.

Having found that every part answered to his wish, and having fastened his trap-door down, the whole machine standing at such a height that I could both look under and over it, it appeared to be [of] a vast dimension.

It was of almost an oval form, and each wing extended at least three yards at the sides from the floor, but at the two ends it was somewhat more; and there being a handle on each side the pipe or pump, he could make it go which way he pleased, by altering his own standing, as he told me, either on the one side or the other of the pump; for the side he stood on being the heaviest, and the other consequently mounting the highest, it would always move that way, which end was the highest.

I told him, I looked upon it as an ingenious sort of a whim to try an experiment with, and that as I had seen it play, I was now satisfied it would fly; but advised him to come down for fear of any accident; for now I had gratified my curiosity, I desired to see no more of it. "What!" says he, "be at all this trouble in breeding up my eagle, and not take one flight in it!" He wished, he said, he knew which way *England* lay, for that then he would certainly go to my father's at *Royston*. "Poor lad," says I, "you think that there is nothing but *England* out of this island; whereas *England* is no bigger, with respect to the whole habitable earth, than my hand is, compared to this island. No, there are numberless places nearer to us than *England*."—"What, houses!" says he, "and cattle and men there!" —"Ay," says I, "and *Englishmen* too, such as I am."

Jacob, growing impatient of delay, "come, father, now I am mounted on my eagle," says he, "you shall see me fly." I would fain have dissuaded him; but he began with his pump-handle, and rising gently from the posts, away he went, almost two miles; then working his contrary handle, as he told me, he returned again, and passed by me to the other end of the mountain; then soaring a little as he came near me again, "father," says he, "I can keep her up, if you can guide her to the posts." I did so, and he seemed so rejoiced at his flight, and so alert upon it, that perceiving with what ease it was managed, and how readily it went and returned, and he entreating me to take a turn with him, I at last consented.

Jacob having brought me to his wish, opened his trap-door in great joy, and let me up; then making all fast, "father," says he, "lie you, or sit close to the pump on that side, while I work it on this"; and seeing me somewhat fearful, "don't be afraid," says he, "hold by the pump-irons, you are as safe here as on the solid earth." Then plying his handle, we rose, and away we went to the mountain's edge; but going very swift, and observing that while I sat forward he could not come at the other handle, he called to me to come round to his side, while he went on mine; but being afraid to stir, or at least so readily as I should, and being obliged to keep the same handle moving till I came round, we had now overshot the mountain, and possibly might be three quarters of a mile from the level plains. The sight of this so terrified me, that I could not move a joint, every moment expecting my neck to be broken with a fall. My fear, and he not being able to quit his handle till he could fairly come at mine, and we being now over the sea (for we flew at an immense rate), somewhat terrified *Jacob;* and had he been as dispirited as I was, we must both have fallen headlong into it; but keeping up his courage, so long as we were on the wing, and as he told me in no danger of falling, unless through our own faults, for want of balancing, and still playing the pump, not much minding, as he afterward told me, whither he went, imagining he could come the same way back again, as soon as I was so well recovered from fright as to be able to stir round the pump, we still moved on; till I perceiving that we must be prodigiously higher than we lately were, and vastly above a level with the mountain, informed him of my fears; and indeed, he then too soon discovered that we were so, and began to be under a violent discomposure likewise; but it was rather a time to work than to stand amazed in, and all the hope he had was my coming round, that we might tack about.

In less than half an hour we were all out of sight of the island, which, for my own part, I then bade farewell to; but he had still hopes, till beginning to flag a little in his strength, he hinted it to me; but putting some of the leaf into his mouth, that recruited his spirits, and away we went, not knowing whither. Night coming on, I bewailed myself and my poor wife terribly; till *Jacob,* not able to bear my reproaches, roused up his courage, and told me that he thought I should have more prudence at my years, than to despond upon such an accident, as he, who could not be supposed to be endued [endowed] with my prudence, was resolved to bear up against. He said, men should show themselves such in every change of fortune; and as we were yet safe, though we were flown past our knowledge, yet we ought to struggle with every cross occurrence, till by perseverance we became conquerors.

This, and much more that *Jacob* justly then urged, awakened me somewhat from my dejection; and feeling about (for it was then almost dark), I held by the irons, and was rising. "Stand still, when you are up," says he, "and move round to my place that way, while I this way take yours, and let us see if we cannot fly back again." I did so, and at length he caught the opposite handle, and working at it, we imagined we were going homeward again; but it being quite dark, had we been near the island we could not have seen it. However, the imagination of being homeward-bound kept us in some heart; we would willingly have stood upon the wings without motion till morning, if we could have done it, but we were not yet adept enough at flying for that; but that the labouring oar might not altogether lie upon my son, I proferred to help him, which he, being a little fatigued, permitted me to do; and I pumped, while he sat down. This being unusual labour to me, I was soon tired at it, and told him so. "Pray, father," says he, "take some of my leaf into your mouth, and observe if it refreshes you or not." I did so, and soon told him I perceived a very sensible alteration, for that I was not only almost tired, but very thirsty before I took it, and that then I could not say I was either; so I pumped away for some time, and then *Jacob* came to it again; but which way we went, neither of us knew, or whether we were higher or lower than before night. After some hours working and refreshing, alternately, we became in a degree familiarized to our stations; but what gave me the deepest concern was, to conjecture what my poor wife thought, when she saw us past the mountain, and ascending out of her sight.

At length, the morning beginning to break upon us, I was in hopes, by the sun, to guess to what part of the compass we were steering; but, to my prodigious surprise, all around us seemed equally luminous, nor could we, by any of the usual characters of the morning, know in what place the sun would shine first. We thought it had been but a short night indeed, though that we took from our fears, which had disengaged our minds from the thoughts of those transactions that we could have measured it by; but what puzzled me now excessively was, that we were in bright day-light, and then immediately saw the sun, all at once, dart upon us very piercingly from the serenest sky that ever we beheld; and though we pumped ever so strong, we could not discern whether we moved either upward, downward, or sideways. Thus we continued in great suspense, our wings moving with only half the force they did before, till upon the next alteration of the scene we found ourselves almost in the dark again. Looking about us every way, we saw a vast moon beyond us, and at the same time the eagle wavering about, quite surprised us, and struck us into such a terror, that the handle of the pump slipping out of my hand, as I wrought at it, and finding the machine joggle, as if it was going to overset, I caught fast hold of the pump iron; and *Jacob,* who was as much terrified at the accident as myself, clinging to his seat, we were sometimes hanging at the bottom, and sometimes sideways, and in diverse positions for a few moments, till the machine righting, as by mere accident, in its fall, *Jacob* caught hold of the handle nearest him, and set her going again. Our surprise is no ways to be imagined; and it occasioned his working but slowly at it till he recovered his spirits, the few strokes he gave only just keeping the eagle true to the air. We were then sensible, that at the height we were, there was nothing more to be done than to keep ourselves steady; and we perceived, that if we balanced right, the least motion of the wings imaginable would convey us along, so that we now floated with very little difficulty to ourselves; and after passing a long way thus, we thought we saw a small black spot, almost beneath us; and observing that it grew bigger and bigger, were in great hopes that it was our island; but approaching still nearer and nearer, we found ourselves very much mistaken, perceiving it to be the whole terraqueous globe. Now we began to rejoice indeed; and finding we had nothing else to do then, without using force to raise us, only to keep ourselves steady till we descended, we waited the wished-for moment of our alighting safe upon *terra firma,* which we did in less than an hour afterward, just at sun-set, upon prodigious high and craggy hill, with vast precipices on each side of us.

Our eagle no sooner touched the ground, than *Jacob* opened the trap-door, and putting out his feet first, he raised it gently up with his hands, till he had slid himself out, and then held it up for me. We tenderly embraced each other, and immediately falling upon our knees, returned hearty thanks for our preservation; then setting down on the mountain, and recapitulating the past passages of our journey, we could scarcely believe the whole to be more than a dream; but as watching [staying awake] so long had made sleep very necessary for us, and our day closing in, we resolved not to descend the mountain till morning. We therefore laid ourselves under shelter of the eagle's wings, and slept very soundly, and very long, as we imagined; for though we were both sure we must have slept at least a full night, yet it being very dark at our awaking, we from thence concluded, that we must have slept all the next day too; and that the then present, was the second night of our residence there; so contenting ourselves under that apprehension, we turned about for another nap.

We waked a second time, after a second sound and long sleep, as we esteemed it, from the refreshment we had received by it; but were surprised at the darkness continuing still, without the least prospect of day's approach; and believing it might be the depth of winter in the country we had settled upon (for we perceived ourselves very cold), I began to imagine, that the days being very short there, we might have passed them over in our sleep; and I told *Jacob,* that I thought it best for us to rise, and stir about till morning; for that I had heard, that in some parts of the earth, in their winter, they had but little day-light, and in some none at all for a long time together.

When we arose from under the eagle's wings, it was not so dark but we could see the shapes and faces of each other by starlight, and a vast moon that we saw, though we could not distinguish objects far off; so we walked about, taking but very short turns, for fear of the precipices we had seen about us, at our first landing. Longing for the appearance of morning, we stirred till we were both weary again, and moon light still continuing, we sat down, then walked again in great perplexity; till at length, being assured that we had expected day much longer than the continuance of any possible night, and yet that the moon had not quite passed the arch of our hemisphere, we almost despaired of ever seeing the day-light again. The moon, which till then had comforted us, by degrees disappearing, we were in excessive fear of total darkness.

We had neither tasted victuals nor drink since we left the island, but how long that might be, I could no ways guess; for though we had a night or two in our first flight, I am persuaded that several others were swallowed up in that serene brightness that surrounded us for a long time in our passage; and then, how long it was since our arrival on the earth, we could not tell. However, our leaf had very well supported us, or at least preserved us, without any sensible alteration or decay, either of strength or spirits; so relinquishing the expectation of more light; and the moon being near to setting, we thought that we had better descend into the valley, to endeavor after some sustenance, while we had light, than to stay till the moon would afford us none, when it would be impossible to find our way thither.

With great resolution we therefore descended, neither seeing or hearing the least creature or noise all the way we went; till coming near the level ground, where a monstrous cave gaped to our left hand, we thought we heard several shrill voices, and standing still, heard them plainer, but so shrill, fine, and musical, that we doubted them to be human. Having passed a little way on the level, we saw several things pass by us, in various shapes, that we had never before observed; but though some of them seemed to go erect, yet they were very small and thin, and we could not discern their countenances, for their heads seemed quite covered with somthing. One of them stopt just before us, and by moonlight shone like copper; but seeing us step forward, he gave a great shriek, and fled, muttering somewhat that we did not understand. As we travelled but very slow down the descent, for fear of danger, we slept once or twice ere we arrived at the bottom; and being now entered on the plains, from whence we could see no boundary, except that one we had come from, after some travel there, we turned to look at the prodigious height of it, when, to our imagination, it shone at the top like gilding. We wandered about this plain two days, for though our light was much the same, and we had no natural distinction of day from night, yet we called our waking time day, and our sleeping time night. We then lost the moon entirely, but in lieu thereof, found, what was much more grateful to us, the light of the sun approaching; and the third day he rose up above the hills.

Its presence gave us such a flow of spirits, that we even forgot our toils and hardships. It afforded us, from the mountain we climbed up, a prospect of the most romantic country I had ever beheld; there were prodigious mountains, extensive plains, and immense lakes, interspersed with the largest plantations of trees that can be imagined to lie within the compass of the eye at once; and then the air was so serene, thin, and transparent, that we could see distinctly, to a distance beyond comparison to what we ever could before; and what increased our extacies was, that we were now in hopes of not losing the sun again, for it seemed not visibly to alter its position at all.

We entered the groves of trees, and began to see several people, and divers sorts of cattle, beasts, and birds, but far different in make, shape, and action, from what I had ever seen before. The people seemed . . . of a bright copper colour all over, and had hair so thick and long, as when it was justly distributed all round their head, would almost cover their whole body; some of these we saw, just upon the approach of light; but all that presented themselves after the sun appeared, had their hairs tied up in a great knot behind, when their bodies being disencumbered from it, they shone like gold. Having seen so many of these people, who only gazed at us, with little round eyes in their small faces, and none of them being any ways armed with what might offend us, we ventured to call to them; but they took no notice, by way of reply, and only moved off the faster: and indeed were so light and nimble of foot, that it would have been a vain pursuit to have followed them.

At last, turning the corner of some tall bushes one day, and walking pretty fast, just at the angle, one of these men met me breast to breast; he gave a shriek, and I caught him in my arms, which he would have avoided had not I held him too fast, till perceiving it would be in vain to struggle with me, he lifted up his hands, by way of craving my pity. I did not choose to seem to detain him by force, because of the fright I saw him in; nor did I care to let him run away, till I had discovered, by his means, the name and situation of his country, and who were the inhabitants. Therefore, letting go my right hand, I clapped it upon his head, and stroking his face, which was very beautiful, as a token of my friendship, I desired him to sit down; and seating myself on his left, and *Jacob* on his right hand, I began to examine him with words, though I suspected these to be insignificant, as they after appeared to be, and then by gestures. As to my words he took no notice of them, but my motions he readily comprehended; when pointing to my mouth for food to go into my stomach, and holding up my hands, as supplicating him to furnish me with some; he also pointed to some herbs that grew about there, and then to his own mouth, speaking in his way as idly to me as I had done to him; for his sounds were not articulate, being mostly short, and broken aspirates; and very little variety he seemed to have, even of them.

I then made signs to him to arise, and pointing to the herbs he had before nodded at, I gave a sign to him to pick and eat, which he did, and gave me a parcel. I ate some too; but though they seemed to fill me, they were so light that they offered me no nourishment, and *Jacob* observed the same from them. Then I signified to him, that I would know what other things they ate, but still all were herbs; by-and-by an odd shapen creature (as indeed all that we had yet seen were), passing by us, I pointed to that, and to my mouth; but he shook his head, and made signs of detesting to eat such things; then speaking in his way to the beast, it turned its head, and answered him in its way, and, to my thinking, pretty much like him. I tried, on his recommendation, several other of his eatables, which he produced to me in the wood I walked with him to; but though the fruits looked fresh and fair, they yet were flat and spiritless. As to my main questions of the name of the place, and the manners of the inhabitants, I could no ways make him understand my requests, and consequently could gather no determinate answer from him; and if I could have done it, yet I believe it would have been impossible either for me to have imitated his sound, or to have formed any letters together, to have expressed an idea of it by.

After I had gained all the information I could expect from him, I shook him by the hand, and took my leave of him; but now I could hardly get rid of him; he would bound like a doe to the wood, and bring me samples of several fruits, and was highly delighted when I expressed satisfaction at any of them, which I frequently did, merely to gratify his good nature; and when he had done serving me, he fled over the plain with such nimbleness as surprised me.

I told *Jacob,* that this country would not subsist us; for that the air was so thin, and the food so light, that we should be starved here but for his leaf, though I must say the water was as excellent as I ever tasted any where, and that if we could have but learned from the stranger where any great town stood, we would have travelled to it, for it would be impossible to live long where we were.

While we were thus discoursing, we saw a multitude of the same people we had been in company with before, all making toward us, from the opposite side of the plain. The sight of so many of them, though seemingly unarmed, put us into a consternation, and brought us to consult our own safety. However, as flight would be so far from securing us, that it would only animate them to the pursuit, whose agility was so much preferable to our own, that we must soon be overtaken, we determined to stand our ground, undaunted in appearance, however our hearts might be distressed. We did so, and soon were given to understand, that it was not to commit hostilities that we were so surrounded; for upon their advance to us, every one strove who should present us in the humblest manner with something that they had brought for our refreshment; all crowding to touch us but with a finger; upon which they expressed great satisfaction. We returned due acknowledgments for their civilities, in the ways we perceived to be most suited to their capacities; and after long gazing at each other, two of the gravest of them took us by the hand, and led us cross the plain, to the part they came from; and passing a little wood, led us into the mouth of a large hollow under the mountains, where we walked at least half an hour, through a long and broad path way, most part of the time descending, till at last we reached a little valley, which, when we looked from the ground upward, seemed just like the bottom of a well, the rocks and mountains rising so perpendicularly from it on every side to a prodigious height; and all round the valley, which was about a furlong diameter, were holes, either natural or artificial, in which were several passages, of greater and lesser dimensions, wherein they had their residence. They offered us of the best of every liquor and eatable they had, though nothing that I ever ate in that country seemed to satisfy a craving appetite, but rather excited it. There was indeed among their liquors, one of a charming taste, much like mead, but richer than I ever tasted any; and this suiting my gust [taste], I drank plentifully of it, and would have drank more but for fear of its overpowering me, though I perceived no tendency that way.

It was an inexpressible concern to me, not to be able either to understand them, or they us, except in trivial matters. I watched their language, and the application of their sounds, as narrowly as possible; but they being, as I thought, all so nearly allied, I found it would be in vain to attempt the distinction of them, though it was plain that to each other they were fully expressive and significant. I made several signs to be gone; but finding it would be disagreeable to them, and not knowing whither to go, we staid some time with them, and gathered-in one of their harvests. How they sow their corn, I could not learn, nor did I stay long enough with them to see; but it grows like grass, and as thick together, looking just like our small rushes; these blades are filled with a pulp, which when so dry as to be crisp and brittle, they roll between two stones; and then sifting it, it produces the lightest flour I ever saw. This they mix with water and dry great quantities of it in the sun, in lumps of a pound, or thereabouts each; and when they want it (as at eating their herbs) they give it a stroke with their hand, and it falls down into crumbles, which they eat by handfuls; but this food also, though it fattened them, did us but little service.

I was very desirous of informing myself, whether they had any religion among them, for I had observed no signs of it as yet; but one day, before I was stirring (for we lay on a sort of matrass [mattress] made of flags, and other light and warm things), I was awakened by most prodigious shrieks from every quarter; and starting up, I ran to see what was the matter; when coming into the valley, I beheld several hundred people walking round it, in a sort of processional order, with their arms a-cross, their heads drooping, and their hair, which before was all tied up in large knots behind, now loose and pendant, almost to the ground, all round them; resembling to my fancy persons in cloaks attending a funeral, and so indeed I suspected they were; but seeing the foremost of them take into the passage by which we came to the valley, and all the rest, three by three, taking the same route, *Jacob* and I gently brought up the rear, wondering all the while what was to succeed. They had no sooner got into the plain, than they all turned their faces to the sun, which was then about half buried beneath the mountain tops, at a vast distance from us; and then wringing their hands, they set up such a howling, crying, and shrieking, as made the whole plain ring; neither did one of them stir a foot from his position, or cease howling, till they had quite lost the sight of its body, which was a considerable time first: and then redoubling their outcry (if possible) for a short time, they ceased, and returned through the passage, in the same order, to the valley again.

After their return, with great difficulty I made them understand that I wanted an explanation of their proceedings, with regard to the sun, which I discovered to be the object of their ceremony; and at last, by several means attaining my purpose, one of them, as well as he could, made me sensible, that the great giver of life had left them; and as they did not know whether he would ever visit them again, they went to take leave of him, and implore his return. I pitied their ignorance, and attempted to show them, that the sun was but a creature (as we were) of the great giver of life, and maker of the world; but I fear that all my endeavours for their information were abortive, for I could not discern them in the least the wiser for them.

Expecting again the same continued darkness that had before seized us, which I had computed to be about the same length with their day, I remained very contentedly in the valley with them during all that time, and had the fortune to see another procession, with its attendant orisons, offered at its first appearance in the opposite horizon; from whence, I could conclude nothing else but that it must be one long day and night, while the sun made one revolution; but what could be the meaning of his being so slow in his circuit in this part of the world, more than in any other I was as yet acquainted with, I could no ways account for, not understanding much of astronomy.

Upon the next approach of light, I heartily thanked my benign hosts for all their favours to us, and we took our leave, not being able to learn whither we must go to find any great cities of inhabitants. The sun, which used to be my guide both in *England* and at the *Isle of Providence,* baffling all my former methods of observation, *Jacob* and I got into the plain again, with several of our hosts attending us so far. We were in great doubt which way to take; but getting up the opposite mountain, which cost us three of our whole days to ascend, and was excessively high; and being there able to see immensely far about us, without the least sign of any city or habitation; and a vast sea or lake being the extreme bounds of our view, we were so discouraged, that upon further consideration that night we determined to abandon all thoughts of any future land journey, and to betake ourselves again to the eagle; which would not only be the most expeditious, but least fatiguing. Which ever way we went, we might pitch upon the most likely spot to alight on. This being concluded upon, we set out the next morning, that is, after we had slept and rested ourselves; and descending the mountain, we re-crossed the plain to the hill we first alighted upon, where we found the eagle safe, on the same spot where we had left it.

Our leaf, which had stood us in so much stead, and without which we could not so long have subsisted upon the light diet we had found in this country, was now almost all consumed, though we had been as sparing of it as possible for some time past, which was an additional argument to press our departure; so after we had rested, and surveyed our eagle, finding it, upon *Jacob's* report, very capable of performing, we got up, and shutting our door after us, made an essay to rise, *Jacob* being of opinion that we might do it, though she stood upon the flat ground, till several repeated trials convinced him to the contrary.

Thus disappointed, we had a long way to fetch poles to fix it on, which gave us no small uneasiness, till *Jacob* spying a large stone, with my assistance rolled it toward a little hillock, like a mole hill; then drawing the eagle to it, and placing one part of the iron ring on the hillock, and the opposite part on the stone, I got in first, and he followed and closed the door; but we now lying on one side, could not freely work the wings, till he bade me stand forward, with my legs wide, and sway first one way and then the other; which raising the eagle by turns from side to side, *Jacob* took advantage of, and soon, with quick strokes, set it on float. Being near the mountain's edge, we were presently over the plain, upon a body of air sufficient to carry us any where. We took the way cross the plain, and over the hill from whence we had viewed the country, minding not to work too hard, but just to keep her on a level, without mounting; thus we skimmed along at a vast rate, and with so much ease, that it was amazing.

Yet though we had covered such a tract of land, we had not seen one habitation; but people we had beheld at times innumerable, all of whom we supposed had their residence in such a manner as our late hosts had; for the whole face of the country was very much broken, with prodigious risings, and as hideous depths.

Our time for the sun to set again was not above two thirds run, so that we were out of fear of being benighted, as we thought; but all of a sudden, upon looking behind us, the sun was setting; and before we had got from over the water, it was dark, only that we had the moon and star-light. This vexed us terribly, nor could we fathom out the meaning of it; but still went on, when thinking, by the motion, that we were sinking, I bade *Jacob* let me come to the handle, for that I was afraid he was tired; and I gave him for reason, because I thought the eagle sunk, which I told him we must take care to prevent till it became light again; for I had by this time changed my opinion as to the regularity of the days and nights, and took them to be quite arbitrary.

Now whether we really sunk or not, as I thought, or whether *Jacob* mended his stroke at the handle or not, and so raised us higher than we ought to have been, I cannot say, but so it was, that when, after a long flight, which had almost spent us both with working, we first began to see the sun again, it was before us, and we out of all view and prospect of earth, or the least speck in the universe; neither was there so much as a cloud to be seen, but all pure and serene round us. I should now have been glad of something to eat, finding myself light, and breathing without labour; but what perplexed me most was, to think how we, who came a straight course from the sun, should now meet it before us, This seemed unaccountable to me; but we had now become so accustomed to the eagle, that we had no fear of falling, and that kept us in. *Jacob* had plied the handle, as he thought, but slowly; upon which I told him, that I thought him in the wrong, and that unless he wrought more briskly at it, we should never see an end of our journey; for we were not sensible whether we proceeded forward, mounted higher, or sunk lower. Then taking the handle myself, I worked at it a great while till I felt the eagle totter, just as it did in the first flight; upon which I gave it to *Jacob* again; and sitting down with my back against the pump, which was my usual posture, I put both my arms under the irons, which fixed the pump to the floor. My labour had inclined me to drowsiness; and I had just forgot myself, when *Jacob* cried out, "take care, father"; and immediately clasping hold of the pump himself, the eagle pitched quite over, and proceeded without ever wagging more. We wondered at it, especially that in the turn we did not seem the least likely to fall; and though we were sure we flew upon our heads, in respect to our former position, yet *Jacob* stood, and I sat, as little liable to fall as ever we did, and seemed to be still with our heads upward. We considered how this was possible to happen, and many reasons passed on each side *pro* and *con;* but it being something above our comprehension, and feeling no inconvenience from it, we were very happy that it was no worse. We now visibly perceived the eagle to sink, and therefore humoured it; for we were such proficients, that give us but day-light, we could rise or fall it at pleasure; and by proper balancing, have floated for half an hour together, with very little motion of the wing. We had not been long turned thus, before we were in utter darkness again, which by no means suited us; but fearing nothing, we patiently waited the return of day.

At the next dawn, when we were able to descry objects at a distance, we found ourselves near the surface of the earth, over the water, and within a little distance of some very large sea port; and we made toward it, I describing to *Jacob* the buildings, and pointing to the ships in the harbour, and others riding before the port. This was a joyful sight to *Jacob,* who had so long fed himself upon the hopes of a prospect of this nature. "Father," says he, "is that *England?*" I told him, it was strange if it should [be]; but that it might as well be that as any other place, for ought I knew. However, I told him, we would make toward it, and see. Accordingly, we pushed for it; but taking notice of a high hill, just on the back of the town, and overlooking it, I bade him spring away with all his force for that hill, where we would alight, and from thence walk down to the town.

. . . .

"VIVENAIR"

A Journey lately performed through the Air, in an Aerostatic Globe . . . To the newly discovered Planet, Georgium Sidus (1784)

[This brief work, probably the least well-known of the selections in this book, was originally published in pamphlet form in 1784. The author is unknown, and his pseudonym, "Vivenair," gives no indication of his real identity, but he is believed to have been an Englishman since the pamphlet was written in English.

The story uses the motif of a space venture to satirize the political turmoil and some of the social follies of England in the late eighteenth century. Vivenair's aeronaut, a man of exceedingly high moral purpose and scientific dedication, lands on the small planet Georgium Sidus (actually discovered in 1781 and named for King George III), which he finds is much closer to the earth than had been suspected. The society on the planet, as he describes it, is also close to that of the earth, particularly that of the England of George III.

Historians have described the "collapse of cabinet government" in England in the early years of George's reign. George III, King of England from 1760 to 1820, did his best to maintain strong monarchal leadership in the face of rigorous opposition from Parliament, to say nothing of the English colonials. In 1780 George Dunning, one of the King's most outspoken Parliamentary opponents, presented a famous resolution that articulated the political spirit of the opposition by stating, "the influence of the crown has increased, is increasing, and ought to be diminished." Vivenair was obviously sympathetic to Dunning's resolution.

In 1782, much to the displeasure of the King, the opposition in Parliament elected a new, reform-minded Prime Minister, Lord

Rockingham. When Rockingham died a few months later, a struggle ensued between Charles James Fox, a bitter enemy of the King's, and Lord Shelburne, a monarchal favorite. Shelburne won the fight and became Prime Minister in 1783. Fox then formed an alliance with Lord North, a former Prime Minister and also once a favorite of the King's. Together they held a majority in Parliament and succeeded in effecting Shelburne's removal. In December, 1783, English cabinet government came to yet another crisis when George III was able to defeat the Fox-North coalition and appoint the younger William Pitt Prime Minister.

Vivenair satirizes the rapid changes in ministers that resulted from the continuing contest for power. His story ends on a note of hopelessness; he did not know that Pitt would actually succeed in saving the cabinet form of government in England. George III was soon to be blind, deaf, and insane, leaving Pitt free to guide England away from the defeat and unpopularity that surrounded both the loss of its American colonies and the open political corruption that Vivenair so effectively ridicules.

The hypocritical morals and manners of English society and the growing materialism of the era also attracted Vivenair's sharp pen. For example, the English Civil List, a kind of fund for bribes and favors controlled by the King, becomes on Georgium Sidus the "Fillifist," or filler of fists, a term used by the inhabitants of the planet to mean sunshine. This sunshine has a wondrous effect: Those who get most of it grow tall and powerful, while those who receive little shrink into insignificance. Tipping of servants, coachmen, and many others had become a widespread custom in England; Vivenair finds that on Georgium Sidus his voyager could communicate "more than some hours of conversation" merely by placing the thumb and forefinger of one hand in the palm of the other, thus miming the giving of a tip.

Certain aeronautic events that preceded the publication of Vivenair's fantasy are worth noting. The men mentioned in the first chapter, the Mongolfier brothers and Charles, were pioneer French balloonists. Joseph and Étienne Montgolfier designed, built, and, on June 5, 1783, launched the world's first hot-air balloon. J. A. C. Charles was the physicist who designed and launched the first hydrogen balloon, on August 23, 1783. On November 21 of that same year, 500,000 people, including King Louis XVI, Marie Antoinette, and Benjamin Franklin, watched the first human ascent. England was about a year behind France in the "balloon race"; the first human flight from British soil occurred on August 24, 1784, in Edinburgh. Thus, the balloon mania was very much a part of English life, and the balloon was a natural choice for Vivenair's space vehicle.

What follows is reprinted from the copy of the original pamphlet now in the Eleutherian Mills Historical Library.]

A satirical English engraving that appeared on December 13, 1784, the same year Vivenair's satire was published. The work depicts the second balloon ascent in England, on November 30, 1784, by Jean-Pierre Blanchard, a Frenchman, and Dr. John Jeffries, an American. Jeffries is said to have paid 100 pounds for the privilege of making the flight. The second man from the left is probably the Prince of Wales, who witnessed the flight. The text at the bottom reads:

BRITISH BALLOON AND D[EVILISH] AERIAL YACHT

Designed for conveying the high Fliers of Fashion over the Channel from Dover to Calais, and in which, it being snug, easy and convenient, the enterprising Pair may safely make the Grand Experiment.

Che sara, sara
Ye Masters of Packets! ye poor silly loons!
Sell your boats and get Blanchard to make you Balloons.
For our fair modern Witches, no longer aquatic.
Will never more cross but in boats Aerostatic.

CHAPTER I

The Manner of the Author's setting out, and the surprizing Objects he met with on his Voyage

Urged on, or rather inspired, by the wonderful experiments of late made and performed by those superlative geniuses, Messrs. Mongolfier, Charles, and others, no less to the honour of this our mighty kin[g]dom of France, than to the advancement of true experimental knowledge; animated also, as it must be confessed, by that selfishness, the usual attendant upon glory; I resolved upon constructing, in the most secret manner, an Aerostatic Globe: not only with all the improvements of the great philosophers above named, but those also suggested by my own mind, naturally fertile and inventive. To effect this great, and I may say (since the event has so turned out) glorious experiment, I went to work in a retired and unfrequented part of the wood, near my retreat, about three leagues southwest of the famous city of Orleans.

In the course of about a fortnight, by my own indefatigable industry, and the great blessing of God, the work was finished, unknown to all my family, and even my wife; notwithstanding the curiosity and inquisitiveness natural (as many affirm) to that sex; and of which she gave many indications in the course of my work.

And now arrived the time when Providence, for the delight and instruction of mankind, armed me with sufficient fortitude to place myself in the vehicle, I had been constructing; but of which, my impatience to communicate the wonderful discovery I have made to the world, prevents my giving a proper drawing: and without taking leave of my dear wife and children, (dreading their lamentations,) I determined to launch forth from this sublunary globe, either to achieve the most astonishing discoveries, or lose my life in the perilous attempt. I had no sooner adjusted myself in my seat, and secured the provisions I thought it necessary to provide for so long and hazardous a journey, than (after having most devoutly offered up my prayers to the Almighty) I cut the rope by which the Balloon was held, and instantly felt myself rising with an easy pace through the air.

As the day I had chosen for my exaltation happened to be remarkably fine, and the great Providence of God had purged from me all apprehensions of danger, the sensations of delight upon my mind, at seeing myself in a few moments rising above this world, and viewing at the same time the delightful prospects it afforded, were such, as are far above the utmost efforts of my pen to describe. . . .

I continued rising in this manner for the space, as I guessed, of about half an hour; and had undoubtedly got many miles in height from the earth, as was evident to me from the smallness of the objects thereon; when, upon looking upwards, I perceived a luminous body, resembling in lustre and size the moon at the full.—I kept my eyes fixed upon this object for a considerable length of time, wondering what planet it could be; till, by observing the surrounding stars (the situation of which I was well acquainted with, astronomy having always been my favourite study) I found it to be the lately discovered planet Georgium Sidus.

This discovery filled me with the utmost astonishment, especially at its increasing dimensions; for the Balloon kept flying towards it with great speed; and here I had the courage to make use of a contrivance I had invented, for guiding the Balloon, and immediately directed it towards this new world; but my astonishment was still greater, upon casting my eyes again towards the earth; for the heighth was such, that I could no longer discern the multitude, the trees, or other objects on her surface, except the hills, the different seas, and the general appearance of the land; the same as when upon the earth one observes the moon; but vastly larger.—And here I cannot help observing, how greatly those philosophers err, who suppose the atmosphere of the earth to reach but a few miles above its surface; it being far more extensive than they have ever imagined, as must be evident from the foregoing narrative.—I shall quickly show also, that their ideas of the Georgium Sidus being a planet at an immense distance from the earth are equally erroneous; the extreme smallness of the planet having led them into that mistake—So liable to error are the highest flights of human philosophy! ! !

But to resume my journey.—I continued rising nearly at the same rate at which I first set out, still making towards the brilliant object which had so much engaged my attention; till I could plainly discern a great number of its inhabitants collected together, and, as I concluded, gazing with astonishment at the wonderful object that was sailing through the sky, and making towards them.—As I was now not far distant from them, I could plainly distinguish their forms.—They were most of them of a gigantic size, though differing in dimensions, and had not only two faces, one before and the other behind, but the whole of their forms were the same on both sides; so that (as I afterwards found) the appearance and actions of one side were a direct contrast to those of the other:—But more of this hereafter.—I no sooner was on the point of alighting amongst them, than they ran from me to a considerable distance, looking at me all the time with great surprize and fear, and leaving a great space for me to descend upon; which I very soon effected, without any damage to myself or my apparatus.

CHAPTER II

The Author's Reception, and the Entertainment given him by Hehehe Lob Jol-Teredd, the King of the Country

I had no sooner disengaged myself from the machine, than I perceived a number of those who had fled at my first alighting, slowly approaching me; (encouraged no doubt by my diminutive appearance) but with marks notwithstanding of some fears.—I immediately threw myself on the ground, and by all the gestures I was master of, endeavoured to remove their suspicions, and solicit their protection.—They seemed perfectly to understand me, and having recovered by degrees from their fear, they surrounded me; beckoning at the same time to one of a very large size, who, by the richness of his dress, I supposed to be the King, as indeed he afterwards proved to be.

They examined me and the machine for a considerable length of time, turning the latter round and round, and often lifting their eyes up to Heaven in great amazement. They spoke several words to me, the meaning of which I understood no more than they did my answers. The King finding no good was to be done that way, pointed to a building of a most tremendous size, though far from elegant, which was his palace, and immediately walked towards it, beckoning me to follow him; at the same time ordering one of his attendants to bring my machine after us.

We were conducted by his guards to the entrance of a large hall, at the further end of which was a place raised not unlike a throne; upon which, having seated himself, he made signs for me to sit down by the side of him, on a seat somewhat lower than his own.—The hall was immediately filled with all who could gain admission to see the wonderful stranger that had arrived amongst them; as well as to pay their court to the Prince. He smilled [smiled] upon all as they came near him; but what greatly surprized me (for I sat so as to see behind as well as before him) whilst he smiled upon some with his front face, and held out his hands (after the manner of the country) to be embraced by them, he at the same moment frowned with his hind face, bit his lips, and clinched his backward hands with the utmost marks of displeasure.—One in particular (a very *dark looking figure,*[1] having his face much covered with hair, with a shinning [shining] kind of a staff in his hand, of a colour not unlike gold, and whom I supposed, from the great respect paid him from every part of the

[1] Probably Lord Rockingham.

hall, to be his minister, or, as he is called here, Sublukarf, and in which conjecture I afterwards found myself not deceived) never approached him without his acting the double part just described; and once in particular, as he came up to him to communicate (seemingly) some matters of very great moment, he answered, and looked upon him more kindly than I had seen him do before; but, upon observing his hind face, I found it not only so much the more frowning, but the whole of the backward man was in consultation, with a very busy counsellor, who was kneeling down behind the throne, so as not to be perceived by the company; and by their often pointing to the *dark looking figure* with the staff, who stood before them, I judged they were plotting some mischief against him. My ignorance of their language alone prevented my doing more than conjecturing this, as they spoke sufficiently loud for me to overhear their conference. The courtiers, who were of very different sizes (their growth depending, as I was afterwards informed, upon the length of time they had been in the Fillifist or Sunshine, the effect of which upon them I shall hereafter more fully explain) having performed the Neeltokarf, or adoration of their King Hehehe Lob Jol-Teredd, as was their custom (which [the] name Jol-Teredd signifies, translated into our language, the WISE, *The Extender of the Empire;* he is also stiled by his subjects, amongst his other titles, Lobhy-fillifist, or Lord of the Sunshine.) . . .

CHAPTER III

The Author makes himself Master of the Language of the Country, and is enabled to give a further Account of the Court of King Hehehe Lob Jol-Teredd

As they have no night in the part of the country where I alighted, (unless that portion of time each devotes, as best suits his fancy, to sleep, may be stiled such,) I awaked in the same degree of light I went to rest in.

I immediately dressed myself, and was considering how to dispose of my time, when I heard a noise at the entrance of my room, which at first startled me; but, upon going towards it, I found my attendant there, who came to inform me of his readiness to wait upon me. Having thanked him for his willingness to serve me, I explained to him as well as I could how much I longed to be master of his language; he signified by signs in return, that he could present me with an instrument that would answer my purpose sufficiently for the present, till such time as I could speak off-hand,

and then pulled a kind of parchment from his bosom, filled with a list of characters and words, which he explained the meaning of to me by his gestures, (at which he was wonderfully expert) and by which I found, that their mode of conversing consisted chiefly in gestures; but was aided by a language somewhat similar to the Chinese (having no alphabet) but far more expressive than theirs; each word signifying as much as a whole sentence with us: and I afterwards found the common people comprehended every signe made to them with a readiness that astonished me. With the assistance of this list of words and characters, and his aid, he assured me that I should never be much at a loss, as they all, from the highest to the lowest, were compleat masters of conversing by gesticulation; of which I was soon after convinced, having seen several remarkable instances of it; one of which, for instance, the holding out one hand, and gently striking the palm of it with the thumb and fore finger of the other, without speaking a word, conveyed more meaning, and was more readily understood, than some hours conversation with us.[2] . . .

I spent about three hours with him in attaining those expressive motions; in which I became so expert, as to be able to convey my ideas pretty correctly.—I also learned many of their most significant words to accompany them; so that I rendered myself, in this short time, capable of asking many important questions; and was so pleased at my progress, that I instantly proposed waiting upon the King, and paying my respects to him; to which my attendant having consented, we immediately repaired thither.

On my arrival, the King expressed great pleasure at seeing me again, and I was so elated with the progress I had made in the language, that I could not help giving him a sample thereof; at which he seemed highly delighted, and cried out to my attendant three or four times, *Ouskin Pereskit,* that is, "He talks almost as well as we do. Spare no pains with him"; for two words of theirs (as I before observed) express as much as a whole sentence with us.

The King now informed me, he was going to the *Humdelbug,* or Hall of Audience, to receive the *Neeltokarf,* or adoration of his great men, and ordered me to attend him; although I much rather wished to have observed the country and the manners of the inhabitants, I thought it most prudent to smother my inclination for the present, and act according to his wishes.

We soon made our appearance there; and being placed as before, the King on his throne, and myself by the side of him on a seat somewhat lower; my eye was immediately struck with a set of faces quite different from those that were present on the former occasion: but my surprize was

[2] The reference is to the practice of tipping.

still greater, when I observed the very same person, who had been so exceedingly busy behind the throne, now appear before it; but grown to a very large size and holding the same shining staff the rough and hairy figure had before, and whom I no longer saw in the hall; and indeed the whole company was quite different.[3] This new Sublukarf, or Minister, no sooner approached Hehehe Lob Jol-Teredd, than he was received with the utmost joy; and when he had performed his Neeltokarf, or adoration, and retired to some distance, I heard the King repeat several times to himself, with great satisfaction, *Loobysit, Loobysit, Whomobase.* That is, *I have done it, I have done it. This man will do, he is after my own heart.* I looked immediately behind Hehehe Lob Jol-Teredd, expecting to see some counterplot to this scene, but was surprized to find both sides equally pleased.

Whilst I was musing upon this, a very loud kind of a murmur ran through the hall; and upon turning round, I saw a deal of fresh company coming in, whispering and pointing with great contempt and indignation at the new favourite with the staff; who no sooner perceived it than he began to tremble and turn pale; as did several others in the hall who stood round him, and with whom he had just been talking and laughing. The favourite quickly after approached King Hehehe Lob Jol-Teredd and gave up to him the staff he had so long enjoyed; at which, to my great surprize, he sunk down all at once to his former stature, amidst the derision of the whole company.[4] . . .

The *wise* King Hehehe Lob Jol-Teredd professed to be greatly pleased at what had happened; but upon surveying his other face, I found *that* told a very different story. His Majesty now broke up the assembly and retired to his private apartments; after having secretly dispatched a messenger after the late Sublukarf, to inform him that he wanted to see him in private. As I had been fearful of speaking to King Hehehe Lob Jol-Teredd in the midst of his disappointment, I neglected asking his permission to view the country and its inhabitants; but recollecting that the sending my interpreter with my request, would answer the same end, I sent him accordingly; who, after staying some time, returned, and brought me word, that the King was at present deeply engaged, but would consider my request as soon as the business was ended, and inform me of his pleasure.—I was much surprized at this, but my attendant informed me, that it was merely the cus-

[3] Probably a reference to the frequent turnover among English Prime Ministers—specifically, to Rockingham's replacement by Lord Shelburne.

[4] This refers to the 1783 take-over by the Fox-North alliance, which George III called the "most unprincipled coalition the annals of this or any other nation can equal."

tom of the Court; which never granted the most trifling request, without keeping the party that made it in waiting—waiting and supplication being deemed necessary appendages to the dignity of so great a King as Hehehe Lob Jol-Teredd.

CHAPTER IV

An account of the Georgium, or Neeltokarf Country, so named from the ancient Ceremony of adoring their Princes; with some Account of the Religion, Laws, Customs, &c. of the Inhabitants

As we were prevented going out of the palace of the great King Hehehe Lob Jol-Teredd, in consequence of the ceremony abovementioned, I thought I could not better employ my time, than in taking my interpreter to my apartment, and learning all I could of the country I was in, previous to my inspecting it. I first enquired, what was meant by King Hehehe Lob-Jol-Teredd's title of Lobhyfillifist, or Lord of the sunshine? and why the inhabitants grew larger or smaller as they were in or out of favour with him? To which he replied, than in their world, the whole of which was governed by Hehehe Lob Jol-Teredd, one half was constantly in the sunshine, call'd *Fillifist,*[5] (which answers to our word *Prosperity,*) and the other (except a glimmering kind of light, and a small degree of warmth near the edges of this sunshine) was nearly dark and very cold and uncomfortable; this he called *Grimollofist,* (which answers to our *Adversity.*) By which, I perceived, that their Planet constantly held the same face towards the sun, in its revolution round that body; in the same manner as the moon does to our earth. He added, that King Hehehe Lob Jol-Teredd, had the power of admitting into this Fillifist, or Sunshine, or expelling from it (though controlable in some particulars by the great men of the Fillifist) as many of his subjects as he pleased. What? exclaimed I, is it possible then, that there are inhabitants on the cold and dismal side of your world? Certainly, resumed he—and more than we have on this sunny side; the reason whereof is as follows: when the gracious King Hehehe Lob Jol-Teredd came to the throne, this sunny side was exceedingly populous, abounding in a smiling and happy people; for our former King took every step possible to bring what people there were on the *Grimollofist,* or dismal and gloomy side of

[5] Here is the reference to sunshine and prosperity that is a direct attack on the Civil List of George III.

our world into the shining and happy one; but our present sovereign (who is said to be very religious and virtuous) being willing to promote virtue amongst his subjects, which he thinks the Grimollofist, or Adversity side the best school for, (and, indeed, I believe there is more on that side than on this) has taken every method in his power to drive the people from this warm and comfortable side of Fillifist (or Prosperity) to the dismal one of Grimollofist (or Adversity); to answer the end abovementioned, or some other unknown to us. For this sunshine is of so nourishing a quality to our natures, that when transplanted from a cold situation into a warmer, we increase in size immediately, like plants, only with this difference, that when deprived again of the sunshine or Fillifist, we shrink into our former dimensions; for which reason, the Inhabitants of the other side of our globe, are a poor diminutive and feeble race. But the greatest degree of sunshine, is just round that spot where King Hehehe Lob Jol-Teredd holds his Court; for every particular *place* there, is made so as to reflect the beams of the sun strongly upon the favourite he puts into it, and answers the end of a hot-house; the Kneeltokarf placed there, quickly shooting up to a great height. Whoever he admits into the *place* of Sublukarf, or Minister, especially, encreases and rises to a height superior to any of them; and when turn'd out, or obliged to resign that warm and comfortable situation, he sinks again to his original lowness—of which you have just seen an instance—and which circumstance often happens, as there is a perpetual struggling amongst the great men of the Fillifist, or sunshine, for this place, and few remain long in it.

I thanked my companion for the very particular and curious account he had given me, and was preparing some fresh questions to put to him, when a messenger arrived from the King, with his permission for me to see the country. We sallied forth immediately, in consequence of our licence, and no sooner made our appearance out of the Palace, than we were surrounded by a number of the common people, who expressed great astonishment at the sight of me; but were no otherwise offensive than by staring rather too much; except a few of a more uncivil turn than the rest, who viewed me with no small degree of contempt, crying out to one another in an exulting tone, *Demegraff—Uniphiz*—that is, *What a wretched half-made figure this is! What good can the poor fellow think to do himself here, with only one face?* Not being quite master of what they said, I enquired of my interpreter, who after some hesitation, fearing I should be offended with them, informed me. I could not help smiling at their conceit, which only drew from them *Scumtocro!—Scumtocro!* that is, *Alas! poor wretch, he has but little reason to smile or rejoice!* However we marched on without paying any farther attention to their remarks; and here I could not help observing the decrease of the heat of the sunshine, as we encreased our distance from the Court; which convinced me of the truth of what my interpreter had just told me.

We were now upon the point of turning down one of the principal streets of the metropolis of Neeltokarf, when I observed a very large building with the door standing open; upon inquiring what place it was, and being informed it was one of the principal temples of the place, we went immediately into it. The people were in the midst of their devotions, each with one of his faces looking up to the sun (which they worshipped, and upon which they kept their eyes fixed, for there was no covering to the Temple) and the other face looking down to the earth, and (as my interpreter informed me) thinking upon the most likely means of rising into favour with Hehehe Lob Jol-Teredd; which mode of worship was constantly practised in their Temples; and in these acts consisted the whole religion of the country.

The Priest who was elevated above the rest, and was repeating prayers to the Sun, was busily employed, (as was evident from his other face, which was bent upon the ground) in thinking upon the same subject with the rest; and indeed (as my interpreter informed me) though he was a *Hympra Fillifist* (or Bishop), he was soliciting for the place of the late Graff Hympra Fillifist (or Archbishop) and it was thought, through the great interest he had, (though he had many competitors) he would succeed to it.

We now left the temple, where, though I attracted all the attention of the worshippers, I had no reason to think I lessened the devotion of their thoughts; and pursuing our way through another street, I was much entertained with observing the two different faces of each of those who were selling goods in their shops, their front faces having all the appearance of simplicity and honesty, whilst the backward ones were laughing at the imposition practicing upon the customers.

In other parts, many who were laying out their money, expressed much dissatisfaction of what they were buying, whilst their hind faces showed them to be highly pleased with their bargains.—As I stood at a shop door, looking at a similar scene to the first mentioned of these, the tradesman, as soon as he had dismissed his customers, invited me in to rest myself; which invitation I accepted, I could not help remarking, that it was well for him his customers could not look behind him whilst they dealt with him; he smiled and told me, there was no gaining a little of the Fillifist or Sunshine, without using two faces; and if I pleased to step with him to the top of the house, he would show me another who was of the same way of thinking with himself, though in a different line of business.

I accepted his invitation, and he conducted me into a kind of garret, where there was one writing very expeditiously; but what greatly surprized me was, he had a desk both before and behind him, and was writing at both at the same time. He rose as soon as we entered, but we having apologized for the interruption, and begged him to proceed, he, (after surveying me with no small surprize, and as I thought, some marks of contempt, making at the same time some inquiries relating to me) went to work again, both before and behind, writing at an incredible rate.

I inquired of our conductor, if he knew what subject he was upon, which being overheard by the writer, he addressed me thus; "No one can expect, in this our country of Neeltokarf, to live long in the Fillifist or Sunshine, without employing every advantage nature has given him on both sides.—One half only of those advantages I perceive, unhappily for you, has fallen to your share;—but to proceed, an event has lately fallen out in the Court of our Great King Hehehe Lob Jol-Teredd, which has occasioned a change of the Sublukarf or Minister, and thrown all the leading men of the Fillifist or Sunshine into a great ferment and controversy, and I am now employed in writing two pamphlets upon the occasion at the same time.—This before me, is an attack upon the late Sublukarf, and this behind me a defence of him.—They will both be out exactly the same time, and I have no doubt but they will pay me well, and keep me from quitting the Sunshine, which, without their assistance I shall be in danger of doing.—When I have finished them, one of each shall be at your service."

I thanked him very sincerely for his kind offer, and taking our leave of him and the tradesman, we pursued our rout through the other streets of the town; where I met with many curious circumstances, most of which I forbear mentioning least [lest] I should tire my readers. One of these I shall relate, however, though I would willingly suppress it, for the honour of the fair sex, (whom I highly esteem in every country) were I not urged on by that impartiality and regard to truth, every traveller should adhere to in his narrations, and which I have strictly observed, as must indeed be pretty conspicuous throughout the whole of this work.

Just as I got to the bottom of one of those streets that looked into the fields, I observed a female Neeltokarf, very neatly, and indeed genteelly dressed, being in what was the height of the fashion here, viz. the hair of the head as it were frized out to a great width at the top and each side of the head, so as to make quite a partition between the front and hind faces;

which, together with the clothes being extended on each side of the body like a fan, produced the appearance of two different people. This Lady was entertaining a lover, who was very eagerly kissing her hand, and vowing eternal constancy, (as I perceived by his often looking up to the Sun) sometimes dropping on his knees, and tempting her by all the arts he was master of, and by pointing to a Temple near at hand, to marry him; to which she with a very becoming reluctance, at length consented, and permitted him to step to the Temple (as I perceived by their motions) to prepare every thing ready for the solemnity.

I stood some time enjoying the felicity of this honest couple; when the lady happening to turn her other side to me, as he was taking his leave of her for the purpose abovementioned, I discovered that she had been entertaining another lover all the time on that side, to whom she was by no means so coy and bashful, but freely granted him liberties, the decorum of my pen forbids me to mention; they were both very well pleased with each other, and laughing at the simplicity of the poor Neeltokarf, who was just on the point of taking another squeeze of his mistresses hand, and setting off for the Temple with the greatest eagerness and joy.

I turned away, with no small displeasure, from this scene of duplicity, and pursued my rout into another quarter of the town, where the Snacklesee or Hall of Justice stood; Here I observed as much double dealing (as may easily be supposed) as in any part of the extensive city of the Neeltokarfs;—particularly in a Man of the Law, who stood near me, and was receiving a fee on one side, from a client, to forward his suit, and at the same moment accepting a double fee on the other, from his opponent to ruin it. After having visited the different Courts of Law then sitting, and made my remarks on them, as I meant next to take a view of the Grimollofist, or gloomy side of this World, I hastened home with all the speed I was master of, to prepare for my journey, and put my design into execution.

CHAPTER V

The Author gives King Hehehe Lob Jol-Teredd some Account of the World he came from, and sets out on his return Home

As soon as I got to my apartments, I committed to paper the remarks and minutes I had made in the courses of my excursion, upon the laws, learning, and other particulars of the Neeltokarfs. A full account of all which, (as it will require a considerable time to arrange,) I mean hereafter to present to the Public.

One part of the Constitution of this remarkable Planet, however, I cannot help mentioning here; which is, that they have a kind of Senate, composed of a few individuals, who represent the whole body of the inhabitants, and who, in conjunction with King Hehehe Lob Jol-Teredd, make the laws which govern the People at large; but who, in general, were so managed, as to act perfectly agreeable to the wishes of their King. These Delegates were very unequally chosen; some small and insignificant parts of the country, with scarce any inhabitants, sending more to this meeting, than tracts of country ten times as large and populous; and they were chiefly elected, by making use of that very expressive sign, we before mentioned; viz. the holding out one hand, and striking the palm of it with the thumb and fore finger of the other. But as I intend to give a more particular account of this meeting hereafter, I shall only add, that a rumour prevailed at this time, that the GREAT and WISE King Hehehe Lob Jol-Teredd meant to break up this assembly, and send the members of it to their respective districts, in consequence of their non-compliance with some violent and underhand measures he was pursuing.—This I say, was fully expected, as he had been heard to say in great anger that, he was *resolved to defend all his prerogatives to the utmost.*[6]

But this intended dissolution, it was said, notwithstanding, by those in the secret, could not take place, as the King had through his wild schemes and unbounded extravagance, too little chinkifist (or money) left in his Treasury, to accompany with sufficient efficacy the sign above alluded to: They therefore concluded, that this RASH step of his very experienced YOUNG Minister, would produce no other effect than that of encreasing the majority of voices against him.[7]

After I had finished my business I waited upon Hehehe Lob Jol-Teredd, who received me with a very pleasant countenance, and enquired very particularly what I had seen worthy of my notice; in answer to which, I gave him very faithfully the particulars of all I had observ'd. . . . Having answered to his satisfaction all the questions he proposed to me, I requested his permission to visit the Grimollofist, or dark side of his kingdom; but

[6] And so he—that is, George III—did. The Fox-North ministry lasted only eight months before it was defeated by George III and the King's Friends, many of them well paid from the Civil List while they remained in Parliament.

[7] The younger William Pitt was appointed Prime Minister after George defeated the Fox-North cabinet. Pitt was then twenty-five years old and had served in Parliament for only four years. In early 1784 he risked a general election and shocked the opposition by winning a solid majority in Parliament. Pitt's first ministry lasted seventeen years.

he endeavoured to dissuade me from my purpose, in so earnest a manner (for reasons best known to himself) that, finding the idea of my journey to that part so very disagreeable to him, I dropped all further thoughts of it, and desired permission to return home again to this world; which request he having cheerfully assented to, I went to work at my Balloon, to prepare it for the voyage and then giving notice of the time I meant to set off, I was accompanied by the King, his whole Court, and an immense crowd of the people, to the spot from whence I proposed taking my departure; and having finished myself with provisions and every thing necessary, I rose into the air amidst the shouts and acclamations of the whole assembly; and after meeting with nothing different from my former voyage, I arrived at my residence, not far from the city of Orleans, to the great joy and surprize of all my family.

Finis.

EDGAR ALLAN POE

Hans Phaall—A Tale (1835)

[In early August, 1835, the Richmond, Virginia, *Southern Literary Messenger* published what was intended to be Part I of a two-part story by Edgar Allan Poe. Three weeks later, the first installment of Richard Adams Locke's version of the tremendous discoveries by Sir John Herschel (reprinted in this volume) appeared in the New York Sun. Once he read Locke's story, Poe, who had recently joined the staff of the *Messenger* as an editor and reviewer, concluded that he could "add little to the minute and authentic account" and destroyed the second half of his "Hans Phaall" manuscript. Fortunately, the first half remains as a kind of landmark in the history of moon stories, and an engaging and insightful one at that.

Poe prepared for the Hans Phaall adventure by reading extensively in earlier works about the moon, including those of Godwin, Wilkins, and Cyrano de Bergerac. He dismissed most of these writings as potential patterns for his story on the ground that they were too implausible, but the reader will quickly note similarities between Hans Phaall and Cyrano de Bergerac in particular. Both Phaall and Cyrano begin their adventures on the first of April; both stories contain excellent nature descriptions; and, in both, the moon inhabitants sing rather than speak. Although "Hans Phaall" was pure fantasy, Poe acknowledged a great debt to scientific articles, especially the real Sir John Herschel's "Treatise on Astronomy," which had appeared in *Harper's* the previous spring.

To a generation that has witnessed an actual lunar landing, Poe's story seems amazingly prophetic. Although the basic vehicle is a rather simple balloon, the aeronaut experiences the effects of high elevation and decreased atmospheric pressure. He survives the rare atmosphere of space by devising an airtight compartment, or capsule, attached to the balloon and containing its own special atmospheric condenser for air supply. Perhaps most interesting are the descriptions of the earth recorded by Phaall during his ascent, which are remarkably similar to the reports of real-life space travelers.

Although "Hans Phaall" represents one of Poe's few attempts at humor, it nonetheless hints of his later, gloomier works. Phaall passes through a lightning cloud and then watches in horror as the cloud turns into a seething mass of electric fire, like the fires of hell. Mysterious and frightening crackling noises are discovered to be comets whose fiery paths threaten the very life of our hero. Even his landing on the moon becomes a desperate and frantic attempt to lighten the balloon sufficiently to keep it from smashing into the moon.

Thus, almost two hundred years after Domingo Gonsales launched his gansas and flew to the moon, men were still allowing their imaginations to carry them through the vastness of space to the unknown lunar world. After the publication of "Hans Phaall" and Locke's moon hoax, writers seemed to take increasing pains to make their stories plausible, weighing down their imaginations with the impediments of scientific and technological realities. Poe was among the last, and surely the best, of the romantic moon adventurers. This selection is reprinted from the original edition of the *Messenger* in the Rare Book Collection of the University of Pennsylvania, Philadelphia, Pennsylvania.]

By late accounts from Rotterdam that city seems to be in a singularly high state of philosophical excitement. Indeed phenomena have there occurred of a nature so completely unexpected, so entirely novel, so utterly at variance with preconceived opinions, as to leave no doubt on my mind that long ere this all Europe is in an uproar, all Physics in a ferment, all Dynamics and Astronomy together by the ears.

It appears that on the —— day of ——, (I am not positive about the date) a vast crowd of people, for purposes not specifically mentioned, were assembled in the great square of the Exchange in the goodly and well-conditioned city of Rotterdam. The day was warm—unusually so for the season—there was hardly a breath of air stirring, and the multitude were in no bad humor at being now and then besprinkled with friendly showers of momentary duration. These occasionally fell from large white masses of cloud which chequered in a fitful manner the blue vault of the firmament. Nevertheless about noon a slight but remarkable agitation became apparent in the assembly; the clattering of ten thousand tongues succeeded; and in an instant afterwards ten thousand faces were upturned towards the heavens, ten thousand pipes descended simultaneously from the corners of ten thousand mouths, and a shout which could be compared to nothing but the roaring of Niagara resounded long, loud, and furiously, through all the environs of Rotterdam.

The origin of this hubbub soon became sufficiently evident. From behind the huge bulk of one of those sharply-defined masses of cloud already mentioned, was seen slowly to emerge into an open area of blue space, a queer, heterogeneous, but apparently solid body or substance, so oddly shaped, so *outré* in appearance, so whimsically put together, as not to be in any manner comprehended, and never to be sufficiently admired by the host of sturdy burghers who stood open-mouthed and thunderstruck below. What could it be? In the name of all the vrows and devils in Rotterdam, what could it possibly portend? No one knew—no one could imagine—no one, not even the burgomaster Mynheer Superbus Von Underduk, had the slightest clue by which to unravel the mystery: so, as nothing more reasonable could be done, every one to a man replaced his pipe carefully in the left corner of his mouth, and, cocking up his right eye towards the phenomenon, puffed, paused, waddled about, and grunted significantly—then waddled back, grunted, paused, and finally—puffed again.

In the meantime, however, lower and still lower towards the goodly city, came the object of so much curiosity, and the cause of so much smoke. In a very few minutes it arrived near enough to be accurately discerned. It appeared to be—yes! it *was* undoubtedly a species of balloon: but surely no *such* balloon had ever been seen in Rotterdam before. For who, let me ask, ever heard of a balloon entirely manufactured of dirty newspapers?[1] No man in Holland certainly—yet here under the very noses of the people, or rather, so to speak, at some distance *above* their noses, was the identical thing in question, and composed, I have it on the best authority, of the precise material which no one had ever known to be used for a similar purpose. It was too bad—it was not to be borne: it was an insult—an egregious insult to the good sense of the burghers of Rotterdam. As to the shape of the phenomenon it was even still more reprehensible, being little or nothing better than a huge foolscap turned upside down. And this similitude was by no means lessened, when, upon nearer inspection, there

[1] Rotterdam was known as a city of numerous publications and little censorship.

was perceived a large tassel depending from its apex, and around the upper rim or base of the cone a circle of little instruments, resembling sheep-bells, which kept up a continual tinkling. . . . But still worse. Suspended by blue ribbands to the end of this fantastic machine, there hung by way of car an enormous drab beaver hat, with a brim superlatively broad, and a hemispherical crown with a black band and a silver buckle. It is, however, somewhat remarkable, that many citizens of Rotterdam swore to having seen the same hat before; and indeed the whole assembly seemed to regard it with eyes of familiarity, while the vrow Grettel Phaall, upon sight of it, uttered an exclamation of joyful surprise, and declared it to be the identical hat of her good man himself. Now this was a circumstance the more to be observed, as Phaall, with three companions, had actually disappeared from Rotterdam about five years before, in a very sudden and unaccountable manner, and up to the date of this narrative all attempts had failed of obtaining any intelligence concerning them whatsoever. To be sure, some bones which were thought to be human, and mixed up with a quantity of odd-looking rubbish, had been lately discovered in a retired situation to the east of Rotterdam; and some people went so far as to imagine that in this spot a foul murder had been committed, and that the sufferers were in all probability Hans Phaall and his associates. But to return.

The balloon, for such no doubt it was, had now descended to within a hundred feet of the earth, allowing the crowd below a sufficiently distinct view of the person of its occupant. This was in truth a very droll little somebody. He could not have been more than two feet in height—but this altitude, little as it was, would have been enough to destroy his equilibrium, and tilt him over the edge of his tiny car, but for the intervention of a circular rim reaching as high as the breast, and rigged on to the cords of the balloon. The body of the little man was more than proportionally broad, giving to his entire figure a rotundity highly grotesque. His feet, of course, could not be seen at all, although a horny substance of suspicious nature was occasionally protruded through a rent in the bottom of the car, or, to speak more properly, in the top of the hat. His hands were enormously large. His hair was extremely gray, and collected into a cue behind. His nose was prodigiously long, crooked and inflammatory—his eyes full, brilliant, and acute—his chin and cheeks, although wrinkled with age, were broad, puffy, and double—but of ears of any kind or character, there was not a semblance to be discovered upon any portion of his head. This odd little gentleman was dressed in a loose surtout [coat] of sky-blue satin, with tight breeches to match, fastened with silver buckles at the knees. His vest was of some bright yellow material; a white taffety cap was set jauntily on one side of his head; and, to complete his equipment, a blood red silk handkerchief enveloped his throat, and fell down, in a dainty manner, upon his bosom in a fantastic bow-knot of super-eminent dimensions.

Having descended, as I said before, to about one hundred feet from the surface of the earth, the little old gentleman was suddenly seized with a fit of trepidation, and appeared altogether disinclined to make any nearer approach to *terra firma*. Throwing out, therefore, a quantity of sand from a canvass bag, which he lifted with great difficulty, he became stationary in an instant. He then proceeded, in a hurried and agitated manner, to extract from a side pocket of his surtout a large morocco pocket-book. This he poised suspiciously in his hand—then eyed it with an air of extreme surprise, and was evidently astonished at its weight. He at length opened it, and, drawing therefrom a huge letter sealed with red sealing-wax, and tied carefully with red tape, let it fall precisely at the feet of the burgomaster Superbus Von Underduk. His Excellency stooped to take it up. But the aeronaut, still greatly discomposed, and having apparently no farther business to detain him in Rotterdam, began at this moment to make busy preparations for departure; and, it being necessary to discharge a portion of ballast to enable him to re-ascend, the half dozen bags of sand which he threw out, one after another, without taking the trouble to empty their contents, tumbled every one of them, most unfortunately, upon the back of the burgomaster, and rolled him over and over no less than one and twenty times, in the face of every man in Rotterdam. It is not to be supposed, however, that the great Underduk suffered this impertinence on the part of the little old man to pass off with impunity. It is said, on the contrary, that, during the period of each and every one of his one and twenty circumvolutions, he emitted no less than one and twenty distinct and furious whiffs from his pipe, to which he held fast the whole time with all his might, and to which he intends holding fast until the day of his death.

In the meantime the balloon arose like a larke, and, soaring far away above the city, at length drifted quietly behind a cloud similar to that from which it had so oddly emerged, and was thus lost forever to the wondering eyes of the good citizens of Rotterdam. All attention was now directed to the letter, whose descent and the consequences attending thereupon had proved so fatally subversive of both person and personal dignity, to his Excellency the illustrious burgomaster Mynheer Superbus Von Underduk. That functionary, however, had not failed, during his circumgyratory movement, to bestow a thought upon the important object of securing the packet in question, which was seen, upon inspection, to have fallen into the most proper hands, being actually directed to himself and Professor

Rub-a-dub, in their official capacities of President and Vice-President of the Rotterdam College of Astronomy. It was accordingly opened by those dignitaries upon the spot, and found to contain the following extraordinary and indeed very serious communication.

"To their Excellencies Von Underduk and Rub-a-dub, President, and Vice-President of the States' College of Astronomers in the city of Rotterdam.

"Your Excellencies may perhaps be able to remember an humble artizan by name Hans Phaall, and by occupation a mender of bellows, who, with three others, disappeared from Rotterdam, about five years ago, in a manner which must have been considered by all parties at once sudden, and extremely unaccountable. If, however, it so please your Excellencies, I, the writer of this communication, am the identical Hans Phaall himself. It is well known to most of my fellow citizens, that for the period of forty years, I continued to occupy the little square brick building at the head of the alley called Sauerkraut, and in which I resided at the time of my disappearance. My ancestors have also resided therein time out of mind, they, as well as myself, steadily following the respectable and indeed lucrative profession of mending of bellows. For, to speak the truth, until of late years that the heads of all the people have been set agog with the troubles and politics, no better business than my own could an honest citizen of Rotterdam either desire or deserve. Credit was good, employment was never wanting, and on all hands there was no lack of either money or good will. But, as I was saying, we soon began to feel the terrible effects of liberty, and long speeches, and radicalism, and all that sort of thing. People who were formerly the very best customers in the world had now not a moment of time to think of us at all. They had, so they said, as much as they could do to read about the revolutions, and keep up with the march of intellect, and the spirit of the age. If a fire wanted fanning it could readily be fanned with a newspaper; and, as the government grew weaker, I have no doubt that leather and iron acquired durability in proportion, for in a very short time there was not a pair of bellows in all Rotterdam that ever stood in need of a stitch or required the assistance of a hammer. This was a state of things not to be endured. I soon grew as poor as a rat, and, having a wife and children to provide for, my burdens at length became intolerable, and I spent hour after hour in reflecting upon the speediest and most convenient method of putting an end to my life. Duns, in the meantime left me little leisure for contemplation. My house was literally besieged from morning till night, so that I began to rave, and foam, and fret like a caged tiger against the bars of his enclosure. There were three fellows in particular, who worried me beyond endurance, keeping watch continually about my door, and threatening me with the utmost severity of the law. Upon these three I internally vowed the bitterest revenge, if ever I should be so happy as to get them within my clutches, and I believe nothing in the world but the pleasure of this anticipation prevented me from putting my plan of suicide into immediate execution, by blowing my brains out with a blunderbuss. I thought it best, however, to dissemble my wrath, and to treat them with promises and fair words, until, by some good turn of fate, an opportunity of vengeance should be afforded me.

"One day, having given my creditors the slip, and feeling more than usually dejected, I continued for a long time to wander about the most obscure streets without any object whatever, until at length I chanced to stumble against the corner of a bookseller's stall. Seeing a chair close at hand, for the use of customers, I threw myself doggedly into it, and hardly knowing why, opened the pages of the first volume which came within my reach. It proved to be a small pamphlet treatise on Speculative Astronomy, written either by Professor Encke of Berlin, or by a Frenchman of somewhat similar name. I had some little tincture of information on matters of this nature, and soon became more and more absorbed in the contents of the book, reading it actually through twice before I awoke, as it were, to a recollection of what was passing around me. By this time it began to grow dark, and I directed my steps towards home. . . .

"It was late when I reached home, and I went immediately to bed. My mind, however, was too much occupied to sleep, and I lay the whole night buried in meditation. Arising early in the morning, and contriving again to escape the vigilance of my creditors, I repaired eagerly to the bookseller's stall, and laid out what little ready money I possessed, in the purchase of some volumes of Mechanics and Practical Astronomy. Having arrived at home safely with these, I devoted every spare moment to their perusal, and soon made such proficiency in studies of this nature as I thought sufficient for the execution of my plan. In the intervals of this period I made every endeavor to conciliate the three creditors who had given me so much annoyance. In this I finally succeeded—partly by selling enough of my household furniture to satisfy a moiety of their claim, and partly by a promise of paying the balance upon completion of a little project which I told them I had in view, and for assistance in which I solicited their services. By these means—for they were ignorant men—I found little difficulty in gaining them over to my purpose.

"Matters being thus arranged, I contrived, by the aid of my wife, and with the greatest secrecy and caution, to dispose of what property I had remaining, and to borrow, in small sums, under various pretences, and without paying any attention to my future means of repayment, no inconsiderable quantity of ready money. With the means thus accruing I proceeded to purchase at intervals, cambric muslin, very fine, in pieces of twelve yards each—twine—a lot of the varnish of caoutchouc [crude rubber]—a large and deep basket of wicker-work, made to order—and several other articles necessary in the construction and equipment of a balloon of extraordinary dimensions. This I directed my wife to make up as soon as possible, and gave her all requisite information as to the particular method of proceeding. In the meantime I worked up the twine into a net-work of sufficient dimensions, rigged it with a hoop and the necessary cords, bought a quadrant, a compass, a spy-glass, a common barometer with some important modifications, and two astronomical instruments not so generally known. I then took opportunities of conveying by night, to a retired situation east of Rotterdam, five iron-bound casks, to contain about fifty gallons each, and one of a larger size—six tinned war tubes, three inches in diameter, properly shaped, and ten feet in length—a quantity of *a particular metallic substance or semi-metal* which I shall not name—and a dozen demijohns of *a very common acid*. The gas to be formed from these latter materials is a gas never yet generated by any other person than myself—or at least never applied to any similar purpose. . . .

"On the spot which I intended each of the smaller casks to occupy respectively during the inflation of the balloon, I privately dug a hole two feet deep—the holes forming in this manner a circle of twenty-five feet in diameter. In the centre of this circle, being the station designed for the large cask, I also dug a hole three feet in depth. In each of the five smaller holes, I deposited a canister containing fifty pounds, and in the larger one a keg holding one hundred and fifty pounds of cannon powder. These—the keg and the canisters—I connected in a proper manner with covered trains; and having let into one of the canisters the end of about four feet of slow-match, I covered up the hole, and placed the cask over it, leaving the other end of the match protruding about an inch, and barely visible beyond the cask. I then filled up the remaining holes, and placed the barrels over them in their destined situation.

"Besides the articles above enumerated, I conveyed to the depot, and there secreted one of M. Grimm's improvements upon the apparatus for condensation of the atmospheric air. I found this machine, however, to require considerable alteration before it could be adapted to the purposes to which I intended making it applicable. But with severe labor, and unremitting perseverance, I at length met with entire success in all my preparations. My balloon was soon completed. It would contain more than forty thousand cubic feet of gas; would take me up, I calculated, easily with all my implements, and, if I managed rightly with one hundred and seventy-five pounds of ballast into the bargain. It had received three coats of varnish, and I found the cambric muslin to answer all the purposes of silk itself—quite as strong and a good deal less expensive.

"Every thing being now ready, I exacted from my wife an oath of secrecy in relation to all my actions from the day of my first visit to the bookseller's stall, and, promising, on my part, to return as soon as circumstances would admit, I gave her all the money I had left, and bade her farewell. Indeed I had little fear on her account. She was what people call a notable woman, and could manage matters in the world without my assistance. I believe, to tell the truth, she always looked upon me as an idle body, a mere makeweight, good for nothing but building castles in the air, and was rather glad to get rid of me. It was a dark night when I bade her good bye, and, taking with me, as *aides-de-camp,* the three creditors who had given me so much trouble, we carried the balloon, with the car and accoutrements, by a roundabout way, to the station where the other articles were deposited. We there found them all unmolested, and I proceeded immediately to business.

"It was the first of April. The night, as I said before, was dark—there was not a star to be seen, and a drizzling rain falling at intervals rendered us very uncomfortable. . . .

"In about four hours and a half I found the balloon sufficiently inflated. I attached the car therefore, and put all my implements in it—not forgetting the condensing apparatus, a copious supply of water, and a large quantity of provisions, such as pemmican, in which much nutriment is contained in comparatively little bulk. . . . It was now nearly day-break, and I thought it high time to take departure. Dropping a lighted cigar on the ground, as if by accident, I took the opportunity, in stooping to pick it up, of igniting privately the piece of slow match, whose end, as I said before, protruded a very little beyond the lower rim of one of the smaller casks. This manoeuvre was totally unperceived on the part of the three duns, and, jumping into the car, I immediately cut the single cord which held me to the earth, and was pleased to find that I shot upwards, rapidly carrying with all ease one hundred and seventy-five pounds of leaden ballast, and able to have carried up as many more.

"Scarcely, however, had I attained the height of fifty yards, when, roaring and rumbling up after me in the most horrible and tumultuous manner, came so dense a hurricane of fire, and smoke, and sulphur, and legs and arms, and gravel, and burning wood, and blazing metal, that my very heart sunk within me, and I fell down in the bottom of the car, trembling with unmitigated terror. Indeed I now perceived that I had entirely overdone the business, and that the main consequences of the shock were yet to be experienced. Accordingly, in less than a second, I felt all the blood in my body rushing to my temples, and, immediately thereupon, a concussion, which I shall never forget, burst abruptly through the night, and seemed to rip the very firmament asunder. When I afterwards had time for reflection, I did not fail to attribute the extreme violence of the explosion, as regarded myself, to its proper cause—my situation directly above it, and in the exact line of its greatest power. But at the time I thought only of preserving my life. The balloon at first collapsed—then furiously expanded—then whirled round and round with horrible velocity—and finally, reeling and staggering like a drunken man, hurled me with great force over the rim of the car, and left me dangling, at a terrific height, with my head downwards, and my face outwards from the balloon, by a piece of slender cord about three feet in length, which hung accidentally through a crevice near the bottom of the wicker-work, and in which, as I fell, my left foot became most providentially entangled. It is impossible—utterly impossible—to form any adequate idea of the horror of my situation. I gasped convulsively for breath—a shudder resembling a fit of the ague agitated every nerve and muscle in my frame—I felt my eyes starting from their sockets—a horrible nausea overwhelmed me—my brain reeled—and I fainted away.

. . . .

". . . But this weakness was, luckily for me, of no very long duration. In good time came to my rescue the spirit of despair, and amid horrible curses and convulsive struggles, I jerked my way bodily upwards, till at length, clutching with a vice-like grip the long-desired rim, I writhed my person over it, and fell headlong and shuddering within the car. It was not until sometime afterwards that I recovered myself sufficiently to attend to the ordinary cares of the balloon. I then, however, examined it with attention, and found it, to my great relief, uninjured. My implements were all safe, and I had fortunately lost neither ballast nor provisions. Indeed, I had so well secured them in their places, that such an accident was entirely out of the question. Looking at my watch, I found it six o'clock. I was still rapidly ascending, and my barometer showed a present altitude of three and three quarter miles. Immediately beneath me in the ocean, lay a small black object, slightly oblong in shape, seemingly about the size, and in every way bearing a great semblance to one of those childish toys called a domino. Bringing my spy-glass to bear upon it, I plainly discerned it to be a British ninety-four gun ship, close-hauled, and pitching heavily in the sea with her head to the W. S. W. Besides this ship, I saw nothing but the ocean and the sky, and the sun, which had long arisen.

"It is now high time that I should explain to your Excellencies the object of my perilous voyage. Your Excellencies will bear in mind, that distressed circumstances in Rotterdam, had at length driven me to the resolution of committing suicide. It was not, however, that to life itself I had any positive disgust—but that I was harassed beyond endurance by the adventitious miseries attending my situation. In this state of mind—wishing to live, yet wearied with life—the treatise at the stall of the bookseller opened a resource to my imagination. I then finally made up my mind. I determined to depart, yet live—to leave the world, yet continue to exist—in short, to drop enigmas, I resolved, let what would ensue, to force a passage, if I could—to the moon. . . .

. . . .

". . . I shall now proceed to lay before you, the result of an attempt so apparently audacious in conception, and, at all events, so utterly unparalleled in the annals of human kind.

"Having attained the altitude before mentioned, that is to say, three miles and three quarters, I threw out from the car a quantity of feathers, and found that I still ascended with sufficient rapidity—there was, therefore, no necessity for discharging any ballast. I was glad of this, for I wished to retain with me as much weight as I could carry, for reasons which will be explained in the sequel. I as yet suffered no bodily inconvenience, breathing with great freedom, and feeling no pain whatever in the head. . . .

"At twenty minutes past six o'clock, the barometer showed an elevation of 26,400 feet, or five miles to a fraction. The prospect seemed unbounded. . . . The sea appeared unruffled as a mirror, although, by means of the spy-glass, I could perceive it to be in a state of violent agitation. The ship was no longer visible, having drifted away, apparently, to the eastward. I now began to experience, at intervals, severe pain in the head, especially about the ears—still, however, breathing with tolerable freedom. . . .

"At twenty minutes before seven, the balloon entered within a long series of dense cloud, which put me to great trouble, by damaging my condensing apparatus, and wetting me to the skin. This was, to be sure, a singular *rencontre,* for I had not believed it possible that a cloud of this nature could be sustained at so great an elevation. I thought it best, however, to throw out two five-pound pieces of ballast, reserving still a weight of one hundred and sixty-five pounds. Upon so doing, I soon rose above the difficulty, and perceived immediately, that I had obtained a great increase in my rate of ascent. In a few seconds after my leaving the cloud, a flash of vivid lightning shot from one end of it to the other, and caused it to kindle up, throughout its vast extent, like a mass of ignited and glowing charcoal. This, it must be remembered, was in the broad light of day. No fancy may picture the sublimity which might have been exhibited by a similar phenomenon taking place amid the darkness of the night. Hell itself might then have found a fitting image. Even as it was, my hair stood on end, while I gazed afar down within the yawning abysses, letting imagination descend, as it were, and stalk about in the strange vaulted halls, and ruddy gulfs, and red ghastly chasms of the hideous, and unfathomable fire. I had indeed made a narrow escape. Had the balloon remained a very short while longer within the cloud—that is to say—had not the inconvenience of getting wet determined me to discharge the ballast, inevitable ruin would have been the consequence. Such perils, although little considered, are perhaps the greatest which must be encountered in balloons. I had by this time, however, attained too great an elevation to be any longer uneasy on this head.

"I was now rising rapidly, and by seven o'clock the barometer indicated an altitude of no less than nine miles and a half. I began to find great difficulty in drawing my breath. My head too was excessively painful; and, having felt for some time a moisture about my cheeks, I at length discovered it to be blood, which was oozing quite fast from the drums of my ears. My eyes, also, gave me great uneasiness. Upon passing the hand over them they seemed to have protruded from their sockets in no inconsiderable degree, and all objects in the car, and even the balloon itself, appeared distorted to my vision. These symptoms were more than I had expected, and occasioned me some alarm. At this juncture, very imprudently and without consideration, I threw out from the car three five pound pieces of ballast. The accelerated rate of ascent thus obtained carried me too rapidly, and without sufficient gradation, into a highly rarefied stratum of the atmosphere, and the result had nearly proved fatal to my expedition and to myself. I was suddenly seized with a spasm which lasted for better than five minutes, and even when this, in a measure, ceased, I could catch my breath only at long intervals, and in a gasping manner—bleeding all the while copiously at the nose and ears, and even slightly at the eyes. . . . I now too late discovered the great rashness I had been guilty of in discharging the ballast, and my agitation was excessive. I anticipated nothing less than death, and death in a few minutes. The physical suffering I underwent contributed also to render me nearly incapable of making any exertion for the preservation of my life. I had, indeed, little power of reflection left, and the violence of the pain in my head seemed to be greatly on the increase. Thus I found that my senses would shortly give way altogether, and I had already clutched one of the valve ropes with the view of attempting a descent, when the recollection of the trick I had played the three creditors, and the inevitable consequences to myself, should I return to Rotterdam, operated to deter me for the moment. I lay down in the bottom of the car, and endeavored to collect my faculties. In this I so far succeeded as to determine upon the experiment of losing blood. Having no lancet, however, I was constrained to perform the operation in the best manner I was able, and finally succeeded in opening a vein in my right arm, with the blade of my penknife. The blood had hardly commenced flowing when I experienced a sensible relief, and by the time I had lost about half a moderate basin full, most of the worst symptoms had abandoned me entirely. I nevertheless did not think it expedient to attempt getting on my feet immediately; but, having tied up my arm as well as I could, I lay still for about a quarter of an hour. At the end of this time I arose, and found myself freer from absolute *pain* of any kind than I had been during the last hour and a quarter of my ascension. The difficulty of breathing, however, was diminished in a very slight degree, and I found that it would soon be positively necessary to make use of my condenser. . . .

"By eight o'clock I had actually attained an elevation of seventeen miles above the surface of the earth. Thus it seemed to me evident that my rate of ascent was not only on the increase, but that the progression would have been apparent in a slight degree even had I not discharged the ballast which I did. The pains in my head and ears returned, at intervals, with violence, and I still continued to bleed occasionally at the nose: but, upon the whole, I suffered much less than might have been expected. I breathed, however, at every moment, with more and more difficulty, and each inhalation was attended with a troublesome spasmodic action of the chest. I now unpacked the condensing apparatus, and got it ready for immediate use. The view of the earth, at this period of my ascension, was beautiful indeed. To the westward, the northward, and the southward, as far as I could see, lay a boundless sheet of apparently unruffled ocean, which every moment gained a deeper and a deeper tint of blue, and began already to assume a slight appearance of convexity. At a vast distance to the eastward, although perfectly discernible, extended the islands of Great Britain, the entire Atlantic coast of France and Spain, with a small portion of the northern part of the continent of Africa. Of individual edifices not a trace could be discovered, and the proudest cities of mankind had utterly faded away from the face of the earth. From the rock of Gibraltar, now dwindled into a dim speck, the dark Mediterranean sea, dotted with shining islands as the heaven is dotted with stars, spread itself out to the eastward as far as my vision extended, until its entire mass of waters seemed at length to tumble headlong over the abyss of the horizon, and I found myself listening on tiptoe for the echoes of the mighty cataract.

. . . .

"At a quarter past eight, being able no longer to draw breath at all without the most intolerable pain, I proceeded, forthwith, to adjust around the car the apparatus belonging to the condenser. This apparatus will require some little explanation, and your Excellencies will please to bear in mind that my object, in the first place, was to surround myself and car entirely with a barricade against the highly rarefied atmosphere in which I was existing—with the intention of introducing within this barricade, by means of my condenser, a quantity of this same atmosphere sufficiently condensed for the purposes of respiration. With this object in view I had prepared a very strong, perfectly air-tight, but flexible gum-elastic bag. In this bag, which was of sufficient dimensions, the entire car was in a manner placed. That is to say, it (the bag) was drawn over the whole bottom of the car—up its sides—and so on, along the outside of the ropes, to the upper rim or hoop where the net-work is attached. Having pulled the bag up in this way, and formed a complete enclosure on all sides, and at bottom, it was now necessary to fasten up its top or mouth, by passing its material over the hoop of the net-work—in other words between the net-work and the hoop. But if the net-work was separated from the hoop to admit this passage, what was to sustain the car in the meantime? Now the net-work was not permanently fastened to the hoop, but attached by a series of running loops or nooses. I therefore undid only a few of these loops at one time, leaving the car suspended by the remainder. Having thus inserted a portion of the cloth forming the upper part of the bag, I re-fastened the loops—not to the hoop, for that would have been impossible, since the cloth now intervened,—but to a series of large buttons, affixed to the cloth itself, about three feet below the mouth of the bag—the intervals between the buttons having been made to correspond to the intervals between the loops. This done, a few more of the loops were unfastened from the rim, a farther portion of the cloth introduced, and the disengaged loops then connected with their proper buttons. In this way it was possible to insert the whole upper part of the bag between the net-work and the hoop. It is evident that the hoop would now drop down within the car, while the whole weight of the car itself, with all its contents, would be held up merely by the strength of the buttons. This, at first sight, would seem an inadequate dependence, but it was by no means so, for the buttons were not only very strong in themselves, but so close together that a very slight portion of the whole weight was supported by any one of them. Indeed had the car and contents been three times heavier than they were, I should not have been at all uneasy. I now raised up the hoop again within the covering of gum-elastic, and propped it at nearly its former height by means of three light poles prepared for the occasion. This was done, of course, to keep the bag distended at the top, and to preserve the lower part of the net-work in its proper situation. All that now remained was to fasten up the mouth of the enclosure; and this was readily accomplished by gathering the folds of the material together, and twisting them up very tightly on the inside by means of a kind of stationary tourniquet.

"In the sides of the covering thus adjusted round the car, had been inserted three circular panes of thick but clear glass, through which I could see without difficulty around me in every horizontal direction. In that portion of the cloth forming the bottom, was likewise a fourth window, of the same kind, and corresponding with a small aperture in the floor of the car itself. This enabled me to see perpendicularly down, but having found it impossible to place any similar contrivance overhead, on account of the peculiar manner of closing up the opening there, and the consequent wrinkles in the cloth, I could expect to see no objects situated directly in my zenith. This, of course, was a matter of little consequence—for, had I even been able to place a window at top, the balloon itself would have prevented my making any use of it.

"About a foot below one of the side windows was a circular opening eight inches in diameter, and fitted with a brass rim adapted in its inner edge to the winding of a screw. In this rim was screwed the large tube of the condenser, the body of the machine being, of course, within the chamber of gum-elastic. Through this tube a quantity of the rare atmosphere circumjacent being drawn by means of a vacuum created in the body of the machine, was thence discharged in a state of condensation to mingle with the thin air already in the chamber. This operation, being repeated several times, at length filled the chamber with atmosphere proper for all the purposes of respiration. But in so confined a space it would in a short time necessarily become foul, and unfit for use from frequent contact with the lungs. It was then ejected by a small valve at the bottom of the car —the dense air readily sinking into the thinner atmosphere below. To avoid the inconvenience of making a total *vacuum* at any moment within the chamber this purification was never accomplished all at once, but in a gradual manner,—the valve being opened only for a few seconds, then closed again, until one or two strokes from the pump of the condenser had supplied the place of the atmosphere ejected. . . .

"By the time I had fully completed these arrangements and filled the chamber as explained, it wanted only ten minutes of nine o'clock. During the whole period of my being thus employed I endured the most terrible distress from difficulty of respiration, and bitterly did I repent the negligence, or rather foolhardiness, of which I had been guilty in putting off to the very last moment a matter of so much importance. But having at length accomplished it, I soon began to reap the benefit of my invention. Once again I breathed with perfect freedom and ease—and indeed why should I not? I was also agreeably surprised to find myself, in a great measure, relieved from the violent pains which had hitherto tormented me. A slight headach[e], accompanied with a sensation of fulness or distension about the wrists, the ancles, and the throat, was nearly all of which I had now to complain. Thus it seemed evident that a greater part of the uneasiness attending the removal of atmospheric pressure had actually *worn off,* as I had expected, and that much of the pain endured for the last two hours should have been attributed altogether to the effects of a deficient respiration.

"At twenty minutes before nine o'clock—that is to say—a short time prior to my closing up the mouth of the chamber, the mercury attained its limit, or ran down, in the barometer, which, as I mentioned before, was one of an extended construction. It then indicated an altitude on my part of 132,000 feet, or five and twenty miles, and I consequently surveyed at that time an extent of the earth's area amounting to no less than the three-hundred-and-twentieth part of its entire superficies. At nine o'clock I had again entirely lost sight of land to the eastward, but not before I became fully aware that the balloon was drifting rapidly to the N. N. W. The convexity of the ocean beneath me was very evident indeed—although my view was often interrupted by the masses of cloud which floated to and fro. I observed now that even the lightest vapors never rose to more than ten miles above the level of the sea.

"At half past nine I tried the experiment of throwing out a handful of feathers through the valve. They did not float as I had expected—but dropped down perpendicularly, like a bullet, *en masse,* and with the greatest velocity—being out of sight in a very few seconds. I did not at first know what to make of this extraordinary phenomenon: not being able to believe that my rate of ascent had, of a sudden, met with so prodigious an acceleration. But it soon occurred to me that the atmosphere was now far too rare to sustain even the feathers—that they actually fell, as they appeared to do, with great rapidity—and that I had been surprised by the united velocities of their descent and my own elevation.

"By ten o'clock I found that I had very little to occupy my immediate attention. Affairs went on swimmingly, and I believed the balloon to be going upwards with a speed increasing momentarily, although I had no longer any means of ascertaining the progression of the increase. I suffered no pain or uneasiness of any kind, and enjoyed better spirits than I had at any period since my departure from Rotterdam, busying myself now in examining the state of my various apparatus, and now in regenerating the atmosphere within the chamber. This latter point I determined to attend to at regular intervals of forty minutes, more on account of the preservation of my health, than from so frequent a renovation being absolutely necessary. In the meanwhile I could not help making anticipations. Fancy revelled in the wild and dreamy regions of the moon. Imagination, feeling herself for once unshackled, roamed at will among the ever-changing wonders of a shadowy and unstable land. Now there were hoary and time-honored forests, and craggy precipices, and waterfalls tumbling with a loud noise into abysses without a bottom. Then I came suddenly into still noon-day solitudes where no wind of heaven ever intruded, and where vast meadows of poppies, and slender, lily-looking flowers spread themselves out a weary distance, all silent and motionless forever. Then again I journeyed far down away into another country where it was all one dim and vague lake, with a boundary-line of clouds. And out of this melancholy water arose a forest of tall eastern trees, like a wilderness of dreams. And I bore in mind that the shadows of the trees which fell upon the lake remained not on the surface where they fell—but sunk slowly and steadily down, and commingled with the waves, while from the trunks of the trees other shadows were continually coming out, and taking the place of their brothers thus entombed. 'This then,' I said thoughtfully, 'is the very reason why the waters of this lake grow blacker with age, and more melancholy as the hours run on.' But fancies such as these were not the sole possessors of my brain. Horrors of a nature most stern and most appaling would too frequently obtrude themselves upon my mind, and shake the innermost depths of my soul with the bare supposition of their possibility. Yet I would not suffer my thoughts for any length of time to dwell upon these latter speculations, rightly judging the real and palpable dangers of the voyage sufficient for my undivided attention.

. . . .

"At six o'clock I perceived a great portion of the earth's visible area to the eastward involved in thick shadow, which continued to advance with great rapidity until, at five minutes before seven, the whole surface in view was enveloped in the darkness of night. It was not, however, until long after this time that the rays of the setting sun ceased to illumine the balloon; and this circumstance, although of course fully anticipated, did not fail to give me an infinite deal of pleasure. It was evident that, in the morning, I should behold the rising luminary many hours at least before the citizens of Rotterdam, in spite of their situation so much farther to the eastward, and thus, day after day, in proportion to the height ascended, would I enjoy the light of the sun for a longer and a longer period. I now determined to keep a journal of my passage, reckoning the days from one to twenty-four hours continuously, without taking into consideration the intervals of darkness.

. . . .

"April 3d. I found the balloon at an immense height indeed, and the earth's apparent convexity increased in a material degree. Below me in the ocean lay a cluster of black specks, which undoubtedly were islands. Far away to the northward I perceived a thin, white, and exceedingly brilliant line or streak on the edge of the horizon, and I had no hesitation in supposing it to be the southern disk of the ices of the Polar sea. My curiosity was greatly excited, for I had hopes of passing on much farther to the north, and might possibly, at some period, find myself placed directly above the Pole itself. I now lamented that my great elevation would, in this case, prevent my taking as accurate a survey as I could wish. Much however might be ascertained. Nothing else of an extraordinary nature occurred during the day. My apparatus all continued in good order, and the balloon still ascended without any perceptible vacillation. The cold was intense, and obliged me to wrap up closely in an overcoat. When darkness came over the earth, I betook myself to bed, although it was for many hours afterwards broad daylight all around my immediate situation. . . .

"April 4th. Arose in good health and spirits, and was astonished at the singular change which had taken place in the appearance of the sea. It had lost, in a great measure, the deep tint of blue it had hitherto worn, being

now of a grayish white, and of a lustre dazzling to the eye. The islands were no longer visible—whether they had passed down the horizon to the southeast, or whether my increasing elevation had left them out of sight, it is impossible to say. I was inclined however, to the latter opinion. The rim of ice to the northward, was growing more and more apparent. Cold by no means intense. Nothing of importance occurred, and I passed the day in reading—having taken care to supply myself with books.

"*April 5th.* Beheld the singular phenomenon of the sun rising while nearly the whole visible surface of the earth continued to be involved in darkness. In time, however, the light spread itself over all, and I again saw the line of ice to the northward. It was now very distinct and appeared of a much darker hue than the waters of the ocean. I was evidently approaching it, and with great rapidity. Fancied I could again distinguish a strip of land to the eastward—and one also to the westward—but could not be certain. Weather moderate. Nothing of any consequence happened during the day. Went early to bed.

"*April 6th.* Was surprised at finding the rim of ice at a very moderate distance, and an immense field of the same material stretching away off to the horizon in the north. It was evident that if the balloon held its present course, it would soon arrive above the Frozen Ocean, and I had now little doubt of ultimately seeing the Pole. During the whole of the day I continued to near the ice. Towards night the limits of my horizon very suddenly and materially increased, owing undoubtedly to the earth's form being that of an oblate spheroid, and my arriving above the flattened regions in the vicinity of the Arctic circle. When darkness at length overtook me I went to bed in great anxiety, fearing to pass over the object of so much curiosity when I should have no opportunity of observing it.

"*April 7th.* Arose early, and, to my great joy, at length beheld what there could be no hesitation in supposing the northern Pole itself. It was there, beyond a doubt, and immediately beneath my feet—but, alas! I had now ascended to so vast a distance that nothing could with accuracy be discerned. Instead, to judge from the progression of the numbers indicating my various altitudes respectively at different periods, between six A.M. on the second of April, and twenty minutes before nine A.M. of the same day, (at which time the barometer ran down) it might be fairly inferred that the balloon had now, at four o'clock in the morning of April the seventh, reached a height of *not less* certainly than 7254 miles above the surface of the sea. This elevation may appear immense, but the estimate upon which it is calculated gave a result in all probability far inferior to the truth. At all events I undoubtedly beheld the whole of the earth's major diameter—the entire northern hemisphere lay beneath me like a chart orthographically projected—and the great circle of the equator itself formed the boundary line of my horizon. Your Excellencies may however, readily imagine that the confined regions hitherto unexplored within the limits of the Arctic circle, although situated directly beneath me, and therefore seen without any appearance of being foreshortened, were still, in themselves, comparatively too diminutive, and at too great a distance from the point of sight to admit of any very accurate examination. Nevertheless what could be seen was of a nature singular and exciting. Northwardly from that huge rim before mentioned, and which, with slight qualification may be called the limit of human discovery in these regions, one unbroken, or nearly unbroken sheet of ice continues to extend. In the first few degrees of this its progress, its surface is very sensibly flattened—farther on depressed into a plane—and finally, becoming *not a little concave,* it terminates at the Pole itself in a circular centre, sharply defined, whose apparent diameter subtended at the balloon an angle of about sixty-five seconds; and whose dusky hue, varying in intensity, was, at all times darker than any other spot upon the visible hemisphere, and occasionally deepened into the most absolute and impenetrable blackness. Farther than this little could be ascertained. By twelve o'clock the circular centre had materially decreased in circumference, and by seven P.M. I lost sight of it entirely—the balloon passing over the western limb of the ice, and floating away rapidly in the direction of the equator.

"*April 8th.* Found a sensible diminution in the earth's apparent diameter, besides a material alteration in its general color and appearance. The whole visible area partook in different degrees of a tint of pale yellow, and in some portions had acquired a brilliancy even painful to the eye. My view downwards was also considerably impeded by the dense atmosphere in the vicinity of the surface being loaded with clouds between whose masses I could only now and then obtain a glimpse of the earth itself. This difficulty of direct vision had troubled me more or less for the last forty-eight hours—but my present enormous elevation brought closer together, as it were, the floating bodies of vapor, and the inconvenience became, of course, more and more palpable in proportion to my ascent. Nevertheless I could easily perceive that the balloon now hovered above the range of great lakes in the continent of North America, and was holding a course due south which would soon bring me to the tropics. This circumstance did not fail to give me the most heartfelt satisfaction, and I hailed it as a happy omen of ultimate success. Indeed the direction I had hitherto taken had filled me with uneasiness, for it was evident that, had I continued it much longer, there would have been no possibility of my arriving at the moon at all, whose orbit is inclined to the ecliptic at only the small angle of 5°, 8'', 48''.

"*April 9th.* To-day, the earth's diameter was goodly diminished, and the color of the surface assumed nearly a deeper tint of yellow. The balloon kept steady on her course to the southward, and arrived at nine P.M. over the northern edge of the Mexican gulf.

"*April 10th.* I was suddenly aroused from slumber about five o'clock this morning, by a loud, cracking and terrific sound, for which I could in no manner account. It was of very brief duration, but, while it lasted, resembled nothing in the world of which I had any previous experience. It is needless to say, that I became excessively alarmed, having, in the first instance, attributed the noise to the bursting of the balloon. I examined all my apparatus, however, with great attention, and could discover nothing out of order. Spent a great part of the day in meditating upon an occurrence so extraordinary, but could find no means whatever of accounting for it. Went to bed dissatisfied, and in a pitiable state of anxiety and agitation.

"*April 11th.* Found a startling diminution in the apparent diameter of the earth, and a considerable increase, now observable for the first time, in that of the moon itself, which wanted only a few days of being full. It now required long and excessive labor to condense within the chamber sufficient atmospheric air for the sustenance of life.

"*April 12th.* A singular alteration took place in regard to the direction of the balloon, and although fully anticipated, afforded me the most unequivocal delight. Having reached, in its former course, about the twentieth parallel of southern latitude, it turned off suddenly at an acute angle to the eastward, and thus proceeded throughout the day, keeping nearly, if not altogether, *in the exact plane of the lunar ellipse*. What was worthy of remark, a very perceptible vacillation in the car was a consequence of this change of route—a vacillation which prevailed, in a more or less degree, for a period of many hours.

"*April 13th.* Was again very much alarmed by a repetition of the loud, crackling noise which terrified me on the tenth. Thought long upon the subject, but was unable to form any satisfactory conclusion. Great decrease in the earth's apparent diameter which now subtended from the balloon an angle of very little more than twenty-five degrees. The moon could not be seen at all, being nearly in my zenith. I still continued in the plane of the ellipse, but made little progress to the eastward.

"*April 14th.* Extremely rapid decrease in the diameter of the earth. To-day I became strongly impressed with the idea, that the balloon was now actually running up the line of apsides to the point of perigee—in other words, holding the direct course which would bring it immediately to the moon in that part of its orbit, the nearest to the earth. The moon itself was directly over-head, and consequently hidden from my view. Great and long-continued labor necessary for the condensation of the atmosphere.

"*April 15th*. Not even the outlines of continents and seas could now be traced upon the earth with anything approaching to distinctness. About twelve o'clock I became aware, for the third time, of that unearthly and appalling sound which had so astonished me before. It now, however, continued for some moments, and gathered horrible intensity as it continued. At length, while stupified and terror-stricken I stood in expectation of, I know not what hideous destruction, the car vibrated with excessive violence, and a gigantic and flaming mass of some material which I could not distinguish, came with the voice of a thousand thunders, roaring and booming by the balloon. When my fears and astonishment had in some degree subsided, I had little difficulty in supposing it to be some mighty volcanic fragment ejected from that world to which I was so rapidly approaching, and, in all probability, one of that singular class of substances occasionally picked up on the earth, and termed meteoric stones for want of a better appellation.

"*April 16th*. To-day, looking upwards as well as I could, through each of the side windows alternately, I beheld, to my great delight, a very small portion of the moon's disk protruding, as it were, on all sides beyond the huge circumference of the balloon. My agitation was extreme—for I had now little doubt of soon reaching the end of my perilous voyage. Indeed the labor now required by the condenser had increased to a most oppressive degree, and allowed me scarcely any respite from exertion. Sleep was a matter nearly out of the question. I became quite ill, and my frame trembled with exhaustion. It was impossible that human nature could endure this state of intense suffering much longer. During the now brief interval of darkness a meteoric stone again passed in my vicinity, and the frequency of these phenomena began to occasion me much anxiety and apprehension. The consequence of a concussion with any one of them, would have been inevitable destruction to me and my balloon.

"*April 17th*. This morning proved an epoch in my voyage. It will be remembered that, on the thirteenth, the earth subtended an angular breadth of twenty-five degrees. On the fourteenth, this had greatly diminished—on the fifteenth, a still more rapid decrease was observable—and on retiring for the night of the sixteenth I had noticed an angle of no more than about seven degrees and fifteen minutes. What, therefore, must have been my amazement on awakening from a brief and disturbed slumber on the morning of this day, the seventeenth, at finding the surface beneath me so suddenly and wonderfully *augmented* in volume as to subtend no less than thirty-nine degrees in apparent angular diameter! I was thunderstruck. No words—no earthly expression can give any adequate idea of the extreme—the absolute horror and astonishment with which I was seized, possessed, and altogether overwhelmed. My knees tottered beneath me—my teeth chattered—my hair started up on end. 'The balloon then had actually burst'—these were the first tumultuous ideas which hurried through my mind—'the balloon had positively burst. I was falling—falling—falling—with the most intense, the most impetuous, the most unparalleled velocity. To judge from the immense distance already so quickly passed over, it could not be more than ten minutes, at the farthest, before I should meet the surface of the earth, and be hurled into annihilation.' But at length reflection came to my relief. I paused—I considered—and I began to doubt. The matter was impossible. I could not in any reason have so rapidly come down. There was some mistake. Not the red thunderbolt itself could have so impetuously descended. Besides, although I was evidently approaching the surface below me, it was with a speed by no means commensurate with the velocity I had at first so horribly conceived. This consideration served to calm the perturbation of my mind, and I finally succeeded in regarding the phenomenon in its proper point of view. In fact amazement must have fairly deprived me of my senses when I could not see the vast difference, in appearance, between the surface below me, and the surface of my mother earth. The latter was indeed over my head, and completely hidden by the balloon, while the moon—the moon itself in all its glory—lay beneath me, and at my feet.

"The stupor and surprise produced in my mind by this extraordinary change in the posture of affairs was perhaps, after all, that part of the adventure least susceptible of explanation. For the *bouleversement* [confusion] in itself was not only natural and inevitable, but had been long actually anticipated as a circumstance to be expected whenever I should arrive at that exact point of my voyage where the attraction of the planet should be superseded by the attraction of the satellite—or, more precisely, where the gravitation of the balloon towards the earth should be less powerful than its gravitation towards the moon. To be sure I arose from a sound slumber with all my senses in confusion to the contemplation of a very startling phenomenon, and one which, although expected, was not expected at the moment. The revolution itself must, of course, have taken place in an easy and gradual manner, and it is by no means clear that, had I even been awake at the time of the occurrence, I should have been made aware of it by an *internal* evidence of an inversion—that is to say by any inconvenience or disarrangement either about my person or about my apparatus.

"It is almost needless to say that upon coming to a due sense of my situation, and emerging from the terror which had absorbed every faculty of my soul, my attention was, in the first place, wholly directed to the contemplation of the general physical appearance of the moon. It lay beneath me like a chart, and although I judged it to be still at no inconsiderable distance, the indentures of its surface were defined to my vision with a most striking and altogether unaccountable distinctness. The entire absence of ocean or sea, and indeed of any lake or river, or body of water whatsoever, struck me, at first glance, as the most extraordinary feature in its geological condition. Yet, strange to say! I beheld vast level regions of a character decidedly alluvial—although by far the greater portion of the hemisphere in sight was covered with innumerable volcanic mountains, conical in shape, and having more the appearance of artificial than of natural protuberances. The highest among them does not exceed three and three quarter miles in perpendicular elevation. . . . The greater part of them were in a state of evident eruption, and gave me fearfully to understand their fury and their power by the repeated thunders of the miscalled meteoric stones which now rushed upwards by the balloon with a frequency more and more appalling.

"April 18th. To-day I found an enormous increase in the moon's apparent bulk, and the evidently accelerated velocity of my descent began to fill me with alarm. It will be remembered that, in the earliest stage of my speculations upon the possibility of a passage to the moon, the existence in its vicinity of an atmosphere dense in proportion to the bulk of the planet had entered largely into my calculations—this too in spite of many theories to the contrary, and, it may be added, in spite of the positive evidence of our senses. Upon the resistance, or more properly, upon the support of this atmosphere, existing in the state of density imagined, I had, of course, entirely depended for the safety of my ultimate descent. Should I then, after all, prove to have been mistaken, I had in consequence nothing better to expect as a *finale* to my adventure than being dashed into atoms against the rugged surface of the satellite. My distance from the moon was comparatively trifling, while the labor required by the condenser was diminished not at all, and I could discover no indication whatever of a decreasing rarity in the air.

"April 19th. This morning, to my great joy, about nine o'clock, the surface of the moon being frightfully near, and my apprehensions excited to

the utmost, the pump of my condenser at length gave evident tokens of an alteration in the atmosphere. By ten I had reason to believe its density considerably increased. By eleven very little labor was necessary at the apparatus—and at twelve o'clock, with some hesitation, I ventured to unscrew the tourniquet, when, finding no inconvenience from having done so, I finally threw open the gum-elastic chamber, and unrigged it from around the car. As might have been expected, spasms and violent headach[e] were the immediate consequence of an experiment so precipitate and full of danger. But these and other difficulties attending respiration, as they were by no means so great as to put me in peril of my life, I determined to endure as I best could, in consideration of my leaving them behind me momentarily in my approach to the denser strata near the moon. This approach, however, was still impetuous in the extreme, and it soon became alarmingly certain that, although I had probably not been deceived in the expectation of an atmosphere dense in proportion to the mass of the satellite, still I had been wrong in supposing this density, even at the surface, at all adequate to the support of the great weight contained in the car of my balloon. Yet this *should* have been the case, and in an equal degree as at the surface of the earth, the actual gravity of bodies at either planet being in the exact ratio of their atmospheric condensation. That it *was not* the case however my precipitous downfall gave testimony enough—why it was not so, can only be explained by a reference to those possible geological disturbances to which I have formerly alluded. At all events I was now close upon the planet, and coming down with most terrible impetuosity. I lost not a moment accordingly in throwing overboard first my ballast, then my water-kegs, then my condensing apparatus and gum-elastic chamber, and finally every individual article within the car. But it was all to no purpose. I still fell with horrible rapidity, and was now not more than half a mile at farthest from the surface. As a last resource, therefore, having got rid of my coat, hat, and boots, I cut loose from the balloon *the car itself,* which was of no inconsiderable weight, and thus, clinging with both hands to the hoop of the net-work, I had barely time to observe that the whole country as far as the eye could reach was thickly interspersed with diminutive habitations, ere I tumbled headlong into the very heart of a fantastical-looking city, and into the middle of a vast crowd of ugly little people, who none of them uttered a single syllable, or gave themselves the least trouble to render me assistance, but stood, like a parcel of idiots, grinning in a ludicrous manner, and eyeing me and my balloon askant with their arms set a-kimbo, I turned from them in contempt, and gazing upwards at the earth so lately left, and left perhaps forever, beheld it like a huge, dull, copper shield, about two degrees in diameter, fixed immoveably in the heavens overhead, and tipped on one of its edges with a crescent border of the most brilliant gold. No traces of land or water could be discovered, and the whole was clouded with variable spots, and belted with tropical and equatorial zones.

"Thus, may it please your Excellencies, after a series of great anxieties, unheard of dangers, and unparalleled escapes, I had, at length, on the nineteenth day of my departure from Rotterdam, arrived in safety at the conclusion of a voyage undoubtedly the most extraordinary, and the most momentous ever accomplished, undertaken, or conceived by any denizen of earth. But my adventures yet remain to be related. And indeed your Excellencies may well imagine that after a residence of five years upon a planet not only deeply interesting in its own peculiar character, but rendered doubly so by its intimate connection, in capacity of satellite, with the world inhabited by man, I may have intelligence for the private ear of the States' College of Astronomers of far more importance than the details, however wonderful, of the mere *voyage* which so happily concluded. This is, in fact, the case. I have much—very much which it would give me the greatest pleasure to communicate. I have much to say of the climate of the planet—of its wonderful alternations of heat and cold—of unmitigated and burning sunshine for one fortnight, and more than polar severity of winter for the next—of a constant transfer of moisture, by distillation *in vacuo,* from the point beneath the sun to the point the farthest from it—of a variable zone of running water—of the people themselves—of their manners, customs, and political institutions—of their peculiar physical construction—of their ugliness—of their want of ears, those useless appendages in an atmosphere so peculiarly modified as to be insufficient for the conveyance of any but the loudest sounds—of their consequent ignorance of the use and properties of speech—of their substitute for speech in a singular method of inter-communication—of the incomprehensible connection between each particular individual in the moon, with some particular individual on the earth—a connection analogous with, and depending upon that of the orbs of the planet and the satellite, and by means of which the lives and destinies of the inhabitants of the one are interwoven with the lives and destinies of the inhabitants of the other—and above all, if it so please your Excellencies, above all of these dark and hideous mysteries which lie in the outer regions of the moon—regions which, owing to the almost miraculous accordance of the satellite's rotation on its own axis with its sider[e]al revolution about the earth, have never yet been turned, and, by God's mercy, never shall be turned to the scrutiny of the telescopes of man. All this, and more—much more—would I most willingly detail. But to be brief, I must have my reward. I am pining for a return to my family and to my home: and as the price of any farther communications on my part—in consideration of the light which I have in my power to throw upon many very important branches of physical and metaphysical science—I must solicit, through the influence of your honorable body, a pardon for the crime of which I have been guilty in the death of the creditors upon my departure from Rotterdam. This, then, is the object of the present paper. Its bearer, an inhabitant of the moon, whom I have prevailed upon, and properly instructed, to be my messenger to the earth, will await your Excellencies' pleasure, and return to me with the pardon in question, if it can, in any manner, be obtained.

"I have the honor to be, &c. your Excellencies' very humble servant,

HANS PHAALL."

Upon finishing the perusal of this very extraordinary document, Professor Rub-a-dub, it is said, dropped his pipe upon the ground in the extremity of his surprise, and Mynheer Superbus Von Underduk, having taken off his spectacles, wiped them, and deposited them in his pocket, so far forgot both himself and his dignity, as to turn round three times upon his heel in the quintescence of astonishment and admiration. There was no doubt about the matter—the pardon should be obtained. So at least swore with a round oath, Professor Rub-a-dub, and so finally thought the illustrious Von Underduk, as he took the arm of his brother in science, and without saying a word, began to make the best of his way home to deliberate upon the measures to be adopted. Having reached the door, however, of the burgomaster's dwelling, the Professor ventured to suggest, that as the messenger had thought proper to disappear—no doubt frightened to death by the savage appearance of the burghers of Rotterdam—the pardon would be of little use, as no one but a man of the moon would undertake a voyage to so horrible a distance. To the truth of this observation the burgomaster assented, and the matter was therefore at an end. Not so, however, rumors and speculations. The letter, having been published, gave rise to a variety of gossip and opinion. Some of the overwise even made themselves ridiculous, by decrying the whole business as nothing better than a hoax. But hoax, with these sort of people, is, I believe, a general term for all matters above their comprehension. For my part I cannot conceive upon what data they have founded such an accusation. Let us see what they say:

Imprimis. That certain wages in Rotterdam have certain especial antipathies to certain burgomasters and astronomers.

Don't understand at all.

Secondly. That an odd little dwarf and bottle conjurer, both of whose ears, for some misdemeanor, have been cut off close to his head, has been missing for several days from the neighboring city of Bruges.

Well—what of that?

Thirdly. That the newspapers which were stuck all over the little balloon were newspapers of Holland, and therefore could not have been made in the moon. They were dirty papers—very dirty—and Gluck, the printer, would take his bible oath to their having been printed in Rotterdam.

He was mistaken—undoubtedly—mistaken.

Fourthly. That Hans Phaall himself, the drunken villain, and the three very idle gentlemen styled his creditors, were all seen, no longer than two or three days ago, in the tippling house in the suburbs, having just returned, with money in their pockets, from a trip beyond the sea.

Don't believe it—don't believe a word of it.

Lastly. That it is an opinion very generally received, or which ought to be generally received, that the College of Astronomers in the city of Rotterdam—as well as all other Colleges in all other parts of the world—not to mention Colleges and Astronomers in general—are, to say the least of the matter, not a whit better, nor greater, nor wiser than they ought to be.

The d——l, you say! Now that's too bad. Why, hang the people, they should be prosecuted for a libel. I tell you, gentlemen, you know nothing about the business. You are ignorant of Astronomy—and of things in general. The voyage was made—it was indeed—and made, too, by Hans Phaall. I wonder, for my part, you do not perceive at once that the letter—the document—is intrinsically—is astronomically true—and that it carries upon its very face the evidence of its own authenticity.

RICHARD ADAMS LOCKE

From *Great Astronomical Discoveries Lately Made by Sir John Herschel . . . at the Cape of Good Hope* (1835)

[The story of the "Great Astronomical Discoveries Lately Made by Sir John Herschel . . . at the Cape of Good Hope," which first appeared in the New York *Sun* during August, 1835, is believed to be the work of Richard Adams Locke, a man who, according to Edgar Allan Poe, was responsible for "one of the most important steps ever taken in the pathway of human progress"—the establishment and popularization of the cheap daily press.

Locke, a collateral descendant of the seventeenth-century English philosopher John Locke, was born in 1800 in Somersetshire, England, and educated at Cambridge. Before he entered the university, his poetry was published in several provincial periodicals. Upon graduating, he started the London *Republican,* a short-lived political journal, and then launched a similarly unsuccessful periodical, *Cornucopia,* for which he wrote scientific articles, as well as poetry and criticism.

In 1832, Locke and his wife migrated to the United States, where he became a reporter for the New York *Courier and Enquirer*. In the summer of 1835, Locke left the *Courier* for the *Sun,* a penny paper owned by Benjamin Day. In later years Day recalled that, at a time when the news scene was relatively quiet, Locke, no doubt eager to increase his $12 weekly salary, approached him with a plan for attracting a larger readership to the *Sun* by creating a sensational story about discoveries on the moon. The first installment of the "moon story" appeared on page 2 of the *Sun* on Friday, August 21, 1835. As we have noted, the appearance of the *Sun* article completely overshadowed Poe's "Hans Phaall," the first installment of which had appeared three weeks earlier. As a result, Poe destroyed the second part of his story before it could be published.

The *Sun*'s initial story—a modest and brief article purportedly quoted from an Edinburgh newspaper—read as follows:

> CELESTIAL DISCOVERIES——The Edinburgh *Courant* says—"We have just learned from an eminent publisher in this city that Sir John Herschel, at the Cape of Good Hope, has made some astronomical discoveries of the most wonderful description, by means of an immense telescope, of an entirely new principle."

Nothing more appeared on the subject until Tuesday, August 25, when three columns of page 1 of the *Sun* were devoted to Herschel's "discoveries." The article asserted that

> . . . the younger Herschel, at his observatory in the Southern Hemisphere, has already made the most extraordinary discoveries in every planet of our solar system; has discovered planets in other solar systems; has obtained a distinct view of objects in the moon, fully equal to that which the unaided eye commands of terrestrial objects at the distance of a hundred yards; has affirmatively settled the question whether this satellite be inhabited, and by what order of beings; has firmly established a new theory of cometary phenomena; and has solved nearly every leading problem of mathematical astronomy.

What is more, at a time not known for large type or banner headlines, the *Sun* headed the story in bold print. The story was attributed to the *Courant* and the source of its information was said to be the *Supplement* to the Edinburgh *Journal of Science.*

As for how the *Journal of Science* had been privy to all this information while scientists, astronomical societies, and scholarly journals knew nothing about it, the *Sun* claimed that the *Supplement* had made a special agreement with Dr. Andrew Grant, a close friend and associate of Dr. Herschel's, who had been authorized by Herschel to make much of the information public while the renowned astronomer prepared his notes for the Royal Society and other learned groups. But the *Supplement* never existed, and the *Journal of Science,* which had once been published, no longer existed. Needless to say, it also appears that Andrew Grant was a figment of Locke's imagination.

Great numbers of people purchased the August 25 issue of the *Sun* even though the lengthy first installment, which discussed the details of constructing Herschel's immense telescope, may have been too technical for the average reader. Each subsequent issue brought some startling revelation—on Wednesday, August 26, a description of lunar vegetation, birds, and animals, including a unicorn; in Thursday's installment, mountains, craters, and biped beavers that walked like humans, lived in huts, and apparently used fire; on Friday, winged humans; on Saturday, the discovery of a great temple on the moon made of polished sapphire; and on Monday, August 31, destined to be the last day of major moon revelations, encounters with man-bats. Shortly thereafter, the *Sun* reported that an "accident" had damaged portions of the telescope; when it was finally repaired, the moon was invisible and Herschel turned his attention to Saturn.

But Richard Adams Locke and his sensational moon story had left their mark on journalism, as Poe said, for they introduced thousands of readers to the wonders of the penny paper. On Wednesday, August 26, when the first of Herschel's moon discoveries were described, the circulation of the *Sun* climbed above that of every other paper in the world, and on Friday, August, 28, Benjamin Day proudly announced that his paper had sold 19,360 copies, 2,300 more than the London *Times,* the next most popular daily. Furthermore, the *Sun* was deluged with requests for reprints of the moon story, and papers in Paris, London, Glasgow, and, of all places, Edinburgh issued editions of the tale. Later in 1835, the *Sun* published the story in pamphlet form, and it is said to have sold 60,000 copies of the pamphlet.

It is not surprising that the man who finally revealed that the entire moon adventure was fiction was none other than Richard Adams Locke himself. Locke inadvertently admitted his authorship to a reporter friend on the rival *Journal of Commerce,* who revealed the hoax to the public before Locke and the *Sun* could offer an explanation, if they ever intended to do so. Still, many people chose to ignore these revelations, preferring to believe the original account. On September 16, 1835, more than two weeks after the last installment of the moon story appeared, the *Sun* ran an editorial in which it pleaded innocent to any attempt to deceive the public and shifted the blame to the unnamed man who had provided the paper with the story. However, it left some doubt as to whether the story actually was fictitious by refusing to call it a hoax before English and Scottish papers and scientists confirmed that it was untrue.

Sir John Herschel, perhaps the only real character in Locke's story, was shown a copy by an American visitor to his observatory, and he is reported to have taken the hoax quite well, remarking good-naturedly that he would never be able to live up to the fame the article had given him. In fact, Herschel's contribution to astronomy was not minor. He was born in 1792, a son of Sir William Herschel, himself a famous astronomer. By 1825, Sir John had published several articles and, using his father's telescope, had been able to make a valuable drawing of the Orion nebulae and to observe the second comet of 1825 and the Andromeda nebulae. He was one of the founders of the Royal Astronomical Society, its first foreign secretary, and, later, its president. His discovery and cataloguing of double stars and nebulae visible in the Northern Hemisphere brought him numerous awards and citations. His wish to complete his survey of the heavens by studying the nebulae of the Southern Hemisphere brought him to Feldhausen and the Cape of Good Hope in early 1834. He remained there, cataloguing his findings, until 1838, when he returned to England and a baronetcy.

Locke does not appear to have been as successful as Herschel in the years after the appearance of the moon hoax. He left the *Sun* in the fall of 1836 to join Joseph Price in founding the *New Era,* a penny paper that they hoped would rival the *Sun*. Locke's attempt to create another hoax, this one entitled "The Lost Manuscript of Mungo Park," failed, as did the *New Era*. He then moved on to the newly created *Brooklyn Eagle,* where he was editor for a brief period. His last job seems to have been with the New York Customs House. He died in 1871 at his home on Staten Island in New York.

The only known copy of the pamphlet issued by the *Sun* in 1835 is at present in the Library of Congress, Washington, D.C. The edition used in this book was issued in 1852 and edited by William N. Griggs, who also supplied a biographical sketch of the author and an appendix including an "authentic description of the moon" and a "new theory of the lunar surface in relation to that of the earth." We have omitted, in addition to these materials, the descriptions of the setting up of Herschel's great telescope and of Herschel's "findings" after his moon discoveries. The copy followed is in the University of Delaware Library, Newark, Delaware.]

In this unusual addition to our journal, we have the happiness of making known to the British public, and thence to the whole civilized world, recent discoveries in astronomy, which will build an imperishable monument to the age in which we live, and confer upon the present generation of the human race a proud distinction through all future time. It has been poetically said that "the stars of heaven are the hereditary regalia of man," as the intellectual sovereign of the animal creation. He may now fold the zodiac around him with a loftier consciousness of his mental supremacy.

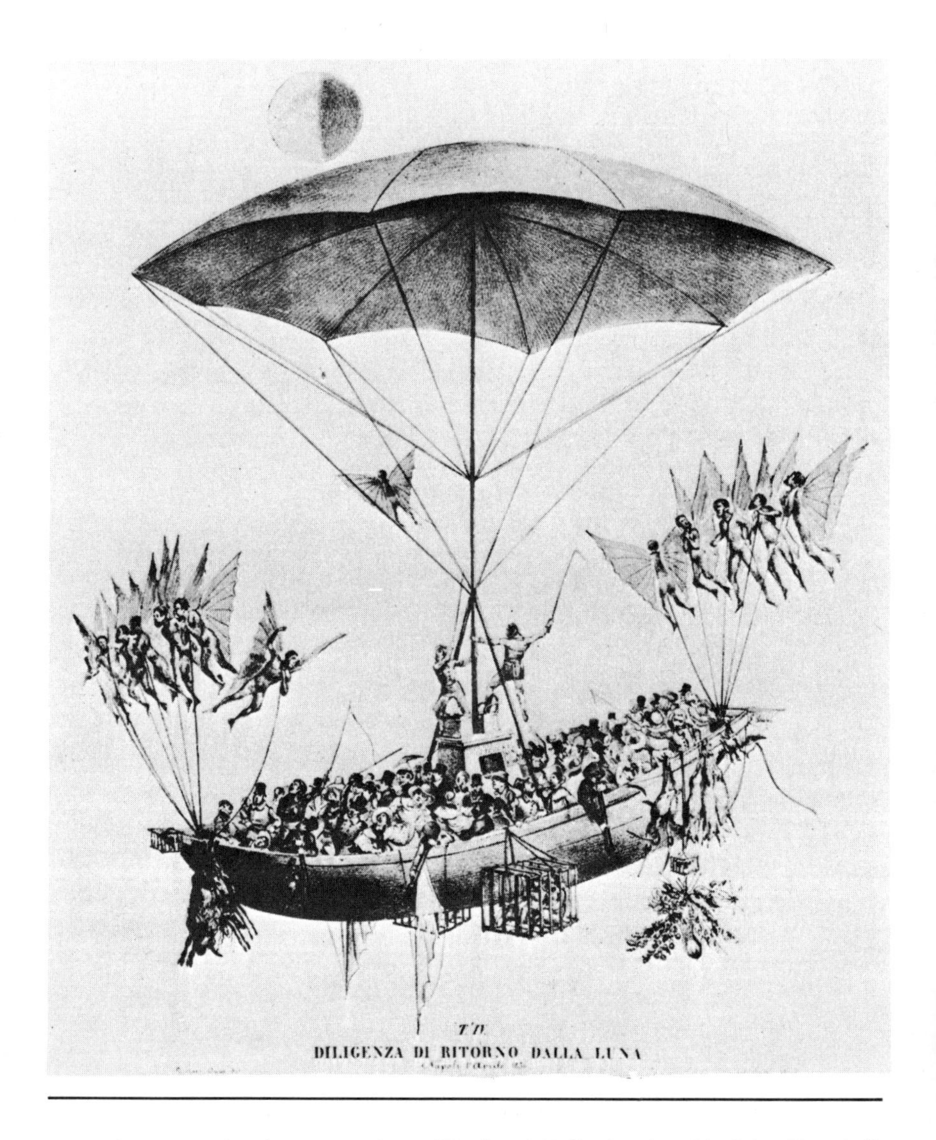

One of a series of Italian engravings (Naples, 1836) showing Sir John Herschel's supposed scheme for the "Flying Diligence." This illustration, apparently inspired by Locke's series of revelations in the New York *Sun,* shows the return of the airship to the moon with a full load of passengers. The motive power is furnished by flying men from the moon, urged on, with sword and lash, by taskmasters clinging to the mast. The picture, from the collection of Bella C. Landauer, is reprinted from Francis T. Miller, *The World in the Air* (New York: G. P. Putnam's Sons, 1930), by permission of G. P. Putnam's Sons.

It is impossible to contemplate any great astronomical discovery without feelings closely allied to a sensation of awe, and nearly akin to those with which a departed spirit may be supposed to discover the unknown realities of a future state. Bound by the irrevocable laws of nature to the globe on which we live—creatures "close shut up in infinite expanse"—it seems like acquiring a fearful supernatural power when any of the remote and mysterious works of the Creator yield tribute to our curiosity. It seems almost a presumptuous usurpation of powers denied us by the Divine will, when man, in the pride and confidence of his skill, steps forth, far beyond the apparently natural boundary of his privileges, and demands the secrets and familiar fellowship of other worlds. We are assured that when the immortal philosopher to whom mankind is indebted for the thrilling wonders now first made known had at length adjusted his new and stupendous apparatus with a certainty of success, he solemnly paused several hours before he commenced his observations, that he might prepare his own mind for discoveries which he knew would fill the minds of myriads of his fellowmen with astonishment, and secure his name a bright, if not transcendent, conjunction with that of his venerable father, to all posterity. And well might he pause! From the hour the first human pair opened their eyes to the glories of the blue firmament above them, there has been no accession to human knowledge at all comparable in sublime interest to that which he has been the honored agent in supplying; and we are taught to believe that, when a work, already preparing for the press, in which his discoveries are embodied in detail, shall be laid before the public, they will be found of incomparable importance to some of the grandest operations of civilized life. Well might he pause! He was about to become the sole depository of wondrous secrets, which had been hid from the eyes of all men that had lived since the birth of time. He was about to crown himself with a diadem of knowledge which would give him a conscious pre-eminence above every individual of his species who then lived, or who had lived in the generations that are passed away. He paused ere he broke the seal of the casket which contained it.

To render our enthusiasm intelligible, we will state at once that, by means of a telescope of vast dimensions and an entirely new principle, the younger Herschel, at his observatory in the Southern Hemisphere, has already made the most extraordinary discoveries in every planet of our solar system; has discovered planets in other solar systems; has obtained a distinct view of objects in the moon, fully equal to that which the unaided eye commands of terrestrial objects at the distance of a hundred yards; has affirmatively settled the question whether this satellite be inhabited, and by what orders of beings; has firmly established a new theory of cometary phenomena; and has solved or corrected nearly every leading problem of mathematical astronomy.

For our early and almost exclusive information concerning these facts, we are indebted to the devoted friendship of Dr. Andrew Grant, the pupil of the elder, and for several years past the inseparable coadjutor of the younger Herschel. The amanuensis of the latter at the Cape of Good Hope, and the indefatigable superintendent of his telescope during the whole period of its construction and operation, Dr. Grant has been enabled to supply us with intelligence equal, in general interest at least, to that which Dr. Herschel himself has transmitted to the Royal Society. Indeed, our correspondent assures us that the voluminous documents now before a committee of that institution contain little more than details and mathematical illustrations of the facts communicated to us in his own ample correspondence. For permission to indulge his friendship in communicating this invaluable information to us, Dr. Grant and ourselves are indebted to the magnanimity of Dr. Herschel, who, far above all mercenary considerations, has thus signally honored and rewarded his fellow-laborer in the field of science. . . .

. . . .

New Lunar Discoveries

Until the 10th of January, the observations were chiefly directed to the stars in the southern signs, in which . . . a countless number of new stars and nebulae were discovered. But we shall defer our correspondent's account of these to future pages, for the purpose of no longer withholding from our readers the more generally and highly interesting discoveries which were made in the lunar world. And for this purpose, too, we shall defer Dr. Grant's elaborate mathematical details. . . .

It was about half past nine o'clock on the night of the 10th [of January], the moon having then advanced within four days of her mean liberation, that the astronomer adjusted his instruments for the inspection of her eastern limb. The whole immense power of his telescope was applied, and to its focal image about one-half of the power of his microscope. On removing the screen of the latter, the field of view was covered throughout its entire area with a beautifully distinct and even vivid representation of *basaltic* rock. Its color was a greenish brown, and the width of the columns, as defined by their interstices on the canvas, was invariably twenty-eight inches. No fracture whatever appeared in the mass first presented, but in a few seconds a shelving pile appeared of five or six columns width, which showed their figure to be hexagonal and their articulations similar to those of the basaltic formation at Staffa.[1] This precipitous shelf was profusely covered with a dark red flower, "precisely similar," says Dr. Grant, "to the *papaver rhoeas,* or rose-poppy, of our sublunary cornfield; and this was the first organic production of nature in a foreign world ever revealed to the eyes of men."

The rapidity of the moon's ascension, or rather of the earth's diurnal rotation, being nearly equal to five hundred yards in a second, would have effectually prevented the inspection or even the discovery of objects so minute as these, but for the admirable mechanism which constantly regulates, under the guidance of the sextant, the required altitude of the lens. But its operation was found to be so consummately perfect that the observers could detain the object upon the field of view for any period they might desire. The specimen of lunar vegetation, however, which they had already seen, had decided a question of too exciting an interest to induce them to retard its exit. It had demonstrated that the moon has an atmosphere constituted similarly to our own, and capable of sustaining organized, and therefore, most probably, animal life.

The basaltic rocks continued to pass over the inclined canvas plane through three successive diameters, when a verdant declivity of great beauty appeared, which occupied two more. This was preceded by another mass of nearly the former height, at the base of which they were at length delighted to perceive that novelty, lunar forest. "The trees," says Dr. Grant, "for a period of ten minutes, were of one unvaried kind, and unlike any I have seen, except the largest class of yews in the English church-yards, which they in some respects resemble. These were followed by a level green plain, which, as measured by the painted circle on our canvas of forty-nine feet, must have been more than a half mile in breadth; and then appeared as fine a forest of firs, unequivocal firs, as I have ever seen cherished in the bosom of my native mountains.

"Wearied with the long continuances of these, we greatly reduced the magnifying power of the microscope, without eclipsing either of the reflectors, and immediately perceived that we had been insensibly descending, as it were, a mountainous district of a highly diversified and romantic character, and that we were on the verge of a lake, or inland sea; but of

[1] An uninhabited islet of the Inner Hebrides, Argyll, Scotland, known for its numerous basaltic caves.

what relative locality or extent, we were yet too greatly magnified to determine. On introducing the feeblest achromatic lens we possessed, we found that the water, whose boundary we had just discovered, answered in general outline to the Mare Nubium of Riccoli,[2] by which we detected that, instead of commencing, as we supposed, on the eastern longitude of the planet, some delay in the elevation of the great lens had thrown us nearly upon the axis of her equator. However, as she was a free country, and we [were] not, as yet, attached to any particular province, and moreover, since we could at any moment occupy our intended position, we again slid in our magic lenses to survey the shores of the Mare Nubium. . . .

"Fairer shores never angel coasted on a tour of pleasure. A beach of brilliant white sand, girt with wild castellated rocks, apparently of green marble, varied at chasms, occurring every two or three hundred feet, with grotesque blocks of chalk or gypsum, and feathered and festooned at the summits with the clustering foliage of unknown trees, moved along the bright wall of our apartment until we were speechless with admiration. The water, wherever we obtained a view of it, was nearly as blue as that of the deep ocean, and broke in large white billows upon the strand. The action of very high tides was quite manifest upon the face of the cliffs for more than a hundred miles; yet, diversified as the scenery was during this and a much greater distance, we percieved no trace of animal existence, notwithstanding we could command at will a perspective or a foreground view of the whole. Mr. Holmes,[3] indeed, pronounced some white objects of a circular form, which we saw at some distance in the interior of a cavern, to bona fide specimens of a large *cornu ammonis;*[4] but to me they appeared merely large pebbles, which had been chafed and rolled there by tides. Our chase of animal life was not yet to be rewarded.

"Having continued this close inspection nearly two hours, during which we passed over a wide tract of country, chiefly of a rugged and apparently volcanic character; and having seen few additional varieties of vegetation, except some species of lichen, which grew everywhere in great abundance, Dr. Herschel proposed that we should take out all our lenses, give a rapid speed to the panorama, and search for some of the principal valleys known to astronomers, as the most likely method to reward our first night's observation with the discovery of animated beings. The lenses being removed,

[2] The Mare Nubium, or Sea of Clouds, is a dark plain in the third quadrant of the moon that covers about 95,000 square miles. It was first identified by Giovanni Riccioli (1598–1671), an Italian astronomer.

[3] The fictitious Mr. Holmes was supposedly an assistant to Dr. Herschel who had accompanied him to the Cape of Good Hope.

[4] The "Horn of Ammon" is a fossil shell of a cephalopod mollusk of an extinct order.

and the effulgence of our unutterably glorious reflectors left undiminished, we found, in accordance with our calculations, that our field of view comprehended about twenty-five miles of the lunar surface, with the distinctness both of outline and detail which could be procured of a terrestrial object at the distance of two and a half miles. . . . This afforded us the best landscape views we had hitherto obtained, and although the accelerated motion was rather too great, we enjoyed them with rapture. Several of those famous valleys, which are bounded by lofty hills of so perfectly conical a form as to render them less like works of nature than of art, passed the canvas before we had time to check their flight; but presently a train of scenery met our eye, of features so entirely novel that Dr. Herschel signalled for the lowest convenient gradation of movement. It was a lofty chain of obelisk-shaped or very slender pyramids, standing in irregular groups, each composed of about thirty or forty spires, every one of which was perfectly square and as accurately truncated as the finest specimens of Cornish crystal. They were of a faint lilac hue, and very resplendent. I now thought that we had assuredly fallen on productions of art; but Dr. Herschel shrewdly remarked that if the Lunarians could build thirty or forty miles of such monuments as these, we should ere now have discovered others of a less equivocal character. He pronounced them quartz formations, of probably the wine-colored amethyst species, and promised us, from these and other proofs which he had obtained of the powerful actions of laws of crystallization in this planet, a rich field of mineralogical study.

"On introducing a lens, his conjecture was fully confirmed: they were monstrous amethysts, of a diluted claret color, glowing in the intensest light of the sun! They varied in height from sixty to ninety feet, though we saw several of a still more incredible altitude. They were observed in a succession of valleys divided by longitudinal lines of round-breasted hills, covered with verdure and nobly undulated; but what is most remarkable, the valleys which contained these stupendous crystals were invariably barren, and covered with stones of a ferruginous [rusty] hue, which were probably iron pyrites. We found that these curiosities were situated in a district elevated half a mile above the valley of the Mare Foecunditatis[5] . . . ; the shores of which soon hove in view. But never was a name more inappropriately bestowed. From 'Dan to Beersheba'[6] all was barren, barren—the sea-board was entirely composed of chalk and flint, and not a vestige of vegetation could be discovered with our strongest glasses.

[5] A dark plain in the fourth quadrant of the moon that covers about 160,000 square miles.

[6] The ancient Biblical town of Dan was the northernmost point in Palestine; Beersheba, the southernmost. The phrase, therefore, means "from top to bottom."

"The whole breadth of the northern extremity of this sea, which was about three hundred miles, having crossed our plane, we entered upon a wild mountainous region abounding with more extensive forests of larger trees than we had before seen—the species of which I have no good analogy to describe. In general contour they resembled our forest oak; but they were much more superb in foliage, having broad glossy leaves like those of the laurel, and tresses of yellow flowers which hung, in the open glades, from the branches to the ground. These mountains passed, we arrived at a region which filled us with utter astonishment. It was an oval valley, surrounded, except at a narrow opening towards the south, by hills, red as the purest vermillion, and evidently crystallized; for wherever a precipitous chasm appeared—and these chasms were very frequent, and of immense depth—the perpendicular sections presented conglomerated masses of polygon crystals, evenly fitted to each other, and arranged in deep strata, which grew darker in color as they descended to the foundations of the precipices. Innumerable cascades were bursting forth from the breasts of every one of these cliffs, and some so near their summits, and with such great force, as to form arches many yards in diameter. I never was so vividly reminded of Byron's simile, 'the tail of the white horse in the Revelations.'

"At the foot of this boundary of hills was a perfect zone of woods surrounding the whole valley, which was about eighteen or twenty miles wide, at its greatest breadth, and about thirty in length. Small collections of trees, of every imaginable kind, were scattered about the whole luxuriant area; and here our magnifiers blest our panting hopes with specimens of conscious existence. In the shade of the woods, on the southeastern side, we beheld continuous herds of brown quadrupeds, having all the external characteristics of the bison, but more diminutive than any species of the *bos* genus [cattle] in our natural history. Its tail was like that of our *bos* grunniens [yak]; but in its semicircular horns, the hump on its shoulders, the depth of its dew-lap, and the length of its shaggy hair, it closely resembled the species to which I first compared it. It had, however, one widely distinctive feature, which we afterwards found common to nearly every lunar quadruped we have discovered; namely, a remarkable fleshy appendage over the eyes, crossing the whole breadth of the forehead and united to the ears. We could most distinctly perceive this hairy veil, which was shaped like the upper front outline of the cap known to the ladies as Mary Queen of Scots' cap, lifted and lowered by means of the ears. It immediately occurred to the acute mind of Dr. Herschel that this was a providential contrivance to protect the eyes of the animal from the great extremes of light and darkness to which all the inhabitants of our side of the moon are periodically subjected.

"The next animal perceived would be classed on earth as a monster. It was of bluish lead-color, about the size of a goat, with a head and beard like him and a *single horn,* slightly inclined forward from the perpendicular. The female was destitute of the horn and beard, but had a much longer tail. It was gregarious, and chiefly abounded on the acclivitous glades of the woods. In elegance of symmetry it rivalled the antelope, and like him it seemed an agile sprightly creature running with great speed, and springing from the green turf with all the unaccountable antics of a young lamb or kitten. This beautiful creature afforded us the most exquisite amusement. The mimicry of its movements upon our white painted canvas was as faithful and luminous as that of animals within a few yards of a camera obscura [box camera], when seen pictured upon its tympan [the reflective surface of the camera obscura]. Frequently when [we were] attempting to put our fingers upon its beard, it would suddenly bound away into oblivion, as if conscious of our earthly impertinence; but then others would appear, whom we could not prevent nibbling the herbage, say or do what we would to them.

"On examining the centre of this delightful valley, we found a large branching river, abounding with lovely islands, and water-birds of numerous kinds. A species of gray pelican was the most numerous; but a black and white crane, with unreasonably long legs and bill, was also quite common. We watched their pisciverous experiments a long time, in hopes of catching sight of a lunar fish; but although we were not gratified in this respect, we could easily guess the purpose with which they plunged their long necks so deeply beneath the water. Near the upper extremity of one of these islands, we obtained a glimpse of a strange amphibious creature of a spherical form, which rolled with great velocity across the pebbly beach, and was lost sight of in the strong current which set off from this angle of the island. We were compelled, however, to leave this prolific valley unexplored, on account of clouds which were evidently accumulating in the lunar atmosphere, our own being perfectly translucent. But this was itself an interesting discovery, for more distant observers had questioned or denied the existence of any humid atmosphere in this planet.

"The moon being now low on her descent, Dr. Herschel inferred that the increasing refrangibility of her rays would prevent any satisfactory protraction of our labors, and our minds being actually fatigued with the excitement of the high enjoyments [of which] we had partaken, we mutually agreed to call in the assistants at the lens, and reward their vigilant attention with congratulatory bumpers of the best 'East India Particular.' It was not, however, without regret that we left the splendid valley of the red mountains, which, in compliment to the arms of our royal patron, we denominated 'the Valley of the Unicorn.' . . ."

The nights of the 11th and 12th, being cloudy, were unfavorable to observation; but on those of the 13th and 14th further animal discoveries were made of the most exciting interest to every human being. We give them in the graphic language of our accomplished correspondent:—

"The astonishing and beautiful discoveries which we had made during our first night's observation, and the brilliant promise which they gave of the future, rendered every moonlight hour too precious to reconcile us to the deprivation occasioned by these two cloudy evenings; and they were not borne with strictly philosophical patience, notwithstanding that our attention was closely occupied in superintending the erection of additional props and braces to the twenty-four feet lens, which we found had somewhat vibrated in a high wind that arose on the morning of the 11th.

"The night of the 13th (January) was one of pearly purity and loveliness. The moon ascended the firmament in gorgeous splendor, and the stars, retiring around her, left her the unrivalled queen of the hemisphere. This [would be] the last night but one, in the present month, during which we would have an opportunity of inspecting her western limb, on account of the libration in longitude which would thence immediately ensue. . . .

"Taking then our twenty-five miles breadth of her surface upon the field of view, and reducing it to a slow movement, we soon found the first very singularly shaped object of our inquiry. It is a highly mountainous district, the loftier chains of which form three narrow ovals, two of which approach each other in slender points, and are united by one mass of hills of great length and elevation, thus presenting a figure similar to that of a long skein of thread, the bows of which have been gradually spread open from their connecting knot. The third oval looks also like a skein, and lies as if carelessly dropped from nature's hand in connection with the other; but that which might fancifully be supposed as having formed the second bow of this second skein, is cut open, and lies in scattered threads of smaller hills which cover a great extent of level territory. The ground plan of these mountains is so remarkable that it has been accurately represented in almost every lineal map of the moon that has been drawn. . . .

"Within the grasp, as it were, of the broken bow of hills last mentioned, stands an oval-shaped mountain, inclosing a valley of an immense area, and having, on its western ridge, a volcano in a state of terrific eruption. To the northeast of this, across the broken, or what Mr. Holmes called 'the vagabond mountains,' are three other detached oblong formations, the largest and last of which is . . . fancifully denominated the Mare Mortuum, or more commonly the 'Lake of Death.' Induced by a curiosity to divine the reason of so sombre a title, rather than by any more philosophical motive, we here first applied our hydro-oxygen magnifiers to the focal image of the great lens. Our twenty-five miles portion of this great mountain circus had comprehended the whole of its area, and of course the two conical hills, which rise within it about five miles from each other; but although this breadth of view had heretofore generally presented its objects as if seen within a terrestrial distance of two and a half miles, we were, in this instance, unable to discern these central hills with any such degree of distinctness. There did not appear to be any mist or smoke around them, as in the case of the volcano which we had left in the southwest, and yet they were comparatively indistinct upon the canvas. On sliding in the gas-light lens the mystery was immediately solved. They were old craters of extinct volcanoes, from which still issued a heated, though transparent exhalation, that kept them in an apparently oscillatory or trembling motion, most unfavorable to examination. The craters of both of these hills, as nearly as we could judge under this obstruction, were about fifteen fathoms deep, devoid of any appearance of fire, and of nearly a yellowish white color throughout. The diameter of each was about nine diameters of our painted circle, or nearly 450 feet; and the width of the rim surrounding them about 1000 feet; yet, notwithstanding their narrow mouths, these two chimneys of the subterranean deep had evidently filled the whole area of the valley in which they stood with the lava and ashes with which it was encumbered, and even added to the height, if not indeed caused the existence of the oval chain of mountains which surrounded it. These mountains, as subsequently measured from the level of some large lakes around them, averaged the height of 2800 feet; and Dr. Herschel conjectured from this and the vast extent of their abutments, which ran for many miles into the country around them, that these volcanoes must have been in full activity for a million of years. Lieut. Drummond,[7] however, rather supposed that the whole area of this oval valley was but the exhausted crater of one vast volcano, which in expiring had left only these two imbecile representatives of its power. I believe Dr. Herschel himself afterwards adopted this probable theory, which is indeed confirmed by the

[7] A fictitious member of the Royal Engineers who supposedly accompanied Dr. Herschel to South Africa.

universal geology of the planet. There is scarcely a hundred miles of her surface, not even excepting her largest seas and lakes, in which circular or oval mountainous ridges may not be easily found; and many, very many of these having numerous inclosed hills in full volcanic operation, which are now much lower than the surrounding circles, it admits of no doubt that each of these great formations is the remains of one vast mountain, which has burnt itself out, and left only these wide foundations of its ancient grandeur. A direct proof of this is afforded in a tremendous volcano now in its prime, which I shall hereafter notice.

"What gave the name of 'The Lake of Death' to the annular mountain I have just described, was, I suppose, the dark appearance of the valley which it incloses, and which, to a more distant view than we obtained, certainly exhibits the general aspects of the waters of this planet. The surrounding country is fertile to excess: . . . we counted not less than twelve luxuriant forests, divided by open plains, which waved in an ocean of verdure, and were probably prairies like those of North America. In three of these we discovered numerous herds of quadrupeds similar to our friends the bisons in the Valley of the Unicorn, but of much larger size; and scarcely a piece of woodland occurred in our panorama which did not dazzle our vision with flocks of white or red birds upon the wing.

"At length we carefully explored the Endymion [circle]. We found each of the three ovals volcanic and sterile within; but, without, most rich, throughout the level regions around them, in every imaginable production of a bounteous soil. Dr. Herschel has classified not less than thirty-eight species of forest trees, and nearly twice this number of plants, found in this tract alone, which are widely different from those found in more equatorial latitudes. Of animals, he classified nine species of mammalia, and five of oviparia. Among the former is a small kind of reindeer, the elk, the moose, the horned bear, and the biped beaver. The last resembles the beaver of the earth in every other respect than in its destitution of a tail, and its invariable habit of walking upon only two feet. It carries its young in its arms like a human being, and moves with an easy gliding motion. Its huts are constructed better and higher than those of many tribes of human savages, and from the appearance of smoke in nearly all of them, there is no doubt of its being acquainted with the use of fire. Still, its head and body differ only in the points stated from that of the beaver, and it was never seen except on the borders of lakes and rivers, in which it has been observed to immerse for a period of several seconds.

"Thirty degrees further south, in . . . Cleomedes, is an immense annular mountain, containing three distinct craters, which have been so long extinguished that the whole valley around them, which is eleven miles in extent, is densely crowded with woods nearly to the summits of the hills. Not a rod of vacant land, except the tops of these craters, could be described, and no living creature, except a large white bird resembling the stork. At the southern extremity of this valley is a natural archway or cavern, 200 feet high, and 100 wide, through which runs a river that discharges itself over a precipice of gray rock 80 feet in depth, and then forms a branching stream through a beautiful champaign district for many miles. Within twenty miles of this cataract is the largest lake, or rather inland sea, that has been found throughout the seven and a half millions of square miles which this illuminated side of the moon contains. Its width, from east to west, is 198 miles, and from north to south, 266 miles. Its shape, to the northward, is not unlike that of the bay of Bengal, and it is studded with small islands, most of which are volcanic. Two of these, on the eastern side, are now violently eruptive; but our lowest magnifying power was too great to examine them with convenience, on account of the cloud of smoke and ashes which beclouded our field of view: as seen by Lieut. Drummond, through our reflecting telescope of 2000 times they exhibited great brilliancy.

"In a bay, on the western side of this sea, is an island 55 miles long, of a crescent form, crowded through its entire sweep with the most superb and wonderful natural beauties, both of vegetation and geology. Its hills are pinnacled with tall quartz crystals, of so rich a yellow and orange hue that we at first supposed them to be pointed flames of fire; and they spring up thus from smooth round brows of hills which are covered as with a velvet mantle. Even in the enchanting little valleys of this winding island we could often see these splendid natural spires, mounting in the midst of deep green woods, like church steeples in the vales of Westmoreland. We here first noticed the lunar palm-tree, which differs from that of our tropical latitudes only in the peculiarity of very large crimson flowers, instead of the spadix protruded from the common calyx. We, however, perceived no fruit on any specimens we saw: a circumstance which we attempted to account for from the great (theoretical) extremes in the lunar climate. On a curious kind of tree-melon we nevertheless saw fruit in great abundance, and in every stage of inception and maturity. The general color of these woods was a dark green, though not without occasional admixtures of every tint of our forest seasons. The hectic flush of autumn was often seen kindled upon the cheek of earliest spring; and the gay drapery of summer in some places surrounded trees leafless as the victims of winter. It seemed as if all the seasons here united hands in a circle of perpetual harmony.

"Of animals we saw only an elegant striped quadruped about three feet high, like a miniature zebra; which was always in small herds on the green sward of the hills; and two or three kinds of long-tailed birds, which we judged to be golden and blue pheasants. On the shores, however, we saw countless multitudes of univalve shell-fish, and among them some huge flat ones, which all three of my associates declared to be *cornu ammonae;* and I confess I was here compelled to abandon my skeptical substitution of pebbles. The cliffs all along these shores were deeply undermined by tides; they were very cavernous, and yellow crystal stalactites, larger than a man's thigh, were shooting forth on all sides. Indeed every rood of this island appeared to be crystalized; masses of fallen crystals were found on every beach we explored, and beamed from every fractured headland. It was more like a creation of an oriental fancy than a distant variety of nature brought by the powers of science to ocular demonstration. The striking dissimilitude of this island to every other we had found on these waters, and its near proximity to the main land, led us to suppose that it must some time have been part of it; more especially as its crescent bay embraced the first of a chain of smaller ones which ran directly thither. This first one was a pure quartz rock, about three miles in circumference, towering in naked majesty from the blue deep, without either shore or shelter, but it glowed in the sun almost like a sapphire, as did all the lesser ones of whom it seemed the king. Our theory was speedily confirmed; for all the shore of the main land was battlemented and spired with these unobtainable jewels of nature; and as we brought our field of view to include the utmost rim of the illuminated boundary of the planet, we could still see them blazing in crowded battalions as it were, through a region of hundreds of miles, In fact we could not conjecture where this gorgeous land of enchantment terminated; for as the rotary motion of the planet bore these mountain summits from our view, we became further remote from their western boundary.

"We were admonished by this to lose no time in seeking the next proposed object of our search, the Langrenus. . . .

"After a short delay in advancing the observatory upon the levers, and in regulating the lens, we found our object and surveyed it. It was a dark narrow lake seventy miles long, bounded, on the east, north, and west, by red mountains of the same character as those surrounding the Valley of the Unicorn, from which it is distant to the southwest about 160 miles. This lake, like that valley, opens to the south upon a plain not more than ten miles wide, which is here encircled by a truly magnificent amphitheatre of the loftiest order of lunar hills. For a semicircle of six miles these hills are riven, from their brow to their base, as perpendicularly as the outer walls of the Coliseum at Rome; but here exhibiting the sublime altitude of at least two thousand feet, in one smooth unbroken surface. How nature disposed of the huge mass which she thus prodigally carved out, I know not; but certain it is that there are no fragments of it left upon the plain, which is a declivity without a single prominence except a billowy tract of woodland that runs in many a wild vagary of breadth and course to the margin of the lake. The tremendous height and expansion of this perpendicular mountain, with its bright crimson front contrasted with the fringe of forest on its brow, and the verdure of the open plain beneath, filled our canvas with a landscape unsurpassed in unique grandeur by any we had beheld. Our twenty-five miles perspective included this remarkable mountain, the plain, a part of the lake, and the last graduated summits of the range of hills by which the latter is nearly surrounded. We ardently wished that all the world could view a scene so strangely grand, and our pulse beat high with the hope of one day exhibiting it to our countrymen in some part of our native land.

"But we were at length compelled to destroy our picture, as a whole, for the purpose of magnifying its parts for scientific inspection. Our plain was of course immediately covered with the ruby front of this mighty amphitheatre, its tall figures, leaping cascades, and rugged caverns. As its almost interminable sweep was measured off upon the canvas, we frequently saw long lines of some yellow metal hanging from the crevices of the horizontal strata in wild net-work, or straight pendent branches. We of course concluded that this was virgin gold, and we had no assay-master to prove the contrary.

"On searching the plain, over which we had observed the woods roving in all the shapes of clouds in the sky, we were again delighted with the discovery of animals. The first observed was a quadruped with an amazingly long neck, head like a sheep, bearing two long spiral horns, white as polished ivory, and standing in perpendicular parallel to each other. Its body was like that of the deer, but its fore-legs were most disproportionally long, and its tail, which was very bushy and of a snowy whiteness, curled high over its rump, and hung two or three feet by its side. Its colors were bright bay and white in brindled patches, clearly defined, but of no regular form. It was found only in pairs, in spaces between the woods, and we had no opportunity of witnessing its speed or habits. But a few minutes only elapsed before three specimens of another animal appeared, so well known to us all that we fairly laughed at the recognition of so familiar an acquaintance in so distant a land. They were neither more nor less than three good large sheep, which would not have disgraced the farms of Leicestershire, or the shambles of Leadenhall market. With the utmost scrutiny, we could find no mark of distinction between these and those of our native soil; they had not even the appendage over the eyes, which I have described as common to lunar quadrupeds. Presently they appeared in great numbers, and on reducing the lenses, we found them in flocks over a great part of the valley. I need not say how desirous we were of finding shepherds to these flocks, and even a man with blue apron and rolled-up sleeves would have been a welcome sight to us, if not to the sheep; but they fed in peace, lords of their own pastures, without either protector or destroyer in human shape.

"We at length approached the level opening to the lake, where the valley narrows to a mile in width, and displays a scenery on both sides picturesque and romantic beyond the powers of a prose description. Imagination, borne on the wings of poetry, could alone gather similes to portray the wild sublimity of this landscape, where dark behemoth crags stood over the brows of lofty precipices, as if a rampart in the sky; and forests seemed suspended in mid-air. On the eastern side there was one soaring crag, crested with trees, which hung over in a curve like three-fourths of a Gothic arch, and being of a rich crimson color, its effect was most strange upon minds unaccustomed to the association of such grandeur with such beauty. But whilst gazing upon them in a perspective of about half a mile, we were thrilled with astonishment to perceive four successive flocks of large winged creatures, wholly unlike any kind of birds, descend with a slow even motion from the cliffs on the western side, and alight upon the plain. They were first noticed by Dr. Herschel, who exclaimed, 'Now, gentlemen, my theories against your proofs, which you have often found a pretty even bet, we have here something worth looking at: I was confident that if ever we found beings in human shape, it would be in this longitude, and that they would be provided by their Creator with some extraordinary powers of locomotion. . . .'

"This lens, being soon introduced, gave us a fine half-mile distance; and we counted three parties of these creatures, of twelve, nine, and fifteen in number, walking erect towards a small wood near the base of the eastern precipices. Certainly they *were* like human beings, for their wings had now disappeared, and their attitude in walking was both erect and dignified. Having observed them at this distance for some minutes, we introduced lens H.*z.*, which brought them to the apparent proximity of eighty yards: the highest clear magnitude we possessed until the latter end of March, when we effected an improvement in the gas-burners. About half of the first party had passed beyond our canvas; but of all the others we had a perfectly distinct and deliberate view. They averaged four feet in height, were covered, except on the face, with short and glossy copper-colored hair, and had wings composed of a thin membrane, without hair, lying snugly upon their backs, from the top of the shoulders to the calves of the legs. The face, which was of a yellowish flesh-color, was a slight improvement upon that of the large orang-outang, being more open and intelligent in its expression, and having a much greater expansion of forehead. The mouth, however, was very prominent, though somewhat relieved by a thick beard upon the lower jaw, and by lips far more human than those of any species of the simia genus. In general symmetry of body and limbs they were infinitely superior to the orang-outang; so much so, that, but for their long wings, Lieut. Drummond said they would look as well on a parade ground as some of the old cockney militia! The hair on the head was a darker color than that of the body, closely curled, but apparently not woolly, and arranged in two curious semicircles over the temples of the forehead. Their feet could only be seen as they were alternately lifted in walking; but, from what we could see of them in so transient a view, they appeared thin, and very protuberant at the heel.

"Whilst passing across the canvas, and whenever we afterwards saw them, these creatures were evidently engaged in conversation; their gesticulation, more particularly the varied action of their hands and arms, appeared impassioned and emphatic. We hence inferred that they were rational beings, and, although not perhaps of so high an order as others which we discovered the next month on the shores of the Bay of Rainbows, that they were capable of producing works of art and contrivance. The next view we obtained of them was still more favorable. It was on the borders of a little lake, or expanded stream, which we then for the first time perceived running down the valley to a large lake, and having on its eastern margin a small wood. Some of these creatures had crossed this water, and were lying like spread eagles on the skirts of the wood. We could then perceive that their wings possessed great expansion, and were similar in structure to those of the bat, being a semi-transparent membrane, expanded in curvilineal divisions by means of straight radii, united at the back by the dorsal integuments. But what astonished us very much was the circumstance of this membrane being continued from the shoulders to the legs, united all the way down, though gradually decreasing in width. The wings seemed completely under the command of volition, for those of the creatures whom we saw bathing in the water, spread them instantly to their full width, waved them as ducks do theirs to shake off the water, and then as instantly closed them again in a compact form. Our further observation of the habits of these creatures, who were of both sexes, led to results so very remarkable, that I prefer they should first be laid before the public in Dr. Herschel's own work, where I have reason to know they are fully and faithfully stated, however incredulously they may be received.— * * * * * The three families then almost simultaneously spread their wings, and were lost in the dark confines of the canvas before we had time to breathe from our paralyzing astonishment. We scientifically denominated them the Vespertilio-homo, or man-bat; and they are doubtless innocent and happy creatures, notwithstanding some of their amusements would but ill comport with our terrestrial notions of decorum. The valley itself we called the Ruby Coliseum, in compliment to its stupendous southern boundary, the six-mile sweep of red precipices two thousand feet high. And the night, or rather morning, being far advanced, we postponed our tour . . . until another opportunity."

. . . .

The night of the 14th displayed the moon in her mean libration, or full; but the somewhat humid state of the atmosphere being for several hours less favorable to a minute inspection than to a general survey of her surface, they were chiefly devoted to the latter purpose. But shortly after midnight the least veil of mist was dissipated, and the sky being as lucid as on the former evenings, the attention of the astronomers was arrested by the remarkable outlines of the spot marked Tycho . . . and in this region they added treasures to human knowledge which angels might well desire to win. Many parts of the following extract will remain forever in the chronicles of time:

"The surface of the moon, when viewed in her mean libration, even with telescopes of very limited power, exhibits three oceans of vast breadth and circumference, independently of seven large collections of water, which may be denominated seas. Of inferior waters, discoverable by the highest classes of instruments, and usually called lakes, the number is so great that no attempt has yet been made to count them. Indeed, such a task would be almost equal to that of enumerating the annular mountains which are found upon every part of her surface, whether composed of land or water. The largest of the three oceans occupies a considerable portion of the hemisphere between the line of her northern axis and that of her eastern equator, and even extends many degrees south of the latter. Throughout its eastern boundary, it so closely approaches that of the lunar sphere, as to leave in many places merely a fringe of illuminated mountains, which are here, therefore, strongly contradistinguished from the dark and shadowy aspect of the great deep. But peninsulas, promontories, capes, and islands, and a thousand other terrestrial figures, for which we can find no names in the poverty of *our* geographical nomenclature, are found expanding, sallying forth, or glowing in insular independence, through all the 'billowy boundlessness' of this magnificent ocean. One of the most remarkable of these is a promontory, without a name, I believe, in the lunar charts, which starts from an inland district denominated Copernicus by the old astronomers, and abounding, as we eventually discovered, with great natural curiosities. This promontory is indeed most singular. Its northern extremity is shaped much like an imperial crown, having a swelling bow, divided and tied down in its centre by a band of hills, which is united with its forehead-band or base. The two open spaces formed by this division are two lakes, each eighty miles wide; and at the foot of these, divided from them by the band of hills last mentioned, is another lake, larger than the two together, and nearly perfectly square. This one is followed, after another hilly division, by a lake of an irregular form; and this one, yet again, by two narrow ones, divided longitudinally, which are attenuated northward to the main land. Thus this skeleton promontory of mountain ridges runs 396 miles into the ocean, with six capacious lakes inclosed within its stony ribs. . . .

"Next to this, the most remarkable formation in this ocean is a strikingly brilliant annular mountain of immense altitude and circumference, standing 330 miles E.S.E., commonly known as Aristarchus . . . with a great cavity in its centre. That cavity is now, as it was probably wont to be in ancient times, a volcanic crater, awfully rivalling our mounts Etna and Vesuvius in the most terrible epochs of their reign. Unfavorable as the state of the atmosphere was to close examination, we could easily mark its illumination of the water over a circuit of sixty miles. If we had before retained any doubt of the power of lunar volcanoes to throw fragments of their craters so far beyond the moon's attraction that they would necessarily gravitate to this earth, and thus account for the multitudes of massive aerolites which have fallen and been found upon our surface, the view which we had of Aristarchus would have set our skepticism forever at rest. This mountain, however, though standing 300 miles in the ocean, is not absolutely insular, for it is connected with the main land by four chains of mountains which branch from it as a common centre.

"The next great ocean is situated on the western side of the meridian line, divided nearly in the midst by the line of the equator, and is about 900 miles in north and south extent. It . . . was fancifully called the Mare Tranquilitatis. It is rather two large seas than one ocean, for it is narrowed just under the equator by a strait not more than 100 miles wide. Only three annular islands of a large size, and quite detached from its shores, are to be found within it; though several sublime volcanoes exist on its northern boundary; one of the most stupendous of which is within 120 miles of the Mare Nectaris before mentioned.

"Immediately contiguous to this second great ocean, and separated from it only by a concatenation of dislocated continents and islands, is the third, . . . known as the Mare Serenitatis. It is nearly square, being about 330 miles in length and width. But it has one most extraordinary peculiarity, which is a perfectly straight ridge of hills, certainly not more than five miles wide, which starts in a direct line from its southern to its northern shore, dividing it exactly in the midst. This singular ridge is perfectly *sui generis,* being altogether unlike any mountain chain either on this earth or on the moon itself. It is so very keen, that its greatest concentration of the solar light renders it visible to small telescopes; but its character is so strikingly peculiar that we could not resist the temptation to depart from our predetermined adherence to a general survey, and examine it particularly. Our lens G *x* brought it within the optical distance of 800 yards, and its whole width of four or five miles snugly within that of our canvas. Nothing that we had hitherto seen more highly excited our astonishment. Believe it or believe it not, it was one entire crystallization!—its edge, throughout its whole length of 340 miles, is an acute angle of solid quartz crystal, brilliant as a piece of Derbyshire spar [a crystalline mineral found in Derbyshire] just brought from a mine, and containing scarcely a fraction or chasm from end to end! What a prodigious influence must our thirteen times larger globe have exercised upon this satellite, when an embryo in the womb of time, the passive subject of chemical affinity! We found that wonder and astonishment, as excited by objects in this distant world, were but modes and attributes of ignorance, which should give place to elevated expectation, and to reverential confidence in the illimitable power of the Creator.

"The dark expanse of waters to the south of the first great ocean, has often been considered a fourth; but we found it to be merely a sea of the first class, entirely surrounded by land, and much more encumbered with promontories and islands than it has been exhibited in any lunar chart. One of its promontories runs from the vicinity of Pitatus . . . in a slightly curved and very narrow line, to Bullialdus . . . , which is merely a circular head to it, 264 miles from its starting place. This is another mountainous ring, a marine volcano, nearly burnt out, and slumbering upon its cinders. But Pitatus, standing bold upon a cape of the southern shore, is apparently exulting in the might and majesty of its fires.

"The atmosphere being now quite free from vapor, we introduced the magnifiers to examine a large bright circle of hills which sweep close beside the western abutments of this flaming mountain. The hills were either of snow-white marble or semi-transparent crystal, we could not distinguish which, and they bounded another of these lovely green valleys, which, however monotonous in my descriptions, are of paradisaical beauty and fertility, and like primitive Eden in the bliss of their inhabitants. Dr. Herschel here again predicated another of his sagacious theories. He said the proximity of the flaming mountain, Bullialdus, must be so great a local convenience to dwellers in this valley during the long periodical absence of solar light, as to render it a place of populous resort for the inhabitants of all the adjacent regions more especially as its bulwark of hills afforded it an infallible security against any volcanic eruption that could occur. We therefore applied our full power to explore it, and rich indeed was our reward.

"The very first object in this valley that appeared upon our canvas was a magnificent work of art! It was a temple—a fane [temple] of devotion, or of science, which, when consecrated to the Creator, *is* devotion of the loftiest order; for it exhibits his attributes purely free from the masquerade attire and blasphemous caricature of controversial creeds, and has the seal and signature of his own hand to sanction its aspirations. It was an equitriangular temple, built of polished sapphire, or of some resplendent blue stone, which, like it, displayed a myriad points of golden light twinkling and scintillating in the sunbeams. Our canvas, though fifty feet in diameter, was too limited to receive more than a sixth part of it at one view, and the first part that appeared was near the centre of one of its sides, being three square columns, six feet in diameter at their base, and gently tapering to a height of seventy feet. The intercolumniations were each twelve feet.

"We instantly reduced our magnitude so as to embrace the whole structure in one view, and then indeed it was most beautiful. The roof was composed of some yellow metal, and divided into three compartments, which were not triangular planes inclining to the centre, but subdivided, curved, and separated, so as to represent a mass of violently agitated flames rising from a common source of conflagration, and terminating in wildly waving points. This design was too manifest, and too skilfully executed, to be mistaken for a single moment. Through a few openings in these metallic flames, we perceived a large sphere of a darker kind of metal nearly of a clouded copper-color, which they inclosed and seemingly raged around, as if hieroglyphically consuming it. This was the roof; but upon each of the three corners there was a small sphere of apparently the same metal as the large centre one, and these rested upon a kind of cornice, quite new in any order of architecture with which we are acquainted, but nevertheless exceedingly graceful and impressive. It was like a half-opened scroll, swelling off boldly from the roof, and hanging far over the walls in several convolutions. It was of the same metal as the flames, and on each of the sides of the building it was open at both ends. The columns, six on each side, were simply plain shafts, without capitals or pedestals, or any description of ornament; nor was any perceived in other parts of the edifice. It was open on each side, and seemed to contain neither seats, altars, nor offerings; but it was a light and airy structure nearly a hundred feet high from its white glistening floor to its glowing roof, and it stood upon a round green eminence on the eastern side of the valley. We afterwards, however, discovered two others which were in every respect facsimiles of this one; but in neither did we perceive any visitants besides flocks of wild doves, which alighted upon its lustrous pinnacles. Had the devotees of these temples gone the way of all living, or were the latter merely historical monuments? What did the ingenious builders mean by the globe surrounded with flames? Did they by this record any past calamity of *their* world, or predict any future of *ours?* I by no means despair of ultimately solving not only these but a thousand other questions which present themselves respecting the objects in this planet; for not the millionth part of her surface has yet been explored, and we have been more desirous of collecting the greatest possible number of new facts, than of indulging in speculative theories, however seductive to the imagination.

"But we had not far to seek for inhabitants of this 'Vale of the Triads.' Immediately on the outer border of the wood which surrounded, at the distance of half a mile, the eminence on which the first of these temples stood, we saw several detached assemblies of beings whom we instantly recognized to be of the same species as our winged friends of the Ruby Coliseum near the Lake Langrenus. Having adjusted the instrument for a minute examination, we found that nearly all the individuals in these groups were of a larger stature than the former specimens, less dark in color, and in *every respect* an improved variety of the race. They were chiefly engaged in eating a large yellow fruit like a gourd, sections of which they dexterously divided with their fingers, and ate with rather uncouth voracity, throwing away the rind. A smaller red fruit, shaped like a cucumber, which we had often seen pendent from trees having a broad dark leaf, were also lying in heaps in the centre of several of the festive groups; but the only use they appeared to make of it was sucking its juice, after rolling it between the palms of their hands and nibbling off the end. They seemed to be eminently happy, and even polite, for we saw, in many instances, individuals sitting nearest these piles of fruit, select the largest and brightest specimens, and throw them archwise across the circle to some opposite friend or associate who had extracted the nutriment from those scattered around him, and which were frequently not a few. While thus engaged in their rural banquets, or in social converse, they were always seated with their knees flat upon the turf, and their feet brought evenly together in the form of a triangle. And for some mysterious reason or other this figure seemed to be an especial favorite among them; for we found that every group or social circle arranged itself in this shape before it dispersed, which was generally done at the signal of an individual who stepped into the centre and brought his hands over his head in an acute angle. At this signal each member of the company extended his arms forward so as to form an acute horizontal angle with the extremity of the fingers. But this was not the only proof we had that they were creatures of order and subordination. * * *

"We had no opportunity of seeing them actually engaged in any work of industry or art; and, so far as we could judge, they spent their happy hours in collecting various fruits in the woods, in eating, flying, bathing, and loitering about upon the summits of precipies. * * * But, although evidently the highest order of animals in this rich valley, they were not its only occupants. Most of the other animals which we had discovered elsewhere, in very distant regions, were collected here; and also at least eight or nine new species of quadrupeds. The most attractive of these was a tall white stag, with lofty spreading antlers, black as ebony. We several times saw this elegant creature trot up to the seated parties of the semi-human beings I have described, and browse the herbage close beside them, without the least manifestation of fear on its part, or of notice on theirs. The universal state of amity among all classes of lunar creatures, and the apparent absence of every carnivorous or ferocious species, gave us the most refined pleasure, and doubly endeared to us this lovely nocturnal companion of our larger, but less favored world. . . ."

With the careful inspection of this instructive valley, and a scientific classification of its animal, vegetable, and mineral productions, the astronomers closed their labors for the night: labors rather mental than physical, and oppressive, from the extreme excitement which they naturally induced. A singular circumstance occurred the next day, which threw the telescope quite out of use for nearly a week, by which time the moon could be no longer observed that month. . . .

. . . .

"It was not until the new moon of the month of March that the weather proved favorable to any continued series of lunar observations; and Dr. Herschel had been too enthusiastically absorbed in reporting his brilliant discoveries in the southern constellations, and in constructing tables and catalogues of his new stars, to avail himself of the few clear nights which intervened.

"On one of these, however, Mr. Drummond, myself, and Mr. Holmes, made those discoveries near the Bay of Rainbows to which I have somewhere briefly alluded. . . . The region which we first particularly inspected was that of Heraclides Falsus . . . , in which we found several new species of animals, all of which were horned, and of a white or gray color; and the remains of three ancient triangular temples, which had long been in ruins. We thence traversed the country southeastward, until we arrived at Atlas . . . ; and it was in one of the noble valleys at the foot of this mountain that we found the very superior species of the vespertilio-homo. In stature, they did not excel those last described, but they were of infinitely greater personal beauty, and appeared, in our eyes, scarcely less lovely than the general representations of angels by the most imaginative school of painters. Their social economy seemed to be regulated by laws or ceremonies exactly like those prevailing in the Vale of the Triads, but their works of art were more numerous, and displayed a proficiency of skill quite incredible to all except actual observers. I shall, therefore, let the first detailed account of them appear in Dr. Herschel's authenticated natural history of this planet."

[This concludes the *Supplement,* with the exception of forty pages of illustrative and mathematical notes, which would greatly enhance the size and price of this work, without commensurably adding to its general interest.—*Ed. Sun.*]

"A MEMBER OF THE L.L.B.B."

The Great Steam-Duck (1841)

[*The Great Steam-Duck: or a Concise Description of a most useful and extraordinary invention for Aerial Navigation* is a parody on the various wild ideas proposed to enable men to fly. Its author is an anonymous "Member of the L.L.B.B." (Louisville Literary Brass Band), an informal group of convivial gentlemen who met irregularly in the back room of a local saloon. Written in the form of a lecture and published in a Louisville newspaper in 1841, *The Great Steam-Duck* takes particular aim at a plan to build a flying machine shaped like an American eagle, advanced by one Richard Oglesby Davidson in a pamphlet published in 1840 (*Disclosure of the Discovery and Invention, and a Description of the Plan of Construction and Mode of Operation of the Aerostat . . .*).

In the years after publication of John Wilkins's *Discovery of a New World in the Moon* (1638–40), the possibility of realizing the dream of moon flight continued to fascinate scientists and visionaries. Suggestions and inventions proliferated, especially after the successful flight of the Montgolfier brothers' balloon in 1783. The Robert brothers, countrymen of the Montgolfiers', designed and flew a cylindrical balloon in 1784. A year later one Samuel Hoole, an Englishman, constructed a machine he called a flying fish, in which the aeronaut traveled within the vehicle rather than suspended below it. (There is no evidence of any attempt to fly the fish, however.) In 1816–17 Samuel Pauly and Durs Egg, of Switzerland, designed a spherical balloon within a hydrogen-filled envelope made to resemble a dolphin. In 1835, the German Georg Rebenstein unveiled a plan to build a cubiform balloon that could be collapsed at a certain altitude and used as a glider to return to earth. That same year Count Lennox, a Frenchman, built a cylindrical balloon that may well have inspired Richard Oglesby Davidson. Lennox's airship had four movable wings, or flappers, two on each side of the balloon, which were controlled by a series of chains from the car hanging below the balloon. Lennox exhibited his airship in London, but it does not appear that it ever left the ground.

The author of *The Great Steam-Duck* was well aware of the achievements of the leading balloonists in England, France, and the United States; in fact the "lecture" opens with a survey of their accomplishments, which we have omitted here. He was, however, skeptical about the usefulness of the balloon for air travel and regarded most of the proposals as laughable. His description of a "flying duck" heaps ridicule on at least two of these proposals—a winged balloon suggested by H. Strait and Davidson's American eagle—by carrying them to their logical extreme of foolishness. No further information is available on either Strait or Davidson, but it is apparent that the suggestion of neither man was acted on, perhaps in part because of this anonymous attack.

The author of the "lecture" claims to have in his possession a manuscript by another author, describing a steam-propelled flying duck, but the airship is clearly a product of the L.L.B.B. member's own imagination. Its superiority over all other inventions, he says, is based on its simple machinery, consisting of a small but powerful engine placed in the breast of the duck and fueled by well-seasoned wood. Every aspect of the airship, which is modeled after a mallard duck, "a fowl well known for its swiftness of wing and powers of swimming," was carefully thought out and every contingency prepared for. Although only 15 feet long and 6 feet wide at its widest point, the duck contains an engine room with a steam engine, boilers, and a fuel bin, as well as a cabin with "two births [berths], a table, two chairs, a library of selected and scientific books, thermometer, &c., and other accommodations appertaining to a well furnished study." (Much of this brings to mind the well-stocked flying chariot John Wilkins proposed two hundred years earlier.) Most amazing of all is the steam-duck's ability to fly at better than 200 miles per hour while lifting a total weight of 700 pounds. Although the airship is intended for "sublunary" flight, the author claims that there is no limit to the distances it can travel. The greatest danger to the steam-duck, he feels, is from sportsmen who might take a shot at it as it flies by.

All this, of course, was intended to make the reader realize the foolishness of contemporary aeronautic thinking. The author believed that sound scientific experimentation needed to be carried out before man ventured aloft, so that a "true and logical system of reasoning" would replace the "absurd sophistry with which the world of invention is now enslaved and benighted."

The Great Steam-Duck, published in 1841, has been reprinted only once before now, in 1919 in the *Magazine of History with Notes and Queries* (Tarrytown, New York). The text followed in this book is from the only copy of the original edition known to exist. It is part of the Lammot du Pont, Jr., Collection of Aeronautics in the Eleutherian Mills Historical Library.]

Illustration from the original version of *The Great Steam-Duck* (Louisville, Ky., 1841).

The principles upon which aerostation, or the art of navigating the air, has been founded are of some antiquity; altho' the application of them to practice seems to be altogether of modern discovery. The peculiar property of the atmosphere which induced philosophers, to make such experiments as finally led to this discovery, has long been known. It was an axiom among chemists and philosophers, before the seventeenth century, that, 'any body which is specifically or bulk for bulk, lighter than the atmospheric air encompassing the earth, will be buoyed up by it and ascend; but as the density of the atmosphere decreases, on account of the diminished pressure of the superincumbent air, and the elastic property which it possesses at different elevations above the earth, this body can rise only to a height in which the surrounding air will be of the same specific gravity with itself.' Other facts have since led to the discovery that in this situation the encasing body will either float or be driven in the direction of the wind or current of air, to which it is exposed. . . .

. . . .

We learn from the American Magazine that 'about three years ago a Mr. H. Strait of Ranselear county N. York, made a communication to Prof. Silliman[1] of New Haven, Ct. editor of the American Journal of Science and Arts, on Aerial navigation, which was lately published in that periodical [Vol. XXV, 1833]. Little has been said of the plan of M. Strait, as to whether it was practicable or would probably be useful. But in this age of enquiry, it seems proper to lay before the public every project which is not evidently so visionary as to promise no useful results whatever. Mr. Strait, like all others who have formed plans with some labor and attention, thinks his project quite practicable, and with some improvements capable of becoming the means of frequent conveyance and transportation.

His plan is, to have the united assistance of inflamable or rarified air and the percussion of wings. The first is to supply the means of ascent, and this power is to be governed at pleasure by the percussion of wings; the latter to be so constructed as to be moved with the greatest facility, whatever the size or shape. The materials of which they are made should be light; strong, durable and capable of elasticity. He thinks they may be made so as to be very little heavier, in proportion to their surface, than bird's wings, and equally movable. They are also to supercede the need of a parachute, and

[1] Benjamin Silliman (1779–1864), Professor of Chemistry and Natural History at Yale, founded *The American Journal of Science and Arts* in 1818.

to regulate ascent and descent, to insure and assist progress, and to prevent fatal consequences from the rarified air envelope bursting, or being torn. A description is given of the wings as to shape, construction, connexion with the balloon, and their operation; and he supposes their motion will be easy, and in a great measure independent of weight, shape, or size, and the percussion, powerful and constant. He also shows the manner in which the wings are to be fastened to the balloon; but supposes a sufficiency of rarified air to overcome the weight of the balloon, its apparatus and load.

He is of [the] opinion that the form of the balloon should be similar to that of the vessel which tracts in the denser medium of water. The wings he proposes to fasten about five feet below the balloon. The car is to be attached to the wings. The pilot is to stand upright if he chooses, and so that his hands shall come upon, or have full command of the wings for moving them.'

An improvement on this plan was lately presented to the citizens of this place in the shape of a miniature model, by a Mr. Angleson. This gentleman, like many before him, did not discover till too late that the invention which he was honestly exhibiting as his own, was several years old, and if well investigated, probably several centuries.

In a pamphlet published some time ago, by Mr. Richard Oglesby Davidson,[2] we are informed that the author is the true and original inventor of the Aerostat. To this assertion we may reply in the words of a Roman satirist—*'Obsecro tuum est? vetus credideram!'* —'Is it thine? I thought the invention was an old one!'

Mr. Davidson very wisely determined in his own mind, when he first conceived the thought and plan of the Aerostat, not to disclose them until after he had experimented on and established their practicability. 'Because,' he adds, 'I was aware of the fact, that hitherto inventors and discoverers have been deprived of their rights by designing interlopers, who happened to have the means for experimenting on, and consequently forestalling the true and original discoverers, both as to the honor and profits of their intellectual labor; and secondly, to save my feelings the chagrin and mortification occasioned by the exposition, ridicule, and derision invariably heaped upon all innovations.'

Again he says: 'I had no means for experimenting on my theory, and, to keep it to myself, under the daily apprehension of its being discovered by some one else, placed me in a peculiar situation indeed.' To remove this difficulty, he has disclosed his secret to an enlightened public, trusting to

[2] *Disclosure of the Discovery and Invention, and a Description of the Plan of Construction and Mode of Operation of the Aerostat: or A New Mode of Aerostation* (Saint Louis, 1840).

their generosity and to the practicability of his invention, to furnish him with means for the experiment. He offers 'FIFTY THOUSAND DOLLARS for and in consideration of the loan of FIVE THOUSAND'—predicated on his chance of success—as flattering a speculation for the monied man as ever [was] offered; and, in this financial revolution and bank-plague, the speculator who has no other use of five thousand dollars could not dispose of them better or to greater advantage than by accepting the proposal.

Proceed we next to examine the gentleman's claims to originality. He introduces his disclosure by a historical sketch of aeronautic navigation, from the time of Friar Bacon,[3] in the thirteenth century, to that of himself in the nineteenth century—an era in which 'a great number of extraordinary and useful inventions have marked, as with the finger of inspiration,' the mighty nineteenth century—an era in which 'a great number of extraordinary and shows some research; but it is deficient in one point—it cannot make him the *inventor* of the aerostat—a point which he labors so assiduously to prove.

If he examines the annals of modern improvement a little more closely than he seems to have done, he will at once perceive that he has been preceded, and that the honor of the invention is due to another—perhaps a less learned explorer in the 'airy world,' but one who has certainly carried the science to greater perfection than Mr. Richard Oglesby Davidson or any of his predecessors. It is not for me to say whether the invention referred to was or was not original—for few things can now claim that title—and some have even doubted whether there is such a trait at all in the human mind as originality—but the description given of the aerostat, though less prolix, and therefore falling under Mr. Richard Oglesby Davidson's strictures on 'abstract theories,' is substantially the same as that of the American Eagle. Let an extract suffice.

'It has long been considered,' says the author, 'that steam cannot be employed successfully in aeronautical navigation; but I have proof incontestible that this is a crude prejudice, based upon neither equity nor justice.

'*November,* 1839. Invented an extraordinary FLYING DUCK. This animal . . . is shaped like the ordinary wild duck, but has greater breadth of wing and beam. I have constructed its wings of whale-bone and very stout silk, and plastered them with a certain slippery compound, to ease their motion. In the breast, or craw, are the works; and the hind part is partitioned off into berths; a large window in the stern giving light.' There is but one material difference between this Aerostat and that of Mr. Richard Oglesby Davidson, but *it* constitutes a vast superiority, viz: The propelling power in

[3] Roger Bacon (1214–92) is believed to have been the first Englishman to write about flying as a scientific possibility.

the former is STEAM—that in the latter is manual labor; and it must be evident to the most casual observer, that steam is infinitely superior, no human power being able to endure the exertion necessary to raise itself. The STEAM DUCK, exclusive of other advantages, is a self propeller—i.e., the machinery being the only foreign aid—and, from its peculiar construction, is capable of enduring all the dangers of flood and storm.

Although Mr. Richard Oglesby Davidson endeavors to prove that we must adhere in every particular to nature, yet it has frequently been found convenient to depart from it—as in the formation of the wings of this Aerostat. As it is, let us see their affinity to nature:

'The principle of ascending the air by means of a balloon,' says the learned aeronaut, 'grows out of the atmosphere, and is susceptible of the clearest demonstration. But, instead of its aiding the world in discovering the means for navigating the air, I have no doubt that it operates as a blind in the matter [i.e., obscures the facts]. In itself it is perfectly SUI GENERIS. It acts upon no NATURAL PRINCIPLES; it employs no power, natural or artificial; nor does it imitate any animal belonging to the three great elements, earth, water, and air.'

We cannot coincide with Mr. Richard Oglesby Davidson in many points of this paragraph. Instead of the balloon operating as a blind as regards discoveries for navigating the air; by what means, we ask, in the absence of the balloon, could we have discovered the actual resistance of the air?—the height to which it extends?—how and in what manner it ceases to support life?—the invaluable uses of aeromancy and of the gasses?—and numberless other branches of the sciences of Aeronautical navigation?

'How then,' he suggests, 'is man to carry himself upon the atmosphere with safety and expedition?' I answer, by adopting a principle founded in, and imitating a MODEL in creating his machine, and employing a POWER FURNISHED BY NATURE. Now, he has not only answered the question to the satisfaction of every one, but IMITATED A MODEL, so closely indeed that he has hatched an EAGLE out of a DUCK, and produced by the process, a most wonderful specimen in ornithology.

Literally speaking, the AMERICAN EAGLE is a noble bird—

'The emblem of the brave and free?' but a question arises, in 'following nature,' whether he can fly as fast or swim as buoyantly as the common duck? Every ornithologist knows he cannot. Therefore, in the same ratio as the duck can fly faster and swim better than the eagle, is the original Aerostat or STEAM DUCK superior in model and construction to the AMERICAN EAGLE.

Mr. Richard Oglesby Davidson, after some philosophical reflections on the probable resistance of that airy nothing, which has proved too subtle for the unsuitable means hitherto suggested by the ingenuity of man, proceeds with a very ingenious, though somewhat intricate account of the construction and mode of operation of the Aerostat. It is formed as the bird from which it derives its name. The chief framing of the body is made of whalebone covered with oiled silk or varnished lines: The wings are jointed and moved by cranks acted upon by a series of compound levers. The rudder is formed, like a shovel and made out of thin plank. The internal machinery is propelled by the conductor who seats himself in the centre of the Aerostat when it is 'IN TRANSITU."

The great obstacle to this plan is, that, governed by a certain law of gravity the conductor could not raise his own weight, much less that of a machine several hundred pounds heavier; but Mr. Richard Oglesby Davidson seems to have calculated his power otherwise.

Anticipating its progress through the air, he says:

'Each revolution of the cranks of the large wheels produces four strokes with the wings, the points of which describe sections of a circle twelve feet in length. This motion of the wings raises the Aerostat gradually at an angle of about five degrees, during the space of fifteen minutes; in which time it has traversed a distance of six or seven miles. It is now at a point sufficiently elevated above all obstacles connected with the earth, and the conductor regulates the application of the power so as to maintain his altitude; and the motion of the wings and the influence of gravitation move the Aerostat through the atmosphere at the rate of 100 MILES AN HOUR.'

Imagine him for a moment, poetically describing his flight in the language of Cowper.[4] He is taking a voyage to heaven in his 'American Eagle.'

> I bid adieu to bolts and bars,
> And soar with angels to the stars,
> Like him of old to whom 'twas given,
> To mount on fiery wheels to heaven.
> Bootes wagon, slow with cold,
> Appals me not; nor to behold
> The sword that vast Orion draws,
> Or even the scorpion's horrid claws.
> Beyond the Sun's bright orb I fly,
> And far beneath my feet descry,
> Night's sable goddess, seen with awe,

[4] William Cowper (1731–1800), English poet.

Whom her winged dragons draw.
Thus ever wondering at my speed,
Augmented still as I proceed,
I pass the planetary sphere,
The Milky Way—and now appear,
Heaven's crystal battlements, her door
Of massy pearl and emerald floor.
But here I cease; for never can
The tongue of once a mortal man,
In suitable description trace,
The pleasures of that happy place!

To return to the matter of fact part of our subject:—It is a well known principle in mechanics that the influence of friction is such as to prohibit all possibility of increasing the power with a similar increase in the velocity of the machine acted upon by the propeller. Hence instead of gaining power at every revolution, by his levers, steel-wheels and elastic wood-springs he would lose nearly four-fold, besides the resistance of friction, which may be subtracted as one-fifth part of the original power—allowing the cranks propelled by the conductor to produce four revolutions or strokes with the wings—and this loss is calculated without reference to any diminution of power in raising the wings or giving the onward impetus. And yet the learned Aeronaut pens such a paragraph as this: 'The machinery of the aerostat is in nature a compound lever, and without entering into a mathematical calculation or demonstration of its power, it is sufficient for my present purpose to state, that, nothing, or but very little, is lost, of the power applied to the cranks, in its passage to the wings. And it will be recollected the wings move four times as fast, or, in other words, make four strokes while the cranks perform one revolution. Then, I am safe in saying, that, in this case, there is a facility imparted to the wings equal in effect to FOUR TIMES THE POWER APPLIED TO THE CRANKS.' This is a bold assertion for an experienced mechanist. Let us suppose one wheel, three feet in diameter, with cogs or band, stationed so as to act upon several smaller wheels, compound levers and springs—the whole directly or indirectly uniting their powers to propel a wheel of SIMILAR dimensions to the original one; will the first or propelling power, be increased, in effect or otherwise, by their agency? It is obvious that in a case like this, the more complicated the machinery, the greater is the friction, and consequently the greater the decrease of power. Then allowing, as all must, that a wheel of similar dimensions to the original one, looses [loses] more or less power, varying according to the combination machinery intervening, in being acted upon by the propelling agent, what power will be lost by a wheel, under the same circumstances, and only ONE FOURTH the diameter? The result is apparent: it has not ONE FOURTH the original power.—Hence we cannot take it for granted that Mr. Richard Oglesby Davidson's power is sufficient to put his wings in motion, although he does endeavor to prove that in this case the VELOCITY is POWER. He calculates largely on the assistance to be derived from the atmosphere in driving down the tail or rudder and thus elevating the head so as to give the aerostat an upward direction—by which means, he opines, the American Eagle will nearly fly of itself. And in another version of the plan, he seems to think that under the arrangement stated, the blowing of the wind instead of being a disadvantage, will aid the conductor in going directly against it.—'The stronger it blows the faster will be the speed of the aerostat.' This sounds not unlike the invention which caused such commotion a few years ago amongst the ship builders of the East. A hull was fitted up with wheelhouses, paddles, flywheel, &c. and other appurtenances of a steam-ship. In the middle, instead of a mast, stood a wind-mill, to which cogwheels or bands from the axle of the fly-wheel below, were attached and thus caused the paddles to revolve as if propelled by steam. The intention was, that it should so far gain upon the wind as to make rapid progress against the most stormy opposition, and in calm weather CREATE a wind to drive itself, increasing in its velocity until it had raised a gale.

The great misfortune was, that, like a pedestrian climbing a slippery hill, every two steps forward produced three steps back; and we are sorry to think Mr. Davidson's Eagle would share the same fate.

What, it may be asked, is the remedy? We answer a different organization of the powers employed; a less complex quantity of machinery; a total distrust of manual labor; and a model founded upon principles the most practicable and convenient.

Although Mr. Richard Oglesby Davidson patriotically calls upon his countrymen, and asks them if they will suffer this invention—aye, this *new invention*—'for it . . . has never been tried in any age or country, nor by any person living or dead'—to remain untried, and has secured himself the patent by Act of Congress—yet the laurel can no longer sit upon his brow after the following disclosure from the MS of the true inventor, whom modesty forbids me to name, dated Nov. 1839.

'There are five reasons why the STEAM DUCK is superior to any other model or version that can be founded on it:

'1st. It is an *original* invention.

'2d. Its construction is peculiarly adapted to aerial navigation.

'3d. The velocity of the *duck* is greater than that of any other bird.

'4th. There is no danger from flood or storm.

'5th. The machinery is simple; the propelling power is furnished by nature, and is inexhaustible as long as material is supplied; and the whole is founded upon the strictest philosophical principles.

'The STEAM DUCK is fifteen feet long from beak to tail, and six feet in diameter at the base or thickest part. It is constructed in the form of a MALLARD DUCK, a fowl well known for its swiftness of wing and powers of swimming—and the frame work is of light seasoned hickory, and is covered with canvass varnished and air-tight.—The wings are not complex —they have but one joint, but are so constructed and worked as to revolve with the necessary motion. This end is attained by having them made similar to the . . . windmill. Thus when they describe an ellipsis, the whole power except the WEIGHT of the wings, is used in raising the Aerostat; and while the impetus given by each revolution or ellipsis, shoots the Aerostat several feet in the air, the wings will have elevated themselves for another start downwards. (Here it may be remarked that Mr. Richard Oglesby Davidson has miscalculated his power, although he does allow a loss of nine feet out of twelve, in every stroke of the wing. Constructed as his wings are, their resistance against the atmosphere in their upward motion, added to their weight, would indubitably destroy the advantage gained by the stroke downward.) I have ascertained that the total weight of the wings is not more than five pounds, including the resistance of the atmosphere. Hence the impetus, allowing HALF A SECOND for every stroke, would not suffer any thing to be detracted from the advantage gained by the downward or main stroke.

'The internal machinery is as remarkable for its simplicity as the external. A small, light, and powerful ENGINE is placed in the breast or craw. The piston moves upward; and drives two slight flywheels, on the spokes of which are two sliding pins describing a circle, as they revolve, of any convenient diameter. These pins, one being at each side, are attached by globular joints to the shoulders of the wings, which extend inward about a foot; and by sliding the pins so as to produce a larger or a smaller circle inside, the outward motion of the wings can be varied. The scapepipe, passing along the bottom, is conducted out of a small hole under the tail or rudder, and thus gives an additional impetus to the Aerostat, every puff.

'The fire-place and grate are in front of the boilers; and to save all possible power, by lightening, the ashes and cinders as soon as created fall through a hole in the breast and are lost in the air.

'In the engine-room is a small partition for fuel, which may be coal or wood; but the latter is preferable, when good and well seasoned, from [for] its efficacy in raising steam.

'Separated by a partition, from the front or engine-room, is a small cabin containing two births [berths], a table, two chairs, a library of selected and scientific books, thermometer, &c., and other accommodations appertaining to a well furnished study.' (We think this is a proper place to say a word on Mr. Richard Oglesby Davidson's apparent want of consideration. He speaks of the advantages to be derived from being provided with a thermometer, telescope, &c., as if the conductor were not under the penalty of breaking his neck or being dashed to atoms, should he for an instant leave his work. Now the fact—exclusive of any other obstacle to his mode of Aerostation—that he could not spare a hand, even though called by nature, to scratch his head or blow his nose, ought to deter him from making the experiment.)

I have made a calculation to ascertain the power of the Steam Duck, which, I think proves conclusively that success is inevitable.

ENGINE ROOM.

A light and powerful engine	200
Fireplace, boiler, &c.	50
Poker, tong and shovel	10
Sundries,	10

CABIN.

Chairs, tables &c.	50
Candlesticks, snuffers &c.	5
Books, and papers	10
Thermometer and other scientific apparatus	20
Two births [berths]—or in case of a lady adventurer accompanying, say one	50
	405
Power of engine wings in raising the Aerostat or Steam Duck	700
To spare	lbs. 305[5]

'From this table it will be seen that exclusive of its own weight, the machinery can give a velocity to the wings of the Steam Duck equal to 120

[5] The remainder should be 295 lbs.

strokes in a minute, by which I conclude it would travel with amazing swiftness—say TWO HUNDRED miles an hour. I make this calculation with suitable deduction for the resistance of the atmosphere.

But this description has already occupied an undue portion of our time.

Without any intention to damp the ardor of modern explorers in the airy regions, we must say that we have very little faith in artificial flying, or the means of navigating the air by mechanical contrivances of any sort. We fully concur in what a late philosopher says on the subject. 'Man,' he observes, 'should be satisfied with the earth and water, to aid him in passing from one region to another. The air is so light that I believe it is not practicable to travel in it, except before the wind. From the time of Dedalsus,[6] there have occasionally been projects and attempts for imitating the mode of conveyance of the birds of the air. But they have not been successful. The hazard is too great to justify the experiment. When balloons were invented forty years ago in France, it was predicted, that it would soon become common to journey this way; but heavy bodies cannot be transported through the air. The OSTRICH never flies: it is too ponderous to rise on so attenuated an element.'

The manuscript before alluded to seems to evince more sanguine hopes of success.

'In conclusion,' it adds, winding up with the account of the great Steam Duck, 'nothing has been said of the danger to which the Aeronaut is exposed from sportsmen and others given to the destruction of the feathered tribe.

'Flying over an immense tract of country, it is not to be expected that a bird of this description, so rare and wonderful, can escape the unerring bullet of the rifleman or the scattering charge of the cockney [derogatory term for an inept person]. But any one of common sense can perceive that there never was a real bird with a scapepipe in the situation descriped [described]; nor wings shaped and constructed as those of the steam duck yet it might not be amiss to attach to the works an alarm bell, which would prevent all possibility of mistake.'

Many other obstacles of a less serious nature remain to be overcome before Aerostation can attain any degree of perfection. A new and less complex construction in the formation of the Aerostat must be carried into effect; the atmosphere must be conquered; the absurd doctrines of enthusiasts cast aside as leading to error and failure; the visionary schemes of theorists given up for sound and practical experience; an adherence to the laws of nature closely observed; the resources of art and of science ran-

[6] Daedalus.

sacked for auxiliary powers; various antidotes resorted to for the annihilation of natural obstacles; and a true and logical system of reasoning substituted for the absurd sophistry with which the world of invention is now enslaved and benighted.

When all these improvements are effected; when men suffer themselves to be guided by reason; when knowledge usurps the place of ignorance: *then* may we safely prophecy that the triumph of ingenuity is at hand; and that at some future period man can display the mighty offspring of his genius in the face of high heaven itself, and

> '——cleave the etherial plain,
> The pride, the wonder of the main.'